I0817901

THE WITCHES OF THE CROSSWORLDS

ISBN
hardcover: 978-0-6456581-8-7
ebook: 978-0-6456581-9-4
Special thanks to all those who have contributed with their feedback
and support throughout the writing of these books.,

Published by Rack and Rune Publishing
rackandrune.com
email: info@rackandrune.com

For my children, Emily and Luke,
who taught me the meaning of fulfillment.

THE WITCHES OF THE CROSSWORLDS

BOOK I

SELLEMAE'S WRATH

CHAPTER 1

Patsy worried the crisp mountain air turning her breath to steam might give her away.

She should have been preparing for when her tutor would arrive, quizzing her about steam driven locomotives and all the other marvels of the modern age. Instead, the reluctant student stood peering around the corner of the house, watching the rickety sulky carry her parents away from the majestic manor and onto the road to Blackheath. Once it was out of sight, and the clatter of horses' hooves had faded into the distance, she stepped away from the house, turned, and skipped her way to the bottom of the garden, away from the housekeeper's ever-watchful eyes.

She sang to herself as she went, "Magpies and kookaburras…" Patsy loved singing; it was her favourite escape from the boredom of the rigid routine imposed by her parents.

It also helped her forget that her tutor, the cranky old widow, Mrs Bradshaw, was due to arrive at any moment.

The very thought of it made her anxious, especially after Mrs Bradshaw had lied so much to Patsy's parents by saying she'd been rude and insolent.

On reaching the bottom of the large yard, she looked over her shoulder and caught a glimpse of Mrs Bradshaw's carriage approaching the house. She took cover behind a shrub. Then, when one of the servants had taken Mrs Bradshaw inside, Patsy slid down the grassy slope and through the bushes leading to the dark world of the creek. Her father had warned her many times to stay away from its snake-infested banks, and Patsy knew she'd be in trouble for avoiding her lessons. But that mattered little as she picked herself up and ran down the creek to her favourite playground. Once there, she pretended not to hear the servants calling in the distance, and celebrated her escape by skipping stones where the creek opened into an expansive pool.

The servants' voices soon stopped as, one by one, they gave up, leaving the cicadas and a multitude of birds singing in the bushes as the only sounds around her, a kookaburra's laugh rising loud above it all. Patsy felt sure she'd be safe for now. She'd rather face her father's anger later in the day than spend the next six hours with a cranky old widow criticising everything she said or did. *Old widow…? More like an old witch*, she thought.

Patsy picked up another stone, crouching low as she drew her shoulder back and prepared to throw. Then something caught her attention. At first, she thought it might have been her imagination, or even one of the servants. But when Patsy focused on the sound, she heard it for what it was: a tiny voice pleading for help.

She called out in reply, careful not to be so loud as to be heard from the house. "Hello?"

There it was again: "Help!" Faint, but nevertheless, a voice.

"Where are you?"

The voice replied, "I'm near the big rock, across the other side of the pool. I'm stuck! Please, help me!"

Crossing would mean Patsy's dress and stockings would be soaked up to her waist, but she was already going to be in trouble, so what did that matter?

She slipped off her shoes and waded across the cold pool.

"Please, do hurry, Patricia!"

Patsy stopped. "How did you know my name?"

"I've known you since before you were born. I knew your mother, and your grandmother, when they were young girls… like you."

Patsy stood in the middle of the pool and folded her arms. There was something about this that didn't seem right. "You say you know my family, but I think you're lying. You're a stranger, and my mother has told me since I was little not to trust strangers."

"Oh Patricia, what can I do to convince you, to help you understand? I am no stranger. I am a fairy… the fairy who watches over you, and has watched the first-born daughters of your family for a hundred generations."

"Hmmph." Patsy wasn't convinced, but her curiosity compelled her to continue crossing the pool, her feet squishing in the mud at the water's edge when she reached the other side. A leech waved its head nearby in search of a host. Watching it for a moment, Patsy thought to herself that where there was one, there were always more, so she would have to be quick.

She leaned against the enormous rock, then twisted around to examine the dark space beyond. "This can't be!" Her jaw dropped, and she wondered if her mind might be playing tricks on her. There, stuck in an enormous and intricate web, was a beautiful fairy, no more than twenty centimetres high, with long slender limbs. A few centimetres from her right hand a small wand dangled, appearing ready to fall any second.

Despite the fairy's size, Patsy saw the relief in her eyes at the hope of rescue. "At last! Now please, Patricia, if you can just take my wand and place it in my hand, I'll be able to free myself. Then I'll grant you any wish your heart desires."

Patsy reached out to do as the fairy requested, then paused. She thought about what she'd read in some of the books on fairy tales in her parents' library. "How do I know you're a real fairy, and not some sort of evil pixie pretending to need help?"

"Excuse me, child? I don't quite understand."

"How do I know I can trust you?"

"I'm not sure I believe this! I could swear I just heard you express doubt. Are you serious? I'm a fairy! Come now, if you can't trust the fairy who watches over you, then who in this world can you trust? As I told you before, I've been watching over your family for countless generations! What more could you need to know? Please, you need to release me, or the spider will come and it will be too late!"

Patsy withdrew her arm, stood up straight and asked, "Why haven't you revealed yourself until now, when you suddenly need my help?"

The fairy let out a long sigh. "Oh Patricia, it's so very hard to come to terms with your doubts. Yes, I've worked hard to stay out of sight throughout your life, but it doesn't mean I haven't watched over you, as all good fairies should. We used to be happy to let children see us from time to time, but there's so few of us left now." She choked back tears. "Those of us who remain aren't prepared to risk being seen. I called for help only because I could see no other choice."

Her resolve softening, Patsy asked, "Why do you insist on calling me Patricia? I hate being called Patricia. You should know that if you've been watching so closely. Why can't you call me Patsy?"

"Oh, sweet, innocent child. We fairies are duty bound to respect the wishes of a child's mother in such matters. It would go against everything it means to be a fairy if I ignored such a fundamental understanding, one that has stood throughout the ages."

Patsy shook her head. "I don't know." She stood in the leech infested water, wondering how it would feel if she were the one stuck in that web. What if the fairy's nose became itchy, or even her foot? How frustrating would that be? "You'll grant me a wish? All I have to do is hand you your wand?"

"Whatever your heart desires, dear child."

Patsy hesitated, then thought of how much she'd love to have her old tutor back. Why did Miss Lawson have to go and get married, leaving her stuck with cranky old Mrs Bradshaw? Focusing on her wish, she leaned over and removed the fairy's wand from the web, taking great care as she placed it in the fairy's right hand.

The fairy gave Patsy a warm smile. "Thank you, sweet child."

The fairy swung her wrist and used the razor-sharp tip of her wand to free her right arm. In mere seconds, she'd cut away the rest of the threads holding her captive. "Oh, it feels so good to be free!" The fairy stretched her limbs, then flew about, circling Patsy's head before coming to rest on the rock. "I fear I'll need to rest awhile before I can fly off. My wings need time to recover from being so restricted within that horrid web."

Patsy looked smug. "Good, you'll have plenty of time then to grant my wish."

The fairy waved an arm dismissively and laughed. "Oh Patsy, you're hilarious! You actually believed the bit about granting a wish? Anything your heart desires? You need to accept reality!"

Already anxious about having to face the consequences of skipping her lessons, Patsy started breathing heavily. She clenched her fists and felt the pressure building in her temples.

But the fairy paid little attention to the danger brewing. "Why would I have been caught in that death trap if I could perform magic? You want to know what our wands are for? Do you ever grab a stick to cut down the spider webs in front of you when walking through the bushes early in the morning? Think about it, Pats. We're flying around all the time. Common sense has taught us we need to wave a stick in front of us as we go. The star at the top is only there to cut through the tougher threads, not weave some sort of magic. Ha! The only real magic I know of comes from drinking nectar, a bit too much magic sometimes. That's how I ended up getting—"

The fairy was cut off mid-sentence as Patsy snapped, picking her up and holding her tight around the waist. "You liar! You promised! You're just like that stupid Mrs Bradshaw! You treated me like an idiot and you lied to me!" She'd started shaking, and tears rolled down her cheeks as her grip on the fairy tightened. "And now, you're making fun of me. Why does everyone have to treat me like I don't matter?" Patsy stomped her foot as hard as she could, making a splash that spread high and wide. The action felt good, as if it was easing the pressure. "You lied to me… you promised me a wish. Why would you do that?"

Desperate to get away, the fairy stabbed her wand into Patsy's hand, triggering a reflex action. The girl cried out in pain as she flung her arm out and sent the fairy hurtling across the pool.

Trying to gain control of her flight, the fairy spread her wings, only to discover they were still too damaged from her time in the web to get her to safety. She hit a tree branch, then a rock, as she plummeted and fell headfirst into the water. "Help! I can't swim, help!"

Although still angry about being lied to, Patsy had no desire to see the fairy drown. She waded across to rescue the fairy once more.

"My wings, they're broken. I may never fly again."

Patsy took great care scooping the fairy out of the water. "That's okay, I can look after you while you get better. My father has plenty of glass jars in the garden shed. I'll keep you in one of those until you're ready to fly again. What do I need to feed you?"

Horrified at what lay ahead for her, the fairy replied with a single word: "Nectar."

A few minutes later, in her father's garden shed, Patsy hummed to herself while punching air holes in the lid of a jar, just big enough to hold the fairy. "I'll take you in through the kitchen. Cook likes to talk about fairy stories. So, can you imagine how amazed she'll be when she sees you?"

With her head slumped, Patsy's captive pleaded with the girl. "Oh, Patsy, please… I really don't think that's a good idea."

"Nonsense! Cook helped me care for a sick bird once."

"Did it survive?"

"No, but we wrapped it in a small cloth and kept it warm. We even managed to get it to drink a bit of water before it passed away. Cook's my favourite person in the whole world. Well, after my mother she is."

The fairy responded with an exasperated moan of anguish before falling silent.

Approaching the kitchen door at the back of the manor, Patsy's excitement was palpable. She burst through the door saying, "Look what I found, Cook! A real fairy!"

"Oh my God, child! Look at you! Covered in mud… and what are you doing bringing that thing into the house?"

Cook snatched the jar from Patsy. "Do you have any idea how worried we've all been about you? It took a good deal of convincing to get Mrs Bradshaw to wait for your return. I've no doubt she'll have cross words for you. You'd best take yourself upstairs, dry off and get into some fresh clothes so you can join her in the library."

"But, what about—"

"I'll not stand for any back-chatting."

•

As Patsy dragged her feet toward the stairs, Cook held up the jar and saw that three of the spider's legs had broken off. The poor creature was barely alive.

Ordinarily, she would have released it into the bushes outside, but on this occasion, she felt it would be cruel to release it when it would be so disadvantaged.

She took the lid off the jar, tipped the spider onto the pavement outside the kitchen door, and brought her foot down to end its misery.

CHAPTER 2

Dried off and wearing fresh clothes, Patsy made her way down the staircase. The household cat (a large ginger tom) greeted her half-way. Looking up at her, he let out a single meow. Patsy smiled, reached down, and picked him up. "Oh, Ferdinand, you're so lucky you don't have to worry about cranky old tutors." She could hear the cat purring as she continued down the stairs, holding him close so his face was next to hers.

Patsy stopped at the door to the library, Ferdinand's purr falling silent when he saw the old woman by the fire. He opened his claws and pushed against Patsy's chest, making it clear he wanted to get away. She let him go, then watched him race toward the kitchen. She wished she could join him, but because of her previous escapade, there would already be consequences when her parents returned.

Mrs Bradshaw closed her book and Patsy took a cautious step into the room. Her black dress, grey hair, and wrinkled flesh was just how Patsy imagined the witches in the fairy tales she'd read might look. After the surprise of seeing and rescuing an actual fairy earlier in the day, she knew they were real, so why not witches?

The widow turned to her, deep black eyes holding the girl in a vice-like grip. She spoke with a cold and flat voice. "Sit."

Patsy walked to the desk where the lessons took place. Her chair made a high-pitched scraping sound as she dragged it across the timber floor. Then, she took her seat in silence.

For at least a minute, maybe two, there wasn't a sound, other than the crackling of the fire. When the woman decided she was ready to speak, each word cut Patsy to the core. "*Never* has anyone treated me with such contempt." Another minute passed. "I want you to understand just how wretched you are to me. I want you to know how it feels to be so utterly rejected, the way you rejected me this morning."

Patsy took a breath, preparing to defend herself, then decided it would be safer to keep her thoughts to herself.

Mrs Bradshaw got to her feet and stared at the fire. "I have already called for the stablehands to ready my carriage." She turned to face Patsy and held up a key. "I will be locking the library door on my way out, and leaving the key with one of the servants. They already have strict instructions that the door remain locked until it is time for you to bathe and prepare for dinner."

Patsy's voice came out as a whisper. "But, I haven't had lunch, and I'm thirsty. I'll be stuck in here for hours."

"How is that my problem?"

As Mrs Bradshaw prepared to leave, Patsy could swear she saw the woman's shadow reach out and try to grab her with gnarled fingers. *That's another sign,* thought Patsy. *She must be a witch.*

Mrs Bradshaw walked from the room, turned, and closed the door. The sound of the key in the locking mechanism was the last connection Patsy would have with the woman for today.

What a relief that was!

Okay, she might be hungry and thirsty for a few hours, but she wouldn't have to face her tutor again for another week. Best of all, she had the library all to herself. It had always been off-limits to her unless she was having lessons or her father wanted to show her a specific book.

Now, for the first time ever, she could explore the library unsupervised. Without hesitation, she crossed the room to inspect her mother's writing desk. It was covered with intricate walnut inlays of strange symbols. The main one depicted three semi-circles, connected like links in a chain. Words, written in a language and alphabet she was unfamiliar with, followed the curves. She traced the symbol with her finger and remembered how Miss Lawson had told her such desks sometimes held secret compartments. She opened the cover, pulled out its myriad drawers to see what lay behind them, then started pressing against anything that stood out as a feature. She was about to give up when her hand brushed against a piece of trim on the right-hand-side of the desk. She slipped her hand under it and pushed up.

Click!

A door on the side popped open. She crouched down and looked in. A bunch of letters sat tied in a red ribbon, and next to them lay an ornate key.

Patsy pulled the bundle of letters out, sat cross-legged on the floor, and began untying the ribbon.

She clutched them to her chest on hearing the library door unlock, then reached into the compartment to grab the key. She stood facing the door, the letters and key hidden behind her back.

Relief swept over her when the door revealed Cook's rosy cheeks. "Shame on that woman, locking you in here without having had something to eat. I daresay Mister McIntyre will be looking for a new tutor when he learns of this. It's little wonder you hid from her this morning."

Patsy asked, "How's my fairy? Have you given her something to eat?"

"I'll not discuss that creature till I've got you fed, young miss. Come on now, I've a bowl of chicken soup and some bread for you in the kitchen."

"Can I take my writing book upstairs first?"

"If you must, but be quick about it, else your soup will get cold."

As Cook turned to leave, Patsy crossed the room, careful to keep the key and letters from any unseen eyes that might be watching. She opened her writing journal and shoved the bundle inside. Then, clenching her fist around the key and tucking the journal under her arm, she raced out of the library and up the stairs to her room.

Halfway up, Patsy stopped.

She'd left the secret compartment open!

There was nothing she could do now. She'd have to sneak back in after lunch to deal with it.

*

Patsy hid the letters and key under her pillow and made her way down to the kitchen.

She looked past the steaming bowl of soup on the table, instead focusing on the empty jar by the door. "My fairy! What happened to my fairy?"

Cook finished packing a stack of plates in the cupboard before she turned to the girl and replied, "Some things are best set free. It's cruel to keep a creature like that in a jar." She didn't have the heart to tell Patsy the truth of what she'd done.

"But it's not fair! I've never seen a fairy before. Now no one will believe me when I tell them how I rescued it from that horrible spider's web."

Cook remained silent.

"Will you at least promise not to tell people I'm lying?" Cook closed her eyes and chose her words carefully, then leaned across the table, looking Patsy in the eye. "I promise you, if anyone asks, I will tell them exactly what I saw."

Patsy smiled. "Thank you, Cook. Knowing that, I'm sure Father will believe me if you tell him too."

"I wouldn't be telling your father of it if I were you. He's sure to suspect you found it down by the creek, and you know how he feels about you going down there."

While Cook continued to get the kitchen in order, Patsy finished her soup then said, "I might go to my room now and have a rest. I'm frightfully tired."

"I'm not surprised after this morning's happenings. You'd best be quick about it if you really do want a rest, I'll be preparing your bath once I'm through here."

Patsy was starting to get up, then stopped and said, "Cook, I think Mrs Bradshaw might be a witch."

"Oh, and why might that be?"

"She's always cranky, and her skin's all spotty and wrinkled."

"Mrs Smith's old and wrinkled, do you think she's a witch too?"

"But that's different." Disappointed that Cook wouldn't agree, she got up, pushed her chair in, and made her way out of the kitchen toward the stairs. Once she was confident Cook couldn't see her, she diverted toward the library.

The door was locked!

Patsy backed away, then turned, ran up the stairs and into her room, closing the door behind her. She leaned against it while catching her breath, and wondered about what might be in the letters. And what about the key… what was that for?

Staring at her pillow, she crossed the room.

Who wrote them?

Who were they sent to?

She lifted the pillow, pulled out the bundle and sat on her bed, the letters resting on her lap as she untied the ribbon.

She lifted an envelope from the top of the pile, holding it up in both hands. Curiously, there was no address or postage mark, just a name, *Neridah.* It must have been either handed to her personally or slipped under her door, rather than sent through the post like most letters.

She pulled the pages from the envelope and began reading.

> *Thursday, April 4th, 1826*
> *My Darling Neridah,*
>
> *I cannot begin to tell you how happy I felt on receiving your reply.*
>
> *It is now almost a year since you were widowed, and it filled my heart with joy last week when I watched from afar as young Meredith took her first steps.*

Meredith? That was her mother's name! Neridah must be her grandmother… the one no one spoke of!

She continued reading.

Your father came to the stables again yesterday, lecturing my uncle about the importance of encouraging me to seek work in Parramatta or Sydney, saying I would find more opportunity in the city. Uncle Jeremiah knows him too well, and later confided to me his belief that your father merely wants me as far away from you as possible.

We are both adults now, and it is time we share what has always been in our hearts.

I'll wait for you before sunset this Sunday, at our special place down by the creek. Hopefully it hasn't been taken over by weeds in the years since we last met face to face.

Forever yours,
Alfred.

After years of asking about her grandmother, with no response from her parents, she was finally getting at least some answers.

She knew her grandmother's name! That, in and of itself, was a revelation.

And who was Alfred?

She grabbed another letter at random and opened it, leaving the first one open on the bed.

Saturday, June 21st, 1821
Neridah,

Since you taught me the art of listening to nature, life is full of surprises. Every walk through the bush is a revelation.

And you were so right about the cicadas and their gossip!

Far more wondrous though than any magic, or quirk of nature, was last week when first we kissed.

My life is forever changed.

I still think longingly of the first time we held hands, watching the pixies down by the creek. Since then, Bandah has become probably my closest friend, other than you of course.

Pixies? So, as well as fairies, there's pixies down by the creek? She tossed the letter aside and grabbed another, desperate to learn more.

Monday, December 1st, 1821
Neridah,

Why? Why must your father be this way? All because I lack the blood of the druids!

He tells my uncle to keep me away, and you run whenever I approach.

All because he heard of our love from one of the servants? I beg you, if our love means anything to you, meet me at sunrise by the creek. We can make our way to Blackheath and get a carriage to Sydney. We can start a new life.

Forever yours,
Alfred.

Patsy knew nothing of her great-grandfather's existence before now, but was already quite sure she didn't like him.

And again, she wondered... who was Alfred?

She was about to open another letter when there was a knock at the door, followed by the sound of the doorknob turning.

The letters on Patsy's lap fell to the floor, and she spread her arms in a futile attempt to shield the ones she'd tossed on the bed.

Patsy tried her best to appear calm, but her rapid, short breaths made the façade seem comical as she called out, "Who is it?"

The door swung open and Mrs Smith stepped into the room. "Nothing to worry about, Miss Patricia, it's only me." To Patsy, she appeared roughly the same age as Mrs Bradshaw, but with a larger frame and a thicker crop of hair. "Cook has started preparing your bath. I told her I'd come up to let you know it will be ready in the next half hour."

Mrs Smith was staring at the letters around Patsy's feet as she began backing out of the room. She stopped and said, "Oh, by the way, you might want to learn to cover your tracks in future. I've enough to do around here as it is."

"What do you mean?" said Patsy, trying to pretend there was nothing unusual about the letters.

"Suffice to say, it might be wise if you learn to close some things after you've opened them."

"Was that you who lock—"

She was cut off mid-sentence when Mrs Smith put a finger to her lips. "Shhh." The housekeeper left the room, pulling the door shut behind her.

Patsy fell back on the bed, a mixture of confusion and relief washing over her. Why had Mrs Smith said nothing of the letters?

At least now she knew who'd locked the library.

Once her heartbeat settled, she reached under the pillow and grabbed the key, examining it and imagining what it may open.

Was it for one of the old bookcases... the ones with the leadlight doors?

No, it looked too ornate for that.

But there were other things that had locks in the library, like desk drawers and cashboxes.

Yet it seemed too big to be used for any of those. Then, she remembered!

There was the big old book, the one on the wooden stand. It had a symbol on its front cover, like the one inlaid on her mother's desk, and it was held shut with an elaborate lock.

She'd asked her mother about it one day and had been told it was the old family bible... that Patsy's great-grandparents had lost the key when her mother was a baby. She explained how Patsy's father had wanted to pry open the lock, but relented when the Reverend Casey advised against it, proclaiming that to do so would be a violation of all that was sacred. Instead, he suggested my father should remain hopeful of one day finding the key.

Patsy lay there, rolling the key back and forth in her fingers. No point going downstairs to try it now, the door was locked.

But then, she had to go downstairs soon anyway for her bath, so why not go down now and check again, just in case? Maybe it was only locked while Mrs Smith was in there closing the secret compartment.

Her curiosity getting the better of her, Patsy collected the letters and hid them at the bottom of a drawer in her dresser. She opened her door and peered out to make sure no one was watching before tiptoeing down the corridor to the staircase. Hiding behind a banister, she was aware anyone looking up from below would likely see her anyway, but it gave her a vantage point where she could look down and see the door to the library. To her great surprise, the door was open!

She made her way down the stairs, clinging to the banisters as she went, and making a point to avoid the fifth step down, the one that always creaked when stepped on.

Darting from the base of the stairs to the library door, she made sure the room was empty before slipping through its grand cedar entrance.

There it was, at the far end of the room.

Patsy felt her heart would explode if it were to beat any harder as she approached the ornate book. It was covered in embossed green leather, with a brass inlay of the linked semi-circles in the middle. Each corner was adorned with a brass corner protector, and a large locking mechanism kept the book shut tight. She held up the key, debating the wisdom of what she was about to do. *Don't worry, Patsy,* she thought, *it probably won't fit anyway.* With a slow, deliberate movement, she slipped the key into the lock and tried turning it anti-clockwise.

Click!

She felt the pressure holding the book shut drop as the lock was released.

Unsure what to expect, she opened the cover and ran her fingers over the first page.

Even though the words and symbols looked meaningless to her, it was obvious as she turned the first few pages of vellum that this was no traditional bible.

A golden ribbon attached to the book's spine bookmarked a page in the middle. Patsy tried lifting the pages to get to it but was stopped when she heard voices approaching.

Her parents were home early!

Patsy shut the book as gently as possible, flipping the locking mechanism back over the cover. She fumbled with the key, panicking as she tried to withdraw it.

It was no good, the key was stuck!

With the voices now just outside the door, she dropped to the floor and crawled behind the desk normally used for her lessons.

CHAPTER 3

Colin McIntyre strode into the library, followed by Cook and his wife, Meredith. "How is it that she wasn't here when Mrs Bradshaw arrived in the first place?" His riding boots hammered on the floorboards as he made his way to the small table where he kept the decanters of rum and brandy, pouring himself a glass of the latter.

Meredith walked across the room, her petite frame appearing to glide as the hem of her long silken white gown hid her feet from view. Her face was framed by cascades of shimmering light brown hair that fell way past her shoulders.as she placed a gentle hand on Cook's shoulder. "Oh, Colin, you know what she's like. You can't expect Cook and the other servants to carry out their duties and know what our daughter's up to every second of the day. And if I had a tutor like that, I'd want to run away too."

"It was my understanding that part of what we pay them for is to do exactly that."

Cook's voice trembled as she stepped forward to defend herself. "Honestly, Mister McIntyre, sir, I never had this problem with her when Miss Lawson was her tutor."

Colin put the glass down and faced the servant. "And now you're suggesting I should dismiss her new tutor, who came highly recommended and at great expense, for teaching her the meaning of consequences?"

"She locked her in here without food or drink, sir. And then left for the day. If I can speak my mind, sir, I'd say she was being negligent."

"I'd call it discipline."

Meredith was quick to reply. "I don't care what you want to call it, I call it cruelty. I'm not prepared to stand here and accept someone treating our daughter that way, and neither should you. I know you want to protect her, and I love you for that, but in the process, you're far too hard on her at times."

Colin took a sip on his brandy. He knew there was no chance of him winning this battle, and that what Mrs Bradshaw had done was wrong. But damn that girl! Did she have to be so feisty? "Very well then, it seems I have little choice. I'll write Mrs Bradshaw a letter of termination in the morning." He looked toward Cook. "There was something else you wanted to tell me?"

"Yes, sir. When Miss Patricia returned from the creek, she'd taken one of your large jars from the garden shed and placed a spider in it. Biggest spider I've ever seen!"

"Go on."

"She insisted it was a fairy… honestly, sir, I worry at times about the imaginings that go on in that girl's head."

Colin and Meredith looked at each. After a small nod from his wife, he turned back to Cook and asked, "So, where is this spider now?"

"It's gone, dealt with it the same manner I always do with such creatures."

"Very well then, Cook, thank you for sharing your concerns."

"Am I free to finish preparing Miss Patricia's bath then?"

"Yes, please do."

"Thank you, sir."

Cook left the room as quickly as she could. Colin walked over to the fireplace, grabbed the poker, and used it to push the burning logs about until their dying flames sprang back to life.

"Colin, we need to tell her."

Colin bit hard on his lower lip. He'd secretly hoped Patsy would be able to go through her life without ever being burdened by the truth of who she was. "But she's still so young."

"She turns eleven next week; she's almost a young woman now. And if she's claiming to see fairies…"

"Yes, I know." He placed a reassuring hand on her shoulder. "Clearly, she has your gifts. The Reverend Casey is among our dinner guests tonight. I think we'd do well to seek his guidance."

"Yes, I agree."

"Speaking of dinner guests, I've matters to attend to in the stables. I'd best deal with them now, in case anyone arrives early and starts knocking at the door."

Meredith smiled, aware of what her husband was thinking. "Would you be thinking of the Danburys?"

"I like Charles, in small doses…"

Meredith placed a finger over his lips, "You busy yourself in the stables and do what you need to. I'll entertain the Danburys, and anyone else silly enough to arrive early."

"Thank you." Colin kissed her forehead, finished his drink, then made his way out of the library.

*

A spider? Cook thought my fairy was a spider? Patsy's foot became itchy, making it hard to focus. Beads of sweat dripped from her brow, and she struggled to keep her breathing slow enough to be silent.

On hearing her father's footsteps echo into the distance, she felt safe to relax a little and peer around the corner. Her mother stood in silence, surveying the room. *The key! Oh please, don't see the key.*

Meredith's eyes moved past the book, then locked on the desk where Patsy hid. Was that a frown on her mother's face? And if she could see her mother, didn't that mean her mother could see her? Patsy felt her lungs would burst if she had to hold her breath any longer. She didn't even dare blink.

After what seemed an eternity, her mother turned and left the room, pulling the door shut behind her.

Patsy felt giddy with relief. She walked over to the book and opened it at the bookmarked page, a folded note slipping out and falling to the floor. Patsy ignored the note as she stared in awe at the page in front of her. There, taking up almost the whole page, was an etching of a fairy, stuck in a web. The illustration was almost identical to what she'd been confronted with earlier in the day. On the opposing page was another image, this one depicting a gigantic spider, with human-like facial features, rearing up in front of an array of small cocoons suspended from the ceiling. Each one had an exposed head that appeared to be singing. Could that be the builder of the web behind the big rock? Surely not! Such a thing couldn't possibly be real.

She reached down and picked up the fallen note, unfolded the fragile page, and began reading.

> *I've little doubt the etchings on these pages convey the truth of my beloved daughter's fate.*
>
> *Now my granddaughter, gripped by the bravado of adolescence, talks of crossing worlds to retrieve her. But I'll not let my only granddaughter sacrifice her own life in such a foolhardy endeavour.*
>
> *I've ceased her training in the craft of our ancestors and will keep the Book of Wisdom closed to her from now on, along with her mother's journals, now safely concealed from her curiosity down where the gardeners keep their tools. Her training can only continue when she grows beyond such reckless ideas.*
>
> *My heart would have me destroy this book, but to do so would be a sacrilege beyond imagining. So, I leave this note as a warning to any who may chance upon the key, or another method of opening its lock. Do not trust fairies lest you meet the same fate as befell my daughter.*

CHAPTER 4

Patsy let her head sink down among the suds of the bathtub as Cook poured in another pitcher of hot water.

Cook's cheeks were bright red, and she shook her head while lecturing the young girl. "I swear child, you'll be leading me to an early grave with some of the mischief you get up to."

Patsy responded by sinking down further in the hope it would drown out the woman's words.

"I had little choice but to tell your parents about that creature you had in the jar, and they'll no doubt guess where you collected it from. Rest assured, when they catch up with you, you'll likely be in a world of trouble."

Thanks a lot, Patsy thought. *Does she have to remind me?*

Cook leaned over the bathtub to ensure she had the girl's attention.

"It troubles me that a girl your age should believe such a thing to be a fairy! You're far too old for such imaginings. I suspect your mother would be wanting to talk with the Reverend Casey about it. He knows a good deal about the workings of the mind and how it can be fixed through discipline and prayer. I've a good mind to have words with him myself."

Patsy raised her head from below the surface. "No! Please, promise you won't. You know the Reverend Casey scares me."

Cook's frown relaxed. "Don't worry yourself. I'll not tell a lie, should I be asked, but I won't be seeking to make trouble for you."

Patsy sighed and slid back down so her shoulders were submerged. "I don't understand why the creek has to be off limits. Father's happy for me to walk everywhere else on the property. He says it's because of the dangerous wildlife, but there are brown snakes and venomous spiders everywhere on the property."

"Shhh, child, you should know better than to question your father's wisdom. Now be quiet and soak for a bit. I need to go help Mrs Smith hang your washing. The poor woman struggles these days with her arthritis."

Patsy closed her eyes, humming as she slid further down in the tub. She hadn't realised she was drifting off to sleep until a sound from the corner of the room caught her attention, snapping her back to reality.

"Psst, Patricia."

She sat up and held her knees to her chest, shocked to discover she was not alone. "Who said that?"

"We need to talk."

Patsy surveyed the room; the only living thing she could see appeared to be a cockroach.

She glared at the bug and said, "That wasn't you I hope."

Rising from the floor to stand erect, the pixie put aside the shield he normally carried over his back for camouflage. He walked towards her and said, "There's no one else here as far as I can tell. But I digress. You created quite a problem this morning and we need to talk about it."

"Ugh! I don't believe this. I've had enough of creatures that aren't real for one day, so I'd appreciate it if you'd kindly disappear."

"Why do you doubt your own eyes? I saw you browsing through the Book of Wisdom. What you saw this morning was real. But more important are the forces you unwittingly unleashed." A dozen other pixies had entered the room, each carrying their own camouflage shield. "This is but a handful of the pixies who'll be gathering to protect you and your family tonight."

"Why? What do I need protection from? You're nothing but a cockroach that my imagination wants me to believe is something else. The fact is, you really are a cockroach, and when I've had a good sleep, I'll see you as such, and nothing more."

Although the Pixie's face was tiny, Patsy noticed his frown. "You'll think very differently by tomorrow morning."

"And why would that be?"

"The danger is coming, and it's worse than anything you could imagine."

Before Patsy had a chance to reply, the pixies raised their shields over their heads and went to ground. Cook's silhouette loomed large in the doorway. "Who's that you're talking to?"

"Oh, nobody, I was just—"

"Oh no! Cockroaches!" With her hands over her head to hold her courage in, the middle-aged woman rushed into the room, determined to stamp out the vermin.

Patsy protested, "No, Cook, no! They're really little people… like pixies. They were talking to me."

Cook froze. "Pixies you say? Talking to you?" The woman's eyes drifted skyward. "Honestly, Patricia, I love you dearly… your free spirit and your imagination… but it's getting too much. This morning you're telling me a spider is really a fairy, and now? Now you'd have me believe that cockroaches are pixies… and that they talk to you! Maybe it would be for the best if the Reverend Casey had a chat to you after all."

Cook was taken by surprise when Mrs Smith appeared behind her. "Oh, really Cook, I don't think that'll be necessary."

Cook replied, "I'm sorry, Mrs Smith, but is this really your concern?"

"I'd prefer it weren't, but the sun is getting low, and you'll be needed in the kitchen. I can get young Patricia dry and dressed."

Cook looked out the window at the sun just above the treeline. "Yes, I suppose you're right." She turned to Patsy. "It's your favourite tonight, and I will be putting turnips with it, so I expect you to eat them without complaint."

Patsy's eyes lit up. "Is it your special mutton pie? Please say it is."

"Aye, that it is. But Mrs Smith is right. Your parents will be having guests for dinner tonight, and there's much for me to be doing in the kitchen."

Once Cook had left, Mrs Smith grabbed a small stool and moved across to the tub. "Now, perhaps you might want to tell me about what you saw today… however strange it may have seemed."

The authority in the old woman's voice left Patsy feeling she had no choice but to comply. "Did you hear about the spider?"

"My understanding is that it was actually a fairy."

"What? Who told you? Was it Cook? Why would she do that?"

"You should understand by now that house staff don't keep secrets from one another, well, not about those things anyway. But trust me, I know far more about your day than Cook, or any of the other servants for that matter. The pixies warned me that the fairy was down there even before you rescued her, but it was too late by then for me to intervene."

"So, it really was a fairy… not a spider like Cook claimed it was?"

"It was both."

"I don't understand, how do you know so much about this anyway? Why would the pixies talk to you, and not the other servants?"

"Because I have been part of an ordeal almost identical to yours. It also involved your grandmother."

"You knew my grandmother?"

"I met her that very day. The outcome of her encounter with a fairy ended quite differently to yours. In her case, she unwittingly swapped her fate for that of the fairy in the web. She didn't know that every two score years, the fairies select one of their own to be left in the Spider Queen's web, so she can take it to sing in her choir."

Patsy said, "I saw the Spider Queen, and her choir. They were in the big book in the library. I'd thought they couldn't possibly be real."

Mrs Smith leaned forward so her face almost touched Patsy's. "Oh, she and her choir are real alright. She calls herself Sellemae. You helped her prize escape today, then hurt and imprisoned the poor dear before handing her over to an old fool who couldn't even see her for what she was." Mrs Smith grabbed Patsy's shoulders. "Listen to me! Sellemae will seek revenge, and it will be tonight. She'll seek to punish both you and Cook, then likely establish a nest in this manor."

Patsy pushed Mrs Smith's arms away from her. "No, I don't believe you! That's just something made up to scare people. It can't be real."

Taken aback, Mrs Smith replied, "With that attitude, it may be better that I don't tell you more of what's coming."

She held up a towel for Patsy to wrap around herself as she got out of the bath. "You need to dry off and get dressed. After dinner's done with, I'll be preparing you for what lies ahead."

"All I'll be preparing for after dinner is a good night's sleep."

"Trust me, you won't be getting much opportunity to sleep tonight."

Patsy set about drying herself off, then paused. Maybe, if she tried a more diplomatic approach, she might get some answers to help her work out what was real and what wasn't. She looked up at the housekeeper and said, "If you expect me to trust you, I'm going to need to know more about what's going on. I've been through quite a lot already today, and the more I think about it, the more some of what's happened just doesn't make sense." She paused again before continuing. "The fairy, the one I rescued today, it told me wands are just for cutting through webs."

"Aye, that she would. Anything to avoid honouring her deal with you. A wand is a powerful tool that can perform all manner of what you might call magic."

Patsy asked, "Why were you there when my grandmother was tricked by the fairy?"

"There's no time—"

Patsy insisted, "I need to know."

Mrs Smith remained silent as Patsy finished rubbing herself down with the towel.

"It was you, wasn't it?"

"Enough of this useless chit-chat." She took the towel from Patsy and handed the girl her petticoat and dress. "You can get dressed and march straight to your room, young miss."

Patsy saw Mrs Smith's refusal to answer as an admission of guilt. She slipped into her clothing then asked, "What happened to her… what happened to my grandmother?"

Mrs Smith sneered as she moved closer and whispered in Patsy's ear,

"I've no doubt your grandmother is alive, cocooned in Sellemae's lair… paralysed, yet conscious. She'll likely remain in that state for many thousands of years."

Patsy reeled back, struggling to keep her balance on hearing the revelation. "My grandmother's alive?"

Silence.

"Maybe there's some way we can rescue her!"

Patsy's attention was drawn to a small voice in the far corner. "Ha! Do you have any idea what that would entail?"

Mrs Smith turned to the pixie. "Don't you have something better to do?"

"She needs to know." The pixie flew toward Patsy then hovered in front of her. "The Queen's lair lies on a different plane of existence. It's barely possible to get there without being able to draw on the power of the Crossworlds… unless the portal opens."

"When will that happen?"

Mrs Smith replied, "Tonight, when the Spider Queen leads her army to seek vengeance on the foolish girl who stole her prize. Now, enough of this talk. There is much the pixie and I need to prepare."

The pixie added, "One thing you should be aware of, you will more than likely discover abilities—"

Mrs Smith cut him off, "Bandah! How is that helpful? She already knows more than she should."

"Bandah?" Patsy asked. "Are you the same… the one who knew Alfred? Tell me, who is Alfred? And what do you mean by abilities?"

Mrs Smith addressed Bandah. "Whatever abilities she may turn out to have, they won't be much help tonight, not on my reckoning."

Bandah replied, "I disagree. Sellemae is coming. Of all the perils in the Crossworlds, she is one of the most dangerous. We're going to need all the help we can muster if we're to see the morrow."

"You're not helping. Off with you, before I grab the fly swatter."

Patsy cried out, "No, I need to know more. Tell me, I need to know about these abilities, and about Alfred."

Bandah looked at Mrs Smith. She let out a sigh then said, "I can see I won't be rid of you till you've had your say. Go on then, get it over with."

Bandah returned his attention to Patsy. "Few people can see fairies for what they are. Those who can invariably have more capabilities. They easily learn to hear the natural world: the gossip of the cicadas, the poetry in magpie songs, and the sarcasm of kookaburras."

Patsy rolled her eyes. "But that's just silly. Cicadas talking? And magpies? They wouldn't even know what poetry is."

She jumped in surprise at the sound of a small, high-pitched male voice behind her. "Are you really so sure?"

She turned to see Ferdinand stepping out from the shadows. Hands on hips, Patsy stared at the cat. "Seriously? This must be a dream of some sort. I know for a fact that you can't talk."

Ferdinand casually sat and licked a paw before replying. "Oh? You might want to think about that."

"You never spoke before, why should you start now?"

"Have you ever bothered to listen?"

Bandah said, "Right now, you're hypersensitive, more able to free up your mind. You're hearing what nature is actually saying, rather than what you expect. Anyone can be taught to listen with practice, but for you, it comes naturally. You just needed a catalyst, like the events today by the pool."

"What else can I expect to discover?"

"I don't know. But one thing's clear, like your mother, and her mother before her, you're a genuine Witch of the Crossworlds."

This was getting ridiculous. None of this could possibly be real. And what gave him the right to call her a witch? "How dare you accuse me of such a thing!"

"Please, Patricia, you need to relax and hear me out."

She rolled her eyes again. "No, I don't believe I do. I know what I am, and I'm certainly not a witch, of this world or any other. I'll be turning eleven in a few weeks. So, stop telling me lies." Patsy's breathing grew short and shallow. She'd had enough of being treated like an idiot. Wanting to stamp out all the lies, she lifted her foot and brought it down hard, as though squashing an insect.

To the surprise of them all, Bandah went flying backwards, slamming hard against the wall.

Ferdinand asked, "Still doubt what the pixie has to say?"

"I've more than likely eaten something that doesn't agree with me. Like I said, none of this is real. It can't be!"

Mrs Smith assured her, "Oh, don't you worry, this is very real. There's little time left to prepare; the guests will be arriving soon. Once dinner's over, I fear events will unfold quickly."

"And what of my parents? Do they know about this? About this Spider Queen, or that I'm supposedly some sort of witch? And you still haven't told me about Alfred."

Mrs Smith frowned. "Enough of the questions, you'd do well to go to your room, NOW!" She leaned forward to add a touch of sarcasm as she continued. "And rest while you can."

"I don't want to."

"I don't recall saying you have a choice. If we're to protect you, you'll be doing as I say. I don't want to be having to tell your parents how you took those letters that you've got hidden in your dresser."

So that was why Mrs Smith hadn't mentioned the letters earlier.

"That's blackmail!"

"Call it what you will. So long as it keeps you in your room till it's time for dinner. I'm not willing to run the risk of you getting up to your usual antics. There's too much at stake."

CHAPTER 5

Patsy marched up the stairs, with Mrs Smith close behind, while Ferdinand ran ahead.

When she entered her room, Mrs Smith remained outside in the corridor. "I'll collect you when it's time for dinner." She pulled the door shut, locked it, then walked away.

Patsy went straight to the dresser and looked for the letters. Seeing they were still there, along with the key, she made her way to the window.

Ferdinand jumped on the bed and set about getting comfortable. "That's twice in one day you've been locked in a room."

"Not for long." She opened the window as far as it would go and looked for a way she might climb down.

Ferdinand jumped on the windowsill. "Are you sure you want to do this? It's a long way down, you know."

Staring at the shed near the bottom of the garden, she replied, "I don't see that I have a choice."

She'd already swung one leg over the windowsill when Ferdinand said, "I wouldn't if I were you."

"Well, you're not me, are you?" Patsy lowered herself down so she was hanging by her hands on the outside, feet just short of the back veranda roof. She knew that if she let herself drop from here, it would make enough noise on the corrugated iron that any servants in the kitchen would be alerted to her latest escapade.

She moved one hand away from the windowsill and searched the sandstone wall for a fingerhold. Reaching out to her right, she found a small gap between the stone blocks, just big enough to work three of her fingers in as far as the first knuckle. It wouldn't support her for long, but should be enough for the second or so she'd need to lower herself to the roof. She gripped the sandstone as tight as she could, then eased her left hand away from the windowsill, not daring to breathe until she felt the roof under her feet.

Patsy sat on the roof with her back to the wall, looking for the safest spot to undertake the next stage of her escape. She could try to jump, but there'd be too great a risk of hurting herself. Looking to her left, she saw where the jasmine vine had spread from its lattice support and onto the roof. There was a risk her mother would be able to see her if she were in her drawing room, but it was a risk she had to take. She had to find those journals! It was her only hope of learning at least some of what was going on… from someone who wasn't going to tell her lies.

Patsy extended her feet toward the vine, then pushed with her hands to slide her backside along the iron, all the while being careful to stick to the parts where she could see it was nailed down. She hadn't gone far when the jagged end of a nail cut through both fabric and flesh. She resisted the urge to scream by gritting her teeth while silently counting to ten.

Once Patsy was within reach of the vine, the scent of the jasmine assaulted her nostrils, reminding her how it often gave her headaches and sneezing fits. *Not now*, she thought, *please... anything but that!* Conscious of an itch building in her nostrils, Patsy swung her legs over the edge and felt around with her feet until they'd found firm footholds.

She'd lowered her whole body from the roof onto the lattice when she sensed the sneeze coming. Closing her eyes, Patsy put a finger under her nose to block her nostrils, then held her jaw shut tight. She managed to reduce the sneeze to something that could barely be heard, then climbed down holding her now watery eyes shut to reduce the irritation, only opening them when she was past halfway.

Inside the drawing room, getting up from her chair and turning to face the window, was Patsy's mother. There was little choice but to jump, or her mother would see her for sure.

Patsy pushed away from the lattice, winding herself when she landed on her back. Confident she hadn't been seen, Patsy crawled behind the bushes until she reached a spot where she could make a run for the shed.

She sprinted away from the house, focusing on nothing but the shed and the cover it would provide. By the time she got there, Patsy was going so fast that she tripped while trying to stop, falling to her hands and knees in the muddy ground behind the small building.

She'd made it!

Looking toward the house to ensure no one was looking, Patsy slipped in through the door, pulling it shut behind her.

Where would someone hide a collection of journals?

She knew they wouldn't be in any of the drawers, but started by checking them anyway, rummaging around and taking out whatever was on top. She reached in with her hand to see if they were somehow concealed above the drawer, somehow wedged under the bench. Or, maybe they were concealed behind the drawers.

Next, she started checking the cupboards. She'd just opened the second cupboard when she heard one of the workers whistling as he approached the shed. Patsy rushed over to the door and pushed herself up against the wall, so as to be concealed by the door when it opened.

The gardener's voice boomed just outside the door. "I'm sure we'll get that one sorted before sunset Mister McIntyre, sir."

Her father was outside as well!

The door opened, and two sets of footsteps entered the shed. There was no mistaking the hammer of her father's boots on the floorboards as he entered the room. "I've no doubt a couple of good nails should hold it in place until we've cut some more timber to replace it."

Patsy held her breath, petrified of making the slightest sound.

The worker reached up to grab the jar of long nails from a shelf, then got distracted by the open cupboard and drawers not properly closed. "Begging your pardon, sir, but it looks like someone's been rummaging around in here."

"Yes, that would no doubt be my daughter. Cook mentioned earlier that she'd grabbed a jar and poked some holes in its lid this morning. I must have another talk to that girl about leaving things as she found them." Colin took a hammer from one of the drawers, then the two men left, pulling the door shut behind them.

Patsy let out a huge sigh of relief, then started checking the boxes stacked under the workbench.

Having searched the last of the boxes, Patsy sat on the floor, looking around and wondering where else they could be hidden. She tried to remember the words of the note… *where the gardeners keep their tools.*

The rafters!

There were more boxes stored in the rafters.

The heavy ladder swayed back and forth as Patsy tried to position it safely. Once in place, she clambered up its rungs then took careful steps along the wooden beams until she reached the two wooden chests. The hinges let out a loud creak as she lifted the lid open.

Empty!

She checked the second one, only to find the same result.

... where the gardeners keep their tools.

Patsy surveyed the room from her vantage point in the rafters, in case there was some possibility she'd missed. She looked at the assortment of shovels, rakes and hoes in the corner.

... where the gardeners keep their tools.

Where would she hide a collection of books she didn't want found? Certainly not in the places she'd looked so far.

... where the gardeners keep their tools.

There was nothing in the message that implicitly said they were inside.

Being on a slope, the shed had been built on piers. Could that be it? Could the journals be *underneath* the shed? The more she thought about it, the more Patsy felt sure that's where *she'd* hide them. She'd put them in a wooden box and wedge them under the floorboards, somewhere safe from the weather and where nobody would be likely to come across them.

Having made her way back down the ladder, Patsy looked through the window to check no one was watching, then slipped out the door and around to the back of the shed.

Choosing the spot where the clearance from the ground was greatest, Patsy crawled under, pausing to give her eyes time to adjust to the dim light before searching for a box that might contain books.

There it was-- two beams away and directly in front of her!

The slime and mud felt repulsive as she crawled across to retrieve the box, but once Patsy was back out in the daylight with her prize, she decided it was worth the effort.

She opened the box, lifted out the collection of books, then opened the first one to a random page.

> *Alfred asked me again today to explain how it is that I came to know the art of listening to nature and talking with animals. Oh, how much easier when all we shared was my lessons in mathematics, the sciences, and English.*
>
> *Father says our language and what we learn from the Book of Wisdom is sacred, and must only be shared among druids and their bloodline.*
>
> *But there are no druids in the Blue Mountains other than us, and I do so enjoy Alfred's company.*
>
> *There are some things in life that mean so much more when shared.*

Patsy turned to the next entry.

> *Today, I caved in. I don't care what my parents think, Alfred deserves to know the truth about my origins, and our ancestral oath to protect humanity from the perils lurking in the Crossworlds.*

The perils of the Crossworlds. Wasn't that the term Bandah had used? She opened another of the journals at random.

I told Alfred the true extent of my powers this morning. To say he was shocked would be an understatement…

She read through the page, realising that her grandmother really did see herself as a witch… a Witch of the Crossworlds. She turned the page and continued reading.

Today was my first experience, outside my dreams, of flying. After I'd snuck up behind Alfred and poked his ribs, he set upon chasing me through the bush. A tree had fallen across the path, and Alfred was sure to catch me if I stopped to clamber over it. Instead, I jumped as high I could, pushing the air aside with my arms, thereby pulling myself through the air. It's so easy to see air as nothing, but should you allow yourself to see it as one sees water, it's surprising how easily one can move through it… and the look on Alfred's face was priceless!

Still struggling to accept the idea she also possessed some manner of magical powers (despite what she'd already seen today, and her conversations with the pixie, Mrs Smith, and the cat), Patsy turned to a page further into the volume, hoping to find more conclusive evidence one way or the other.

It was my turn to be surprised today. A rare occurrence took place when a fairy appeared near the portal at the pool. The most amazing part was that Alfred could see her too!

The only explanation I can think of is that his ancestry

must link back to the druids as well! I can't wait to tell Father when he returns from Parramatta tomorrow.

Eager to learn of her great-grandfather's response, Patsy turned to the next entry.

Why must Father be this way? He says Alfred seeing the fairy meant nothing, other than that he is draining power from me, through a kind of osmosis ... and that I should have nothing more to do with him.

I won't abide by his ruling.

I shall continue to see Alfred in secret.

She skipped a few pages and read on.

Father was cross with me again today, after he heard the cicadas singing to everyone that they'd seen me with Alfred by the creek.

Do they have to be so indiscreet? I know it's just their way of celebrating all that is good, but is there no way that two people in love can share time together in true privacy?

Meanwhile, Father continues to grow weaker. His powers have failed him, and his eyes have lost their sparkle. He says it's a sign that humanity no longer needs our protection.

Yet, my own powers grow stronger by the day, and Alfred managed to move a small rock today with the power of his will.

Aware she'd soon have to return to her room, Patsy flipped to another page.

I met the man today that I'm told I should marry.

Father no longer seems concerned with the need for me to wed a man with druid blood, but maintains his contempt toward Alfred.

My husband-to-be is the son of a wealthy squatter. He seems a good man, too good a man to tell the truth of what is in my heart, that it still lies with Alfred, and always will. I shall fulfil my duty. I shall marry him, and bear his children, accepting that to do so will mean leaving behind all I've learnt from the Book of Wisdom.

Patsy picked up another volume. It appeared on first inspection to be less used than the others. When she opened it, she could see why—there were just two entries.

Should I feel guilty? Am I somehow a lesser person for my failure to weep at my husband's funeral, and my inability to mourn him in the months since his passing?

I will always mourn the loss of a good man from this world, yet I still resent having been forced into marriage, and never once felt the connection a woman should toward her husband.

The only joy left in my life is baby Meredith's smiles and laughter.

I noticed Alfred watching from the stables today. Meredith took her first steps while we were in the garden enjoying the sunshine.

Oh, how I miss his arms around me and the tenderness of his lips on mine.

Patsy turned to the final entry.

> *Bandah finally told me the truth today, the real reason Father is on his deathbed, and why Alfred has developed powers of his own.*
>
> *It's not me that Alfred draws his power from, it's Father.*
>
> *The natural order has declared its hand, anointing Alfred to be my Father's successor as a protector of the Crossworlds.*
>
> *Bandah says the only way this process can be halted is for Alfred to leave. Tomorrow, when we meet by the creek, I will accept Alfred's offer to take Meredith and myself away from here.*
>
> *We will make our way to Sydney, where we will live as though married and start a new life together.*
>
> *Mother will then be able to use her knowledge from the Book of Wisdom to nurse Father back to health, while Alfred and I will be able to leave the burden of my druid heritage behind.*

If she wanted to piece the rest of the puzzle together, Patsy felt certain she'd need to learn more about Alfred.

The sound of a guest's carriage arriving reminded Patsy of the need to be back in her room by the time Mrs Smith came to collect her.

Patsy packed the books back in their box, and wedged it between the bearer and the floorboards once more. She kept low as she ran up the garden to the house, disturbing a pair of grazing wallabies on the way.

Having checked that no one was looking, she snuck into the laundry, confident it would be free of servants whilst so many preparations were underway in the kitchen. Patsy grabbed a sponge, wetting it so she could wash the mud from her hands and face, and grabbed a clothes peg before crawling past the bushes that lined the veranda. On reaching the lattice, she put the peg on her nose and climbed like a monkey.

A minute later, Patsy was back in her room. She removed the muddy dress and hid it under her bed, then collected a fresh one from her wardrobe. Ferdinand lay on her bed grooming himself. He paused to look up and ask, "Learn anything interesting?"

"I want to know who Alfred is."

"Oh, that tells me a lot. By the way, you might want to brush your hair before you go downstairs as well. We wouldn't want your parents believing the servants were sloppy about grooming you." Having said his piece, he went back to his own grooming.

Patsy looked in the mirror above her dresser. Her hair would have to do. She glared at the smug cat. The hard part wasn't so much getting used to the idea that he could talk, it was more about dealing with his attitude.

She'd just managed to get fresh stockings and shoes on when she heard the key turn in the bedroom door.

CHAPTER 6

Patsy took her seat at the table by the side of her mother, careful to ensure that nothing she said or did would embarrass her parents.

Colin sat at the head of the table, with Meredith to his right, and Charles Danbury on his left. *Damn it*, thought Colin. He was sure he'd instructed the servants to direct Charles and his wife to the other end of the table. Now, he was stuck with Charles getting in his ear about the virtues of moving to Bathurst and capitalising on the booming economies of the goldfields. "Can you imagine it, Colin? Between us, we could build the biggest hotel in the region. I've been told there's enough gold up there to keep the mines going for centuries..."

He'd heard it all before. Last week, Charles was extolling the very same virtues of Ballarat. And his grand ideas always hinged on Colin and Meredith selling their property.

There were a dozen or so guests for dinner tonight, a normal situation for a Friday. Among them was the Reverend Casey. Patsy couldn't help but notice how he glared at Mrs Smith as the old woman helped Cook serve out the entrée. She was taken aback when he turned his attention to her and asked, "So tell me, child, how was your day? Did anything out of the ordinary take place?"

Patsy recoiled in her chair. It was the first time in years the Reverend had even acknowledged her existence. "I had a very normal day, Your Reverence."

"Is that so? I wonder if the servants may have a different understanding of how your day was." He grabbed Cook by the arm as she passed the back of his chair. "Tell me, Cook, was there anything out of the ordinary that you may have observed?"

Cook's cheeks flushed bright red. She wanted to protect Patsy, but was aware of what a poor liar she was. "There was nothing of importance. Young Patricia found an injured spider in the garden, but it was of no great interest."

"A spider you say?" The Reverend turned to Patsy. "And where did you come across this 'spider,' my dear?"

The room went quiet, the guests feeling the urgency of the Reverend's questioning. Patsy looked to Mrs Smith for assurance, only to be dismayed when the woman ignored her. She was about to reply when her mother spoke up. "Spiders? Oh, come now, Reverend, do we really want to talk of such things at the dinner table?"

"There are many things in this world that are evil in their nature, and it is good to discuss them with the young. It can be the difference between them following an enlightened path or descending to a world of depravity."

Patsy's father took a sip on his wine then stood, his every word slow and deliberate. "Reverend Casey, you are here as a guest in my home for dinner this evening, and I will not have you talking to my wife and daughter in such a manner. Nor will I accept you manhandling my servants as you did just now with Cook. The only reason you've not been asked to leave already is that you are purportedly a man of God."

The Reverend pushed his plate forward, then stood himself. He was an imposing figure, despite his years, and taller than Patsy's father. His hands alone were almost as big as the plates they were eating off, and his balding head was framed by his long grey beard. "That being the case, I shall excuse myself. I have matters to attend to anyway." He stared accusingly at Mrs Smith. "I fear there are ungodly things happening in these parts, and I intend to deal with them as I must."

*

The Reverend Alfred Casey collected his hat and coat from the parlour, then walked out into crisp night air, feeling the occasional drop of rain. There would be a storm soon, of that he had little doubt.

As the priest approached his sulky, a cockroach flying by caught his attention. He reached out and snatched it from the air.

Bandah let out a strong protest. "Hey, there's no need for that! I was coming in to land anyway. What's your problem?"

"I'm not happy with the allegiance that's been forced on us, but I understand it's need. However, regarding what happened today... to be honest, I'd come to doubt that I'd see it again in this lifetime." He opened his fist, so the pixie could feel free to fly away if he wished.

Bandah put his shield to one side, lay back, and stretched before settling into the comfort of his friend's hand. He had a brief chuckle before replying. "Oh yeah, I totally agree. Allowing Mrs Smith to believe

I'd help her betray Patricia never sat well. But hey, we know what she's up to now, and it's exactly as you predicted. By the way, you did well in there. I could see that Mrs Smith was none the wiser about the charade you and Colin orchestrated."

The Reverend laughed. "That's doesn't surprise me in the slightest. She never was the brightest. I'm just glad Colin picked up on my signals. For someone making it up on the spot, the man was convincing."

"We need to make sure we're underway before she realises she's been conned. She plans to take the girl through the portal before Sellemae comes through, hoping to appease her by offering Patricia in place of the fairy. She's convinced herself that if she betrays me as well, Sellemae will restore her to her old fairy state."

"And no doubt string her up to spend eternity singing in her infernal choir."

"I don't think Mrs Smith cares about that. Her arthritis is a constant reminder of her mortality in human form. She'd prefer an eternity of servitude than face the reality of aging."

The Reverend shook his head. "She always was a fool. It's little wonder the fairies chose her as their offering." He climbed onto the sulky and set the horses in motion. "What of the girl? What does she know of what's going on?"

"She knows enough now that she may be useful in helping us pull this off. She's seen the book, and Neridah's journals. She's already found some of her power, and I believe she'll be formidable by the time she faces true danger."

The Reverend shook his head. "You're expecting too much of her. Formidable power without wisdom driving it will be our undoing. We must ensure she's relaxed and keep her protected. Once we've returned with Neridah, she can join her mother and grandmother in a trinity of power to close off the portal, and keep that vile creature in her own realm where she belongs. I'll park the sulky near the bridge, somewhere out of sight. Then we can work our way down the creek by the light of my lantern. We'll need to try to reach the pool before this storm breaks."

*

The mood in the dining room was sombre, punctuated by the sound of thunder from the approaching storm. Patsy watched on as one guest after another stood and made their apologies. With each flash of lightning, Patsy saw the departing guests' shadows appear on the wall as hideous creatures, leering at her with evil intent. Her mother took her hand. "Don't worry yourself, Patricia, it's just a storm. Although I fear it will be a big one."

Her father stood and addressed the departing guests. "While I understand the discomfort some of you may have felt over the Reverend's departure, I bid you please, stay till the storm has passed. I'd not want to see any of you get caught in the downpour and gale that's coming our way."

One of the departing guests replied for them all: "While we thank you for your concern, we all live within a half hour ride of here, and would like to ensure all is secure before the storm hits. Thank you so much for a wonderful meal as always." They were grateful the impending weather gave a cover for their early departure.

Within minutes, there was just Patsy, her parents, Cook and Mrs Smith remaining in the room. As Cook was preparing to leave the room with the barely touched plates of food, she was stopped in her tracks by the booming voice of Patsy's father. "Tell me, Cook, what exactly did you do with the spider my daughter showed you today."

This was the last thing Cook wanted. How could he ask such a thing in front of Patsy? "Begging your pardon, sir, but the creature was suffering. It needed to be put out of its misery."

"And she'd explained to you that it was actually a fairy?"

"Aye, sir, that she did, but I could see with my own—"

"Don't worry, Cook, you're not in trouble. Please, put the plates on the table and take a seat. There'll be plenty of time to clean up after we've finished discussing Patricia's spider. Mrs Smith, I'd be pleased if you could take a seat and join us as well."

The two servants looked to each other, then took adjacent seats, a few chairs away from the family.

Colin McIntyre chewed on a mouthful of mutton pie, then took a sip of wine. "I'm curious, Cook. Tell me, what else did Patricia tell you of her spider?"

"It was in one of your jars, sir, and she'd punched holes in the lid." Her lips were quivering as she continued. "She kept insisting all day it was a fairy, sir." She cast her eyes down as though she'd suffered a terrible defeat by having to betray Patsy.

"I'm pleased to know my daughter has such a vibrant imagination, and that my staff are capable of such sound judgements. Cook, I thank you for your honesty, and for preparing such a delicious meal this evening. It's sad so little has been eaten. You can feel free to return to cleaning up, but please, have the day off tomorrow. I'm sure we'll be able to hold the place together without you for at least one day."

"Thank you, sir! The market will be on in Blackheath, so I'll enjoy the chance to relax and walk among the stalls."

"Wonderful! I'll see to it that one of the stablehands drives you into town, and that he brings you home safely in the evening."

As Cook collected her stack of dishes and left the room, Colin

McIntyre turned his attention to his daughter. "I've told you before about going to the creek."

Patsy refused to look at him as she asked, "What makes you think that I got the spider from there? There's spiders everywhere around our property, especially in the stables and the laundry… even in your shed."

"Yes, there are. But this one, this one looked to you like it was a fairy."

"So?"

"There's only one place I've ever known of anywhere where spiders who look like fairies come from, and that's the large pool down at the creek."

Patsy's mother interjected, "Colin!"

"Something's going to happen tonight, Meredith. You and I both know it. The Reverend Casey knows it too. This may be our only chance to get your mother back."

Meredith's eyes betrayed her surprise. "Do you really think it's wise to talk of such things when Patricia knows so little?"

Mrs Smith replied, "It's not just wise, ma'am, but I believe it's now critical that you tell her all you can. She's already learned enough today that she needs to know some more. Your daughter has powers, and I believe they'll be beyond your own. You had little guidance to help you develop yours after your grandmother passed away. But today, young Patricia learned to listen to nature without so much as being taught the normal methods. Sellemae is angry about the theft of her offering, and intends to cross the worlds tonight and seek her vengeance on young Patricia and Cook for denying her the joy of another voice in her choir." She turned to Colin. "But you knew of this anyway, did you not?"

"Am I that transparent?"

"I've known you since you and the mistress were newborns. You can't hide anything from me, Colin McIntyre. No one else saw the signals that passed between the Reverend Casey and yourself, but they were clear as day to an old fairy like me. You seem to forget, I've lived for many thousands of years."

Patsy looked at her father and whispered, "It's all true." She turned and stared at Mrs Smith, then blurted out, "I knew it! I knew it was you!"

Colin looked at his daughter. "According to Mrs Smith, you've already shown you have powers. Do you have any understanding yet of what they may be?"

There was so much more Patsy wanted to say, but the words refused to come out. The uncomfortable pause in the conversation was broken by Ferdinand, who'd just taken his place on the chair across from Patsy. "Apart from talking to animals and using her anger to throw pixies around, she doesn't seem to know yet."

Patsy found her voice again as she watched her father listen to the cat. "So, you can hear him too?"

"Oh yes, your mother taught me how to listen years ago. There's a great deal I've learned from your mother."

Patsy turned to her mother. "Does that mean you're a witch too?"

Meredith was taken aback. She hadn't expected to face dealing with these issues so soon. "While I have some powers, I'm not one that should really be called a Witch of the Crossworlds, not like your grandmother. She learned from the Book of Wisdom, the big book in the library. But she was fooled, by a particularly nasty fairy."

Mrs Smith squirmed in her seat, wishing she could avoid having to respond. "You've no idea what I sacrificed that day."

"Oh, but I do… you've told me at least a hundred times a year since I first met you."

Mrs Smith opted to tell her again anyway. "As a fairy, I was immortal. Now, I feel the pain of arthritis and so much more. I'd lived thousands of years without aging before I became human. Now, in the mere space of forty years, I've been reduced to this."

Meredith was nonchalant. "Well, tonight, you have the chance to help us change the result of your deception."

"Oh yes, and how wonderful that will be. I'll extend my life by thousands of years, stuck with all the pain and aging I've endured as a human."

Meredith replied, "You should be more grateful, Mrs Smith. My grandmother took you in, and gave you a job as a servant, all thanks to the pleading of the Reverend Casey's uncle."

"Aye, that she did. And as gratitude, I did marry the man."

"Then led him to an early grave."

"It was the bottle that put him in the ground. And furthermore, I have to ask… who is it that benefits most from this arrangement? I can't help but feel your family has had the better part of it. I've worked tirelessly to protect your child from all manner of threats."

Colin McIntyre stood up. "Codswallop!"

Meredith reached across and touched his arm. "It's okay, Colin, we can deal with these details later."

"Oh, can we now? This storm that's coming, it's not natural. You know that as well as I do. There was just one thing I asked of you throughout these years, Mrs Smith, and that was to keep my daughter away from that pool. Of all days to relax your guard, you chose today?"

Mrs Smith's face contorted into a frown. "I find it so strange that you worked so hard to keep her from a place where you and the Mistress spent so much time together in childhood. Perhaps, if she'd been made more aware of what's down there, we wouldn't be facing this situation."

Ferdinand looked at Colin. "She has a point, you know."

"I didn't ask your opinion."

Ferdinand rolled his eyes and went back to grooming himself.

Throughout the exchange, Patricia felt she had little choice but to sit in silence. The fearful images of the guests' shadows as they'd left still disturbed her. As they swirled around in her head she whispered, "The shadows…"

Soft as her voice may have been, it still grabbed the room's attention. Her mother took her hand and asked, "What about them? Did they seem unusual?"

"When the guests were leaving, their shadows looked hideous, like the most horrible creatures. They resembled the demons the Reverend once showed me in one of his books. It was the same with Mrs Bradshaw earlier, her shadow even tried to reach out and grab me as she was leaving."

Meredith turned to her husband. "They're going after him!"

Colin replied, "Yes, and it would seem you were right about the need to look for a new tutor."

Patsy asked her mother, "Who are they? And who are they going after?"

"They are mind thieves, and if you've seen them, I've little doubt what their intentions are."

"What's a mind thief?"

Meredith took Patsy's hand in hers. "They're in league with the fairies. I've never seen one, and I obviously don't have that capability, or I'd also have seen them tonight."

Mrs Smith scoffed, "In league with the fairies? That's a good one! They were the ones who made the deal with Sellemae, promising to lure a fairy into her web every two score years, just as they did with me. They're no friends of mine, but that's indeed what she saw. I saw them too."

Colin's jaw dropped. "I don't believe this. You saw them, and you chose not to tell us?"

Mrs Smith chuckled as she replied, "Ha! Do you take me for that big a fool? My night will be so much easier if the Reverend doesn't make it to that pool."

Meredith said, "After all these years, and everything my family's done for you, you still care about no one but yourself."

Patsy groaned, "Ugh! You still haven't answered my question."

Colin stood up. "I'll have to go after him!"

Meredith tried to calm her husband, standing with him and placing a gentle hand on his shoulder, encouraging him to take his seat again. "Darling, there's nothing you can do against them now." She leaned closer and whispered, "Bandah is with him, at least we know he'll stand a chance."

Mrs Smith strained to listen in. If Meredith was trying to keep something from her, it could only mean one thing. "That infernal pixie! He's betrayed me!" She rose to her feet. "I must go after them, or this will never—"

She was cut off mid-sentence as she was flung against the wall. Patsy stood across the table, her arm pointing in Mrs Smith's direction. The old woman was at least a metre above ground level with her arms outstretched on the wall.

Patsy's breathing was heavy as she glared at the woman. "I asked a question and I want an answer. What's a mind thief?"

CHAPTER 7

Forty years prior, Alfred sat by the pool at sunrise, anxiously waiting in hope. He was almost ready to give up when Neridah came walking down the path, the early morning light glowing in her thick mane of red hair.

She walked up to him, reached up to place her hands on his broad shoulders, then ran her fingers down his arms till she took his hands in hers and leaned in to gently kiss his lips. "I'm coming with you." She rested her head on his chest. "I should never have listened to my father. Having been through a loveless marriage, I know now, more than ever, I want to be with you, and always have done."

"And what about your mother? Will she be okay, with your father on his deathbed?"

"I told her my intentions last night, and we have her blessing. She'll be bringing Meredith down to join us once she's had breakfast and dressed. Father doesn't respond to the herbs she gives him for the pain now, and even her most powerful healing methods do nothing for him. She says it's unlikely he'll even be aware of my absence."

Alfred held her, losing himself in the depth of her eyes. "You've made me happier today than I thought was possible. I've arranged everything. If we make our way to the Danburys', they've promised to give us a ride to Blackheath in their carriage. From there, we can get a coach to Sydney. My uncle has given me money from his savings to cover the fare, and enough for two weeks' lodgings."

"It's wonderful of Jeremiah to be so kind."

"He said it's to be a wedding gift. So, we'd best make sure we've taken our vows before we see him again. Bandah believes that once we leave, there's a chance of your father recovering. That his illness is due in large part to my presence draining him of the strength he draws from the Crossworlds."

Neridah shook her head. "I doubt that. He's been unhappy since the move from Ireland. It wasn't his desire to move here, but he felt compelled to follow the re-alignment of the portal. The climate doesn't agree with him, and Mother says he's been miserable since they first stepped off the boat from Ireland."

There was a long silence before Alfred said, "I saw a fairy down here one day. It must have been a year and a half ago, while you were still with child. She told me we'd be together one day."

Neridah put her arms around him and closed her eyes as she tightened her embrace. "Let's hope this is one occasion when a fairy actually tells the truth." Neridah eased her hold on him, lifting her head as though listening intently. She looked toward the rock on the far side of the pool. "Did you hear that?"

"What, the cicadas?"

"No, it sounded like a cry for help."

Listening closely, Alfred could hear it too: a faint distress call. "Help me please, I'm stuck in the Spider Queen's web."

The cicadas went silent, creating an eerie feeling around the pool.

Neridah stood up, pulled her dress up around her knees and entered the water. "Come on, Alfred, it sounds like a fairy. Let's see what her problem is."

Alfred removed his shoes, despite his misgivings. "Is this wise? Weren't you just questioning the trustworthiness of fairies?"

"Don't be silly, neither of us are fools." She continued making her way across the pool. "Trust me, we'll be alright."

Alfred waded in after her. "I'm really not liking this. Why'd the cicadas go quiet?"

Neridah stopped, then let out a groan. "Ugh! Will you please not be so boring? As well as having the strength of the Crossworlds behind us, we can both see and hear them for what they are. We've nothing to fear."

On reaching the other side, Neridah peered behind the large rock to see a fairy hopelessly tangled in a web, her right hand still gripping her wand, but unable to move. The fairy looked at her and breathed a sigh of relief. "Oh! Thank you for coming to my aid. If you can just touch the tip of my wand, it will draw enough power from the Crossworlds to set me free. But please be quick. I've been stuck here for ages, and I fear the Spider Queen is approaching as we speak."

Alfred was halfway across. "Neridah, please... don't be doing anything she tells you."

Neridah looked back. "Don't be silly, I'll be fine. It's just a fairy."

As she reached out to touch the wand, Bandah appeared from nowhere, trying to drag her hand away. "No! Don't do it! She's tricked you."

Neridah shook her hand, flinging away the pixie. She'd had a lifetime with her father telling her what to do. There was no way she was going to start her new life being ordered around by a pixie.

She touched the end of the wand and was immediately engulfed in a ball of shimmering light.

Alfred watched in horror as the light faded, revealing that Neridah and the fairy had exchanged places.

The fairy stuck in the web now bore Neridah's features and the young woman standing by the rock bore those of the fairy.

The woman who had been a fairy burst out laughing. "Yes! I'm free! Sellemae, Queen of all the Spiders, I offer you a wondrous tribute! Behold, I give unto you a Witch of the Crossworlds… in fairy-form. Come now and take her that she may decorate your lair." As Alfred looked on, Neridah faded away from sight, dissolving into nothingness within the web. The woman standing before him turned. "Now, I shall see to it that the witch's daughter is raised appropriately, that one day I may use her to return to the immortal fairy-state."

Alfred pointed an accusing finger. "Stay away from the child, or so help me—"

"So help you what? What's the matter? Lost for what to do without your little witch around to help?"

A voice calling from the opposite side of the bank interrupted them. It was Alfred's uncle, Jeremiah Smith. "Alfred! What are you doing? Who's that woman with you? Where's Neridah? I thought you'd be halfway to Blackheath by now."

Alfred had no idea how to explain what had just happened. When the woman turned to face Jeremiah, the man's jaw dropped. He couldn't remember having gazed on such a beautiful woman.

Two months later, the woman who'd once been a fairy married

Alfred's uncle, becoming Mrs Jeremiah Smith.

Stricken with grief, and unable to turn to his uncle any longer for support, Alfred sought counsel from the only friend he trusted. "I still can't accept this, Bandah. Surely, there must be some way to get her back."

"Not without the aid of a Crossworld Witch. Even then, it would be a journey fraught with danger. If you're going to attempt it, you'll need to spend a lifetime preparing for the hazardous trek into Sellemae's domain. I'll teach you all I can, but there is much you need to learn about yourself as well. You'll need to lead a life of discipline, so you can learn to focus your mind."

It was then that Alfred Casey made the decision to join the seminary and train as a priest.

*

The Reverend Alfred Casey heard a horse whinny from behind the bushes by the roadside. Eager to confirm his suspicions, he brought his sulky to a stop and dismounted. The light of his lantern revealed a path where tea trees had been flattened, leading to where Mrs Bradshaw's carriage and horses had been abandoned.

Bandah called out to him from the other side of the vehicle. "You might want to come around here and look at this too."

The driver was facedown beside it with a bloody rock next to his head. The Reverend Casey hadn't counted on Mrs Bradshaw being among those who would attempt to stop him. He now realised that he had less time than he'd anticipated. "It might be prudent if you fly ahead and see where the perpetrator may be. I'll continue on as planned, but if I'm to walk into an ambush, I'd like to know where it will be."

"I suspect whoever did this has been taken over by a mind thief. I've no doubt there'll be others who have been taken over nearby."

The Reverend climbed back onto his sulky as he replied, "I'd prefer you put your time into finding out rather than waste time speculating." He cracked his whip beside the horse and it took off. "I'll meet you downstream of the bridge."

He continued down the road till he reached a small bridge, its timbers rattling as he crossed. There was a clearing on the other side where he tied the horse to a hitching post.

As he crossed the road, the thunder of approaching hooves caused the Reverend to take a step back. A large riderless mare, that must have been at least seventeen hands at the shoulder, raced by, almost bowling him over when it passed within inches of him. As it disappeared into the dark night, he made his way down the bank and began wading through the icy water toward his date with destiny, a lantern in one hand and an ornate cane in the other.

A few minutes into his walk, he found Bandah waiting for him.

Bandah whispered in his ear, "The guests from the dinner tonight, all of them, they've been taken by the mind thieves. They're not much further downstream, and they've set themselves up on either side, lying in wait. Mrs Bradshaw seems to be leading them."

"Then I'd best make my way up the ridge and forge a path around them."

"No. That'd be far too risky. I've got a better plan."

CHAPTER 8

Mrs Smith struggled to breathe as she answered Patsy. "The mind thieves… they possess people. They go inside people's heads and make them do things. It wasn't Mrs Bradshaw who chose to lock you in the library earlier today. It was the mind thief controlling her." Satisfied with the answer, Patsy released Mrs Smith, letting her drop to the floor.

No one said a word as they watched Mrs Smith struggle to her feet, Meredith coming forward in a reflex action to help.

Then, a scream rang out from the kitchen.

Colin McIntyre raced out of the dining room, eager to find the cause. He froze when he reached the kitchen door.

He'd never seen so many spiders!

Cook was standing on a chair in the middle of it all, unable to take her hands away from her eyes.

Colin took a cautious step into the room. "Meredith, Patricia, you both need to come here right away." When Meredith and Patsy reached the door, Colin turned to his daughter and asked, "What do you see?"

"There must be at least a hundred."

"A hundred what?"

"Fairies, of course, don't you see them?"

Colin looked to his wife. "And what about you, darling? What do you see?"

"I see some fairies, but mostly spiders… lots and lots of spiders."

Brimming with confidence, Patsy entered the room. "Don't worry, Cook. I understand they may look like spiders to you, but they're really fairies, and I'm not scared of them."

One of the fairies turned to Patsy. "Well, you should be, especially after what you did to our sister. You couldn't have been more disrespectful if you tried."

Much to the fairy's surprise, Patsy ignored her, continuing to move forward. "I wasn't scared the first time I met a fairy, and I'm not scared now. Didn't you know? It turns out that, apparently, I'm a witch … a Witch of the Crossworlds! And while I don't yet know exactly what I'm capable of, neither do you."

The fairies (or spiders, depending on where you were looking from) started to back away. "You can't protect her right through the night, witch. You'll soon be facing Sellemae in battle. This has been foretold!"

"I don't want to fight her."

"The great battle is already written in the future's history. Soon, the outcome will become clear to all as the words of the ancient texts come into focus."

Meredith stepped forward, putting her arm around Patsy's shoulder. "I've had enough of this! You fairies, spiders, or whatever you are. Your offerings achieve little more than to buy time from an evil creature to whom you owe nothing."

The lead fairy stood its ground as the others hastened their retreat. "It's not about debts, it's about respect."

Meredith replied, "Fairies know nothing of respect! Believe me when I promise you this, Cook will be safe tonight, because she'll be with us."

The fairy laughed. "I don't believe you people! Who are you to talk? You can't even see half of us for who we are. What an appalling way to go into a battle you're already certain to lose."

Ignoring the fairy, Meredith strode up to Cook and took her hand. "It's okay, Cook. Trust me, we'll keep you safe through the night."

Cook cried in loud sobs as she fell into Meredith's arms and watched the spiders dissipate.

*

The Reverend Alfred Casey took off his coat, as Bandah had suggested, and placed it on the creek bank next to his lantern. Hundreds of pixies silently flew in from the surrounding bushes, working their way through his coat and linking their limbs together as they went. Bit by bit, the coat began to fill out, until every gap was gone and it rose as a complete reconstruction of the man.

At first, the replicant swayed back and forth while the pixies grew accustomed to the coordination required to pull off their cunning scheme. Then, picking up the lantern, it made a gesture of farewell before heading downstream.

Just before reaching the area where the mind thieves lay waiting, the pixies diverted to a side trail, so as to take an alternate route along the ridge.

The Reverend watched from behind a bush as Mrs Bradshaw stepped out into the middle of the creek, holding a lantern of her own. "What a fool, believing he could outwit us." She looked up the hill at Alfred's lantern as the pixies carried it into the distance. "We'll split up." She pointed to the Danburys. "You two, go downstream to the pool, then climb up the ridge toward his light. The rest of you, come with me, and we'll pursue him from behind, cutting off the option of retreat." Without hesitation, they set off as directed.

Alfred waited until Mrs Bradshaw was well and truly out of sight and the sound of the Danburys splashing through the creek had faded into the distance. Although the mind thieves had fallen for the deception, they weren't likely to be fooled for long. But with luck, it would give him enough time to head downstream to where he could move through the Crossworlds without distraction.

This would be his first experience of crossing the thresholds between worlds since learning the secrets of how to do so from Bandah during his early days of training. He'd promised himself that he wouldn't cross between worlds until he was sure he had a chance to bring Neridah back with him.

Although the clouds from the approaching storm were closing in and a steady drizzle had started, there was still hope of finding his way by moonlight, but not for much longer.

He moved through the icy water, preparing himself mentally and reciting the mantra he'd been taught by his friend: "Umbah yimbah lundah, umbah yimbah lundah, umbah…"

After several minutes of walking, and bringing himself to the necessary state of mind, he came upon the area where the creek flattened out and expanded into a wide pool, the pool where Patsy had encountered her first fairy and the Reverend Casey had sat with Neridah as a young boy.

The Reverend could hear the Danburys scrambling up the ridge, but was unconcerned now about the consequences of being seen.

He pulled the handle out from his cane to reveal a long, slim sword. He held it over his heart as he continued the mantra, slowly fading away from this world and moving into another. A world dominated by darkness and chaos.

CHAPTER 9

Sellemae danced elegantly about her throne room, dangling her prize possession by a thread from the talon-like finger that extended from the end of one of her many limbs. "Oh, the joy! Yesterday I had but one witch, tonight I shall have, not just a second, but a third as well! What do you say to that, hmmm?"

Wrapped in a cocoon of silk with just her head exposed, Neridah ignored her.

"Oh, come now! That's so boring! After two score years hoping for the unlikely scenario where your lot may change, you still refuse to play by my rules?"

She stared down the queen, challenging her. "If your prize was taken from you, then my family's ready for whatever you may plan. My daughter will have had forty years to study and learn the craft. By now, her knowledge and power will be formidable. You have but one choice: you must accept defeat, before the battle begins."

Sellemae laughed, then turned to address the dozens of fairies in similar cocoons that hung by threads from the ceiling. She made a sweeping gesture with three of her limbs. "Sing a song of joy for me, my lovely guests."

The cocoon bound fairies burst into a beautiful melody that lit up the room with its sweet harmonies. The lyrics however, revealed a darker truth.

All hail the great Sellemae,
May her evil reign forever stay.
Her poison is so strong,
We know to sing our song,
Or else she'll make us pay.
For when we do not play,
She revels so in our fears,
And loves to see our tears.

The captive choir stopped when the doors to the chamber burst open. A contingent of the rogue fairies (fairies who voluntarily descended to the world of the Spider Queen in exchange for her granting them power to move more freely between the Crossworlds) entered the chamber.

Sellemae reared up, ready to strike. "How dare you barge in while I'm immersed in joyful preparations! Within the hour, I will open the gateway to the human world. Then I, the great Sellemae, shall avenge the theft of what was mine." She rolled all eight of her human-like eyes upward and continued, "What a sweet vengeance it will be! I shall take the witch and feast on the wretched human who squashed my prize underfoot. Then, I'll rid the manor they built so near my doorway of its vermin infestation. It will make a fine nest for my eggs. The human world shall become mine, as did this one… ten thousand years ago."

One of the rogue fairies stepped forward. "We know you've got these great plans for tonight, but we've heard news that may force you to make a few… alterations."

Sellemae swiped one of her eight arms at the rogue, only to be frustrated when the fairy flashed into a different world, coming back an instant later. "Grrr, you try my patience, fairy pest! Tell me, what is it that emboldens you to risk my wrath?"

"I meant no disrespect, Your Greatness, but I think you'll agree the matter is of great urgency. We received word the humans and the child-witch are preparing to descend to our world before we have the chance to rise into theirs."

"Ah, wonderful news! They'll save us the trouble of rounding them up in their world!"

"Be that as it may, there is more. The mind thieves told us the priest they've been warning us of also intends making the journey, aided by a horde of pixies. They're being led by a pestilent nuisance who calls himself Bandah."

"Interesting…" Sellemae brought several of her limbs around the rogue to embrace her. "You shall be richly rewarded for your dedicated service, and your recognition of the need to keep me informed." Her embrace became an ironclad grip. "However, I do not appreciate being interrupted during my entertainment! Do you dare to think such loathsome creatures could ever pose a threat to me in my own realm?"

The rogue tried to flash across to another crossworld once more, but found herself robbed of the ability to do so. Sellemae used two of her free limbs to wrap the fairy in silk.

"Your reward shall be rich indeed! One thousand years of service to my choir! Then you may understand the importance of leaving me in peace when I'm enthralled by the dulcet tones within the songs of praise to my greatness."

The rogue fairy was speechless as she was hoisted up to join the others in the void of the vast chamber.

Sellemae turned to the other rogues gathered by the door. "I will not have these pitiful creatures invade my realm! Saddle up the rats and summon the rest of the mind thieves. There can be no delay now in our departure."

•

The replicant of the Reverend Casey continued moving along the rugged track that ran up the hill, then down toward the creek again. The mind thieves began gaining ground, coming within a few metres of their prize just as its path forward was cut off by the Danburys.

Without warning, the pixies flew in different directions, letting the lantern and coat fall to the ground. In a moment, the 'human' form disintegrated. Within seconds, every pixie had crossed between worlds.

Realising they'd been fooled, the mind thieves released their captives, fleeing back to Sellemae's world. They hoped to warn her before she learned of the Reverend and the pixies from other sources.

Mrs Bradshaw and the dinner guests collapsed when the mind thieves departed. Men and women alike were exhausted, having been pushed beyond their physical capacity by their captors.

Their flesh and clothing torn, a sense of disbelief kept them silent. To make it worse, the lanterns had all gone out as the guests fell to the ground, and the storm clouds had covered the moon, leaving them in darkness.

They fumbled their way down the ridge in the darkness until they reached the relative safety of the pool. They looked up as one at the sound of Colin McIntyre's voice: "Who goes there?"

Charles Danbury, holding his tearful wife close, replied, "It's your dinner guests. Your somewhat traumatised dinner guests. What manner of poison did you dish up to us? We've all dined with you many times before, why do you choose now to show the kind of host you really are?"

Colin stepped forward, carrying his lantern. He had a flintlock in his other hand and a revolver holstered on his belt along with two large hunting knives. Close behind him were Meredith, Patsy and Cook. "I can assure you, Charles, what you've experienced has nothing to do with what you ate tonight and everything to do with forces you cannot hope to understand."

"I understand that my wife and I, along with your other guests, were unwillingly compelled to pursue the Reverend after you had rudely insulted a man of God at the dinner table."

Colin replied, "I've no time for dealing with your wounded pride. Tell us what you saw—what you remember."

Charles's wife, Lily, stood up, addressing her husband first, "What we've just been through? It's not his fault, nor his cook's." She turned to Colin and continued, "It was horrifying, as though we were taken over by demons. I remember everything, but as if in a dream. Whatever it was that controlled my body, I could hear its mind. We were following the tutor, Mrs Bradshaw, and chased what we thought to be the Reverend Casey, but it turned out to be something else. My captor vanished before I could understand what he thought it was, but I remember it cursing as it called out a name… Bandah."

"So, the Reverend Casey got away?"

"I believe so, but I learned more than that from the dreadful thing's thoughts. The one that they serve seeks to cause great harm to your daughter, and your cook. In fact, your whole family is in great danger, as I fear the rest of us are too."

Colin was distracted by the sound of splashing water downstream. He turned as a flash of lightning revealed Mrs Smith working her way through the far end of the pool, having used the nearby path. She was surrounded by what Colin saw as large spiders that appeared to run through mid-air.

Patsy looked across and exclaimed, "The fairies! They're helping Mrs Smith." She turned to her father. "We need to stop them!"

She was preparing to run over to them when Meredith grabbed the girl's shoulder and held her back. "It's okay, it'll be better for us if she's there anyway. If we wish to bring your grandmother back, she could be helpful in one way or another. She wants to trade places with her, even though it would mean an eternity of slavery. You see, she fears death. Fairies don't comprehend what it means to have a life like ours. They perceive it as too short to have meaning."

A crack of thunder followed another lightning flash, heralding the start of a downpour.

Colin had to yell as loud as he could to be heard above the rain. "Lily, I need you and Charles to take everyone back to the house. Feel free to help yourselves to warm blankets and a brandy if you wish. We'll see you back there soon and explain it all then."

The guests collected themselves together, relighting their lanterns to guide them along the path. A distant light from the McIntyre home became a beacon of hope as they struggled along.

Meredith asked Patsy, "Are you ready?"

"Yes, I think so."

Another lightning flash showed Mrs Smith and the fairies had disappeared.

Meredith nodded to her husband and they started wading into the pool. She looked back toward Cook. "Do you wish to join the others, or follow us as we cross over?"

Cook stood by the edge, refusing to budge. Her voice was barely audible against the background of the rain. "I'll fancy my chances better if I join the others at the house. I fear an unholy death waits for you if you go ahead with this." She turned and ran, wishing the Reverend Casey were at the house to offer some form of spiritual protection.

Patsy called out to her, a hint of panic in her voice, "Cook! Come back!"

"It's okay," said Meredith. "Cook will be safe there now Mrs Smith and the fairies have crossed over. Tonight's journey will be perilous, of that there's no doubt. Her fears of an untimely death are well founded."

They continued into the pool, the water now up to Patsy's knees. She looked up and asked her mother, "Do you fear death, Mother?"

"We all have to die sometime, and I've no desire to live my life captive to the fear of how and when that might be. So, no… I see nothing to fear in death. It's simply the thing that happens when life ends. What matters more than what might happen after death is that life itself isn't wasted."

When the water reached Patsy's waist, her father turned to his wife and daughter. "Okay, this should be deep enough. I think—"

Patsy interrupted, "No, we need to be closer to the rock! That's why the web's there, to be close to the centre of the portal."

Colin looked to his wife.

Meredith took his hand in hers. "We need to trust her instincts. They're stronger than mine."

Reluctantly, Colin moved in the direction of the rock, holding his firearms above his head to keep them dry.

A few metres from the rock, Patsy called out, "This is it, right here, I can feel it."

Meredith spoke, anxious to ensure Patsy understood the procedures they had to follow: "As witches, there are several ways we can cross between the worlds, but to take your father as well, there is just one. We need to encircle him with our arms and hold hands. Then, we need to close our eyes as we allow ourselves to be somewhere else. Do you understand? It's not about trying to be elsewhere, it's about letting it happen."

Patsy nodded and did as her mother asked… minus the closed eyes. She wanted to watch what was happening and couldn't see how some silly detail like having to close your eyes could be a problem.

As soon as she took her mother's hands, she felt the power. At first, it was like pins and needles circulating through their hands and lower arms. After a few more seconds, Patsy realised she could hear her mother's thoughts, even tap into her memory. A unique understanding ran through her mind as her mother's knowledge of witchcraft became her own. Then, she noticed the rain had changed direction, and was following with the flow of energy swirling around the three of them. The speed built up, and as it did, the water around them in the pool began following the rain. It built up until they were standing free of the water, surrounded by a swirling vortex. Patsy's eyelids dropped. There was nothing she could do to keep them open.

The next thing she knew, they were in darkness on a cold stone floor.

CHAPTER 10

As the Reverend Casey rose to his feet, a giant rat leapt at him. Without hesitation he thrust his sword toward it and the creature fell to the ground in front of him. A rogue fairy jumped off its back and hovered in the air before him.

"So, priest! Do you think your god can save you now? Do you think he'll be able to defeat the might of the great Sellemae?"

"My god doesn't need to lower himself to such tasks… not when he has me here to deal with scum like you!"

As the rogue lifted its wand to attack, the Reverend lowered his sword and extended the palm of his left hand toward the fairy. It hurtled backwards as a surge of energy from the priest's hand lit up the darkness, revealing what seemed an endless sea of approaching rats, some ridden by rogues, others by spiders.

The Reverend showed no hint of fear as he braced himself for the onslaught. He threw his sword javelin-style at the largest of the approaching beasts. His aim was true, bringing the creature's advance to an abrupt halt. At the same time, he swung his other hand across his chest, drawing strings of energy from multiple crossworlds to create an energy surge that forced dozens of rats to rear up and send their riders flying.

A spider the size of a large dog came within a metre of him and prepared its fangs to strike, only to feel them knocked away by the heel of the Reverend's foot striking hard.

The rats, wary now of the priest's power, held back as more spiders approached. The Reverend moved with the grace of a ballerina as he halted the advance of one wave after another, slowly working his way to his sword. He watched in horror when a mounted rat reached the spot where he'd crossed over and promptly faded away, travelling through the portal to the world of humanity.

Retrieving his sword, he swung it in broad arcs, sending broken spiders and their limbs flying in all directions. But he was unaware of a rogue fairy coming up behind him, close enough now to use its wand.

The rogue targeted him, preparing to send a surge of lightning-like energy toward the Reverend's heart. The first the priest knew of its impending attack was when he heard a gunshot ring out and turned to see the fairy drop to the ground dead.

Looking for the source of his salvation, he found the steely gaze of Colin McIntyre, a small puff of smoke rising from the barrel of his revolver. His face was lit by a glowing ball of energy Meredith was fashioning from the air in front of her. Patsy stood by her side, mimicking her mother's movements but having little success at creating her own light source.

As the dark army withdrew into the shadows, Colin stepped forward. "It seems our time of arrival was somewhat fortuitous."

The Reverend replied, "Aye, that it was. But let's not fool ourselves, our reprieve will be short-lived. We are greatly outnumbered, and they know it. Until Bandah and his pixies join us, I fear that, even with my power and that of your wife, we'll struggle to fight our way through this."

"I don't know about that. Don't underestimate what my daughter might be capable of." Colin approached the Reverend and placed a firm hand on his shoulder. "My apologies for my rudeness at the dinner table tonight, but I saw no other way of hastening our guests' departure so we could prepare. As soon as Meredith and I learnt of what was coming, it was clear we'd need to arrive here before Sellemae had the chance to cross over. I saw the mimicked conflict between us as the best way to create an excuse for you to make an early departure, while encouraging our other guests to leave as well. I thought we both managed to put on quite a show for them."

"No offense was taken, I can assure you. For my part, I was grateful that you recognised my need for a hasty exit. I suppose it would be appropriate to apologise for some of my choice of words as well. Even when used as a deliberate deception, such things can be hurtful. But the ruse served its purpose." He glanced at Patsy, then turned his eyes back to Colin and continued. "It's curious, McIntyre. Before today, it seemed unlikely your daughter had any powers at all."

"It appears they're triggered when she gets angry. After your departure, she lost her temper with Mrs Smith and effortlessly managed to hurl her against the wall of the dining room."

The Reverend raised an eyebrow then turned to Patsy, causing her to freeze under the weight of his gaze. "How are you coping, child?'

There's nothing to be afraid of, she thought. *He's here to help us.*

"I'm alright." Patsy took a step towards him. "I've always feared you in the past. I've heard you say such horrible things, both to me and others. But now I think that's all been a charade, like your argument with my father."

The Reverend Casey acknowledged her with a nod. "There are truths that are scarier than anything I've told you of. And I've no doubt we'll face many of them tonight. I'll be interested to learn more of what you're capable of when we do."

Meredith stepped forward, handing the glowing orb of energy to her daughter. "My power to use the craft became stronger the instant we crossed over. So much so, that this orb was almost effortless to create."

The Reverend Casey said, "That'll no doubt be because there are now the three generations in the one world: the Trinity of Power. Your mother told me often of the extraordinary access to strings of energy in the Crossworlds that would be accessible when three generations of Crossworld Witches come together."

Patsy looked up at the Reverend. "You're him, aren't you? You're Alfred!"

The Reverend Alfred Casey looked at her, but remained silent.

She stared into his eyes and saw the pain etched in his face, the forty years spent dedicated to the hope of one day finding the woman he loved. She said, "I've read your letters."

The Reverend cast his eyes down, as though they were dragged to the ground by his memories.

Seeing a need to change the subject, Meredith said, "I'm confident the orbs will last at least an hour. If we create a trail of them, it'll be simple to find our way back when the time comes to return home."

Colin shook his head. "No, we can't risk it. They'd merely give our foes a clearer target."

Patsy said, "Maybe we can still use them to help us." She rolled the orb in her hands, massaging it and stretching it as she teased and coaxed strings of energy through the countless layers of the Crossworlds. It grew and became brighter, to the point where it became difficult to look at. She released it and let it rise higher, continuing to grow as it went. The creatures of darkness surrounding them were uncomfortable in such light and backed away further as the illumination spread.

The Reverend glanced at Colin. "At least now we'll be able to see the foul beasts as they approach. Without darkness, there are few places for them to hide in this world. Tell me, Meredith, since your enhanced powers prove you've established a link with your mother, can you now sense the direction we must follow if we're to reach her?"

"I can only feel her ever so slightly. But if Patricia and I link hands, her location should become clearer."

Meredith looked deep into Patsy's eyes, taking the girl's hands in hers and once more feeling their instant connection and accentuation of power.

The power continued building within them, until Patsy felt compelled to release her grip. She stumbled for a moment, struggling to remain balanced. "I saw her!" She held a hand to her chest as she regained her breath. "I know where she's being held! We have to hurry, or we'll be too late!"

Without warning, Patsy prepared to run, stopped only by the Reverend Casey's strong hand locking on her shoulder in a vice-like grip. "Slow down, girl. We must consider our actions carefully, as each one could be our last. Our greatest danger tonight is the temptation to act in haste."

Colin McIntyre watched on as his daughter's frustration rose. She clenched her teeth, saying, "Let me go! My grandmother needs me!"

The Reverend Casey replied, "She needs us all, and she needs us alive."

Remembering her grandmother's journal entry where she described swimming through the air, Patsy flung her arms up, catching the Reverend Casey by surprise and breaking free of his grip. She jumped and pulled her hands back, lifting herself higher as she emptied her mind of all else and allowed it to be. Colin dived forward in a desperate attempt to stop her, managing to grab the heel of her shoe with his fingertips. Patsy kicked out, struggling to break away. "Let me go!" Another kick, and her foot slipped free of the shoe. She rose high above them, then looked down and said, "My grandmother needs me."

She turned to the east and headed off, travelling toward the distant palace of the Spider Queen. The others ran after her but struggled to keep up.

Realising there was no chance of catching her on foot, Meredith came to a stop. She pulled her muscles tight while reciting a mantra in the ancient tongue of the druids that roughly translated to, "Break these bonds and set me free, break these bonds and…" The fasteners on her formal dinner dress burst apart, allowing the gown to fall to the ground. Her modesty was protected only by the full length slip she wore underneath.

She closed her eyes, preparing to push herself into the air as her daughter had. *It's just like crossing between worlds,* she told herself. *Don't try, just let it happen.* She pushed up and left the ground.

To keep herself from falling, she found it necessary to keep her limbs moving, like treading water. Once she had the hang of it, a couple of frog kicks brought her close to Colin, albeit some distance above his head. "I'm going after her."

"We'll be right behind you." Colin and the Reverend did the best they could to follow from the ground as Meredith swam after Patsy, but they soon lost sight of her as well.

Seeing the two men were now more vulnerable without the witches by their side, the creatures of darkness were more prepared to brave the light cast by Patsy's energy orb.

As they ran, Colin hastily reloaded the revolver he'd fired earlier, then turned to the Reverend. "Now would be a good time for your pixie friends to make an appearance."

•

The fairies threw Mrs Smith to the chamber floor. The Spider Queen brought her face down to Mrs Smith's level. "So, the human that once was a fairy wishes to return to that which she once was. How quaint!" The old woman groaned as she struggled to lift herself enough to kneel in a sign of subservience. Grimacing at the arthritic pain in her knees, she tried composing herself, reaching out to the fang-tipped limb Sellemae extended to her. She drew the fang to her lips, kissed it and declared, "Oh great Sellemae, Spider Queen and rightful ruler of the Crossworlds, I come to you this day pledging eternal service in exchange for one small favour… that I may trade places once more with the witch you hold captive, and live an eternal life in your service as she withers away and dies."

Sellemae lifted Mrs Smith's chin with her fang, so she could look her in the eye. "You do appreciate the consequences of such a deal? That you shall carry the pain of old age through countless millennia?"

"Oh yes, Your Greatness. I am well aware of that. But I'd rather live in eternal pain than wither away and die in this pathetic form."

"Yes, but I prize so much having my witch, and it would be such a shame to watch her shrivel up and die while an old and decrepit crony like yourself lives on. You do see my point?"

"I also have information that may aid you in the capture of the other two witches invading your realm."

Sellemae flicked the fang of her extended limb, sending Mrs Smith to the floor with blood flowing from a deep gash on her brow. "How dare you suggest I may have need of your pitiful information to help me capture what has wilfully brought itself to me! You may be in human form, but you still think with the narcissistic delusion of a fairy! I'm always seeking new forms of entertainment, and tormenting you for a few thousand millennia does appeal to my sense of fun."

The Spider Queen reached up to the area where Neridah's cocoon hung. A fine strand of silk shot out from the tip of her talon-like fang, wrapping around the thread that held Neridah suspended from the ceiling. Sellemae pulled back and the line snapped. Mrs Smith gasped in shock as she watched Neridah's cocoon fall from the top of the dimly lit cavern. It seemed certain that Patsy's grandmother was about to hit the floor headfirst when Sellemae shot out another strand of silk, capturing her and pulling the cocoon to her feet. Her eyes stabbed at Mrs Smith as she turned to face her. "You will have your wish, fairy… but on my terms."

Sellemae slashed the cocoon open, lifting it slightly to spill its contents to the cavern floor, then gestured for the trembling Mrs Smith to take her place. She crawled toward the fairy-sized cocoon, still wearing her housekeeper's uniform, complete with apron.

Neridah lay there, still unable to move a muscle below her neck, as had been the case for many years. She looked up at the aging face of the woman who was once a fairy, the one responsible for her forty years of suffering. Was Mrs Smith seriously volunteering to reverse the spell, and as a consequence, experience countless millennia in this state?

It seemed she was.

The old woman extended a shaking finger to touch the tip of the wand that was firmly planted in Neridah's unmoving right hand. The spell reversal required desire on Neridah's part to trigger the transformation.

Nothing happened.

"Why should I?" asked Neridah.

"Why wouldn't you?" replied Mrs Smith. "Your daughter and granddaughter have crossed over. They wish to come and set you free. Your old boyfriend is with them."

"Alfred? Here? I don't believe you!"

"Reach out to them, feel them, and learn the truth for yourself."

Sellemae slapped a leg to the ground and laughed. "Hah! 'Your boyfriend is with them.' 'Reach out to them.' I so enjoy moments like these. If you can't convince her, then maybe I should string you up in front of her, so she can watch as you shrivel up and your bones crumble to dust." She looked at Neridah. "It would be a fitting and constant reminder of your lack of… dare I say it… humanity."

Neridah closed her eyes, unsure what to do. She knew Sellemae well enough to know she'd likely be freed from the fairy-sized cocoon, only to find herself strung up in a human-sized one. Then, she heard the distant call: it was her daughter and granddaughter, they were on their way! Not only that, but she could sense that her beloved Alfred really was with them. She looked up at Sellemae and said, "Okay, I'll do it."

Mrs Smith once again reached out and touched the wand, letting out a sigh of relief as energy surged through her veins. Yes! At last, she'd be free from the bane of humanity's pitifully short lifespan. The chamber was filled by a flash of light and the transformation was complete.

Sellemae picked up the limp Mrs Smith, once more in fairy form.

"Foolish little fairy. You allow the witch to release herself and become what she was, and at the same time condemn yourself to such prolonged pain at my leisure."

"At least I won't die in the blink of an eye like those wretched humans and witches."

Neridah fell to the floor in shock, dressed in Mrs Smith's housekeeping garb. It was several sizes too large for her petite frame and hung loose on her shoulders. After four decades spent paralyzed below the neck, the sudden freedom of movement was like being reborn. The situation was still dire, but she had something that had been in short supply for throughout her years in captivity… hope.

And it was more than just the regained freedom of movement feeding that hope. Her daughter and granddaughter were here, creating a Trilogy of Power. Like Meredith, Neridah had never felt so powerful.

She sensed Patsy moving toward her at speed, and that she was closer than Meredith… close enough that she could reach out to the girl with her thoughts. Closing her eyes, she focused on what she wanted to tell her granddaughter. *I need you to be here. Release yourself from the restrictions of your senses. Don't come, just be here.*

In an instant, Patsy appeared, floating in mid-air above her grandmother as though treading water. Neridah explained as much as she could through their shared thoughts, desperate to share what she could while they had the chance. *Now we've established the Trinity, there are crossworlds you can move in and out of wherever and whenever you want… as long as the Trinity holds together. But beware, if you spend too long in another crossworld, the Trinity will be broken. I sense amazing power in you, and can feel through you that your mother has many gifts that she's yet to—*

Sellemae cut her off. "And all those gifts will be mine in but a few short minutes, along with the measly powers that you shall both no doubt try to use on me."

The Spider Queen lassoed Patsy and dragged her down. "You do know, don't you, that I can choose to draw your power out with my fangs? That is, if you choose to disobey me."

"Then why does my grandmother still have powers?"

Neridah spoke softly, "She has milked my powers many times, but there were not so many she could gain access to while I was in a fairy form. As time passes, the powers slowly restore themselves, allowing her to feed again and again."

Sellemae's laughter echoed through the chamber as she enveloped Neridah with two of her limbs. "And now, your grandchild can watch me drain all your powers before I consume hers."

Patsy's eyes narrowed as she got to her feet, still bound in Sellemae's silk. "Leave her alone!" She stamped a foot and the ground shook, surprising Sellemae so much that she loosened her grip on Neridah.

"Well, well, you are a feisty little witch! I'll have to find a very special place in my choir for your sweet young voice." Sellemae dragged Patsy closer. "Sing for me child, let me hear what qualities you will bring to the harmonies I so enjoy."

"I'll never sing for you, especially not after what you've done to my grandmother for all these years."

Sellemae lifted Patsy, dangling the girl before her eyes. "Oh, what a sadly misguided child you are. Have you not thought about the bigger picture? Look at how youthful your grandmother is. It's amazing, isn't it? I believe she looks younger than your mother. But that will change, when I drain her, not just of her powers, but of her life force! The choice is yours, little witch. Your grandmother's life, or my choir."

CHAPTER 11

Once Cook had seen to everyone having food and blankets, she called aside two of the men. "We need to gather what we can to use against any spiders we might see—just the big ones mind you." As she spoke, a spider the size of a dinner plate raced toward her. Screaming in fright, Cook fell back, landing hard on her generous backside.

With Cook winded and unable to move, the spider leapt at her, only to be cut down as a hunting knife sliced through the air. The blade came to land next to Cook's hand, tip firmly wedged in the grain of the cedar floorboards.

The knife thrower was Vincent Donaldson, a wealthy squatter who enjoyed hunting. He addressed her as he walked up to take his knife. "I have to agree with you, Cook. The way this evening has panned out so far, the more protection we have, the better. We should make our way to the shed and collect whatever manner of shovels or pick-axes we can find." He helped Cook to her feet then retrieved his knife from the floor. "But we must stick together. We'll be safer in a group."

Everyone rose to their feet, most with blankets wrapped around themselves. The rain had just eased off and, as they made their way down the path towards the shed, Vincent felt the unnatural silence filling the garden. All the usual noises of the night—crickets, frogs and flying foxes—were curiously absent. Normally, after a storm like tonight's, the frogs would be deafening.

They had just about reached the shed when a loud screech broke the silence. Vincent looked over his shoulder then yelled to the others, "Quick, inside the shed."

Vincent's lantern cast just enough light to let him know he had no chance of evading the rodent bearing down on him.

The rat's weight almost crushed him as it pushed him to the ground. The beast opened its jaws, ready to bite, teeth scratching the side of his face as he drove his knife deep, bringing its attack to an abrupt end.

Vincent struggled to breathe under the weight of the dead rat. A large spider crawled off the rodent's back and approached his exposed face. The arachnid used one of its front legs to lift a lock of Vincent's hair from his eye, and the rogue fairy who appeared to Vincent as a spider allowed him to hear her voice. "Such bravery, yet so foolish. The question I have to ask myself is this, do I kill you or your friends first?" The spider's face was now a hand width from Vincent's. "The fun part of me wants the latter, but the—"

The spider's spiel was cut short by a garden fork coming down. The shock made her camouflage vanish for a brief moment, so she appeared as the rogue fairy she was, and a lucky one at that, the fork having pierced more clothing than flesh.

Cook lifted the fork and addressed what she saw as a struggling spider. "I've had about enough of you spiders… or fairies… or whatever you are. I've had it with being scared!" She lowered the fork to the ground and dispatched it the same way she'd dealt with Patsy's spider earlier in the day.

Cook turned to the dinner guests huddling inside the door of the shed. The rain started pouring down again as Cook called out, "Come on, we can't leave the poor man stuck under this foul beast."

Reluctantly, the guests came out, banding together to try and drag the rodent off their friend. They'd barely shifted it an inch when Charles was distracted by a glowing light coming from the direction of the pool. "I think we've got another problem."

•

The Reverend Alfred Casey looked across to Colin as they ran on. "We'll need to be wary of mind thieves as well. They're almost impossible to detect in our world, yet alone this one. If you feel a voice trying to enter your head, you must resist. Even if you're engrossed in fighting a battle, you must keep a part of yourself free to brace against them taking hold of your will."

Colin was distracted by the screech of a giant bat just metres from his head. In a reflex action, he raised his revolver and fired, bringing it crashing to the ground in front of him.

Turning as he ran, the Reverend pushed his palm toward another descending bat. Energy from dozens of crossworlds coalesced in his palm then shot out at their attacker, felling it as though it had been struck by a spear. More bats came at them. Colin had brought a good deal of ammunition with him, but unless he could find time to reload during the onslaught, it would be little help.

He could see at least a dozen bats overhead with hundreds of rats and giant spiders closing in around them, but had only five bullets still loaded in his revolver. "I hope you've got plenty of attack left in you, Alfred."

The Reverend pushed out another wave of energy drawn from the Crossworlds, bringing down an attacking bat. "I fear my strength will become exhausted by the time the rats are upon us, and I can bring down only one at a time with my sword."

Being careful to ensure no bullets were wasted, Colin waited till the next approaching bat was almost on top of them before firing. The bat's momentum kept it moving forward, making Colin leap aside to avoid being crushed. Rolling on the ground, he watched the Reverend send out energy pulses with both hands in quick succession as the winged primates converged on him.

A bat approaching the back of the Reverend's head was preparing to grab him with its razor-sharp claws. With no time to aim, Colin reached out and fired, hoping the bullet would hit its mark and not injure the Reverend by mistake. It tore through the bat's wing, causing only a brief pause in its attack, but giving enough time for the Reverend to bring his sword around in a sweeping action that sent the bat to its death.

Turning to Colin, he pushed his left hand forward, sending forth a burst of energy to cut down a giant spider that was preparing to plunge its fangs into the back of the man's neck.

More spiders approached, with the rats close behind. Colin brought down three of them in quick succession, then heard a dull click as he tried to fire an empty chamber. He stood up and grabbed the loaded flintlock from his back, swinging it like a club against three of the approaching arachnids, then aimed at the closest of the rats and fired, hitting his mark with deadly accuracy.

The Reverend's energy pulses grew weaker, until he had no choice but to rely on his reflexes and sword.

They were forced to climb atop a pile of the fallen vermin as they continued defending themselves. Colin slashed from side to side with the two hunting knives while the Reverend Alfred Casey was ready to resign himself to bringing down a few more creatures of darkness before being brought down themselves.

He slashed at a pair of rats, but failed to bring them down. He stabbed a second time at the first and grabbed the other by the fur on the back of its neck when, out of the corner of his eye, he saw a flicker of light in the distance.

Bandah and his horde of pixies had arrived.

•

Distress overran Meredith's mind, alerting her to Patsy's predicament. Instinctively, she emptied her mind of all distractions and allowed herself to be with her daughter.

The small flash of light that heralded her arrival in Sellemae's chamber distracted the Spider Queen.

Meredith wasted no time. She thrust her right hand forward, fingers extended toward the thread that held Patsy dangling before Sellemae's face. The energy surge was sharp and focused, snapping the thread and sending the girl crashing to the floor with a dull thud, still bound by the remaining silk.

The Spider Queen was outraged. "How dare you! You pathetic little witches dare to come into my domain, defiling the respect my loyal subjects feel toward me!" She slapped Meredith with one of her fang tipped limbs, sending her flying back onto the cold stone floor, her head hitting the ground so hard she blacked out.

Neridah raced to her side and cradled her daughter's head in her lap. It was the first time she'd seen her in forty years. "Oh Meredith, my sweet child. How beautiful you are."

"ENOUGH!" Sellemae stood towering over Neridah as she held her daughter. "It's time you experience the knowledge of real pain." Wearing a wide grin, she turned away and approached Patsy.

With no choice but to try escaping, Patsy staggered to her feet and tried to run, only to have her legs pulled from under her as Sellemae cast another thread and lassoed her ankles.

Neridah took a deep breath as she rose up, standing tall with her arms by her side. Closing her eyes, she took another breath, raising her now glowing hands high above her head. Her words were slow and deliberate. "Stay away from my granddaughter!"

Sellemae picked up Patsy and slung the girl over her shoulder, smirking as she faced Neridah. "Oh, and why would I do that? Who's intending to stop me? Would that be you?"

Neridah flung her arms at Sellemae, sending a bright surge of power toward the Spider Queen. Before it struck, Sellemae opened her mouth wide and let out a deep bellowing sound that wrapped itself around Neridah's energy surge, compressing and dissolving it as the sound wave pushed the energy into another crossworld.

Neridah, having put everything she could into the surge, swayed back and forth, struggling to remain conscious.

The last thing she saw before passing out was the Spider Queen laughing at the hopelessness of her attack.

CHAPTER 12

Much to the relief of Colin and the Reverend, the glow they saw proved to be more significant than Bandah had originally promised. There must have been tens of thousands of pixies.

Once positioned above the general area of the two men, they worked together to generate a blinding surge of light and heat, accompanied by an ear-piercing sound. Colin and the Reverend fell to the ground, struggling to protect their eyes and ears.

The reaction from the rats, bats and spiders was far more dramatic. Being used to a world of darkness, they reeled back in shock, giving squadrons of pixies the opportunity to swoop down on the attackers and prod them on pressure points, leaving them paralysed for several seconds, just long enough for the pixies to collectively raise the men above the fray of the battle.

They flew high, heading in the direction of the Spider Queen's palace, with bats constantly swirling around, unwilling to take on such a large horde of pixies.

Bandah hovered like a hummingbird before the Reverend's face as they moved along. "You look a little worse for wear and tear, my friend."

"Oh really? And why might you be saying that?"

Bandah laughed before replying, "It might have something to do with the tears in both your clothing and your flesh. In all honesty though, you two have done remarkably well."

"Aye, that may be so, but we looked certain to meet our maker before you finally arrived. Did you stop for supper before joining us? Or do you have a more rational explanation for the delay?"

"Come now, Alfred, surely you're capable of better than that. The moment you arrived here, there were pixies observing you from up high, way beyond the heights where these vermin could detect them. I've been traversing the Crossworlds, building as large an army as I could. Had we arrived even just a minute earlier, I fear our numbers would have been insufficient to snatch you from that rabble down there. Right now, though, you should rest, so you can recover while we carry you to your date with destiny."

Bandah was right. The Reverend looked at Colin McIntyre, admiring the way the man still looked so resolute and alert. But drawing the power from across worlds had left the Reverend exhausted. He took a long, deep breath, crossed himself, then recited a mantra he'd practised for decades in preparation for today: "Limbah yumbah, limbah yumbah…" Seconds later, he was in a trance-like state, in which each minute helped rejuvenate his powers far more than would happen through natural sleep.

•

Patsy decided she'd had enough. So what if she was bound in Sellemae's thread? She was angry, and she wasn't going to sit by and let an oversized arachnid hurt her mother and grandmother for one moment longer. "You'd better let us go," she demanded of the Spider Queen.

Sellemae took great joy in swinging Patsy before her eyes. "This should be good. Tell me, what are you going to do about it? Are you going to have a little tantrum?"

"You don't want to push me!"

"I wonder, should I be scared?"

Meredith had just started to come to, and panicked at the sight of Sellemae toying with her daughter. She took her mother's hand, sending energy through Neridah to make her aware of Patsy's dilemma. Neridah opened her eyes and squeezed tight on Meredith's hand. The two exchanged a glance, acknowledging they understood what to do.

The two witches thrust their free hands forward, summoning strings of energy from the Crossworlds that coalesced in a glowing ball. It floated before them, growing till it was three metres across. Then, with a gentle flick of their fingers, they sent it hurtling toward the Spider Queen.

Once again, Sellemae used a wave of sound to defend herself. But this time, she'd been caught unprepared, and was forced to drop Patsy in the process. She braced herself against the ball of energy as it broke through her sound wave (albeit with its power greatly diminished). Sellemae's head pulsed with pain when the energy ball struck. Neridah and Meredith worked to create a new ball, feeling they had the chance to take down their adversary.

But Sellemae was too quick for them. Just as they were about to unleash their next ball of energy, the witches' feet were dragged out from under them by one of Sellemae's web lassos. She dragged them across the chamber to be within striking distance. "You pitiful witches disgust me. How dare you defy me! Tell me, which one of you do I drain first. Oh, but wait, I don't really have to make that choice, I can drain you both together!" She raised her uppermost limbs high, aiming for the women's abdomens, and brought them down hard, only to have them come to an abrupt halt just centimetres from making contact. Frustrated, she raised them again for another attempt, but once more they stopped short of their targets.

Sellemae looked to where she'd left Patsy moments before. The girl was standing, her right arm extended toward her mother and grandmother.

She looked up at Sellemae. "I told you before, leave them alone!" She drew her hand back and made a sweeping motion toward the Spider Queen, sending the ball of energy, similar to that which the others had made, but with greater force than the previous one. Sellemae was unable to respond in time, feeling the full impact of the energy ball as it struck her in the face, sending her reeling back against the wall of the chamber.

Patsy raced up to Meredith and Neridah. The witches embraced, bringing the three generations together for the first time. Each felt an enormous surge of energy run through every inch of their veins.

Sellemae screamed in rage, "COME TO ME, LOYAL FRIENDS OF DARKNESS! Attack these vermin who dare to harm your queen. Make them understand what it means to feel fear!"

From out of the darkness, a multitude of glowing eyes came forth. There was all manner of creatures among the horde: rats, spiders, bats, and rogue fairies. Patsy could even sense the presence of mind thieves.

Sellemae regained her feet, and moved forward with her minions who were hurling spears and rocks at their targets.

The Trinity of Crossworld Witches, now telepathically linked, positioned themselves in an outward facing triangular stance. They shared each other's perception, enabling them to see everything around them. To conserve energy, they used the simplest powers at their disposal to divert the spears and rocks, making sure they fell short, or missed their targets entirely.

Working together, they emitted a glow that expanded outward as a protective dome. Whatever the forces of darkness threw at them simply bounced off.

Some of the creatures tried running through the glowing field of energy, but they too were repelled, receiving shocking burns as a reward for their efforts.

However, Semellae's army had numbers. They continued hurling themselves at the barrier, causing it to recede slightly with each hit. Semellae stabbed at it with multiple legs, shrinking it further with each blow.

Patsy shared a thought with her mother and grandmother: *I know how to beat her, but I can't do it while we're holding this shield.*

Meredith replied, *If we break this link, even for a moment, the barrier will collapse, and we'll be overwhelmed in seconds.*

Neridah disagreed. *If we don't do something soon, they'll be upon us anyway. We need to act while there's at least some distance between them and us. We need to trust in Patsy's power.*

CHAPTER 13

Colin looked at Bandah. "What's happening? Why have they stopped circling us?"

Bandah was also curious as to why the bats had changed course and were now heading toward the palace of the Spider Queen. "My guess is they've been summoned, which means your family must, at the very least, still be alive."

Colin asked, "Can't you fly any faster? At this pace, they'll get there long before us."

Bandah's annoyance was apparent, but he chose to remain silent. There seemed little point in explaining the obvious, that without the burden of ferrying Colin and the Reverend, the pixies would have arrived at their destination long ago.

An uncomfortable silence accompanied them for the following few minutes of their flight, only broken when the Reverend Alfred Casey emerged from his meditative state. He brought his head upright and opened his eyes. Bandah asked, "How do you feel?"

"I'm ready."

Bandah called out to the rest of the horde, "Okay, time for the crossworld jump. The three generations of Crossworld Witches are together, so we'll be able to find them more easily. That, and the strength of the Reverend's power will be enough to take Mister McIntyre with us when we allow ourselves to be with his family." He moved toward Colin and confessed, "I couldn't let you know we could do this jump until Alfred was ready. Sorry if you find that disturbing."

"I'll get over it, one day."

Bandah called out, "Okay, let's do this!"

A few seconds later, pixies began disappearing. Initially, it seemed at random, but Colin was sure he saw a pattern emerge as the pace of the disappearances increased.

The wave of vanishings swept up Colin and the Reverend, sending them headlong into the middle of Sellemae's chamber, directly above the Trinity of Crossworld Witches, but outside the remains of their protective shield.

For the first time in forty years, Neridah and the Reverend made eye contact, albeit for the briefest of moments. Yet within that moment, they conveyed all the hope and love they'd ever felt for each other, and the realisation that to hold each other, they would have to survive a battle with the odds stacked against them.

It gave the Reverend a renewed sense of purpose.

He let out a yell of defiance, throwing himself clear of the pixies and landing among the advancing beasts. He pushed out with his hands and made a sweeping action as he hit the ground, energy surges flowing forth from each palm. The creatures of darkness were sent tumbling back, as though caught in the raging current of a flooded river. Sellemae was preparing to bring a fang tipped limb down on the Reverend when Colin fired his flintlock, hitting one of her eyes. It distracted her enough for the Reverend to see the threat and evade the claw-like fang.

The Spider Queen was outraged. "You! The lowest of all the pitiful creatures in my realm tonight… you dare to throw your firecrackers at me? I'll enjoy watching my babies feed on your flesh!"

Colin replied by pulling out his revolver and firing bullet after bullet at the Spider Queen.

Sellemae laughed as she absorbed each of them. When the revolver's chamber had emptied, she moved closer. "Now, puny human, prepare to meet a painful end!"

She stabbed with one of her forward limbs, aiming for the centre of Colin's chest. It was stopped short, a pillar of metal having appeared from nowhere, with Sellemae's fang-like claw embedded deep within it. She struggled to remove it, but the pillar was anchored in many more crossworlds than this one. "Which of you vermin is responsible for this? I DEMAND TO KNOW!"

Patsy stepped forward. "No one calls my dad puny!"

Sellemae cast a web toward Patsy, only to have it dissolve as soon as it touched her. Another metal pillar materialised, encasing the end of the limb she'd just employed. "What is this? How dare you! Know this, girl, my vengeance is like nothing you can comprehend. Release me now, or pay the price."

"I'm not scared of fairies, and I'm not scared of you." Patsy focused hard, bringing forth power from several thousand crossworlds. She focused on the harmony of the dancing strings of energy, each threading its way through all the known crossworlds. She summoned them to herself and used her will to pull them through into the one crossworld… the crossworld of the Spider Queen. They instantly coalesced and solidified, transforming into six additional super-dense pillars, each holding captive another of Sellemae's limbs.

Patsy then looked to the approaching creatures of darkness. "Anyone wish to challenge me?"

The creatures began backing away while Sellemae screamed, "Come back you cowards!" She turned her gaze to Patsy and prepared to hit her with a sound wave, only to be thwarted by an energy surge that took her by surprise.

It had come from Meredith.

With Sellemae reeling and barely conscious, Meredith raced forward and embraced her daughter. "Oh, my darling! I'm so glad you made it through."

Patsy smiled and fell into her mother's arms.

The Reverend Alfred Casey approached Neridah. Tears formed in his eyes, blurring his vision so much he had to wipe them away to see her clearly. "You've not aged a day."

"Under the circumstances, I suppose that's to be expected. But Alfred, I'm astonished. You waited for me? For all these years?"

"Aye, that and more. I've dedicated my life to preparing for this night. I never gave up hope of bringing you home."

Neridah looked at his torn body and saw the strength he'd built through constant training. She looked at his face, saw the grey of his hair, the beard and the etched lines that seemed an apt counter for the years. Lastly, she looked deep into his eyes, and the years became meaningless. In them, she saw his innocence, commitment, determination, and his heart of gold. But most of all, she saw his love for her. Tears streaming down her cheeks, Neridah draped her arms over his shoulders and pressed her cheek to his chest.

Patsy walked up to the Spider Queen and placed her hands on her hips. "I'm going to leave you like this in the belief your minions will look after your needs until the power holding you in place fades. By then, I'll have made sure you'll never be able to find your way to my world again."

"Ha! You know nothing of magic or the power you possess!"

Patsy looked toward her mother and grandmother, then back to Sellemae. "Maybe not, but I know one thing. I couldn't hope for better teachers." She took in a deep breath, then thrust a hand toward the spider, sending a powerful surge toward her face. Sellemae's head went limp as she lost consciousness.

Colin stepped forward, a sense of urgency in his tone. "We need to leave."

He was surprised to hear a voice from among the cocoons suspended above them. It was Mrs Smith, sounding distant due her reduced size. "Please, don't leave me here. I don't deserve this!"

Colin spat out his response, "You deserve everything that's coming to you."

Patsy was horrified. "No Father! How could you even think such a thing! No one deserves this! We should free them all, whatever they may or may not have done."

Bandah landed on Colin's shoulder. "She's right you know, there's no avoiding it. Before we leave, each and every one of those cocoons needs to be cut open."

Colin sighed as he looked away. He thought about it for a moment then replied, "It would appear I have little choice in the matter, other than to accept the dictates of my daughter and a pixie."

Meredith said, "Whatever we do, we need to be quick about it. I doubt those creatures of darkness are just retreating, I think they're heading for the portal."

The Reverend replied, "I agree, we'd best cut these fairies down and be on our way." He turned to Colin. "With some help from Bandah and his crew, you and I can deal with this. Your family should head back now to defend your home. We can join them once we're done releasing this choir."

Neridah grabbed his arm, her fingernails digging deep. "No! Surely, there must be some other way. Why must we be separated again? I'll stay, and—"

Alfred placed a gentle hand on her shoulder and put a finger to her lips. "No, you three are only safe against those hordes for as long as you stay together. It'll take us little time to set these fairies free, and the three of you can get there faster than the rest of us." Seeing the tears welling up in Neridah's eyes, he backed away from her. "Go woman! There are innocent dinner guests at the house, they need you. I'll not be far behind."

As the Reverend turned his back on the only woman he'd ever loved, Bandah flew over and hovered in front of her. "Don't worry yourself, I'll see to it that he returns unharmed. The Trinity needs to hold together if you're to take on what's likely already passed through the portal. But you may need more than just the Trinity, so I'll send some of the pixie squadrons to help drive them back while you await our return."

"Then, can't Alfred join us now too?"

Bandah shook his head. "Should Sellemae stir, we'll need his powers as well as Colin's guns to help hold her back while we make our escape."

Neridah spoke through tears. "But, there must—"

"There isn't! Go now! Lives are at stake!"

CHAPTER 14

Heartbroken, Neridah turned away and joined hands with her kin. They allowed themselves to be back at the house and the darkness of Sellemae's chamber faded away, replaced by the familiar walls of the dining room. Patsy asked her mother, "Why didn't we need to use the portal, like before?"

"With three generations of us together, we can create an echo portal, allowing us to cross worlds some distance from the real portal's centre."

Neridah walked around the table, marvelling at the walls she'd not seen in decades. So little had changed in the years she'd been away. She ran her hands over the texture of the wallpaper, then, remembering their purpose, she asked, "Where are your guests?"

Meredith replied, "Perhaps they've gone to the kitchen. I wonder, what would our guests do in this situation?"

Patsy replied, "I'd look for a way to protect myself."

Neridah looked at Meredith and said, "She's right, that's what I'd do too."

Meredith asked, "How? With what?"

Patsy answered, "I'd go down to the shed, the one at the bottom of the garden. There's plenty of tools down there… all manner of large forks, hoes, and shovels."

Neridah walked to a window, pushing aside the curtains. "Yes, of course! Look Meredith, there… Patsy's right. Do you see the lights burning down by the shed?" Meredith and Patsy joined her by the window. "We'd better get down there, quickly."

They formed a circle, closed their eyes and held hands, allowing themselves to be elsewhere. A few seconds later, they were standing next to the shed in the pouring rain. The dinner guests were still struggling to get Vincent out from under the giant rat.

Cook looked at the three women, fear filling her eyes. "By all the saints in heaven, I ask you, what is this?" She looked at Neridah. "This cannot be! I've not seen you since I was a wee child and my mother worked for your father. You went missing decades ago! How can this be? You've not aged a day! Are you a ghost, come back to haunt us? Are Lady Meredith and Patricia ghosts too?" She backed away, crossing herself as she went. "Is that how you came to appear, as if by some form of witchcraft?"

Neridah approached Cook, hoping to ease her anxiety. "I can assure you, we are all very much alive. You have nothing to fear. Yes, we are witches, but not as you understand witches to be. We are descended from a long line of Witches of the Crossworlds. For countless centuries, our ancestors have helped maintain the natural order, protecting this world from those who would seek to do it harm. We are all that's left of the family line that once numbered in the hundreds."

Patsy said, "It's okay, Cook, there's no need to be scared. At least, not while we're around."

Charles Danbury pointed toward the distant glow that emanated from the pool, silhouetting a small army of Sellemae's minions. "Judging by the shadowy creatures coming from down there, I'd say we have a good deal to fear."

Meredith stepped forward, taking her mother and daughter by the hand. "We can create a protective shield, like we did in the chamber. It can hold them at bay and keep everyone safe until Colin and the Reverend return."

Patsy approached Mrs Bradshaw. The old widow's wet hair had fallen out of its bun and clung to her face in strands resembling rat tails. She was shivering, despite the blanket wrapped tight around her. Patsy said, "I understand that what you did before was because of the mind thief, and that you're probably not like that at all."

"Is that what you think? Huh! I've never encountered such an ill-disciplined child. I didn't need that infernal creature in my head to see the importance of teaching you some manners."

Patsy's jaw dropped. She was about to say something when Meredith put a hand on her shoulder and said, "Don't worry about her. We've far more important issues to deal with. She'll be replaced before your next lessons anyway."

The old woman stared at Meredith, her eyes conveying her utter contempt. "Good luck to you with that. I've certainly no intention of ever returning."

Meredith led Patsy away from the old widow as Bandah's pixies arrived. They took the utmost care lifting the dead rat away from Vincent, finally allowing him to get a decent breath into his lungs.

Cook ran to him once he was freed, helping the man to his feet.

He was only a few years older than Cook but had kept in good shape. The pain in his chest told him he'd broken at least a few ribs. "You saved me, Cook. God love you, you saved me from that wretched spider."

Cook replied, "I'm not scared of those terrible things now." She looked across at Patsy, then back to Vincent. "I used to be, but not anymore, not while I've got a shovel and a good shoe on my foot."

Neridah addressed the pixies: "You need to hurry. You need to get to the pool and stop those things coming through. But whatever you do, don't seal the portal yet. Colin and my Alfred still have to return. Once they're back, we'll shift the portal's alignment to link with a different crossworld, so we're safe from Sellemae forever."

Charles called out, "Those things are getting closer!"

Neridah looked at Meredith and Patsy. "Okay, let's do this." The witches held hands and stood with their backs to each other while creating a fresh ball of energy, illuminating the bottom of the garden as it grew.

Neridah called out to the guests, "You must all step within the ball of light. It will keep us safe. Once it hardens, those outside will have no choice but to remain there."

The guests were hesitant at first, then Lily Danbury stepped forward. "This is all so confronting… and terrifying. But I feel there's little choice but to trust you three… and your pixies." She looked at Meredith; strong, proud, and drenched through as she stood wearing nothing but her full-length slip and jewellery. "I certainly trust you more than those other creatures. And I don't ever want to experience again what we went through earlier tonight." Her husband, Charles, took her hand and followed her.

Next to step forward were Vincent and Cook. Those remaining found themselves feeling more vulnerable being outside, particularly with the creatures of darkness getting closer.

One by one they moved into the protection of the shield… all except one.

Mrs Bradshaw stood defiantly outside the circle. "I don't trust you people. I don't trust any of you!"

Charles Danbury called out to her, "Don't be foolish, woman. Didn't you see that thing that attacked Vincent? You need to get in here now."

As Charles extended his hand to her, she backed away further. "I don't trust any form of so-called protection that relies on that petulant young girl… or any of her family for that matter."

Charles moved to the edge of the shield, arm still extended, and pleaded with her. "Don't be foolish, woman, you'll be far safer with the rest of us. If you're not prepared to come willingly, then I'll be forced to go out there and drag you in. One way or the other, it's going to happen. So, spare us all the angst and take my hand."

Mrs Bradshaw collapsed to her knees and broke down crying. "You just don't understand, do you? *I liked it!* I enjoyed the power I felt when I shared my mind with that thing. I've been one with it for years. It understood what I wanted. It wanted to help me attain all those things I'd ever…"

Charles cut her off. "Enough! I don't care how much you may wish to protest, I'm not prepared to sit here and watch those beasts take you." He left the protection of the circle, slipping and sliding his way through the mud till he reached the woman.

Mrs Bradshaw struggled to her feet, desperate to get away, only to lose her footing and fall flat on her face. "Why can't you just leave me be?"

"Because I want you to live."

The light of the shield started fading as it began to harden. The time for talk was over. Charles threw the reluctant widow over his shoulder and began the arduous and slippery few steps back to the safety of the shield.

The dwindling light of the hardening ball was still enough to illuminate a giant bat swooping down on Charles before he was even halfway there. He dived forward, sliding to a stop just short of his goal. A pair of shadows swept through them. Charles immediately recognised the mind thief for what it was, focusing hard to shut it out, and determined not to be taken over again.

Mrs Bradshaw was a different story. She welcomed the mind thief with open arms. Once fully under its control, she burst out laughing, then said, "Oh please, save me, Charles! Let me tear you all apart from within the safety of your fragile little shell. One way or the other, you will all die to—"

Charles put a hand over her mouth and pulled her to the ground. He dragged her with him as he pushed into the glowing light of the shield. Although it felt like walking through a sea of molasses, he was still able to struggle through its outer layers till Vincent reached out and grabbed Mrs Bradshaw from him, dragging her through just before the shield had sealed. Charles felt the hardening energy push him back until he collapsed to the ground exhausted.

He was shut out.

Inside the shield, Mrs Bradshaw lunged at the witches. The guests responded quickly, bringing her to the ground and holding her there. Madness filled her eyes as she screamed, "Fools! You'll wish you were dead by sunrise!"

Meanwhile, outside the shield, Charles raised his head from the mud just in time to see a bat preparing to grab him by his shoulders.

Patsy felt his distress as the claws sank into his flesh and lifted him off the ground.

A sound like a crack of thunder echoed and the bat fell to the ground, releasing its cargo.

Colin McIntyre was pleased that his marksmanship hadn't let him down.

Patsy couldn't contain her excitement. "Father's made it back!"

Meredith expelled a sigh of relief, while Neridah anxiously waited for some sign of Alfred's return.

Dozens of giant bats and rats crashed into the shield with each passing second, bouncing back with serious burns where they'd made impact. Charles lay on the ground, attempting to be as still as he could in an effort to avoid attracting attention. But it was no good. The rogue fairy who'd ridden the now dead rat approached him. "It took me years to tame that bat. You'll pay for this, pitiful human scum."

Patsy turned to Neridah and Meredith. "I need to rescue him."

Her mother shook her head. "You can't. It's too great a risk."

Neridah disagreed. "Hush, Meredith! Listen to her… there's a man who needs saving, and we must do what we can. It's been our duty for countless generations. You and I can hold this barrier for at least the few seconds it will take for her to help him."

Meredith protested, "It should be one of us! She's just a child… my child."

"She's also my grandchild, and the most powerful one among us, by a long way. Neither you nor I would have as good a chance of success as she will." Neridah glanced down at Patsy. "Go on, do as you must, bring him to safety."

Patsy allowed herself to be outside the shield, standing next to

Charles Danbury. She stared at the rogue. "You should know by now. I'm not scared of fairies."

The rogue sneered and drew back her wand. "Well, you should be."

"You don't want to know what happened to the last fairy who said that to me." A frown grew across Patsy's brow as she stomped her foot. A reverberation ran through the ground, throwing the rogue off balance.

The rogue brought her arm forward, aiming the wand toward Patsy. But the girl was too quick, sending forth a small surge of energy that knocked the fairy to the ground. Patsy wrapped her arms around Charles's shoulders.

"Don't worry Mister Danbury, if you can just empty your mind, I can take you to safety."

He looked across at Mrs Bradshaw, struggling against the guests holding her down. "But, if I empty my mind, won't I be vulnerable too?"

"Mister Danbury, you may think of me as little more than a child, but you must know by now that I'm more than that. I promise, I will get you to safety."

Charles looked into her eyes, convinced by her confidence that his best option was to trust her.

He closed his eyes.

When he opened them a second later, they were inside the fast-shrinking shield.

Meredith called to her, "Quickly, Patricia… we can't hold this any longer without you."

Realising every second mattered, Patsy allowed herself to be standing with her mother and grandmother, saving the time it would have taken to walk the few steps otherwise. Meredith was speechless. She'd couldn't believe how much confidence her daughter was developing in her capabilities… capabilities she'd known nothing of just twelve hours earlier.

"You've mastered the craft more tonight than I have in my entire life."

Neridah smiled and added, "Perhaps she's felt more reason in this one night than you had throughout your life. I'm guessing that you've mastered your skills more tonight than throughout the rest of your life as well."

"Yes, that's true. I've never looked to do much more than listen to nature. After your disappearance, and Grandfather's passing, my grandmother had little appetite to teach me the craft. But it didn't matter, I don't think I ever had the appetite for such things anyway."

"Oh, Meredith, my darling daughter. You've grown to be such a strong-minded woman, and I believe you to be a far more powerful witch than you realise. It's because of who you are that Patricia is so powerful."

The sound of further gunshots drew their focus back to the battle. Meredith watched the constant flow of beasts bouncing off their shield. "We can't hold this in place forever, and I fear there's too many beasts for Colin and the Reverend to deal with, even with Bandah and his pixies helping them. One of us needs to go out and join them, or these creatures will wear us down. Mother, you and Patsy are strong together. I'll go and you two can hold the shield in place."

Neridah broke away from the circle. "No! It has to be me."

Meredith was horrified. "Mother! No, you can't!"

Neridah replied, "There's no other way. Patricia is stronger than both you and I together. If you maintain focus, her strength is enough that the two of you can hold the shield. You're her mother." She looked down at Patsy. "She'll need you more than she'll need me." Turning back to Meredith, she continued, "If I don't make it back, I'll have gone down fighting for what I believe in." In the next instant, Neridah was gone.

Meredith was dumbstruck. She spoke to the empty space where her mother had been. "You'd better make it back here! If you don't, we're doomed!"

•

The pool was unrecognisable, the water now a spinning vortex with a hollow centre. Where its bottom had been there was now an open portal to darkness.

More creatures came through. It had become akin to a magnet within the Spider Queen's realm, sucking creatures in like a strong rip current at a surf beach.

Having freed the fairies in Sellemae's choir, Colin and the Reverend couldn't escape being caught up in the surge.

As they were swept along, the Reverend had a word with Bandah. "You need to stop them using the portal once we've passed through. There must already be hundreds of these vermin on the other side by now."

"We'll make a net with the silk from Sellemae's cocoons. As well as stopping more going through, it can catch anything you may be able to send back from the other side."

"Will that not take time to weave?"

"You underestimate what a few thousand pixies can achieve working together."

Colin asked, "How will you get back when we've closed the portal from the other side?"

Bandah laughed. "We'll be fine. Pixies don't need portals to travel between crossworlds. Now go, you've no time for idle banter, the witches will need your help."

The Reverend and Colin were drawn toward the portal, side by side with the creatures of darkness, swinging their blades from time to time when the turbulence brought them close enough to strike at their foes.

They lost control of their movements as they were sucked through the portal, the force sending them flying into the bushes near the creek, as though they'd been flung by a catapult.

On getting his breath back, Colin reloaded his revolver and flintlock while the Reverend slashed with his sword at anything that came close. Seeing the pixies poking and prodding the creatures that had already made it through (like a hive of hornets attacking a herd of animals), the Reverend said, "I'm glad to see the pixies doing what they can to slow the beasts down."

Colin replied, "Yes, but they're greatly outnumbered, and hitting pressure points does little more than buy us time."

The Reverend looked up toward the garden shed. "Aye, that may be the case, but can you see the glow? Your family are protecting the guests and themselves with a shield."

Colin stood on a rock to gain a better view. "Yes, I can see that, but look, there's someone outside the shield. It looks like Charles, and there's a bat bearing down on him!" Colin raised the flintlock to his shoulder and fired, bringing the beast to the ground. "We need to provide some cover if we want to give Meredith and the others a chance to get him in."

"There's not much I can do from this distance. If I try to send anything that far, it'll almost certainly lose most of its power by the time it gets there."

"Then we need to get closer."

The two men ran forward with scant regard for their safety. As they ran, the Reverend noticed the flow of creatures coming through the portal had stopped. "Bandah's been as good as his word. Time to send some of these foul beasts back from whence they came." He stretched his arm toward the bat closest to the portal and flung his hand downwards. It was as though an invisible rope connecting his arm with the beast had sent both bat and rider hurtling back toward the portal.

Colin called out, “I’ll take out the biggest.” He continued running as he fired his revolver, each shot hitting its mark with his usual accuracy.

The Reverend’s pace slowed as he continued throwing the creatures back to the portal. Those who’d been stunned by the pixies hitting their pressure points were the easiest targets, but there were still hundreds more to be dealt with. “We’ve no chance if we continue this way. We need to use more facets of the craft than I’m versed in if we’re to send all these vermin back to their foul home.”

As if on cue, Neridah appeared next to him. She took his hands and drew him in close. “Alfred! Thank God, you made it back!”

“Aye, that we did. But it’ll be for naught if we don’t do something to drive these beasts back.”

She took his hands in hers. “Do you trust me?”

“I’d not have dedicated my life to crossing between the worlds to get you back if there were any doubt of that.”

“Then hold my hands, do as I do.” Neridah began reciting a mantra: “Tishbah reign de nigh, tishbah reign de nigh…”

The Reverend joined in and their eyes locked on each other, as though they were boring into each other’s souls. Their feet started rising and they drifted as far away from each other as their extended arms would allow.

As they rose further, the two of them appeared to be lying on their bellies in mid-air. Then, they started to spin. Very slowly at first, but picking up speed as they went. Realising what they were up to, the creatures of darkness turned their attention away from the shield and the house guests.

The pixies formed themselves into a barrier surrounding Neridah and the Reverend, immobilising any who came near.

The pair rose and drifted till they were spinning directly above the portal, their arms pulling hard against each other from the centrifugal force.

With the spell in full flight, there was no longer any need for them to continue the mantra.

Their strategy seemed to be working. The creatures who'd come through the portal were now being drawn back to it.

Unfortunately, that included Colin.

When he felt himself starting to be sucked toward the portal, he grabbed hold of a nearby tree with a trunk that was almost half a metre in diameter. He put his flintlock on the far side of the tree and grabbed hold of it from either end just as the wind rushing toward the portal lifted his feet from the ground. Once satisfied that his grip was strong enough to hold him, he looked up and watched as the creatures of darkness were sucked into the portal.

Neridah looked at the Reverend. "I don't think I can hold on for much longer... my hands... they're slipping." The Reverend tightened his grip as much as possible, but he could tell she was right. It was not a matter of if she'd slip from his grasp, but when. Neridah continued, "When I let go, the portal will snap shut, and whatever's left here shall remain."

The beasts tried to resist the force of the spell drawing them to the portal, but it was to no avail. Dozens were hurtling in, the pace increasing as Neridah and the Reverend spun faster and faster.

Colin's grip on the flintlock was slipping too. He began worrying that it may come apart under the force, throwing him back into the Spider Queen's realm.

Eventually, his fingers had slipped too far, and he went hurtling toward the darkness at the pool's centre.

Neridah's grip failed as well, causing her and the Reverend to fall, crashing to the pool below as the portal snapped shut, with Colin right at its outer edge. A tenth of a second longer, and he would have been gone.

Neridah and the Reverend stood up, their clothing weighing them down in the metre-deep water. Hand in hand, they made their way to the shore in silence. For now, their powers were exhausted. It would be up to Meredith, Patsy and the pixies to deal with the remaining creatures of darkness.

Colin watched them approach the shore as he reloaded his gun. He called out as loud as he could, hoping to be heard over the rain, "Did you notice how many are left?"

The Reverend shook his head. "My guess is there's likely at least fifty."

A flash of lightning revealed a giant spider preparing to bite down on Colin's shoulder. The Reverend, too exhausted to use his power, and no longer in possession of his sword (it had been stripped from him by the centrifugal force), reached for his boot where he kept a small blade. In one fluid action, he brought it to the surface and sent it flying through the air. Colin felt it whistle past his ear before it found its mark. The spider was wounded, but not enough for it to give up. Colin, having finished reloading his revolver, fired just before the spider's fangs could pierce his flesh.

No sooner had the spider fallen than a rat leapt from the bushes. Colin fired two more shots, causing the creature to let out a blood-curdling squeal as it came down on top of him, knocking the revolver from his hand. A rogue fairy climbed off the rodent's back and laughed as she drew back her wand. "Well, this should be easy. I'll end your misery, then drag those two fools back to face their fate at the hands of Sellemae."

A flash of light, brighter than anything they'd seen that night, was accompanied by a deafening crack of thunder. The ground moved as if being carried on a wave. Trees were uprooted, and giant boulders went flying. The rogue stood frozen as she realised the origin of the earth tremor. There, at the central point from which the wave had come, stood Patsy, the upheaval having been the result of her stomping her foot in anger. "Leave my father alone!"

The rogue grinned, then turned to Colin. "Prepare to die, you useless waste of breath and flesh."

The rogue was pushed hard against a nearby tree. Then Patsy lifted her finger and the rogue flew into the air, completely at her mercy. She pointed toward the centre of the pool, sending the rogue toward a miniature portal she'd opened with barely a thought. Once the first rogue had been dispatched, she began flinging her arms about, each movement capturing several creatures of darkness that she then threw back into Sellemae's world. When the last of the creatures had been expelled, Patsy collapsed and blacked out, utterly exhausted.

Colin ran to his daughter while the Reverend and Neridah dragged themselves from the pool as its waters swept in to fill the void the closing portal had created.

A noise from the centre of the pool drew the Reverend's attention. It was Sellemae! One of her fang-tipped limbs was rising above the water, followed a moment later by another.

Meredith had already started to run down the hill to be with Patsy. When she saw the Spider Queen's legs coming through, she knew it was up to her, and her alone.

She had to end this.

While the pixies could possibly buy her time, she was the only one there who could potentially shut the portal that Sellemae held open. She drew her arms back and took a deep breath, focusing everything she had on drawing strings of energy from as many of the crossworlds as possible. She felt immense power surge through her, making her glow like the sun. She drew so much energy that bringing her hands down by her side triggered a flash of lightning and a crack of thunder, along with another wave that moved earth, rocks and trees, just like her daughter.

When the power surge reached the centre of the pool, Sellemae's limbs disintegrated, leaving behind droplets of water that fell harmlessly back to the pool with the rest of the rain.

The portal to Sellemae's world was finally closed, once and for all.

Meredith swayed on the spot for a few seconds before her knees gave way and she fell to the ground.

Three generations of witches and the Reverend Casey were all passed out. Colin slumped his back against a tree, then looked up and opened his mouth in the hope of catching some rain.

It took a while for him to register the voice calling out to him. It wasn't until it was almost directly next to him that he bothered to turn and pay attention to where it came from. There was Cook, full of concern, Vincent by her side. Cook asked, "Mister McIntyre! Are you alright, sir?"

"Yes, Cook, I don't know how, but I believe I am."

"Oh, but begging your pardon, sir, we still have the problem of Mrs Bradshaw. It's taking eight people to hold her down, and they're all getting frightfully tired, sir."

A mind thief! At least there was just the one to deal with. "Vincent, may I ask a favour?" He didn't wait for a response before continuing. "Be a good man and grab some rope from the shed to tie her up until we're all indoors and dried off. We'll need Bandah's help with this. Everyone else with powers seems to be taking a well-earned rest."

Vincent nodded and headed off to the shed while Cook helped Colin to his feet.

Colin told her, "He's a good man you know, never married either."

"Now don't you go getting any harebrained ideas in your head, Mister McIntyre."

Colin surprised himself by smiling and somehow finding the energy to let out a whole-hearted laugh. He thought to himself that sometimes, good things were indeed born out of the bad.

Colin and Cook worked their way up the hill, while the pixies banded together to transport the three unconscious witches and the Reverend to the house. The rain was easing, and the first light of dawn was visible as the guests carried the tied up, and struggling, Mrs Bradshaw.

Once at the house, Bandah instructed the guests to place her on the kitchen table. A hundred pixies gathered around her and began pushing their hands in and under the surface of her flesh, like people searching with their hands for an object in muddy water. Eventually, one of them called out, "I've found it!" He pulled his hand out, revealing part of a shadow. The rest of the pixies joined him, tugging and pulling at the shadow until it was fully out.

Mrs Bradshaw then fell into a deep sleep.

The mind thief, feeling vulnerable and outnumbered, disappeared into another crossworld.

Lily Danbury asked Bandah, "Will it be back?"

"Oh yes, but not in this household. Mind thieves come and go in your world all the time. They like to target politicians and kings, even business leaders. There is more of what you might call magic, good and bad, happening around you every day than you're aware of."

•

A day later, the dinner guests were in good spirits. None of them had any memory of what had taken place, just that their weekend had been somehow extraordinary. They were grateful that Colin had sent stable hands to retrieve their horses that had escaped in the Friday night storm.

Mrs Bradshaw's driver had no idea what the injury had been that led to the bandage wrapped around his head. All he knew was that he had a frightful headache as a result.

As Mrs Bradshaw climbed into the carriage, she said, "Driver, take me away from this wretched place." Once seated, she looked out the window at Meredith and declared, "You need to find yourself another tutor. The idea that I should spend any more time with that petulant child is incomprehensible."

Meredith replied, "I'm glad there's something we can agree on." The driver cracked his whip and the carriage took off.

Vincent approached Cook. "I'll be heading down to Sydney next week to listen to the opera. Would you care to join me? That is, if Mister McIntyre is agreeable to you having the time off work." Cook looked up at Colin and his smile told her everything she needed to know. Vincent climbed onto his horse, tipped his hat at Cook, and rode off.

Neridah walked with the Reverend Alfred Casey to his sulky. "So, you chose to be a man of the cloth?"

Alfred responded with a silent nod.

"Are you sure you have to go?"

"Aye, but I promise you, I'll be back… soon."

As they walked, Neridah grabbed his arm and made sure she had eye contact. "I never knew how powerful a thing love can be. Your whole life, devoted to an impossible dream of bringing me back."

"A dream that has finally come true."

She stopped walking and took his hands in hers. "If you want me, Alfred, I'm yours, and I always will be, whatever may happen."

"I know." Alfred gave Neridah one last hug, then climbed onto his sulky and rode away without another word.

•

Down by the pool, Meredith and Patsy sat listening to the rescued fairies sing joyful songs celebrating their freedom.

As one song finished and another began, Patsy turned her focus to stroking Ferdinand's back as the cat lay purring on her lap. "Tell me what you really think, Mother. Can we trust these ones?"

Meredith looked at her and smiled. "They'll be fine."

The cat stuck his head up to offer his opinion. "You would hope so. After all, you did save them from an eternity of suffering."

But there was one rescued fairy who wasn't singing, and that fairy was Mrs Smith.

She looked dejected as she sat on a nearby bough, well away from the other fairies. Glaring at the witches she grumbled, "Ha! Why would I be grateful? I'd have been happier if you'd left me behind to sing in Sellemae's chamber."

Meredith gave a puzzled look. "Really? I'm curious why you feel that way, Mrs Smith."

Patsy looked the fairy in the eye. "Yes, come on, Mrs Smith, how about some gratitude. After all, you don't want to make me angry, do you?" Patsy tried her best to look serious, but broke out giggling as the pretence faded.

The laughter came to an abrupt halt when Patsy noticed a glow emanating from the centre of the pool. Ripples of water bounced around and a creature Patsy hadn't seen the like of came through the portal.

In a way, it appeared similar to the other fairies, but then she noticed the distinct lack of substance. It seemed almost as though the creature was half in this world and half in another.

It flew towards Patsy and whispered, “She is coming.”

A moment later, the creature was gone.

THE WITCHES OF THE CROSSWORLDS

BOOK II

HUNTER

CHAPTER 1

Ferdinand raised his head when the kookaburras started laughing. Keen to know what the raucous was about, he leapt off Patsy's bed, raced out the door, down the stairs, then through the house until he reached the kitchen.

The aroma of crackling bacon made him almost forget his urgent mission to get outside. Then something extraordinary caught his attention. The cicadas were singing, now, at first light, during the cusp between autumn and winter. It took a while to make out their song, but the more he listened, the clearer it became: "She is here! She is here…"

Desperate to attract Cook's attention, he rubbed himself against her legs then looked up, letting out several short and insistent meows.

Maintaining focus on the eggs she was cracking into the cast iron frying pan, Cook told the cat, "You'll have to wait. I'll not let breakfast be ruined for your sake."

Ferdinand thought to himself, If only she would bother learning to listen like Patsy and her parents.

With the last of the eggs in the pan, the rosy-cheeked woman watched the ginger tomcat move toward the back door, each meow more urgent than the last.

"Okay, hold your horses." Wiping her hands on her apron, she made her way to the door, Ferdinand slipping through the gap as soon as it opened.

Cook stood in the open doorway, her breath turning to steam on contact with the crisp mountain air. She watched the cat race off toward the bushes at the bottom of the garden then stood still for a moment, puzzled as to why there were cicadas making such a racket when it was so cold outside.

•

Having worked his way through the bushes and down the bank to where the creek opened into a large pool, Ferdinand hid behind a small tea tree. A choir of fairies were circling a shimmering glow at the pool's centre. Like the cicadas, they were singing in harmony, "She is here! She is here…"

Then the singing stopped.

The fairies fled as the top of a woman's head broke the surface at the pool's centre. She had golden hair, crowned by a garland of daisies that appeared to look one way then another, as though searching for something. Her eyes were closed and she took measured strides toward the bank, rising further with each step.

Ferdinand backed away, concerned by something odd. No water dripped from her, nor were there any signs of moisture in her hair or on the loose white dress that rippled as though touched by a non-existent breeze.

She looked to be a few years older than Patsy, but not as old as the others in the household.

The young woman turned to him, then opened her eyes.

The cicadas called out, "Run, run, run…"

The cat turned to flee but found himself struggling, as though stuck in a sea of molasses.

A voice whispered in his head, *Do not run, Ferdinand. Stay by my side. Guide me. Tell me what I need to know.*

Ferdinand moved out from the bushes and sat on a sandstone step, part of the pathway Patsy's great-grandfather had laboured over when the family first immigrated from Ireland.

The cicadas screamed even louder, "Run, run, run…"

The young woman raised her arms to the side. Once they were level with her shoulders, she flicked her wrists downward.

The cicadas went silent.

The mist swirling above the pool and the rising sun created a backdrop of light beams as the young woman continued toward the bank. She was a vision of pre-Raphaelite splendour, dawn's warm light highlighting the simple gold-threaded girdle around the waist of her sleeveless white dress.

Her left foot emerged from the water and sank into the mud of the bank. Tiny violets sprang to life around it, blossoming in a multitude of colours, their rapid growth like a dance celebrating the essence of life.

She walked forward, flowers filling each of her footsteps, even as she walked along the solid surface of the sandstone path.

She reached where Ferdinand sat waiting and said, "Go now and bring them to me… but remember nothing of what you saw."

As the cat ran up the hill, the girl looked up at the trees, raised her arms and smiled. The cicadas renewed their song. "She is here! She is here…"

•

The roar of the cicadas jolted Patsy from her sleep.

Cicadas? At this time of year?

Fumbling in the dim light, her hands searched for the slippers she knew were under her bed. She crawled out of the cocoon created by her blankets and mattress, then lay on the floor, making sweeping motions with her arms to bring the slippers out of hiding. With the wayward slippers retrieved, she grabbed her dressing gown from the back of the door.

She ran into the corridor and headlong into her grandmother, Neridah, who grabbed her by the shoulders and whispered, "While we need to go see what's happening, can we do so without causing injury?"

"What do you think it is?"

"I suspect the portal has opened and something has come through. You, your mother and I need to go down together and see what's happening."

A male voice boomed over the top of Neridah's. "I'll be joining you on this reconnaissance, along with my flintlock and revolver." Patsy's father, Colin, was already dressed for riding, and his purposeful stride made each step reverberate like a hammer coming down on the floorboards. He was followed by Patsy's mother, Meredith. Like Patsy and Neridah, she wore her nightclothes and dressing gown.

Neridah grabbed Colin by the arm. Although many years his senior, circumstance had led to her appearing far younger. "If you take guns down there, you risk antagonising a delicate situation. The portal has realigned. We don't know anything about where and when it's aligned to."

Colin replied, "After what came through last time, I'm not taking chances, not until we know who the 'she' is that the cicadas are referring to."

Neridah rolled her eyes. "No, you need to let *us* see what's come through first." She turned and took Patsy's hand so they could go down the stairs together.

Meredith put a hand on her husband's arm. "Don't worry about my mother, you know what she's like."

"A stubborn old woman in a teenage body, that's all I see most days."

"Yes, I know what you mean, but I agree with her in this case. Please darling, just this once, listen to her and let us see what's there first. It's not like we can't look after ourselves."

Meredith let go of his arm and followed her mother and daughter, leaving Colin to contemplate whether he'd handled the situation in the best possible manner.

•

Cook looked up from her breakfast preparations as the three generations of Crossworld Witches entered the kitchen. "If you're looking for the cat, he's gone out and run down to the creek."

Meredith replied, "Thank you, Cook, we'll be back soon for breakfast."

Cook's cheeks glowed redder than usual and her breath became shorter. "Begging your pardon, ma'am, but shouldn't you have Master

Colin escort you down there… in case there's trouble afoot?"

Meredith frowned, turned away from Cook, and opened the door. She took a step back as Ferdinand raced inside.

The cat looked up at Patsy. "You need to hurry! You have to come meet her!"

Patsy squatted to give the cat a pat and asked, "Who is she?"

"She's here! You need to meet her!"

The cat ran back out the door, the witches following close behind. Cook called after them, "Breakfast will be ready in five minutes." After none of them acknowledged her she closed the door. A moment later, Colin entered the kitchen. "Will you be going after them, sir?"

He stared out the window. "Not just yet." He turned to Cook and asked, "Can you hear that?"

"The cicadas?"

"No, there's something else."

CHAPTER 2

The frost crunched underfoot as Patsy ran out the kitchen door and across the lawn with her mother and grandmother. After only a few strides her slippers were soaked through and her feet numbed with cold.

They were halfway to the bottom of the garden when the cicadas fell silent once more. Then the young woman emerged, climbing the steps leading up from the pool.

Patsy watched in awe at the trail of violets growing in her footsteps.

"Hello." The young woman's greeting startled Patsy. It was as though she'd somehow transported herself from being a good distance away to within a few feet of the three witches. "I'm Hunter."

Meredith stepped forward. "I'm Meredith." She gestured toward Patsy. "My daughter, Patricia, and my—"

"Why call her Patricia when she refers to herself as Patsy?"

Neridah stepped forward. "I'm Patricia's grandmother, and—"

"You look younger than your daughter. Why?"

"That's a long story that can wait till later."

"When can I meet Alfred?"

Neridah's eyes narrowed. "The Reverend Casey will be here when it's appropriate." She stood between Hunter and her family, putting her arms out slightly in a gesture to hold them back as though she were a kind of sentinel. "Where are you from?"

"Why does that matter?"

"If you want us to trust you, I need to know."

Hunter turned and looked toward the creek as she answered, "I'm from one of the other places. You call them 'crossworlds'."

"How do you know we call them that?"

"Your thoughts linger everywhere, speaking to me, especially near the door."

Neridah asked, "The door?"

"Yes, the one in the water. You call it a 'portal'? I believe that's what I heard in the memories floating above the pool's surface."

Neridah replied, "I'm very particular about cleaning up my memories, wherever they may be. And I was especially careful to ensure I'd removed them from around the portal."

Hunter tilted her head to one side. "Why?"

Meredith stepped forward and positioned herself close to her mother to create a barrier between Hunter and Patsy. She answered on her mother's behalf: "In case they attracted unwanted guests."

"Who?"

Neridah replied, "To begin with, there are the mind thieves. They take any piece of information they can find in their bid to control the wills of others. They already control many powerful people, but if they had access to *our* knowledge, this world would be in grave danger."

Meredith glared at her mother. Did she really need to share this information with a stranger?

"I know of these creatures you call 'mind thieves.' We call them 'Nasqa.' They are a nuisance. It's better to be rid of them altogether."

Patsy nudged her way through between her guardians. Knowing it would be futile to try to stop her, Neridah placed a protective hand on the girl's shoulder. Patsy asked, "What's your world like?"

Hunter looked at her and smiled. "It is much like this, except mine is ruled by those with the knowledge. My father is the leader of my world and many others." She cast her eyes across the three witches. "Why do you keep your powers hidden from those around you?"

Meredith replied on behalf of them all: "We seek not to rule, but to maintain order."

Hunter paused before responding. "So, you let the Nasqa do as they please?"

Patsy answered, "I don't, they're scared of me."

Hunter gave a gentle nod in acknowledgment and said, "I think they are wise to be scared of you."

Patsy blurted out, "I can see them better than anyone else." She cast a nervous glance toward her grandmother before looking down to avoid eye contact. *What a dumb thing to come out with,* she thought to herself.

"I can see you and I will be good friends, Patsy." Hunter turned her attention back to Neridah. Her words were cold and deadpan. "I want to meet Alfred."

"Why?"

"He fills your thoughts. He must be very special. Why aren't you together, when your thoughts are so entwined?"

Neridah frowned. "It's complicated."

Patsy couldn't help but tell Hunter what she knew of the Reverend's plans. "The Reverend will be coming to dinner tonight." She didn't notice the glare of disapproval from her grandmother. "Would you like to join us?"

Hunter smiled. "Yes, I would like that very much."

*

Colin said to Cook, "I could swear I heard Mrs Smith calling from outside."

Cook continued her preparations as she answered, "I'd rather not be talking of that woman."

"But did you hear her?"

Cook stopped and turned to face him. "Aye, or at least I thought so. I'd dismissed it as coming from my imagination… until knowing you'd heard it too."

"What did you hear?"

"It can't be her, sir. We've not seen her in almost a year."

Colin closed his eyes and took a deep breath. "Cook, just tell me what you heard."

"It sounded like a warning, sir." She looked to the ceiling as she tried to recall the words. "You cannot trust her."

"Hmm, I might have a look outside." Colin was halfway out the door when he stopped and added, "You may want to set an extra place at the table for breakfast. I suspect we'll be having a guest."

He pulled the door shut behind him and looked around the bushes. Sure enough, within two paces of the door, he found a large spider. "It's okay, Mrs Smith, you might as well reveal yourself."

Where the spider had been a moment ago, Colin now saw the aging fairy that was Mrs Smith.

Colin squatted and quietly asked her, "So, how about you tell me who it is that we shouldn't trust?"

"It feels wrong."

"But tell me, what is it that feels wrong, and why would I trust a warning that comes from the likes of you?"

"To be honest, I don't know who she is, but I know this: she's powerful. You shouldn't—"

She was gone.

Colin cursed her for disappearing mid-sentence, then stood up and made his way down the lawn to where the witches were talking to Hunter. On hearing her father's boots crunching on the frosty lawn, Patsy called out, "Father, Hunter said she can join us for dinner tonight when the Reverend Casey comes over."

He looked at Hunter's trail of violets as he replied, "I'm assuming your mother is happy with this?" He turned his gaze to Meredith for an answer. She, in turn, looked to Neridah, her mother's stern expression letting her know she'd need to find approval elsewhere.

Patsy asked, "Please, Mother, please say it's okay for her to join us."

Meredith placed a hand on Patsy's shoulder, then turned to face Hunter. As Hunter's smile grew, Meredith's indecision vanished. "Yes, of course she can." She turned to Hunter. "We'd love to know more about you." Then, she gestured toward Colin. "This is my husband, Colin."

Hunter took a step toward him. "I'm Hunter."

"Well, Hunter, I'm pleased to meet you. Tell me, the violets, are you able to stop them growing in your footsteps?"

"Why would I do that?"

Colin smiled, feeling disarmed by the innocence of her question. "To be discrete. If you're to join us for dinner, none of our servants or guests should know you have powers."

"You don't have the knowledge."

The bluntness of her comment made Colin bite his tongue and wait a moment to calm himself before replying. "No, I don't, but Meredith and I have long had an understanding about such things. Our servants might fear 'the knowledge' as you call it." By the time he'd finished his answer, any sense of irritation had not only passed but had been forgotten.

"I can make it stop for a time, but I will have to release the build-up later in the evening."

"How?"

A wide smile grew across Hunter's face. "I will come out here and dance."

Despite her charm, Colin was firm. "Perhaps you can go back to your own world and release it there? I don't know that it's fitting for you to stay beyond dinner."

"But I wish to stay for a few days. There's much that your family and I can learn from each other. When I go back, I'd like you all to come with me and meet my father."

"We'll discuss the possibility of that later. For now, I'll invite you to join us for breakfast. I've already told Cook to prepare another setting at the table." He turned to Patsy. "Patricia, can you escort Hunter up to the house? The rest of us will join you in a few minutes."

Patsy gave him a hug. "Thank you, Father."

As Patsy took Hunter's hand and started up the hill, Colin called after them, "It would be best not to arouse Cook's fears with the violets either. She's already on edge today."

Neridah grabbed Colin's arm and waited till she was sure Hunter was out of earshot before whispering, "I don't trust her."

Colin nodded. "Mrs Smith expressed misgivings as well, then vanished mid-sentence."

Meredith took his other arm, encouraging him to start slowly up the hill. "She deserves the benefit of the doubt for now. Patricia's already taken a shine to her."

Neridah retorted through clenched teeth, "We know nothing about this young woman, and you've already invited her into our home. If Mrs Smith warned you—"

Colin snapped, "I don't know that a warning from Mrs Smith is sufficient reason to distrust someone outright. However, I must concede, the nature of how she vanished while passing on her warning is disturbing to say the least. I will make a decision about the girl after we talk to her over breakfast."

Neridah released her son-in-law's arm, raising her hands in the air to free some of her frustration. "Am I the only one in this family who sees something wrong here? And since when was it up to you and you alone to make such decisions?"

Walking up the hill, arm in arm with Meredith, Colin replied without turning to face his mother-in-law. "It became my right to make such decisions the day Meredith and I took our vows. I will trust the girl until she gives me reason not to, as I do with everyone who comes to this property."

Neridah replied, uncaring as to whether or not her words were heard, "My daughter may have done so, but I never made a vow to honour and obey you. Mark my words, one day society's attitude will change, and marriage will be seen the way it should be… as an equal partnership. Who knows, men like yourself may one day even learn to respect their elders, whatever their gender." Neridah looked to the ground and lifted her gown slightly as she prepared to walk up the hill. How was the danger of taking the girl into their home not as obvious to the others as it was to her?

Then, something drew her attention.

Was that rotting vegetation she could smell?

She looked back at the path of violets and noticed something odd. As the violets grew, the nearby grass wilted. Determined to point this out to the others, she started after them.

As soon as she'd turned her back on the violets, all memory of what she'd just observed was gone. She headed up the hill, knowing there was something she'd wanted to say. By the time she was halfway there, all she could think of was her eagerness for breakfast.

*

Patsy laughed as she and Hunter burst through the kitchen door. They took Cook by surprise and almost knocked the tray with its plates of bacon and eggs out of her hands. "Oops! Sorry, Cook."

"Heaven forbid!" Cook put the tray down on a sideboard and made a show of placing a hand over her heart. "You know better than to come barging through like that, particularly with a guest… a guest you should rightly be bringing into the house through the front door rather than my kitchen."

"Oh, but Cook, you simply must meet Hunter."

Hunter looked at Cook and smiled. "Hello."

Cook made a subtle nodding gesture. "Hello, Miss Hunter, I'm pleased to make your acquaintance."

"Are you?" Hunter giggled, as though someone had told a joke. "Why?"

Cook ignored the question, picked up her tray, and headed toward the dining room. She glanced over her shoulder and said, "I'd be pleased if you can take your seats at the table. Breakfast is being served now."

Patsy turned to Hunter. "I like Cook ever so much. Do you like Cook?"

Hunter shrugged her shoulders. "She has no knowledge."

"Oh! No! That's not true! Cook knows lots of things, that's what I love about her."

As the two of them made their way to the dining room, Hunter asked, "What sort of things does she know?"

"Well, to begin with, she knows that sometimes, if you want the things that make you happy, you have to do other things that you don't want to." Patsy led Hunter to their seats at the highly polished red cedar table. She pulled back a chair for Hunter. "You can sit here."

Hunter ran a finger along the ornate carving on the chair before asking, "I don't understand, why would you do something you don't want to?"

Patsy laughed, then said, "Oh, come on." She sat down and patted the seat of Hunter's chair, encouraging her to sit as well. "We *all* do things we don't want to sometimes. I don't like taking a bath, but I like it when I feel warm and clean afterward."

Hunter took her seat and smiled. "You can feel that way without taking a bath… I can show you how."

Conscious of not wanting to be overheard by Cook, Patsy whispered in Hunter's ear. "I already know how to do that, but Mother says that it's best to do things without magic when you can. She says it gives your power more meaning when you use it."

The sound of Colin's boots on the floorboards in the kitchen heralded the others' arrival. He entered the room then turned to Cook and said, "Cook, you can spend the rest of the morning as you please. We'll take our own plates to the kitchen once we've finished."

"Very good, sir. I'll return and tend to the dishes before lunch."

Once Cook had left, Colin addressed the table. "Well, it's our great pleasure to host a visitor from another world! Welcome, Hunter, may your visit prove fruitful to us all."

Hunter's eyes stared in the direction of her plate, but she seemed oblivious to its contents. She spoke as though the two girls were the only ones in the room. "I don't understand. Why is it your father who speaks instead of the most powerful of you?"

Patsy's jaw dropped. She shook her head and said, "This is my father's property."

Hunter stared at her. "But he has so little knowledge, so little power."

"He has lots of power; it's just different to yours and mine. And he's very good at listening. He understands the cicadas and some of the animals too."

"He discourages your mother from using her knowledge."

Feeling the impolite nature of the girls' conversation had gone far enough, Meredith interrupted. "No, he doesn't. Patricia's father has always supported me doing as I wish, and I love him for that."

Glaring at their guest, Colin grabbed hold of Meredith's arm to keep her from continuing. "I must say, having overheard your commentary, I find your attitude rather, shall we say… confronting. But I understand that where you come from, the concept of what's normal is obviously different from ours." He released his wife's arm and put some bacon on his fork. "I'm curious to know more about where you come from."

Hunter smiled. "Would you like to visit my world? Then you and your family could meet my father."

Colin chewed his bacon, savouring the flavour before he swallowed. Everyone at the table watched in anticipation as he had a sip of his tea before answering. "I think such arrangements might be a little premature at this stage."

Hunter's smile grew broader, almost to the point of breaking out in laughter. "I think you'd like him." She paused for a moment then asked, "Can I let my violets grow now that the cook has gone?"

"Oh, no!" Meredith replied. She wiped the edge of her mouth with a serviette before explaining. "We try to keep all evidence of our magic to a minimum, especially indoors."

Hunter cast her eyes downward. "This is so hard for me to understand. In my world, if we can do what needs doing using the knowledge, then we do so. Magic then feeds on magic. Where I live, there is no physical labour. People think of what needs to be done, then those with the knowledge make it reality."

Neridah, seated directly across from Hunter, spoke for the first time since they'd sat at the table. "You do understand that using magic comes at a price, don't you? If you use magic in one place, its power comes from another. As a group, we're already deeply indebted to other worlds for the power we've used."

Hunter's eyes narrowed. "So, this bothers you?"

"Yes, it bothers me. It bothers me that I don't know which worlds my powers have been drawn from. It bothers me that by saving lives in this world, it may have cost lives in others." Neridah paused, waiting for support that never came. She picked up her knife and fork. "Perhaps I'm better off just concerning myself with breakfast."

Meredith asked, "How old are you, Hunter?"

"I lost track many years ago."

"Do you have memories of being a little girl?"

She laughed. "Yes, there was a time when I did little more than play. My father says you learn a great deal from play. Yet I enjoy life more since I've been older. The more you know, the more interesting it is talking to people."

As he cut another piece of bacon, Colin asked, "So, you like learning from the people you meet?"

"Sometimes people will tell me things I don't know, and I enjoy that. It doesn't happen often though."

Patsy grinned. "I think there's lots I can tell you that you don't know."

Hunter smiled. "I'm sure there is. Perhaps there are things I can tell you as well." She turned and looked at Neridah. "I look forward to listening to Alfred's stories too."

Neridah frowned. "Why are you so interested in the Reverend?"

"It's rare for men to acquire the knowledge. My father has it, but he is one of the few in my world."

Patsy touched Hunter's arm, seeking her attention. "My great-grandfather was a powerful druid priest." She turned to Neridah. "Wasn't he, Nana-Neri?"

"Yes, he certainly was." Neridah pushed away her plate, having eaten only a few mouthfuls. Everyone cringed at the sound of her chair scraping on the floorboards when she pushed it back and rose to her feet. She looked at Colin, wearing a cynical smile. "If you'll excuse me, I have matters to attend to." She turned and left the room.

Hunter turned to Patsy and said, "I like your grandmother."

Patsy struggled to hide a naughty giggle as she replied, "I don't think she likes you much though."

Hunter tilted her head slightly and looked up before bringing her eyes back to Patsy. "I don't understand. Why?"

Colin sipped on his tea then replied on his daughter's behalf. "Hunter, based on what you've told us, your life is considerably longer than ours. Because our lives are so short, compared to yours, emotion plays a greater role in our choices. While you may be able to dwell on decisions for years, like whether or not to trust someone, our time is somewhat more limited."

Meredith cut him off. "Darling, is it really wise to make such assumptions? Are Hunter's years the same duration as our own? Maybe her age isn't that different from a teenager in our own world. There's so much we need to learn before jumping to conclusions."

She could see by Colin's expression that he didn't agree. An uncomfortable silence hung over the table till he stood up. "I have preparations to attend to before the Magistrate arrives."

His passage toward the door came to a halt when Hunter asked, "Why are you so concerned about the Magistrate?"

He clenched his fists and almost began to reply, then thought better of it and left the room.

*

The Reverend Alfred Casey shivered at first as he strode into the icy-cold swimming hole and made his way to the waterfall that fed it.

There were many things in life that made him feel blessed, but few more so than having his home and church right next to such a majestic location.

Once he'd made his way far enough into the pool, he dived under, then pushed up from the bottom and let out a cry of joy as he broke the surface. He'd done this every morning since he'd discovered this spot within days of his arrival at the small church just out of Pulpit's Hill. He let himself drift under the falls and closed his eyes as he soaked up the sensation of the frigid water coming down on him.

A small voice snapped him back to reality. "Hey, shouldn't you make sure you're alone when you have your bath?"

"Bandah! Of all the times to stop by. We've not seen each other for months, and you choose now? You've known for years of my morning rituals."

The pixie laughed as he fluttered in the air just clear of the falling water. "Trust me, old friend, I would've much preferred to wait till you were through, but someone's come through the portal, and she's already throwing reality out of balance."

"I promised Neridah I'd be there for dinner this evening."

"You can't go earlier?"

"No, I've a funeral to perform this morning. And Colin has already informed me that he'll be receiving the Magistrate before lunch."

"In that case, I'll head over there on my own and keep a low profile while I learn what I can."

"Thank you, my friend." As the pixie flew off, the Reverend Casey let his head sink below the surface.

CHAPTER 3

With breakfast finished Patsy asked her mother, "Can I show Hunter the stables now?"

"As long as you make your bed first."

"Can't one of the servants do that for me? Just this once?"

"Patricia, you know my feelings on this matter. I'm sure Hunter will be happy to wait here for you, then you can show her the stables and find ways to keep yourselves entertained until lunchtime."

Patsy rolled her eyes then looked at Hunter. "I promise I'll just be a minute." She dragged her feet as she left the room, making the promise appear somewhat unrealistic.

Meredith turned to Hunter. "I hope you don't mind, I have matters I must attend to. Will you be fine on your own until Patricia returns?"

"Yes, I'm quite happy to sit and wait. I like Patsy. I like you too."

"I'm glad to hear it." Meredith's smile dissolved as she turned to leave the room. She was uncertain about leaving Hunter on her own, but there were matters she wanted to discuss with her husband before the Magistrate arrived. More importantly, she wanted to consult the Book of Wisdom regarding their new guest.

Within seconds of Meredith's departure, Hunter looked to where Bandah was peering through the window. She reached out with her hand then pulled back, dragging Bandah through the window and onto the table as if she'd lassoed him.

Although taken by surprise, the pixie felt no sense of fear. He wasted no time getting to the point. "Who are you, and why are you here?"

Hunter leaned forward and smiled. "A pixie! How cute." She flicked a finger in his direction and Bandah vanished, much the same as Mrs Smith had done earlier.

•

Meredith walked out the front door to join her mother and husband.

Neridah was in full flight. "I don't trust her."

Colin replied, "Don't you think you're being a little harsh?" He looked away momentarily before continuing. "Look, she may come across as rude and arrogant, but she's from a different world. We don't know what's considered polite where she comes from."

Meredith squinted as she walked out into the bright sunlight then took hold of Colin's arm. "Colin's right, Mother. She was quite sweet a moment ago, telling me she likes Patsy, and me as well."

Neridah turned to her daughter. "You left her alone in there? How could you be so naive? Colin should be firm and let her know she's not welcome. Then when she leaves, we need to do whatever it takes to realign the portal. The longer she stays, the harder it will be to be rid of her."

She tensed when Colin placed a reassuring hand on her shoulder. "Let's just try to stay calm for a while. No doubt Bandah will turn up later with Alfred. There's every chance the pixies may be familiar with her, and her world. I'll be very interested to hear what his thoughts are. Then, if collectively we have concerns, we can ask her to leave."

"It'll be too late by then. We need to make her leave as soon as possible."

"Any minute now we've got a magistrate arriving from Sydney with intentions to force us into parting with a good deal of the property. I'm not prepared to let this issue interfere with what will be a delicate situation. We'll consider our position on Hunter after dinner this evening. Until then, the matter is over."

Neridah brushed his hand off her shoulder. "Don't patronise me." She turned and stormed off into the house, leaving Colin shaking his head.

He glanced across at his wife and grumbled, "I swear, if we don't find alternative accommodation for your mother, I'll lose my temper with her one of these days."

"Oh really? So, you haven't already lost your temper with her on an almost daily basis?"

Colin stared at the empty space where his mother-in-law had been. "She just won't listen."

"Would it be different if she appeared as old as her years? She spent all of four decades deprived of her liberty, unable to move for all that time. Can you blame her for being apprehensive?"

As Meredith spoke, Colin nodded his head and closed his eyes. He'd heard this argument so many times that he expected it now whenever he raised objections to Neridah's behaviour. "That doesn't excuse her talking down to me in my own home."

"She grew up here, Colin. It's only your home now because you and I are married. She'd never even met you before she was taken captive."

Colin opened his mouth to respond but was distracted by the sound of a neighing horse heralding the approach of a sulky. "It seems the Magistrate's arrived early."

*

Bandah was flung out of this world and into the void between worlds with an ease that took him by surprise. He moved as close as he could to the boundary, allowing him to view a shimmering vestige of reality.

This was not a good place to be. Before fully leaving one world, it was important to have a foot firmly placed in another. While pixies were adept at jumping between the crossworlds without reliance on portals, they had little knowledge of how to escape from the void.

He was trying to focus on the hazy image of Hunter walking away when he heard a voice. "Of all the living creatures between Heaven and Hell, it has to be you that I'm stuck with."

He turned and asked, "Mrs Smith?"

"Wonderful, isn't it? Here we are, stuck in a state of limbo where we'll never age. We'll be getting to spend the rest of eternity trying to learn to get on with each other."

The pixie stared at her. "You have a knack for making things seem even worse than they are."

Mrs Smith approached the boundary, staring at the house as she replied, "Could it get much worse than this?"

"There is still a way out you know."

"Not one within our control."

Bandah nodded in acknowledgment. "I know that, but it's still possible."

Mrs Smith turned to him and asked, "What, you think someone's going to just wander up, knowing we're here, then reach in and grab us?"

"That's the basis of what I had in mind."

"They can't hear or see us!" Mrs Smith exclaimed. "I know of no being that can sense what lies in the void between worlds."

"Alfred will hear me."

"Oh?" She rolled her eyes and laughed. "And what makes him so special that he'll hear you?"

"We have a strong and unique connection."

"How can you believe such a thing when you've known the man for little more than a half-century?"

"I trust him like no one I've ever known. More than even my fellow pixies."

"Well then, won't you be disappointed when he ignores your cries for help."

*

Patsy broke into a run as she led Hunter to the stables. She looked over her shoulder. "I'll bet you can't keep up."

Hunter smiled, then lifted her dress and laughed as she tried to match Patsy's pace. Having been suppressed since she'd entered the homestead, a flurry of violets spread from each footfall. Hunter placed a hand over her lips. "Oops, sorry, I forgot to stifle the flowers." She came to a stop. "I've betrayed my word."

Patsy replied. "I don't think you have. It hasn't happened indoors, and they look beautiful."

Hunter giggled behind her hand and started running with Patsy once more. Patsy felt that, despite her age and powers, Hunter wasn't used to being able to be so carefree.

When they arrived at the stables, Patsy called out, "Darcy?" She looked around but couldn't see the young stablehand anywhere. "It doesn't matter, I know most of the horses well enough to introduce you." She walked up to the first stall. "This one's called Milly. She's the oldest and she's the mother of most of the other horses in the stables."

As Hunter approached the stall, Milly came forward and threw her head out, seeking attention. Hunter reached out to her saying, "Hello Milly, I've not met a creature of your kind before, although I've met countless others who are made beasts of burden." She placed her arms around Milly's neck in an embrace.

Patsy responded, "Oh, but Milly's not a beast of burden. She's quite happy."

"Then why isn't she set free, to roam as she would please?"

"If we did that, she might run off, or be stolen by a bushranger."

"I don't understand. You can hear all the creatures, but you don't always listen. Her thoughts tell me that's what she wants… to run free. Can't you hear them?"

"I hear her happiness when she whinnies with joy at being fed… or when I enter her stall to join Darcy as he rubs her down."

Hunter looked down at the ground, disappointed that Patsy didn't understand. "You talk to the cat, you listen to insects. But you don't bother to listen to their deepest thoughts-- they tell an altogether different story. Those with the knowledge are able to listen to each other's thoughts instinctively … that's why we understand each other despite growing up speaking different tongues. How can you believe you understand them when you don't delve deeper into their feelings?"

"Nana-Neri says that's a line we should never cross."

"Why?"

"Because that's what it says in the Book of Wisdom."

Hunter opened the door to Milly's stall as she asked, "Why would you do what a book tells you to do? I think it would be better to let Milly have control over whether she comes or goes."

Patsy drew in a deep breath. "I don't think that's a good idea."

"She won't leave. She likes it here. But she wants the door open."

"I don't think you under—"

Patsy was interrupted by Darcy calling out, "Hey! What are you doing?" The stablehand was leading the Magistrate's horse into the stables to give it food and water, preparing it for the long journey back to Sydney. When Hunter turned and faced the stallion Darcy was leading it panicked, rearing up and throwing the young man off balance.

Hunter threw up an arm, causing both Darcy and the horse to be frozen in time.

Patsy's jaw dropped. She turned and saw that Milly and the other horses seemed unaffected. "How did you…?"

Hunter was already moving toward the stallion. "I'll explain after. This beast is controlled by Nasqa." As Hunter got closer to the stallion, it showed signs of recognition but was held too tight in the time freeze to do anything of consequence. "We only have a few more seconds before it breaks free. Watch, and I'll show you how to deal with what you call a mind thief."

The horse was starting to show signs of struggled movement by the time Hunter was upon it. Without hesitation, she reached into its head, as though reaching into a bowl of liquid, and began to pull back. At first, whatever she was pulling at seemed to fight back, dragging her for a moment closer to the beast. It appeared the struggle would be sustained indefinitely, then Hunter pulled back hard, and a shadow that vaguely resembled a horse was dragged out and fell at her feet. The shadow rose up from the ground in an abstract form and appeared to beg for mercy. None was shown. The daisies that made up Hunter's garland broke away and leapt upon it, taking on animal-like characteristics. They tore the shadow apart and devoured it as though it were a favourite meal. One of the daisies burped before they all elegantly drifted back into place as part of Hunter's dancing garland.

Patsy was shocked. "You've killed it!"

"No, the parts of it still live, but not in this world."

"I don't understand. Mother and Nana-Neri say we can free people from being possessed by these creatures, but even the pixies don't know of ways to do what you've just done. Your flowers tore it apart. How can it not have been killed by your actions?"

Hunter looked toward the ground at Patsy's feet and smiled, as though Patsy's concerns were of no consequence. "Its parts are now strewn across the voids that separate the worlds. Sent to places where they can do no harm. Each part will remain aware for as long as it survives and have time to contemplate its actions."

Patsy returned the smile, but within herself she held back a feeling of discomfort. Something in her heart told her it was important to keep this feeling from rising to the surface.

For the first time since meeting Hunter, Patsy felt uneasy about her newfound friend. Looking at Darcy, she worried that the stablehand and stallion remained frozen in time, while all other life seemed to move on regardless. As if to reinforce the point, a kookaburra swooped from a tree outside the stables and grabbed a baby brown snake. Neridah had told her the Book of Wisdom explained how to do such things as time freezes, but that it was better avoided, as the consequences could be severe.

Hunter turned to Patsy. "Tell me more about this Book of Wisdom you just thought of again."

Patsy snapped back, "It's rude to read people's thoughts."

Hunter smiled then let out a little giggle, as though Patsy's retort was silly. "Is that what your grandmother tells you?"

"I don't need anyone to tell me that. It's pretty obvious, don't you think? Don't you prefer that your thoughts are private?"

"I'm happy to share my thoughts with you." She let out another laugh. "Or anyone else for that matter."

Patsy thought to herself, *I don't believe you.*

Hunter cast an angry glare in her direction. She hesitated for a moment, then, turning her attention back to Darcy and the horse, flicked her wrist. They came back to life. Darcy tipped his flat cap in a sign of respect before asking in a sing-song Irish accent, "Hey, Pats, who's your friend?"

Patsy smiled at the fourteen-year-old boy. She found herself wondering why she couldn't remember seeing him enter the stables. In fact, she struggled even to remember Hunter and herself arriving. Somehow, that seemed of little importance right now. She was always happy to see Darcy. There were few children or teenagers that she had the chance to meet, and she had enjoyed Darcy's company since he and his father had started working for the McIntyre family the week after her last crossworld encounter. "Hi, Darcy, her name's Hunter. She only arrived this morning."

Darcy couldn't help but stare at Hunter. He'd never seen such a beautiful young woman. "Hello, Miss Hunter." He extended his hand. "The name's Darcy, Darcy O'Sullivan."

Sensing his admiration, she adopted a coy expression and, knowing that he'd be unable to understand her without having the knowledge of how to listen, she replied in her native tongue, "Mouwn-kancher gainna-onger yonter." She smiled. "Mouwn-trember mouwn-limbray sauwn-dintar."

Darcy stood as if mesmerised. He removed his hat and ran a hand through his thick red curls. "I've not heard such a language before." He turned to Patsy. "I heard many languages when I travelled here from Ireland, but nothing remotely like your friend Hunter speaks. Do you know what she was saying?"

"She says she arrived a short while ago." Patsy giggled. "And, she says she might grow to like you.'

Hunter feigned embarrassment and waited a moment before turning to Patsy. "Nasqa! Sauwn-drendy ga abessee."

Patsy looked up at Darcy. "I'm sorry, we'll have to come back later. Hunter just heard Father calling."

"Oh, are you sure about that? When I left him just now he was having what seemed to be a serious talk with the Magistrate."

Hunter sent Patsy a thought. *We need to hurry.*

Patsy turned to Darcy as they started to make their way out of the stable. The memory of what Hunter had done to the Nasqa possessing the horse flooded back. If there were mind thieves, or Nasqa as Hunter called them, threatening the family home, then it was important to act. "We'll come back later, I promise."

Darcy called out, "I'll be looking forward to it."

•

Bandah followed Patsy and Hunter as they headed toward the stables.

Mrs Smith called after him, "What on Earth do you hope to achieve by following those two?"

"I want to learn whatever I can about this young woman."

"Fat load of good that'll do you. Mark my words, if that one senses you're watching her, she's liable to reach in here and grab you, then hurl you somewhere even worse."

The pixie looked over his shoulder and called out as he continued, "That's a risk I'm prepared to take."

The rotund fairy that was Mrs Smith got to her feet, cursing the pain that exploded in her knees. If only she'd been able to transform back to her fairy state before the arthritis had set in. She mumbled, "I don't believe I'm doing this." She leaned forward and beat her wings, lifting into the air as she called out, "If you're going to insist on this fool's errand, you'll be better off accompanied by someone with a bit of common sense."

Bandah paused in mid-air to allow her to catch up. "Could this mean that you've found a conscience lurking somewhere within yourself?"

"I'd just rather not spend eternity feeling responsible for your demise because of letting you run off on your own."

"Why, that almost sounds like you care."

"Hmmph."

They continued in silence until they reached the stables. Mrs Smith asked, "Can you hear them?"

He was struggling to focus on the hazy image of Patsy and Hunter at Milly's stall. "It's even harder to hear than it is to see. Their words are mixed with their thoughts, and I can't make out what Hunter's saying at all… her thoughts aren't making sense to me." He was startled when Mrs Smith placed a hand on his shoulder, turning him to face the stable entrance.

"Look at this. She's done a partial time freeze."

Bandah stared in disbelief at the sight of Darcy and the horse standing frozen in time. The nature of the time freeze made their images become clearer in the void. If the freeze was held for long enough, they'd start to become visible in adjacent crossworlds as well. "Can you see it? Can you see the shadow?"

"It's not, is it?" Mrs Smith asked.

"It's hard to say for sure from here, but I'm pretty sure it is. That's the Magistrate's horse. And if his horse is controlled by a mind thief, it's a sure bet that he is too."

"I can't see that it matters a great deal, and there's certainly nothing we can do about it from here."

Bandah shook his head. "Just when I begin to think there's hope for you—" He stopped mid-sentence when Hunter took him by surprise, looking down at him and smiling. "How can she know where we are?"

"I think there's a lot more we're going to discover that this young lady's capable of."

Bandah looked at her. "Young lady? Are you sure you're not letting your human experience affect your judgment?"

"I swear she's no more than a thousand or so years old."

"Yet she took us both by surprise when she threw us into this void."

"Aye, that she did." As she spoke, Hunter approached the Magistrate's horse and reached into it. "And I think we may have more surprises to come."

Bandah flew closer to see what was happening. His jaw dropped at the sight of the daisies tearing the mind thief apart. "No sentient being deserves this."

Mrs Smith scoffed. "Don't be so silly, it happens in the insect world all the time."

Before Bandah had the chance to reply, he was forced to leap aside as a fragment of the mind thief came through the barrier between worlds and into the void. “Whoa!”

Mrs Smith and the pixie watched in horror as more fragments entered the void. Some passed straight through and went elsewhere, while others landed at their feet or nearby. They backed away as the mind thief fragments started coming together. Bandah couldn’t help but look up when Hunter’s thoughts spoke to him. *Here’s a little gift for you, pixie.* Her smile added to the insult.

Bandah stood as tall as his five-centimetre height would allow. “Again I ask, why are you here?”

Hunter looked away and ignored him as though he hadn’t been heard. Mrs Smith sought to bring his attention back to their present predicament. “You might do well to watch what’s happening here.” Bandah took another step back as he watched the mind thief fragments coalesce, like mercury drifting together, barely audible screams of agony coming from each fragment.

Bandah turned to Mrs Smith. “I don’t like the look of this.”

Although the fairy was twice his height, she chose to take cover behind him. “You pixies have always been clever at dealing with these creatures. Do something.”

CHAPTER 4

Darcy saw the Magistrate approaching and, knowing that Colin would want the horse to be given food and water, walked across from the stables. The Magistrate ignored him, coughing as he struggled to alight from his sulky.

Meredith whispered in her husband's ear, "Shouldn't you offer to help?"

Colin answered her with a cold stare, then stepped forward and turned his attention to the Magistrate, reaching out to offer a hand only when he saw the Magistrate no longer needed one. "Justice Johnson, welcome. I hope your journey from Parramatta was a smooth one."

"Spare me the platitudes, McIntyre. You know what that road's like, and I'm not here for pleasantries."

Colin said, "Perhaps the steam train would have been a better option?

I could have arranged for someone to meet you at the railway station."

"Hmph! I'm not inclined to trust those stinking metal contraptions. Spend half a day choking on coal dust and smoke while your bones are rattling along? I'll use a more natural mode of transportation, thank you very much." He looked across at Darcy. "You, boy, get my bags off this infernal buggy then tend to my horse's needs."

Darcy looked at Colin for approval, waiting for the gentle nod to come from his employer before following the Magistrate's bidding. Meredith gripped Colin's arm as she watched the drooling, obese form in front of her pull a dirty handkerchief from the pocket of his black coat to mop some of the sweat from his brow. His jowls trembled as he addressed Colin while his eyes drifted to leer at her. "What's she doing here? We have business to discuss."

Meredith took her husband by surprise. "My grandfather established this property and worked hard to make it what he passed on. I have every right to be present while its future is discussed."

Still leering, the Magistrate barked, "Nonsense! How about you make yourself useful, woman, and get me a brandy?"

Colin closed his eyes for a moment and sought to calm himself. Striking a magistrate, even one as foul as the Justice Johnson, would not help their situation. "Your Honour, while I appreciate that you are here to discuss business, both our interests will be better served if you refrain from speaking to my wife in such a manner. While I respect the fact that the decisions and agreements to be made will be between you and me, my wife has every right to be privy to such matters, and I'll not have you speak to her as though she were a common servant."

Having placed the Magistrate's bags by the man's side, Darcy set about freeing the horse from its constraints and taking it to the stables. The Magistrate turned away to cough before replying, "Hah!

What use is a wife if she doesn't behave as a servant who also bears your children?"

Meredith released her husband's arm. "Darling, I think it might serve our purposes better if I join Mother inside after all. I trust you'll do the best you can for the family."

Colin gave her hand a gentle squeeze before she offered an awkward smile and walked away. The Magistrate called after her, "Know this, woman. He'll do as I bid, or else I'll be taking it all."

Colin spoke through clenched teeth. "I'll have you know that I have friends on the Legislative Council."

"As do I, McIntyre. On top of that, I have an understanding with Governor Pritchard, one that allows me to do as I please with land throughout the Blue Mountains that has previously been claimed by squatters such as your good wife's grandfather." He turned his attention back to Meredith and mopped some spittle from the corners of his mouth as he watched her retreat to the house. "She's feisty, that one. You'd do well to teach her some manners."

Colin's fists tightened so much the knuckles were white. He struggled to maintain control. "You said you came here to discuss business. I'd prefer we restrict our conversation accordingly."

"Hmph, very well then. Help me with my bags and we'll adjourn to your library so you can sign over your pastoral lands. I trust you've organised appropriate lodging for me for this evening. I've no desire to make that dreadful journey twice in one day."

The prolonged silence that followed was broken by a magpie's song, its beautiful melody providing a stark contrast to the tension of their conversation. Colin took a deep breath. "There's a hotel in Blackheath that I'm sure you'll find more welcoming."

"You'll no doubt reconsider that when you appreciate the reality of your circumstance. Now, pick up my bags and we'll get into the warmth of your home where we'll see if your hospitality makes you worthy of remaining as a tenant on what will soon become my lands."

"My understanding was that we're discussing only the pastoral areas of the property."

"That was before you suggested I should find lodgings elsewhere. You'll find me a fair man to those who treat me with due respect. Now, pick up my bags, man!"

Colin could feel the blood pulsing through his temples. He wanted to say, *Pick up your own god-damned bags.* Instead, he swallowed his pride and picked up the Magistrate's bags. As they entered the house, Colin wondered how much longer he could withhold his rage.

•

Bandah and Mrs Smith watched on as the fragments of the mind thief came together.

Mrs Smith mumbled, "I really don't like this."

Bandah replied, "Let's just wait and see what happens. It's not like there's anywhere for us to go and seek cover."

The mind thief started to develop a form, one that included what could vaguely be perceived as a kind of orifice, or maybe even a mouth. Mrs Smith grabbed hold of Bandah's arm when it spoke, the words sounding more like different tones of whistling wind than spoken language. "Mosh-ko klon-ar?"

It made for a pitiful sight, seeing Mrs Smith hiding behind a pixie half her size. She dug her fingernails into his arm. "Can you make out what it's saying?"

Bandah was surprised. "You can't?"

"During those dreadful years in human form, it wasn't just my body that deteriorated. My memory of what I'd learned over the millennia paid a hefty price as well."

The mind thief fragment repeated its question, this time with greater urgency. "Mosh-ko klon-ar?"

Bandah looked at the grovelling shadow, then back to Mrs Smith's puzzled expression. He almost felt sympathy for the woman. If she was suffering from some form of dementia, she'd done a good job of hiding it till now. "It's pleading for help."

Mrs Smith released her grip on the pixie ever so slightly. "What do you mean?"

"I mean what I said… it's asking us for help. Mosh-ko klon-ar… it means, *can you help me?*"

"We can't trust it! It's a mind thief!"

He broke free of her grip. "Right now, we need all the friends we can get."

"But it's just a shadow of a being. It's nothing unless it's controlling another. It's like a virus."

"That's what we've always believed." He turned back to gaze upon the shadow. "But here's a fragment of such a creature that's reaching out, pleading for help." He paused as he watched it patiently wait for his response. "I think it deserves the benefit of the doubt."

"I still don't trust it."

The shadow reached out and touched Bandah's shoulder. "Mosh-ko klon-ar!"

Bandah replied, "Yes, we'll help you. And together, we'll help each other find a way out of here."

The shadow replied, "Ko zandiss"

Bandah turned to Mrs Smith. "He says we are kind."

Mrs Smith laughed. “You pixies are such foolish creatures. Don’t you see? It may change its mind once it gets to know us better… when it finds a weakness to exploit. You’re not seriously going to trust this abomination, are you?”

“Like with any creature, I’ll trust it until it gives me cause to do otherwise. I’d advise that you do the same.”

Mrs Smith took a defiant stance with hands on her hips. “Oh? And why would that be?”

“Because situations like this tend to bring out the best in all sorts of creatures.”

Mrs Smith pointed at the shadow and sneered. “Even mind-sucking creatures like that thing?”

“Yes, absolutely. But you know what’s even more amazing? This situation might just bring out the best in you as well.”

A sound came from their shadowy companion that sounded reminiscent of a guttural laugh.

Mrs Smith looked at the shadow and smiled. “At least your new friend has a sense of humour.”

Bandah snapped his fingers and said, “I have an idea!”

*

As Hunter and Patsy ran toward the house, some of the daisies on Hunter’s garland broke free and moved a short distance ahead. Razor-sharp teeth emerged from around the flowers’ centres in multiple rows that snapped wildly, as though eager for ripping into another mind thief, or Nasqa. Each flower that broke away would return to its place in the garland after a few seconds, unable to maintain their life force for long if they strayed too far from the host.

The girls raced up the steps to the veranda and through the front door. Cook approached the library with a tray of hot scones and was about to open the door when Hunter almost knocked the tray from her hands as she passed, throwing the door open with Patsy close behind.

Colin was in the process of pouring brandy for the Magistrate and himself. He frowned, put down the decanter and looked past Hunter to his daughter. "What's the meaning of this? Do you have any idea how important this meeting is? I'm disappointed, Patricia. You know better."

Patsy responded by pointing at the Magistrate. Colin turned and saw a look of abject fear on the man's face as he looked at Hunter.

The Magistrate tried to push himself back further into his chair as Hunter slowly approached. His voice trembled. "What are you doing here? What do you want?"

The daisies in the garland began swirling, their teeth gnashing so much it filled the room with a sound like dozens of mouse traps repeatedly snapping. Hunter's eyes grew wide. "Lis koo-sauwn vee, Nasqa?" *Why are you here, Nasqa?*

Surprised that he couldn't understand using the knowledge of listening Meredith had given him, Colin turned to his daughter. "Do you understand?"

Patsy nodded. She was about to offer a translation when she glanced at the Magistrate, noticing the dark, wet patch around his crutch where he'd wet himself.

The Magistrate's voice was punctuated by a shortness of breath. "The portal… we need to control it. I was sent to make sure we take control of the land around it." He cast his eyes toward Colin. "You need to make her leave, or she'll kill you all."

Colin took a sip on his brandy then turned to Hunter. "Tell me, what exactly are you intending to do?"

Hunter continued her slow walk toward the Magistrate. "I will free this man of the Nasqa that infects him and ensure it harms no one else, in this world, or any other."

Colin turned to his daughter.

"I've seen her do it, Father. She did it to his horse… she set it free."

Colin looked at the doorway and saw that Cook was standing frozen in time. He wasn't sure he liked what he was witnessing in his home. Turning back to Hunter he asked, "What have you done to Cook?"

"I am protecting her from her fears."

"Wouldn't it have been better to simply wait till she'd left the room?"

She was standing directly in front of the Magistrate, the Justice Albert Johnson. "You cannot waste time when it comes to dealing with Nasqa."

"And yet, here you are, revelling in the man's fear."

Hunter smiled. "It's not the man's fear, it is the fear within the Nasqa." She extended her arm and pushed it into the man's chest. The Magistrate screamed, slipping from his chair to the floor as she reached deep inside him and ripped out the shadow of the mind thief, throwing it to the ground. The daisies broke away from her garland and tore into it like a school of piranhas, ripping it into a thousand pieces. As the daisies swallowed the pieces they passed from our world into the void between worlds.

Colin clenched his fists. "I will not condone such violence taking place in my home!"

Hunter looked at him with a puzzled expression. "But it is Nasqa."

"I don't care what it is. What we've just witnessed can only be described as cruelty."

"You need not worry too much. In a few moments, you'll completely forget what you saw."

A voice from the doorway interrupted the conversation. "I won't."

Neridah stood, arms folded, in front of Cook in the doorway, Meredith by her side.

Hunter smiled. "Are you sure?"

Patsy placed a hand on Hunter's shoulder to get her attention. "We believe in showing respect for life, in all its forms."

Hunter pushed her hand away and took a step back. "Your actions suggest otherwise… all of you." She looked directly at Colin. "You wanted to greet my arrival carrying guns. Do they have a purpose other than to kill? If you respect life, why would you own such a thing?"

A groggy moan from the Magistrate drew everyone's attention, relieving some of the mounting tension in the room. Meredith rushed to him. "Are you okay?"

Leaning on his right elbow, he used his free hand to rub his eyes. "Yes, I believe I am. Perhaps better than I've felt in years." He looked at Hunter. "You, you freed me from hell." Aware that his weight was too great for Meredith to help him to his seat, he turned to Colin and reached out. "McIntyre, would you be kind enough?"

"Yes, of course." By the time he'd spoken the words, Colin was already lifting the man back into his chair.

The Magistrate took out his handkerchief and wiped his brow. "Thank you. If it's okay with you, I could certainly do with that brandy you were pouring."

Neridah approached the Magistrate. "How long were you possessed by that thing?"

He took his brandy and drained it in one go, then replied, "Since I first dined with Governor Pritchard almost two years ago." He extended the glass toward Neridah and asked, "Please?" Feeling sympathy for the man, she took the glass and refilled it as he continued. "The Governor, and all those around him, they're all under the control of these things."

He looked at Hunter and waved his finger as he searched for the words. "In all the time I was under that creature's control, I've not known it to feel fear… until today. As soon as you entered the room it felt terror."

Hunter shrugged. "My family have dealt with these Nasqa for countless generations. They have nothing worthwhile to offer."

"You're not of this world."

Neridah handed the Magistrate his refilled brandy. "Perhaps it's better for you to recover before pursuing this conversation further?"

The Magistrate nodded in agreement as he took the glass. "Probably the wisest words I've ever heard."

Meredith turned to Patsy. "Can you take Hunter to the stables and check that the Magistrate's horse has been attended to? I've no doubt the poor beast would have been spooked if it had to experience the same ordeal."

Patsy protested, "But, I saw Darcy tending to it—"

Colin snapped, "Patricia! I'll not have you argue with your mother. I still have matters of business to discuss with the Magistrate. Now go!"

Hunter was staring at the Book of Wisdom when Patsy grabbed her hand. "Come on." She looked back at her parents and made a show of saying, "It seems we're not wanted here." Hunter continued looking over her shoulder at the book as Patsy led her from the room.

They were already out the door when Meredith called out, "Hunter, could you please release Cook? I think the Magistrate could do with a hot scone now."

Hunter shrugged her shoulders in response. A moment later, Cook was entering the library with her tray of steaming hot scones. She looked at Meredith and Neridah with a surprised expression then turned back to Colin. "Oh, my goodness! Had I realised your good wife and mother-in-law were in here as well, I'd have brought in more… and a pot of tea."

Neridah watched Hunter as she left the room with Patsy. There was a lot that she didn't like about this girl's ways. She was not a good influence on her granddaughter. And there would be a hefty price to pay for the time freeze she'd imposed on Cook.

*

The Reverend Alfred Casey gave a nod to the gravedigger, signifying it was time to fill the grave. There were no mourners, no parents, no friends, no children. A lonely burial of someone who'd not yet reached their prime inevitably meant it had been preceded by a lonely existence. The Reverend always found these services difficult to perform, but he did his best to give the departed a final moment of dignity and recognition. At least on this occasion, there was someone to dig and fill the grave for him. But there'd be no marker other than the simple wooden cross that he'd plant at the head of the grave once the hole was filled. No one would ever know the name of the young man whose remains lay here.

Tonight would be better.

Tonight he'd be able to spend time with the one and only woman he'd ever loved. They'd dine together, talk, enjoy each other's company, and maybe even share a tender moment alone with just each other. A moment where they might share an embrace, or even a kiss, before he returned to Pulpit's Hill to retire for the evening.

There were at least four hours between now and when he'd need to make his way to the McIntyres', ample time to explore parts of the bushland he was still unfamiliar with. That was one of the things the Reverend most loved about living in the Blue Mountains. After all these years, there was still so much to explore. Today, he was thinking about a wallaby track he'd noticed about an hour's ride away.

He stood next to the bedraggled gravedigger filling the hole, then reached into his pocket and pulled out two shillings. They'd been all that was in the dead man's pocket, and the Reverend figured they were of little use to a corpse. "For your troubles." He placed them into the man's hand, causing his near toothless smile to light up his face.

He responded in a thick Irish accent. "To be sure, sir, you're more generous than most. I'll remember you in my prayers." He returned his attention to his work, smiling as he thought of how he'd enjoy spending his new-found wealth at the tavern in Springwood.

The Reverend headed toward the stables to saddle his horse. How long would he have to wait before Bandah returned with information about what was happening at the McIntyre household? How could he not be concerned knowing something had come through the portal? The last time the portal opened, he'd conspired with Colin and his family to rescue Neridah from Sellemae's lair, but it had nearly cost their lives.

With the bridle and saddle in place, he went to the barrel by the stable entrance and grabbed an apple for the horse, talking to the mare as she gratefully took it from his hand. "We'll have a good ride now, Elsa. But in the afternoon I'll be hitching you up to the sulky for the ride to the McIntyres'." The horse whinnied as though it understood, then the Reverend ruffled its mane affectionately before hoisting himself into the saddle. As he turned her to the stable entrance, Elsa seemed to read his mind. She let out a loud snort and took off in a canter.

The gravedigger, otherwise known as Sean O'Malley, tipped his hat as the horse passed through the small church graveyard. "God bless, Your Reverence, sir." He stood watching until the horse was out of sight, then put his shovel aside and stepped into the shallow grave. He hummed to himself as he brushed away the dirt from the dead man's clothing. Finding the pockets to be empty, he spat at the man's face, as though the lack of reward were an insult. Then, he spied the man's shoes. They were nothing special, but they were better than his own. Sean took pride in the fact that, as a result of his occupation, he hadn't paid for a single item of clothing in over ten years. A dead man buried beneath a few feet of dirt was unlikely to tell anyone of his theft.

As the gravedigger clambered back up from the hole, the mind thief that controlled him felt something. One of his own was calling out to any who would listen.

*

Mrs Smith shook her head in disbelief. "You're putting a lot of faith in this creature's supposed goodwill. Something, I might add, we've seen little evidence of."

The pixie asked, "Do you have a better idea?"

"I preferred your original plan, the one where we wait till your priest friend arrives and we see just how 'special' your relationship with him is."

"As much as I do believe that I'll be able to connect with Alfred when he arrives, there's no time for that now. That girl is a danger every minute she continues to run amok out there. And our new friend seems as keen to get out of here as we are."

"I still think it's crazy."

"What choice do we have? The mind thieves can communicate with each other even when they're in different crossworlds. Our friend can create a bridge, one that will allow us to communicate with the witches so they can create a sub-portal that frees all of us."

"You call it your 'friend.' Do you even know its name?"

Bandah sighed. It seemed pointless trying to reach the bitter old fairy.

The next moment, the shadow that was the mind thief remnants spoke in his defence. "Ak-bo-nasqa nub ney bask. Ak po-ee-dah, sass-op ardah." The shadow stretched out as though trying to embrace Bandah and Mrs Smith. "Ak kor poo-ee-dah. Ar-mosh treen-yer li-gak ye ar-dat."

Mrs Smith threw her hands up in the air. "Well, I don't know what the hell it's saying. You could at least let me in on the little secrets it's telling you."

Bandah bit his lower lip to keep himself from expressing his true thoughts. "He says the Nasqa don't need names. They are as one unless inside another."

"I can't see how that helps us."

"If you'll let me finish… he goes on to say that we three are as one. He says that he can reach out to others of his kind and ask that they tell the witches of our plight."

"It's little wonder you pixies generally travel together in your thousands. As individuals, you're so easily fooled."

"I trust him."

A scream of anguish from a short distance away drew their attention. It was the same sound that had pierced their ears when the mind thief fragments first came into the void. Without hesitation, they all raced to where Hunter's daisies were tearing apart the mind thief that had till now controlled the Magistrate.

The few fragments that fell into the part of the void they inhabited were even more tattered than those that had come through from the horse. Their shadowy colleague carefully moved to catch each fragment as it came through, absorbing them and growing in size and stature with each one that it captured.

Once the carnage was over, the creature had grown threefold in size. Stronger and more confident, its shadow rose high over Bandah and Mrs

Smith. “Ar-ee brunkt bow. Ar-mosh hoy nasqa jas. Ar-gosh ki lon-cun prac-bo-tunda.”

Bandah’s excitement was palpable. “It says it’s stronger now, that it can feel another mind thief nearby that it will call to help us. It’s a gravedigger! Alfred had a funeral to perform this morning. He’ll be there... he should get the message.”

Mrs Smith half raised an eyebrow. “I hope you’re right.”

CHAPTER 5

Hunter asked Patsy, "Why do you let them tell you what to do?"

"Because they know better than I do." Patsy stopped walking, wanting to ensure she had Hunter's attention. "What I want to know is, why have you let them tell *you* what to do? You've been alive longer than all of them put together, and you're much more powerful."

Hunter laughed. "Sometimes, it can be helpful to let people believe you respect them. They see in me a girl not much older than you. Even though they know otherwise, their thinking is influenced by what they see."

Patsy thought to herself, *You underestimate them.*

Hunter responded, *No, I don't think so at all. They underestimate me.*

Patsy put a hand on Hunter's shoulder. "You know what, Hunter? As much as I like you, I'd prefer that we keep our thoughts to ourselves."

Hunter's smile was so broad that it lacked sincerity. "But I thought we were friends."

While Hunter held her smile, Patsy couldn't help but notice the daisies in her garland turn toward her. Although they lacked faces, it was clear to Patsy they had a menacing intent. Aware that Hunter had noticed her attention drift to the flowers, Patsy looked her in the eye. "I'd like to be friends, but even friends have things that they keep from each other. I'm sure there are things about yourself you'd prefer I don't know."

Hunter stepped back, pushing Patsy's hand away from her shoulder. "What are you talking about? Do you feel there are things I've hidden from you?"

Patsy gave a reassuring smile. "There's so much about you that's a mystery to me, like the daisies in your garland. They tore apart a mind thief, not once, but twice! They seem bound to you, through some sort of loyalty."

In the back of her head, Patsy heard a voice call out, *Come and join us... be one of us. Join the garland of power.*

Patsy stared at Hunter's garland, searching for the origin of the invasive thought. Her suspicion of the source was confirmed when Hunter reached up and extracted one of the flowers, squeezing it between her fingers. She tried to hide the malice of her action behind a smile that changed to an expression of surprise when she realised Patsy could hear the tortured soul's brief plea for mercy. *Please, no! A thousand years of devoted service...* The thought never reached its conclusion as Hunter rubbed her fingers hard, breaking the daisy apart till its pieces fell from her fingers.

The tension was broken by Darcy's approaching voice. "Miss Hunter, I feel privileged to be crossing your path once more." He removed his battered flat cap, ran a hand through his hair, and straightened his worn waistcoat. "Some would call it fate."

Having been distracted from her train of thought, Patsy's memory of what had just transpired with the garland was gone in an instant. Hunter smiled at Darcy. "Py-sauwn trembar mouwn franze?"

The boy turned to Patsy and asked, "What did she say?"

Patsy giggled. "She asked if you think she's pretty."

Darcy blushed and found himself unable to look her in the eye. He fidgeted with the rim of his cap. "To be honest, you're truly the most beautiful woman I've laid eyes on."

Hunter reached out and gently lifted his chin, so he was facing her directly. She took him by surprise when she asked him in a deeply accented and broken English, "Do you, Mister Darcy O'Sullivan, like the flowers I wear in my hair?"

"Oh yes, my lady. They're like a gilded frame around a beautiful painting."

Hunter smiled as she thought to herself, *And sometime very soon, Darcy O'Sullivan, you'll be a part of that gilded frame.* While they stood staring at each other, Hunter asked, "Tonight… here, after dinner?"

Darcy fidgeted with his cap some more. "What, you and me?" He looked at the expectation in Hunter's eyes and shifted his feet, seeking the courage to come up with a more definitive reply. "The bottom of the garden can be lovely at night, and it should be a full moon. Would you care to go for a walk with me when we meet?"

Hunter and Patsy looked at each other, giggling behind their hands. Then Hunter turned back to Darcy and smiled as she replied, "Yes, I would like that. I would like it very much."

A voice called out from the rear of the stables, "Darcy O'Sullivan? Where in God's name would you be?"

Still blushing and fidgeting with his cap, Darcy looked over his shoulder then turned back to the girls. "That's my father calling, I guess I'd best be off." He looked at the ground for a moment, then looked into Hunter's eyes. "I'll see you this evening." He turned, placed the cap on his head, and walked at a brisk pace toward his father who'd stepped out from behind the stables. The middle-aged Jimmy O'Sullivan shook his head and smiled when he saw that his son had been in conversation with such an attractive young woman.

•

The Reverend Alfred Casey revelled in the thundering of Elsa's hooves as she pounded down the trail. There was little he needed to do to guide the beast. It was as though she knew where he wished to go. So much so, that when they reached the wallaby track he wished to explore, the mare came to an abrupt halt. He dismounted, then retrieved a wooden bowl from his saddlebag and poured half his water bottle into it. Holding the bowl up to the horse he said, "Don't worry, Elsa. I know this isn't much, but I won't be long."

Once Elsa had finished the contents of the bowl, he loosely secured her reins to a nearby tea tree then crouched low to commence his journey into the unknown.

The path was no doubt popular with wallabies and other wildlife as it was clearly defined at ground level. But a man of the Reverend's height had little choice but to bend his knees and back as he walked. He enjoyed the sound of every lizard or snake moving out of his path after they heard his approach. The magic of his journey was further enhanced by the continuous songs of the bellbirds inhabiting the area and the aroma of the rich rainforest soil.

After some twenty minutes, the forest grew darker. The Reverend felt glad to be wearing his coat as the temperature plummeted. He entered the deeper part of a gully, majestic tree ferns rising on either side of the creek that meandered through boulders twice the Reverend's size.

After clambering over a multitude of rocks, a well-defined pathway led up from the creek toward a cave-like opening in a massive wall of rock. Seeing signs of light at the other end, the urge to continue his exploration was impossible to ignore.

"I sometimes wonder about the foolishness of my pursuits." He crossed himself and entered the narrow tunnel, hands pushed against the walls on either side to counter the slippery nature of what was underfoot. After he'd moved forward just a few paces, the tunnel began to slope downward. He lost his footing and his grip on the walls, falling on his backside and sliding the rest of the way. Unable to control his passage, he bumped his head, and every other part of his body, as he accelerated toward the light.

His head bumped hard on a piece of rock jutting out from the wall and he felt like he was about to pass out when the rock fell away from under him and he hit the freezing cold water.

It took a few seconds for him to realise what was up, and what was down. When he recognised the rocks near his face as the bottom of the pool, he placed his feet against them and pushed up to the surface.

As his head broke through, and he captured a much-needed lungful of air, he looked around in wonder. Not one, but two waterfalls fed this pool. It was surrounded on all sides by steep walls. His only way out would be from where he came… unless he dared climb the sheer cliffs that surrounded him. He turned his head and saw that there was at least a shore on the far side where he could catch his breath before attempting to find his way back.

His wet clothing made the swim an unwelcome chore as he struggled toward the shore. He was almost halfway there when he heard a feminine voice next to his ear, "Do you have any idea what you've done?"

The Reverend flicked his head around to face the pixie, his long grey hair spraying water across the surface. "What in God's name would you be talking about?"

The pixie fluttered so close to his face that it forced the priest to go cross-eyed. "You sent him, didn't you? Isn't that what you always do?"

The Reverend took time to contemplate his response. "So, I'm assuming that you're referring to Bandah?"

"Of course I am. He's my cousin."

"Well, that would be of no surprise. It's my understanding that you would be one of thousands of cousins. What would your name be?"

She hovered in front of the Reverend just above the surface of the water. She was slim, although more shapely than the male pixies the Reverend was used to. "They call me Talia."

"You say that as though you prefer to go by a different title."

"My real name is Frydah, but they call me 'Talia' because in the tongue of the pixies it means 'rebel.' Why should that matter to you though, priest?"

"I've found trust works much better when two people understand exactly who they're talking to. I've not met a female pixie before."

"Although rare, we do exist, as do males among the fairies. Now tell me. Where did you send my cousin?"

"I didn't send him anywhere. However, he did make a choice to go the McIntyres' to investigate after someone, or something, accessed the portal between worlds."

Although the pixie's face was tiny, the Reverend recognised the anger in her expression. "And you let him go alone?"

The Reverend shrugged as he continued his journey across the pool, his feet having now found the bottom. The pixie continued to hover in front of his face as he dragged himself from the icy water. "What would you have had me do? In the time I've known your cousin, I've always found him to be single-minded. He wanted to know what was going on, and so did I."

"Why didn't you accompany him?"

"I had a funeral to perform." He found a rock to sit on and pulled off his boots. "I'm curious to know the reason for your anger. Bandah has always been a good friend of mine, and if he's in a perilous situation, I'd like to know of it also, so I can do what's in my power to help."

"For some reason, he's crossed over from this world."

"He does so often. I don't see why that in itself should have you so concerned."

Talia landed on his knee. "He hasn't shown up in any other crossworld."

"How can you be sure? My understanding is that there are countless crossworlds."

"But he's my cousin. I should be able to *feel* what world he's in. That's why we pixies are able to travel between the worlds with such confidence. The only thing that makes sense is that he's somehow trapped in the void between worlds."

"If that's the case, I understand your concern. The idea of being trapped between worlds is indeed frightening."

"I need your help to find him."

"How so? You're able to sense if he's in another crossworld. That's something I'm certainly not capable of."

"You have formed a bond with him we pixies call 'grundai.' You are closer than brothers. He has largely forsaken his own kind to be with you. Female pixies are rare, but what's even rarer is for pixies to form grundai bonds with those of another kind I can feel him if he's in another world, but I can't hear him from across them. My hope is, if he's in the void between the worlds, you may be able to hear him if he calls out to you." She flew up and sat on his shoulder, then took on a harsh and demanding tone of voice. "As his grundai partner, you have a duty to help."

"Bah! You fool yourself. It is my choice, not yours, whether or not I will help to find him. He is my friend, and he went on his own only because I was otherwise indisposed. Of course, I will help to find him, but because I wish to help my friend, not because of your demands." He looked up at the escarpment surrounding him. "But first, I'll need to find my way out of this deep hole."

"You won't be able to go back the way you came. It's far too slippery and treacherous. There is but one safe way for you to climb out of here. I'll guide you and help make sure you put your hands and feet only where they are safe."

"I guess I'd best put my boots back on then."

•

After Cook had left the library, Meredith closed the doors to ensure they had privacy to continue their discussion with the Magistrate.

Colin watched as the man threw down his brandy. "Can I offer you another, Your Honour?"

The Magistrate extended his arm with the empty glass in Colin's direction. "Please, yes. And you can refrain from the formalities while we're in the privacy of your home. Feel free to call me Albert." He turned to Meredith. "My lady, I must apologise for my appalling behaviour earlier. I treated you disrespectfully and in a manner that I deeply regret."

"That's quite alright. I understand that it was the creature who possessed you that spoke."

"But still, the words were delivered by my mouth."

Colin handed the Magistrate his refilled glass. "So, tell me, Albert, are you aware of what the creature was, and what it was thinking?"

He took a sip before replying, "Oh yes. Very much so. I've been a prisoner within my own body for years… until now. I was unable to control anything, but aware of it all. It's a wonder I have my sanity still intact." He leaned across and grabbed Colin's arm. "As I said before, in all that time, I'd never known the creature possessing me to feel fear… until today, when that young lady approached." The memory of the mind thief's fear made him throw down the rest of the brandy in one go. "It was terrified. It called her a 'boom-qua.' The closest words in English to describe what it means that I can think of would be 'under-god.' You need to ask yourselves this, is Hunter her name, or her title?" He turned to Meredith and Neridah. "It knew about you two and your daughter, Patricia… the trinity of witches. They see you as powerful, but also as vermin." He turned back to Colin. "I don't suppose I could trouble you for one more brandy? This is all horribly confronting."

Colin replied, "Yes, of course."

Neridah, not wanting to see Colin treated as though he were the Magistrate's servant, said, "I'll get it."

The Magistrate mopped his brow. "You need to be aware. Governor Pritchard is controlled by these 'Nasqa,' as they call themselves."

Meredith cut in. "That's what Hunter calls them too."

He nodded. "I sensed that their conflict goes back thousands of years and that the under-gods generally come out on top. But, I must tell you, as much as I don't think you should trust her, she may be worthwhile keeping around. Pritchard knows about the portal, and he wants to control it."

Neridah refilled his brandy glass. "We've dealt with mind thieves before. We can deal with them without Hunter's help."

Colin asked, "How did Pritchard learn about the portal?"

"You had a tutor who worked here… Mrs Bradshaw… was that her name?" When Colin nodded in agreement he continued, "She wasn't too happy about you freeing her, you know. But I digress. The Nasqa, or 'mind thieves' as you call them, communicate over vast distances using messengers… birds and the like that are also possessed. She'd let the Governor know about the portal as soon as she became aware of its existence, hoping it might create an opportunity for her. That's why your dinner guests were all taken over that night. After you'd freed her, she headed for Sydney, begging the Governor to have her taken over once more."

Colin asked, "Did he comply?"

"No. He took great joy in giving her false hope. He employed her to tutor his own children and saw to it that they made her life a living hell. I believe she's gone quite mad now and was recently admitted to a lunatic asylum. There's certainly no honour among the Nasqa."

Neridah asked, "But what about Pritchard and his plans… that is why you're here, isn't it?"

"Yes, indeed it is. And I must tell you, he won't give up on this."

Colin asked, "Will you personally be endangered on your return to Sydney?"

"No, there are only a few on the Legislative Council that are controlled by the Nasqa. On my return, I will make my change of allegiance as visible as possible. That will give me security. For all their powers, the

Nasqa can't override the reality of the political process. At least, not yet. But I warn you, Pritchard will not give up on trying to take control of that portal. The Nasqa will do whatever it takes."

Neridah said, "I think our more pressing problem might be what you refer to as an 'under-god.' I don't trust her intentions. My father travelled here from Ireland to continue the tradition of protecting the portal after it shifted its physical location from his homeland. I've no intention of letting that ancestral duty fail now."

The Magistrate replied, "Noble words, but I suspect they may be in vain. If this girl is feared by the Nasqa, you might just be out of your depth."

Neridah clenched her fists as she replied, "Do not underestimate what we are capable of when we come together."

There was an uneasy silence in the room for a few moments that was broken when the Magistrate burst out in laughter. "I swear, these creatures, as you say, have obviously underestimated you." He turned to Colin. "What would you wish me to do from here?"

Colin took a sip of his own brandy. He wasn't accustomed to drinking alcohol at this time of day, but the current situation made him feel comfortable about making an exception. "I think we should wait until this evening to make a decision, when the Reverend Casey joins us for dinner. I've always appreciated his counsel on such matters."

The Magistrate nodded. "I'm aware of him through the Nasqa's thoughts that I've overheard. Are you sure you trust him?"

"More than anyone else I know."

*

Sean O'Malley threw the shovel aside when he heard the plea for help. Maybe this would be his chance to shift to a more worthy host.

I need your help... the vermin let an under-god through, and I've been cast into the void.

Deep within Sean, his true persona held onto the grim hope that maybe this would be the opportunity for the thing that controlled him to move on and that he'd be freed from this curse of possession he'd lived with for so long.

The gravedigger walked up the hill and kicked in the door to the Reverend's house, hoping to find some money to take with him on his journey into town where he'd seek others to help him. Not being foolish enough to consider facing an under-god on his own, he knew he'd need money to buy drinks and food to help convince the occupiers of lowly bodies like his own to join him. He was aware of at least three such people in the barracks at Springwood alone, treated as madmen by some because their hosts resisted their possession. They remained in the corps only as a result of the protection offered them by the Nasqa-controlled captain who was the barracks' commanding officer. Maybe, if he worked it right, he'd even be able to enlist the captain's support.

He strode into the Reverend's house. It was a simple cottage, with one large room and a kitchen attached to the back. Although humble in size, its lathe and plaster walls were lined in wallpaper, and the doorways were framed in cedar. The furniture throughout the room was, for the most part, finely crafted silky oak. As O'Malley rummaged around, he cursed the priest. "Why would any man want so many books?" He pulled them from their shelves, whole rows at a time, sending most scattering across the floor.

Spying the piano, he thought there might be something hidden inside its stool and brought his foot down hard to smash it open. Nothing! He walked to the silky oak buffet, pulling its drawers out and emptying them of their contents.

He rubbed the coarse stubble on his chin before turning toward the kitchen door, kicking it so hard it nearly came off its hinges. He couldn't believe it. More books! This time, in huge stacks on the kitchen table. Why? Why would anyone want to waste time reading? He kicked the table over, then went through the cupboards. Nothing again.

Returning to the main room, he approached the writing desk, opened the cigar box and smiled a toothless grin. He'd finally found something worthwhile.

Looking around again he noticed two bottles of brandy sitting on the buffet. At least the cigars and brandy would warm him on his ride to the barracks.

He walked to the fireplace and lit a cigar from one of the burning embers, then grabbed a bottle, pulling its cork out with two of his remaining teeth. He spat the cork aside and took a deep swig from the bottle, followed by a drag on the cigar. He smiled as he picked up a few sheets of the Reverend's writing paper, then crouched by the fire as he set them alight. Shielding the small flames with his hand, he carried the burning paper across to where some of the books lay scattered on the floor, then let them fall. He stood and laughed when the first books ignited, flames rising as their pages distorted and curled as though tortured by the heat. Knowing the books would be reasonably slow to catch, he strode back to collect his bottles of brandy and the box of cigars, tucked them under his arm, then meandered to the door. He paused in the doorway to splash some brandy over the smouldering books, causing them to burst into flame.

By the time he'd collected his shovel and mounted his horse down by the graveyard, the Reverend's house was a blazing inferno.

CHAPTER 6

Neridah looked at the Book of Wisdom, wondering what it had to say about under-gods, then turned to Colin and asked, "Do you think it might be worthwhile moving the conversation to the drawing room? The sun should be shining through the windows now to make it warm, and it's such a beautiful outlook at this time of day."

The Magistrate waved dismissively. "Nonsense woman! The fireplace is burning and the brandy warms the soul. Drawing rooms are for women to practice their embroidery and talk of things that lack significance." The silence that ensued made the Magistrate realise how poorly his reply had been received. "I'm truly sorry, good lady. I must apologise. I've been possessed by that creature so long that I guess I've lost a degree of sensitivity."

Meredith responded on her mother's behalf. "Perhaps that sensitivity is something that had still to be learned beforehand?"

Not knowing where else to look, the Magistrate gazed at his shoes and let out a long sigh before raising his eyes to meet Meredith's. "Hmm, that could well be the case." Feeling humbled, he turned to Colin. "What say you, McIntyre, do we remain by the warmth of the fire, or adjourn to the drawing room?"

Colin looked at his wife, he knew her well enough to read in her expression that she agreed with her mother. Although he generally felt uncomfortable in the more feminine decor of the drawing room, he understood that resistance would cause him pain later that he could do without. "It's the best view we have over the property, and at this time of the afternoon, it's undoubtedly the warmest room in the house. If we settle in there for the next hour or two, we'll be well placed for a grand view of the sunset."

The Magistrate burped, then extended his hand. "Very well then. If you insist on treating me as a woman, I guess I've little choice but to acquiesce."

Colin helped the Magistrate from his chair while protesting, "That's not the—"

The Magistrate cut him off, grabbing at his chest and gasping for breath. His weight was such that Colin was unable to support him after the strength had gone from the old man's legs. The Magistrate collapsed to his knees. Meredith helped Colin ease him down so he was stretched out on the floor. Then, Meredith and her mother ran their hands over him to read his life force and ascertain what action they should take. The blank look on their faces told Colin everything he needed to know. The Magistrate was dead, and there was no bringing him back.

•

It was a two-hour ride at the best of times from Pulpit's Hill to Springwood, but Sean O'Malley was on a mission, and it didn't matter to him if his horse dropped dead of exhaustion when they arrived. He was sure the Nasqa at the barracks would be able to find some way to provide him with another one.

It would've been easier if he'd been able to enlist a lesser Nasqa to control his horse, a common path for the Nasqa to build their individual prestige. But that only worked if you held a high station, like a magistrate, military officer or governor. He pondered his ill fortune since arriving in this world. Always forced to take on the body of someone already close to the end of their life, helping find dirt on others that may help Nasqa inhabiting those of a more prestigious station. He felt deep resentment over having been sent to the Blue Mountains to keep an eye on the priest who'd caused trouble for the Nasqa when they'd helped Sellemae. As far as Sean was concerned the real reason he'd been sent was because the Nasqa controlling Governor Pritchard wanted to take over the land hosting the portal and didn't want the priest getting in his way.

Sean pulled one of the brandy bottles from his saddlebag, careful to time his movements to match the steady groove of the horse's gallop. He took a long swig then tossed the empty bottle aside.

He rode on. Salty sweat ran off his brow and stung his eyes. Rubbing them with his greasy fingers made it worse. At least the afternoon sun was at his back as he continued his eastward journey.

His horse was covered in frothy sweat and its breathing was laboured when Sean O'Malley reached a squatter's homestead. He rode to the stables, dismounted, and began transferring his saddle to a strong-looking chestnut mare that must have stood all of seventeen hands.

The owner of the homestead emerged, wearing boots and a coat. His square face bore strong features and deep-set eyes, framed by dark hair and thick sideburns. He carried a flintlock in one hand and a stock whip in the other. "Hey, what do you think you're doing?"

Sean continued saddling the horse.

"Did you hear me, man? To steal a man's horse is a hangable offence."

Sean turned to face him. "How far from here to Springwood Barracks?"

"You'll know that answer when you find yourself facing the Captain of the barracks... once I've bound you and led you in there on the back of my cart."

Sean O'Malley went back to ignoring him.

The squatter unfurled his stockwhip, making it crack. Both the mare and O'Malley's horse reared up. O'Malley continued ignoring the squatter and focused on calming the big horse. The squatter came closer, drawing his arm in readiness to crack his whip once more, this time with the intention of striking O'Malley. But the Nasqa was ready. O'Malley reached out and caught the whip, not even flinching as it wrapped around his arm and tore at his flesh. He pulled back hard, causing the squatter to fall to the ground and release his grip on the whip. He prepared himself to aim the flintlock and fire it at O'Malley, but he was too late. The gravedigger had jumped on the horse's back and rode it straight over him, crushing his right shoulder and pelvis.

He rode a short distance then, listening to the man's screams, decided to turn back.

He dismounted and approached the squatter.

"Please, for God's sake, man... help me."

O'Malley bent down and picked up the stockwhip and flintlock. "Now then, good sir, if I were to do that, you might go telling fibs about what happened here just now."

"I, I give you my word… no one will ever know. Just please… help me."

O'Malley watched the squatter's face contort as he tried to deal with the pain. He then sauntered back to his new stead as the man resumed his agonised screams. Once he was back on the horse, he fired the flintlock at the squatter's chest, bringing the screams to an abrupt end. He tossed the flintlock aside and said, "You certainly won't be telling anyone now." He stabbed his heels into the horse's side and rode off toward Springwood Barracks.

When he arrived at the gates twenty minutes later, the guards, who'd been sitting in the shade of a nearby tree sharing a bottle of rum, stumbled to their feet and rushed to block his path. One of them, a man with a mop of curly dark hair and a deep scar under his right eye, slurred his words together as he asked, "Who goes there?"

O'Malley replied, "What would you care?"

The guard burped. "We can't let you pass unless you've good reason to be here."

"I'm here to see the Captain."

The other guard, a lanky man who seemed less affected by the rum, looked O'Malley in the eye and said, "The Captain doesn't like your kind."

His colleague asked, "What would you be talking about?"

The lanky guard gestured toward O'Malley. "He knows what I mean." He stared at the gravedigger and communicated telepathically: *You lowly scum. You don't choose when to talk to us, we choose when to talk to you.*

O'Malley spoke his response. "When the Captain finds out the information I have for him, he'll be pleased you chose to let me through." He followed up the statement with a thought: *There's an under-god has come through.*

Looking to his colleague again, the lanky guard said, "We should let him through. He'll get what's coming to him when he meets the Captain." He turned back to Sean. "I'll escort you to his quarters."

•

Patsy said to Hunter, "Seeing we're clearly not wanted back at the library, let's go for a walk down by the creek. There's lots of lovely wildlife down there, and sometimes the fairies come out and sing."

"Okay, I'd like that."

As they made their way down the path Patsy said, "I can't believe that you're going to meet Darcy later." She giggled then asked, "Have you ever met with boys before?"

Hunter appeared puzzled by the question. "Oh yes, many hundreds of times over the years."

"Have you ever kissed one?"

For a moment, Patsy thought she detected a hint of anger in Hunter's eyes, but then the girl giggled as she had before. "Have you?"

"That's not fair. I asked you first. And besides, you're older than me. Why, my father would be horrified at the thought of me kissing a boy."

"But you are nearly twelve now. Have you never thought of kissing a boy?"

Patsy rolled her eyes upward and bit her lower lip while she thought of how she should respond. "I'm not saying… not until you've told me your answer."

"My father would be very angry if I were to kiss a boy that he hadn't approved of."

"See? We are alike." Patsy did a little pirouette as she continued down the path. "So, have there been any boys your father approved of you kissing?"

"What about you? Is there anyone you ever wanted to kiss?"

Patsy blushed. "I don't think I want to answer that."

"Is there a boy that you ever did kiss?"

Patsy's jaw dropped. "No! Of course not."

Hunter walked ahead, feeling free to let the violets grow in her footsteps now that it was just Patsy and herself.

Patsy looked at the violets. "How do you do that?"

Hunter stopped. "Do what?"

They were at the creek now, and Patsy took Hunter's hand, guiding her to the left, upstream and away from the pool with its portal. "The flowers… how do you make them appear in your footsteps?" She looked down at Hunter's feet, watching her stepping over rocks and in shallow pools at the creek's edge. Whether her foot hit soil, sand, rock or pebbles underwater, the violets always sprang up.

"I don't do anything. It just naturally happens when I take a step. The effort goes into stopping it."

"Does everyone do it where you come from?"

"Only those with the knowledge."

"It must be a very colourful world." As Patsy spoke, she noticed the foliage to either side of Hunter's trail of violets had died off. She turned to Hunter to ask about it then found herself distracted by the daisies in Hunter's garland. "What about your garland? Why do the daisies move around like that?"

"What do you mean?"

"They move like they're looking at me… like they're alive."

"I think you must be imagining things. Would you like a garland of daisies? I could show you how to make one."

They reached an area where the creek opened into a broad shallow area. Patsy looked at the daisies in Hunter's garland. For now, the movement seemed restrained, but Patsy was sure she had seen movement among the flowers when she'd looked at them before. And there was something else… there were thoughts, individual ones, coming from each of the flowers. She thought to herself, *I wonder if there's anything in the Book of Wisdom about the garland… and about the flowers.*

"Patsy?"

"Oh, sorry. Yes, I suppose so."

"What's this Book of Wisdom you keep thinking about? Is that where you get your knowledge from?"

Patsy picked up a stone and skipped it across the surface of the water. "It's a book my family has learned from for generations. My grandmother says no one knows how old it is. No one even knows how many pages there are in it. No matter how many pages you turn, there are always more to follow."

"It sounds like a very special book. Can you show it to me?"

"I'd have to ask my grandmother first. She says it's sacred, and it should only ever be read by those with the duty of protection. Even my father's not allowed to read its contents. You have a duty to protect your world, don't you?"

Hunter picked up a stone, like the one Patsy had skipped across the water. "My father and I protect many worlds."

Patsy smiled. "Then it'll probably be okay. I'll still have to ask though."

Hunter crouched low and flicked her wrist, sending her stone skipping across the water. Each time it bounced off the surface, a spray of tiny flowers radiated out from the point of contact.

•

The Reverend Casey grabbed hold of the ledge. He knew that as soon as his left hand released its hold on a small crack in the rock, he would need to swing his body to bring his left arm over the top of the overhang, with nowhere for his feet to hold onto. It had taken hours to get this far, but the huge climb was almost over.

Talia stood at the cliff's edge. "Come on, Alfred. Hanging around isn't going to make it any easier."

The Reverend shook his head in dismay before responding. "Your comments may be better kept to yourself."

"And, if I were you, I'd be putting my efforts into the climb rather than providing a critique to the voice that's been your guide. Come on, your hand will just end up slipping if you keep waiting."

The Reverend knew she was right, but he didn't appreciate the reminder. He took a deep breath, closed his eyes, and focused. Energy from a dozen crossworlds surged through him. He released his left hand's grip on the rock and swung his arm around. He then reached up and brought it over the top of the ledge, leaving his feet swinging in the air. His grip was tenuous, so there was no time to catch his breath again. He pulled hard until he was able to bring his head above the edge, allowing him to reach out further with his right arm, enough to bring his shoulders and chest onto the safety of the clifftop. He gave himself a moment to draw breath before dragging his hips and legs up. Once clear of immediate danger, he rolled onto his back.

Talia clapped. "Well done. I didn't think you had it in you to do a climb like that."

"I'm grateful then that you showed the wisdom to keep such thoughts to yourself." The Reverend turned his head to the side and saw a column of smoke rising in the distance. "I'm not feeling good about the source of that smoke."

Knowing, as the Reverend did, that his home was the obvious source of the fire, Talia placed her tiny hand on his shoulder. "Sad as this loss may be, I believe you'll be facing bigger issues in the hours and days ahead. Right now, Alfred Casey, there are those who need you."

"Aye, that may be so, but how can you be so dismissive with regard to the fire? It's almost as though you expected it."

"Come on, Alfred, you did realise the gravedigger had been taken by a mind thief, surely?"

The Reverend tightened his fists. He didn't appreciate the obvious being pointed out to him, particularly when he had only just worked it out for himself. There was no point taking it out on the pixie though, she was trying to be helpful. Were it not for her, he'd be languishing at the bottom of the hole. He felt quite sure he would've struggled far more to find his way out without her help. "In hindsight, I should have suspected. I just cannot help but trust in people until given reason to do otherwise."

Talia paused and looked up to the sky for a moment before shaking her head and turning back to the Reverend. "Ah, such a rare trait, particularly in humans. Bandah's always been the same way. I can see now why he likes you… and why he feels protective of you."

CHAPTER 7

Colin, Meredith and Neridah stared at the Magistrate's body in stunned silence.

Neridah stood up and said to no one in particular, "Well, that makes things a little more complicated."

Colin glared at his mother-in-law. "A man has just died. Must you always be so lacking in sensitivity?"

Neridah rolled her eyes and let out a sigh. She looked into space for a moment with her hands on her hips as she collected her thoughts.

Meredith bowed her head, closed her eyes, and rubbed a hand against her brow. She didn't want to listen to Colin and her mother arguing, not now. It was painful at the best of times. At least her mother was pausing to choose her words now, as opposed to her usual reactive manner.

Neridah glanced at the Magistrate's corpse then looked back to Colin.

"I'm not wanting to argue, and I don't wish to be disrespectful. This man would have died years ago were it not for the mind thief."

Meredith concurred. "Mother's right, darling." She stood up to be on the same level as her husband and mother. "I can feel it too. His heart failed after the creature had left him. It turns out his body was incapable of surviving on its own."

Colin nodded as he remembered times when his wife had told him of someone's cancer long before the sufferer or their physician had known of it.

Neridah looked back to the corpse. "Lungs, kidneys, liver, bones. The man was riddled with it."

Colin asked, "Why was he able to live while under the mind thief's control then?"

"The mind thieves control the whole body and everything in it. They can make a disease slow dramatically in its progress. Or even hold it in a kind of stasis. This man was likely at death's door when first taken over."

"The pain must have been unspeakable."

"The mind thief wouldn't have felt that… he'd have left that for the Magistrate to deal with."

"Do you think he knew?"

"A cancer that advanced? Yes, but he must have kept it to himself. I doubt the mind thief would have chosen him as a host had it known beforehand."

Colin replied, "Unless it was concerned more about what the Magistrate's title would allow it to achieve. I wonder how long the mind thief would have remained in his body after the papers transferring my title on the land were signed."

Neridah nodded in acknowledgment. "You may be onto something with that."

Colin put his hand on Meredith's shoulder. "I'll go to the stables to fetch Jimmy and his son. They can help carry him through to the kitchen. Then we can wrap him in wet blankets and place him in the larder overnight. In the morning, I'll take him to the barracks at Springwood. They should be able to deal with transporting him to Sydney from there."

*

Patsy looked at Hunter and asked, "Can you teach me how to do that?"

"What? Skipping stones? I just followed what you did. It's you that's taught me something."

Patsy smiled at the idea that she could have taught Hunter even the smallest thing. "It's not that. It's the flowers that came out as the stones skipped. Can you teach me how to do that?"

Hunter feigned a look of bewilderment. "But that is something that just happens, like when I walk. I don't know that I could teach it when it's not something that's willful."

Feeling patronised, Patsy folded her arms in a gesture of defiance. "I don't believe you. You're able to stop the violets in your footsteps if you try. So, that shows you know how and why they happen. I think it's the same with the flowers when you skip stones."

Hunter narrowed her eyes but said nothing.

Patsy asked, "Is it to do with your garland?"

Some of the flowers in the garland turned in Patsy's direction. Hunter frowned for a moment then softened her expression, letting out a small laugh before replying, "Why would you think that? It's just some flowers woven together."

"But they move… and they think. I know they do."

Hunter remained silent, but thoughts ran through Patsy's head. *You must not think such things. Forget you ever thought of them.*

Patsy replied, "I don't like it when others use thoughts to try and tell me what to do."

Hunter screwed up her face as though confused. "Why would you say that? Are you accusing me?"

"No, it's not you." Patsy pointed at the garland. "It's them."

"Why would you say that?"

"I can hear them. They're telling me not to think about them and trying to make me forget."

This time, Hunter didn't respond. She stood and looked at Patsy. *How could she know?*

Patsy's breathing was getting heavier. "They've done it to me before. There's something you did at the stables, and now I can't remember. I remember things then forget them again. And you wanted everyone to forget what you did to the mind thief you took out of the Magistrate."

Hunter looked at Patsy with a cold stare. "And they will forget. By the time the man is wrapped in blankets, they'll remember only that he had a heart attack. But you won't forget. I can see now, you're different. You're like—"

Patsy stamped her foot, putting a crack in the rock she was standing on and sending out a shockwave that knocked Hunter to the ground, making a splash as she landed on her backside in a shallow puddle. Patsy's teeth were clenched as she said, "I told you before, don't patronise me."

*

After Colin left the library, Meredith said to her mother, "I'll go and ask Mrs Banks to organise some blankets. Are you happy to stay with the Magistrate until Colin returns?"

Neridah replied, “Yes, that’s fine. I wanted to look something up anyway.”

“What, in the Book of Wisdom? Do you think that’s wise when Colin will be back soon with Jimmy and his boy?”

“I’ll be very quick.”

Meredith stared at her mother as she backed out of the room. Sometimes she saw her mother’s teenage appearance and wondered if she had the immaturity to match. It was little wonder her husband and mother clashed so much. “I’ll close the door, so you have a moment of warning when someone enters. At least that might give you time to close the book.”

Neridah smiled. “Thank you, that’s very thoughtful.”

As soon as Meredith had closed the door, Neridah went to the writing desk and opened the secret compartment that held the key to open the Book of Wisdom. There was very little time, but she had a plan to change that. Hunter had imposed a time freeze on an individual, but what she wanted to do was different. She wanted to isolate time within the library. Yes, there were still consequences, but not so great as when imposing a time freeze on others. All magic had consequences anyway. She’d seen the page she was after before. Her own mother had warned her against its contents. The words were still clear in her head. *Spells that invoke the changing of time extract a heavier price than most other spells. You could take time away at a critical moment for another or cause a delay where none should exist. The consequences can be catastrophic, and there is no way of ever knowing what you may have been responsible for.*

Neridah went to the book and unlocked its clasp, throwing the book open to roughly where she remembered the page was when she’d asked her mother about it as a child.

The cost is potentially so great you'd have to wonder why anyone would want to learn about such things. There would have to be no other choice.

It was clear to Neridah. There was no choice.

She didn't trust this powerful and timeless entity that presented itself in such a youthful body. And that garland. There was something very disturbing about the garland.

What annoyed her most of all was that she could feel the foggy mask that hid many of her memories relating to Hunter. If she didn't use the spell to alter the passage of time within the library, she may lose the memory of what she needed to learn.

Neridah was seeking time to look up and read about the garland, without interruption. And she wanted to look up other concerns she had about Hunter, things she couldn't quite put a finger on.

She looked down at the page. It was exactly the one she'd hoped for. That's how the Book of Wisdom worked for those who knew its secrets. It sensed what you needed to know and guided your hand to the page.

Neridah took a deep breath before reciting the incantation. "Ka Dae marsie karn, com-ba swa-ba keb vog." *The time right here must stop, until I swing my arm aloft.*

Being in the library, Neridah was isolated from the sounds of nature that might let her know whether the spell had worked. There was no choice but to trust that it had. She'd gone beyond boundaries that she'd held sacred before today, but there were no regrets.

She placed one hand to the left extreme of the book, and the other to the right, closed her eyes and thought of what she needed to know. *Garlands that live, garlands that dance.* She kept the thought running through her head as she moved her hands along the edges of the book's pages, waiting for the sensation that would tell her where to open the book. The pages felt as though they were moving under her touch, as thousands of them flipped in and out of existence. Of the millions of pages that co-existed across so many crossworlds, it was likely only one would have the information she sought. The movement stopped. The page Neridah needed had made itself known to her right hand. She opened her eyes and carefully opened the book to that page. It revealed an illustration of a garland of daisies, almost identical to the one worn by Hunter.

The text was In a language unfamiliar to her, an indication of how far into the history of the book she'd had to search. If she was patient and waited a few minutes, her eyes would adjust and learn to see the words as ones that she understood.

She ran a finger over the ancient illustration of the garland, then turned her head in response to a knock at the door. The spell hadn't worked! She tried to sound relaxed as she called out, "Who is it?"

She closed the book as gently as she could while the reply came. "It's Mrs Banks, ma'am. Mrs McIntyre requested I bring blankets."

"If you give me a moment, I'll get the door for you." She turned the key in the book's lock then returned it to the secret compartment of the writing desk on her way to the door.

She adjusted her dress and took a moment to settle her breathing before opening the door.

There was nobody there.

*

Captain Taylor poured Sean O'Malley a glass of rum. "You were right to come to me with this information."

"So, we'll be riding there this evening?"

"No."

"Begging your pardon, sir, but there's an under-god there, and it's tortured not one, but two of our own."

"You speak recklessly, almost as though you let the alcohol affect your thinking as it would your host. The Governor has plans for that property. He sent our kin there for a reason. We'll not be doing anything rash without his consent."

"Hah, you say that from the comfort of your position in these barracks." He leaned across the desk and pointed an accusing and trembling finger at the Captain. "What if it were you that were torn apart and thrown into the void?"

Captain Taylor watched the finger as though he was keeping his eye on a mosquito. "And what would you have me do to this under-god?"

O'Malley threw his arms into the air. "Kill the body it inhabits and let it know how it feels to suffer."

Captain Taylor walked to the window then glanced over his shoulder at the decrepit gravedigger. "This attitude you're displaying, it's why you've been designated the host you have rather than one of higher station. I will acknowledge you've done the right thing to report this matter to me rather than recklessly pursuing your own vengeance. But mark my words, try to tell me what I should do again and you will find yourself given a far lesser creature to control."

As if to emphasise the point, he opened the window and let out a quiet whistle. A few seconds later, a screeching flying fox appeared at the windowsill. He spoke to the host in the language of the Nasqa: "Pra-li-ar mondee. Har-gen bo-dah ok-gen li-scew bo-gardae pee-lone buckah gu-dah boom-qua. Gi-gen boobi-gen yandee re-ak li-kae." *Go to our leader. Tell him the one he sent to secure the portal has been disabled by an under-god. Ask him what he wishes for us to do.*

As the mind-thief-controlled primate flew away, he sent it another thought. *Bring me a response before dawn, and the gravedigger's body will be yours to control.*

The flying fox screeched its approval then flew into the night.

Unaware of the Captain's offer, Sean O'Malley finished his rum then burped loudly.

•

The sun was getting lower by the time the Reverend and Talia made it back to his horse. "It'll be getting dark by the time I reach the McIntyres' now."

Talia said to him, "Not if we go straight there."

He mounted the horse as he replied, "I'll not go there till I've had the chance to check and see if anything remains of my home and church."

"Honestly, you humans! I'll never understand why you worry so much about that stuff."

"Your manner of speech is much like your cousin. And just as dismissive. Regardless of what you may think, I'll not ride to the McIntyres' until I know what remains for me. If you wish for my help in finding your cousin, then I suggest you try to be more patient." He kicked his boots into Elsa's side and the horse took off.

Talia flew just ahead of the horse. "Some friend you are."

The rest of the ride to the Reverend's home was punctuated by a tense silence.

When they reached the graveyard, the Reverend pulled up Elsa at the spot where he'd stood performing his lonely burial service earlier in the day. He shook his head as he looked at the partially covered body with the missing shoes.

Talia landed on his shoulder. "Please, tell me you're not. That can wait till the morning, surely?"

The Reverend turned to her with a cold glare. "I'll not leave the body here uncovered overnight. It's a wonder the scavengers haven't already taken their share."

"Does it really matter?"

The Reverend ignored the question. He dismounted and led Elsa up to the smouldering remains of his home. At least the church and stables were still intact. Leaving Elsa to graze on the grass a few metres from the charred remains, he walked into the ruins, making his way toward where his bed had been. The woollen blankets and stuffing of his mattress had retarded the flames just enough that the floorboards beneath them were blackened but not fully destroyed as most of the timber structure had been. He used his boot to brush away what remained of the mattress from a spot near where the wall had been. There were two short boards of identical length. He crouched down and lifted them, revealing a silky oak box. No bigger than a loaf of bread, it showed no obvious signs of hinges or a lid.

Talia flew over and fluttered in the air near his face. She looked toward the box with its intricate marquetry. "So, that's why it was so important for you to come by here?"

"Aye."

"What's in it?"

The Reverend turned his cold gaze to the pixie. "That's of no concern to you." He walked back to Elsa and led her to his sulky by the stables. He then secured the box to the seat with a length of rope before grabbing a shovel and making his way down to the graveyard, insistent on finishing the job he'd paid Sean O'Malley so generously for.

Talia watched the sun sink lower. As the Reverend laboured she shook her head and mumbled, "Humans."

CHAPTER 8

Hunter sat in the shallow pool shivering. "It's so cold… and my dress!" She threw her hands up in the air. "It's wet!"

The daisies in her garland were tearing themselves outward, snapping back in like they were bound to Hunter's head by rubber bands. As they reached out, tiny squeals escaped their central cores.

Ignoring the writhing daisies, Patsy extended a hand, offering to help Hunter to her feet. "Come on, you'll dry off quicker if we go into the paddock and take in the afternoon sun."

Accepting her hand, Hunter looked up at Patsy and rose to her feet. "I don't understand why, or how, you did that."

"You were acting like I don't matter. As though you can make me think and do what you want me to. I want to be friends, but friends don't do things like that to each other."

"You want to be friends? You made me fall. You took me by surprise." Back on her feet, she pointed to the puddle. "I was unable to protect myself from the wetness and the cold of the water."

Patsy shrugged her shoulders. "You made me angry." She looked up at the sky. "My grandmother says that when I get angry the impact is probably felt across all the crossworlds."

"I think your grandmother is good at exaggerating."

Patsy thought about it for a moment then replied, "Maybe, but I think most of the time she's right." Again, she took Hunter's hand. "Come on, you really need to dry off. Let's go up to the paddock by the house. We can sit in the sun." Patsy smiled. "The way you're shivering, you'll likely catch a cold otherwise."

Hunter's teeth were chattering. "If a sickness tries to take hold of me, I will purge it as though it were a Nasqa." She dragged her legs forward and out of the puddle, using her free hand to try and pull the wet dress away from her legs. "It feels so horrible; the way it sticks to the flesh." She had to stop walking for a moment. Her head went back in an involuntary action. Her eyes closed, then she lurched forward and let out a sneeze.

Patsy replied, "I don't mind so much getting wet, and it's been ages since I caught a cold." She laughed to herself at the thought of Hunter trying to get rid of a cold the way she'd dealt with the mind thief. "Colds aren't like Nasqa. Mother says that, one day, people will learn that sickness is caused by lots of tiny creatures that invade the body."

"Then I will rip them out one at a time."

Patsy led Hunter through a shortcut to the paddock. It meant risking tears in their dresses as they followed narrow wallaby tracks, weaving through tea trees and tree ferns. Patsy preferred it to the pathway, and she was concerned about the need to get Hunter into the full sun as soon as possible. She thought about what Hunter had said. "That'll keep you busy. Mother says there are thousands and thousands of them."

"How does your mother know what people will learn in the future?"

"It's in the Book of Wisdom."

This book, it even has knowledge from the future? Father was wise to send me here, for more reasons than just seeking out Alfred.

As they scrambled to the top of the bank and entered the sunlit paddock, Patsy asked, "Why are you so interested in the Reverend Casey?"

Hunter's daisies turned to face Patsy, staring at her in surprise as Hunter replied, "I thought you didn't like us reading each other's thoughts."

"But they were so loud, I couldn't help but hear them. It was like you were screaming them out for the world to hear."

"It must be the wetness. I'll try to keep them more quiet in the future." She reeled back then let out another sneeze.

Patsy sat down in the sun. "You haven't answered my question."

Hunter joined her, choosing to lie on her belly so the sun would be on the wettest parts of her dress. Violets sprang up all around where she lay. "As I said before, in my world, it's rare for men to have the knowledge. When Alfred and your grandmother closed the portal, they used power from so many worlds that it left memories of what they'd done drifting into portals within many of the worlds they drew power from." Hunter paused, then rolled over onto her back. Her dress was already dry, as though the flowers had absorbed the moisture as they grew. "At first, my father was angry that someone would dare to draw power from our world. But then, when he felt the male presence in the memories, he saw hope for the future in them."

"In what way?"

"I won't say more till my father has met with Alfred."

"I don't know that the Reverend is keen to cross worlds again. He's only ever crossed once, and that was solely for the purpose of rescuing my grandmother."

A smug smile spread across Hunter's face. "He will."

*

Standing in the doorway to the library, Neridah heard Colin's voice approaching the front door of the house, closely followed by that of the Magistrate.

How could this be? She looked to where the man's body should be… it was gone!

Had she gone back somehow in time?

Desperate not to have to face Colin in this situation, she slipped out of the library and raced toward the dining room door, managing to get through just before she would have been seen by the two men.

"How about you get your mother-in-law to join us in the library, McIntyre? Rumour has it she's even better on the eye than your missus."

Colin walked on beside the Magistrate in grim silence as they entered the library.

Neridah struggled to maintain control. She could feel the blood pulsing through her temples. Although aware he would soon pass away, she couldn't help but think of what she would like to do to that man.

She was lost in imagined justices being carried out when she was confronted by something she'd never imagined herself having to deal with… the sound of her own voice approaching.

"Seriously, Meredith, we have to intervene. From what you tell me, there's something about the Magistrate that just isn't right. I wouldn't mind betting he's controlled by a mind thief."

The strangest part of it was that she remembered speaking those words. She knew what would happen next and, more importantly, where she should hide to avoid being seen. She knew that Patsy and Hunter would race past the doorway any second now… rushing to the library… that Cook would enter the corridor from the kitchen door next to the stairs carrying a tray of scones… and that Cook's appearance would cause Meredith and the other version of herself to hesitate before entering the library themselves.

Concealing herself behind the door, she watched Meredith and the other version of herself march through the dining room.

Her breathing became heavier and she felt faint. This couldn't be real. She had to call it out for what it was.

She must have passed out and was having a dream.

The best remedy, the only remedy, was to bring this dream to an end. She had to reach out to the image of herself.

Neridah stepped out from behind the half-closed door she'd been hiding behind and prepared to make her presence known, only to go mute when Meredith looked over her shoulder, made deliberate eye contact, and placed a finger over her lips.

•

Colin shook his head in despair. "I shudder to think what they'll think in Sydney when they learn of what's happened."

Darcy and his father remained silent while they shared the burden of the Magistrate's weight as they carried him through to the kitchen.

Cook was ready for them. "I cleared the table as soon as I heard of what happened. Mrs Banks has brought ample blankets to wrap the poor fellow. She told me no one answered when she knocked at the library door, so she brought them straight here. I've already moistened them for you."

Colin said. "Thank you, Cook. I wouldn't have expected anything less."

Ferdinand had followed the men in. What sounded like a meow and a purr to the others was clear to Colin. "You can tell, can't you? This isn't what it seems."

Colin looked at Cook. "Can you do one more thing for me? Can you please get that cat out of here?"

A few seconds later, Darcy and his father heard a sigh escape the dead man's lips. Jimmy O'Sullivan put a hand on his son's shoulder and said, "This happens sometimes. It's not something to worry yourself about."

Having learned the art of listening, Colin had heard a word within the dead man's sigh: *Flee.*

He rubbed a hand against his brow as he processed what was happening. For some reason, his memory of the day's events was hazy. As far as he could recall, the Magistrate had arrived earlier than expected, then there was a hole in his memory regarding what had happened before the man had a heart attack and passed away during a heated discussion in the library. He remembered sending Hunter and his daughter to the stables. It must have been to spare them having to deal with seeing the corpse. Come to think of it, even the memory of Hunter's arrival that morning was vague. Bringing himself back to the moment, he turned to Jimmy and asked, "Will you and Darcy be good enough to help Cook wrap him in the blankets and carry his body to the larder?"

Jimmy replied, "Aye, Mr McIntyre, consider it done."

Cook asked, "What about dinner, Mr McIntyre, sir? Are you still expecting the Reverend Casey?"

Colin replied, "Yes, we've no way of contacting him now to change the arrangements. So, we'll continue as planned. I expect he'll be here soon."

Cook looked at Jimmy and Darcy. "Well then lads, we'd best get done here so I can continue preparations." She turned to Colin as he was leaving the room. "Dinner should be ready in a bit over an hour."

*

As the sun fell below the horizon, Patsy and Hunter made their way back to the house. They'd shared an uncomfortable silence after the discussion about the Reverend. Despite that, Patsy still enjoyed the company of this amazing girl who came from such a different world.

They entered the back door leading into the kitchen just after Jimmy and Darcy had carried the Magistrate to the larder. Cook looked up from the soup she was preparing and said to Patsy, "It's about time. I boiled the water for your bath ages ago, young miss."

Patsy rolled her eyes. "Urgh! Do I really have to? What's Hunter meant to do?"

Cook folded her arms. "It's one thing your mother has always been strong about, that you should bath daily, before dinner. What Hunter does in the meantime is not my concern." She looked at their guest and asked, "Perhaps you'd like to have a bath too, Miss Hunter?"

Hunter looked at the bathtub and giggled, then said to Cook, "I bathed in the creek earlier."

Cook put her hands on her hips. "Oh, did you now? It's a wonder you haven't come down with a chill then. What, with how cold that water is and all."

The two girls looked at each other and snickered behind their hands. Patsy said, "I'm sorry. It won't take too long."

Hunter smiled and replied, "It's okay. I can go back to the stables. I liked it there."

Patsy giggled again, then tilted her head to one side as she swung her shoulders back and forth. "You just want to see Darcy again."

Hunter smiled, then looked at Cook. "I'll come back soon. I promise I won't be late for dinner."

Cook shook her head then turned her attention back to the soup as Hunter left the room. "I'll not say that I approve of a young lass like her going off to the stables to meet a young man like that."

•

It was already dark when the Reverend arrived at the McIntyres' for dinner. Darcy came out and greeted him as he dismounted from his sulky. "I'll look after Elsa for you, Your Reverence." He extended his hand, which the Reverend warmly received, grasping it in both of his own. Darcy smiled. "It's good to be seeing you again."

The Reverend put a hand on the boy's shoulder and said, "Aye, and it's good to see you as well. How's your father?"

"Getting older, but up to no good regardless." The voice came from Jimmy O'Sullivan as he emerged from the shadows near the stables. He addressed Darcy, "Come on, son, let's take Elsa so the Reverend can go inside and relax. I believe he had a funeral to deal with today."

The Reverend untied the cord holding his silky oak box in place so that the stablehands could feel free to take the horse and sulky. "There's no great rush, Jimmy. It's good to see you. I'm more than happy to share a moment of my time with the likes of you two scoundrels."

They all turned their attention to the McIntyre residence as the front door opened to frame Neridah's silhouette. Jimmy looked at the

Reverend and said, “We can catch up another time.” He gestured to his son. “Come on, let’s give Elsa the food and water she deserves.”

The Reverend stood speechless as Neridah slowly approached.

She wanted to run to him, but not while the stablehands were still nearby. Once they were out of sight, she picked up her pace for the last few steps then threw her arms around the Reverend. “Oh, Alfred, I’ve missed you so much.”

The Reverend couldn’t help but reciprocate, enjoying the warmth of her as they embraced. “Aye, and I’ve missed you as well.”

Neridah took in a breath then stepped back, looking the Reverend in the eyes. “I can smell smoke on you.” She pulled back further and looked him up and down. “And your clothes are torn! What happened?”

He lifted a hand and ran it through her hair, just behind her left ear. “I’ve had a difficult day, and I’m afraid I don’t have a home to go to tonight.”

She embraced him once again. “Oh, my poor darling.” She took a step back, still holding him. Her eyes made her look akin to a lost puppy.

He held up the silky oak box. “This is all I have left.”

Again, she pulled herself close to him. “You know there’s always room for you here.”

The Reverend’s response was deliberate and cold. “I think that’s a decision for Colin to be making, don’t you?” He stared deep into Neridah’s pleading eyes, careful not to offer encouragement. “It’s certainly not my place to accept such an offer without his approval.”

Neridah pulled away, letting her hands fall by her side. “Why do you do this? Every time there’s an opportunity for us to be together, you find a reason why we shouldn’t.”

“I took vows.”

“Yes, I know the story.” She wiped a tear away from her cheek then pointed a finger into his chest. "You took vows so you'd have the strength to one day save me; something you dedicated your life to." Her teeth clenched. "And you did it!" She grabbed hold of his arms at the elbow and shook them. "You saved me." She was taking several short and rapid breaths between each phrase. Venom dripped off every word. "Isn't that what your precious vows were all about?"

The Reverend's expression remained the same, as though carved from stone. He asked, "Don't you want to know what happened?"

She threw her arms in the air, like an adolescent throwing a tantrum. "Arrgh! You just don't get it! Do you seriously think you're the only one who's had a hard day?"

The Reverend could feel his blood pressure rising. "For the love of God! My house burnt down, woman." He gestured toward the two-story homestead with a slight movement of his head. "I believe yours is still standing."

She clenched her fists and stamped her foot before speaking through tears. "It's not my house. I just grew up here. Then, when you finally get around to rescuing me after forty long years of waiting, I discover it's now owned by my daughter's husband. And in case you hadn't noticed, he doesn't like me very much."

The Reverend looked away from her and stared at the house. He had no desire to continue having what was bound to be a circular argument. It was painful enough that he loved the woman. Did she have to make it so much harder? As he looked at the house, Talia appeared at his shoulder.

Neridah pointed at the pixie. "Oh, it gets better. You've got a new pixie travelling companion… a female one at that."

The Reverend ignored her as Talia looked at the house and asked, "What do you think?"

He responded in a soft, deadpan voice. "I'm thinking that something out of the ordinary might have taken place here today."

Neridah replied, "What? Like a timeless young beauty, with powers beyond anything I've ever seen, coming through the portal? Or a magistrate arriving from Sydney to strip Colin of half the property, then suddenly dying? But then the best part was when I tried to do a time freeze spell and found myself thrown back in time and had to watch myself do what I'd already done… topping it off with having my daughter bid me be silent!"

Talia asked her, "You did a time freeze spell?"

The Reverend shook his head in disbelief. He tugged at his beard while searching for the best response, only to be saved when Colin called out from the veranda, Meredith standing by his side. "Alfred, it's good to see you. No doubt Neridah has told you of our eventful day."

"Aye, that she has."

Neridah put her arm through the Reverend's. She looked up at him and smiled as she began leading him to the house as though no cross words had been spoken. "Poor Alfred's had a difficult day as well. Far more difficult than ours. It seems his house burnt down. I told him he's more than welcome to stay here."

Colin and Meredith stepped down from the veranda to approach the Reverend. Colin said, "Oh my God, Alfred, that's terrible news. Come inside and tell us about it over a brandy. And I insist you take up residence here until your own home is ready for your return."

The Reverend tipped his hat and replied, "Thank you. I'll gladly accept your offer." Neridah's grip on his shoulder tightened. She couldn't contain the smile that broke out in a broad grin as she began to blush. The Reverend continued as though he was unaware of her excitement. "I must ask you though, Bandah left my company this morning to investigate the girl Neridah says came through the portal this morning." He gestured toward Talia. "His cousin, Talia, came to me later in the day. She was most concerned, having concluded he'd vanished from this world and all others she can feel."

Talia flew out to be closer to Colin. "Actually, I lied when I told Alfred I'm Bandah's cousin. I'm actually his wife."

Meredith raised an eyebrow. "It seems we've got lots to talk about."

•

Hunter made her way down the path to the pool and its portal. She had no intention of going to the stables just now. Looking over her shoulder, she noticed the Reverend's sulky arriving. In the darkness, she was confident that no one would notice her. Although the sunlight was gone, she could still see the path, her eyes adjusting to the dark like those of a cat. The crickets began singing praise to her as she walked by, causing her to raise a finger to her lips. They went quiet in response to her unspoken command.

She stood at the water's edge. "Albiorix come, Albiorix come…" She continued the mantra as she raised her arms. Water in the middle of the pool began spinning in a vortex, droplets breaking away from the surface and rising several metres in the air. "Albiorix come, Albiorix come…"

More and more droplets rose above the vortex and came together until they formed the shape of a man. He had a heroic figure and wore a robe not much different from Hunter's dress. His chiselled features were framed by a mane of hair and a long beard, much like the Reverend. As Hunter lowered her arms, the watery figure spoke: "How goes the hunt, daughter?"

"The priest has just arrived."

"Splendid! When shall you return?"

"I shall bring him in the morning."

"That is good."

Hunter asked, "What of the trilogy of witches?"

"They are not your concern."

"The daughter is powerful. She made me fall."

The watery figure paused to reflect for a moment, then his brow furrowed before he continued: "Surprising as that may be, it is of little consequence."

"Also, Father, their book of spells seems to have great power within its pages. Perhaps I should bring that as well?"

The watery figure thrust an arm toward Hunter. The ground beneath her feet shook and she fell to the ground. "I am Albiorix! It is not for you to make suggestions. I sent you to bring the priest. We are under-gods! We have no need of books, they are for lesser creatures."

Humbled, Hunter rose to her feet. "I shall return in the morning with the priest."

"Good. Now go." The figure of Albiorix fell back to the pool as the vortex came to a stop. Within seconds, the surface appeared still. Hunter turned and walked up the pathway.

CHAPTER 9

Colin and the Reverend sank into the library's high-backed leather chairs. The Reverend's silky oak box was on the floor next to his chair. Neridah had chosen to sit on the settee with her feet up. After closing the ornate cedar door so they had privacy, Meredith poured Colin and the Reverend a brandy before taking a seat near the writing desk. Talia was hovering above the Book of Wisdom with her hands on her hips. "So, this is the famous book, huh?"

Neridah looked across and frowned. "What do you mean by famous? The only people who have ever read its pages have been those of our bloodline."

Talia flew up to her. "Ah, but here's the riddle for you. Your bloodline has been around for a long time. The book is older than humanity, at least in this world. The book co-exists in thousands of worlds but in each world it is also unique, reflecting the differences between those worlds. There have been legends told about it for tens of thousands of years. Much of our knowledge has come from those with access to its wisdom in other worlds… wisdom that custodians of the book have chosen to share with us. We—"

She was interrupted by the Reverend. "Hush… did you hear that?" He stared at the ground near his feet. "I could swear that I heard something just now. For the briefest of moments, there was something there." Talia immediately flew over to inspect the area of his eye line. "Can you feel anything of your husband?" asked the Reverend.

She looked up and shook her head. "I wish I could say otherwise, but no."

Colin said, "After a day like we've all had, it's easy to let our minds play tricks with us, to imagine the things we wish for to the point where it feels as though they're real."

Talia stared at Colin in disbelief, then turned to Meredith. "You actually chose to marry this man?"

Colin snapped, "I don't care if you're a pixie, a human, or some kind of god. When you are a guest in this household, you will treat me, and all the other occupants and guests, with respect."

Talia was about to speak when the Reverend asked Colin, "You wanted to know more about today's happenings?"

Colin nodded to the Reverend. "Please, I'm eager to hear your story."

"My day started with Bandah interrupting me while I bathed. He told of someone coming through the portal and his wish to learn about who or what it was. When I told him of my busy day, he insisted on coming here to see for himself."

Colin said, "I never saw him." He gestured to Meredith and Neridah. "Did either of you?"

Neridah said, "I've sensed gaps in my memory today. I wonder if one of us might have encountered him, but the memory is gone."

Colin said, "I haven't felt that." He turned to Meredith. "What about you?"

Meredith shrugged her shoulders. "I can't really say." Neridah stared at her, sure that she was keeping something to herself.

Colin put his hands together below his chin, the index fingers forming a steeple. "What of your house though, Alfred? I want to know how it came to be that it's burnt down."

The Reverend was about to speak when he looked to his shoulder. "There it is again."

Talia flew up to his shoulder and bent over, sniffing as though she were a bloodhound. Realising the whole room was watching her, she looked up and said, "There's nothing I can grasp onto to say where he is, but I can feel him. I'm sure that Bandah is with us." She flew toward Colin. "It has to be that girl, the one who came through the portal today." She turned and looked toward the base of the Book of Wisdom's stand. "There's something else too... I can sense a mind thief."

They all looked up when there was a knock at the door. Meredith called out, "Who is it?"

Mrs Banks replied, "It's just me, ma'am. Cook asked if I could let you know that she's about to serve dinner."

Colin stood up. "Oh well, it seems we'll have to hear the rest of Alfred's tale over dinner."

Talia protested, "But, what about Bandah? He's in here... I'm sure of it."

Colin replied, "Well then, you can stay in here and seek him out while the rest of us eat."

*

Patsy was waiting at the kitchen door when Hunter arrived back at the house. "Come on, Cook's already serving up dinner." She looked at the direction Hunter had come from. "I thought you were going to the stables?"

Hunter looked up with a half-smile. "I'll be seeing Darcy later… and I found myself missing home when the light had faded, so I went down to sit by the creek for a moment."

"In the dark?"

"Darkness doesn't bother me." She paused and sniffed the air.

"Doesn't it smell wonderful?" Patsy led her through the kitchen then looked over her shoulder. "I enjoy the smell of dinner almost as much as I enjoy eating it."

When they entered the dining room, the others were already seated, and Cook had placed Hunter and Patsy's bowls of soup on the table ready for them. Patsy pulled a chair out for Hunter. "Here, you can sit where I normally do."

Hunter almost looked nervous as she took her seat. When Patsy was seated as well, she looked down at the bowl of soup. She turned to Patsy and asked, "What's in it?"

"All sorts of things. Cook's friend, Mr Donaldson, gave her the recipe when he came back from a trip to the goldfields near Bathurst."

"What sort of 'things' are among the 'all sorts of things' you speak of?"

Patsy used her spoon to scoop out a piece of mutton. "Well, to begin with, there's mutton, and carrots, and corn. Cook says it's the ginger and mutton that give it most of its flavour." Patsy tore off a piece of the damper sitting on the plate next to her bowl of soup. "I like to dunk bread in it, especially while it's hot."

The rest of the table was silent. Colin let out a little cough to draw his daughter's attention.

Patsy put the bread back down on its plate. "Oh!" She was struggling to hold back a snicker. "Sorry, Father."

Colin gestured toward Hunter then moved his arm toward the Reverend. "Hunter, I'd like you to meet the Reverend Alfred Casey."

Hunter smiled. "Hello, I've been looking forward to meeting you."

The Reverend raised an eyebrow. "Oh, and why would that be?"

"My father thinks you're very important."

"Does he now?"

Meredith interrupted, "We can discuss such things with more clarity on a full stomach. Can I suggest we start on the soup before it goes cold?"

Hunter stared at the Reverend. "Why did you bring a pixie with you?"

The Reverend took a sip of his soup before responding. "I don't know that it's any of your business whether or not I share the company of a pixie on my journeys, young lady."

"I'm not young. I'm older than you could imagine."

"Then perhaps you should display more wisdom when choosing your words." The Reverend tore off a piece of damper and dunked it in his soup. He was about to take his first bite when he paused, then turned to Colin and asked, "What time do you intend to leave in the morning for the barracks?"

Colin finished chewing a piece of mutton and swallowed before replying, "Before sunrise. I don't want to be arriving with a body that has started to create a stench around it."

The Reverend asked, "Would you like some company on the journey? I've no commitments for the morning, and I believe the distraction would serve me well."

Hunter snapped, "No! You can't! You have to meet my father!"

Neridah couldn't resist a quiet comment. "This'll be interesting." She continued eating her meal as she watched. The others appeared as though frozen in time, fearful of how the Reverend might react. "It's normally Patricia who gets scary when she's angry."

Patsy pricked her ears up. She was surprised her grandmother would make such a comment. "Hey! I'm right here you know… at the table. It's not like I can't hear you."

The Reverend cast a cold stare toward Hunter. "Understand this, Miss Hunter, there is nothing and no one, on this world or any other, that will make me do something unless it is my own choice to do so."

Hunter returned the stare, made all the more threatening by the way the daisies in her garland turned toward the Reverend. "You will come with me in the morning to visit my father, and it will be your choice."

The room waited for the Reverend's reply in silent anticipation. "What is your father's name?" he asked.

"Albiorix."

"I thought as much." He pointed to her garland. "You'd do well to train your flowers to remain calm. They don't help you pull off your deceptions."

"You know my father?"

"I know of him."

"Then you'll agree to visit with him?"

"I'll decide what I wish to do when I'm ready." The Reverend broke off eye contact and returned to eating his soup.

Hunter looked around and asked, "Where's the pixie you brought with you?"

"Trying to figure out what you've done to her husband."

Neridah interrupted, "I thought Albiorix was just a legend."

The Reverend turned to her. "Aye, and legends are generally born from some form of reality. Before she died, your mother summoned me to her deathbed. There was just one thing that she asked of me: *Should my daughter return, protect her from the one called Albiorix who wears the crown of dancing daisies.*"

Hunter said, "I think it's best if you all just forget this conversation and enjoy the soup your cook has prepared."

Colin said, "To be honest, I haven't followed much of the conversation at all. I've been trying to listen, but I guess the long day has rendered me too tired to keep up."

Meredith added, "I must admit, I'm struggling a bit too." She smiled and grasped her husband's hand to reassure him.

The Reverend didn't bother to look at Hunter as he said, "I'll make two things clear to you, Miss Hunter. The first one would be that your parlour tricks don't work on me. The other is that you should avoid making the mistake of underestimating what these women can do. If you make them angry, I guarantee you'll regret it."

Patsy smiled and touched Hunter's arm. "He's right you know… on both counts. I could feel you trying to fog my understanding of the discussion, but it didn't work." She let out a little laugh. "I actually think it's kind of funny now."

Neridah gave Patsy a puzzled look. "I'm not quite sure what you're talking about."

Meredith chimed in, "I'm not following the discussion either."

Colin gestured toward Patsy and said, "At least there's a little laughter at the dinner table for a change." He raised a glass. "I propose we change the subject and enjoy the evening. After all, poor Alfred has had to endure the tragedy of his house burning down, and in the morning, he'll be transporting through the portal to meet with Hunter's father. As for myself, I'll be up before the dawn tomorrow to deal with the Magistrate, so I'll be looking to retire shortly after dinner. So, let's enjoy each other's company while we can."

The Reverend cast his eyes toward Colin. "A man has died today in your home. It's unlike you to be so frivolous of such matters."

Although Hunter was still looking into her bowl of soup, the flowers of her garland all seemed focused on Colin. He looked at the Reverend and said, "I'm really not sure what you're talking about."

Meredith glanced at her husband as she mopped her lips with a napkin, choosing to remain silent rather than draw the attention of Hunter and her garland. She was unwilling to even think about her concerns.

Neridah squeezed the Reverend's hand. "I'm so glad you've agreed to go with Hunter to meet her father." While Hunter smiled and cast her eyes down to her soup, Neridah glanced at Patsy and gave her a knowing wink. Patsy gave the gentlest of nods in return.

Hunter looked up from her soup and toward Colin. "I tire of this meal. It's not the sustenance on which I thrive." She made an attempt at politeness. "If it's okay with you, I'd like to leave the table now, so that I can go outside and dance. I've spent all day withholding the violets when I walk, and long to let them out while dancing."

Patsy leaned across and cupped her hand over Hunter's ear as she whispered, "Father never accepts the idea of someone leaving the table while others are still eating. He says it's very rude."

Hunter smiled as Colin replied, "Of course. Do as you must." As she got up and left the table, she looked at Patsy with a wry smile.

Patsy asked her father, "Can I join her? I think I've had my fill."

Hunter was halfway to the door, her daisies still facing those at the table. Colin leaned back in his chair, a puzzled expression on his face.

"Patricia, you surprise me that you'd even ask such a thing while we're all still eating."

"But Hunter just—"

Seeing her husband's anger rising, Meredith placed a gentle hand on his wrist and looked across at her daughter. "Patricia, you know better than to talk back to your father." She was looking forward to Hunter leaving the room, hoping that once that had transpired, Colin might regain control of his thoughts.

Her heart sank when, even after Hunter was gone, she observed the tiredness and confusion in his eyes.

*

With Elsa brushed down and happy in a stall, feedbag around her neck, Jimmy placed a hand on his son's shoulder. "I'll be off to our quarters. Mrs Banks intimated she might enjoy sharing a rum together before dinner, and that's an offer too good to refuse. She's been widowed a long time and deserves to spend time in the company of a gentleman like myself."

Darcy smiled and said, "Have a good time then. I'll do my best to make sure I embarrass you when I come up to join you for dinner."

"Oh? Will you now? I'd be minding my own business if I was you… else I might come snooping when you meet your new lady friend."

Darcy looked at the main house, then turned back to his father. "The McIntyres and their guests will be done with their dinner soon. I expect Hunter might come out anytime now. She told me she'd meet me here after dinner."

"Well then, I guess I'd best be getting out of your way." Jimmy laughed to himself as he walked into the darkness. It was a long time since he'd enjoyed life so much. Working with the McIntyre family had given him a great deal of joy and satisfaction.

No sooner had Darcy's father left the stables than Hunter appeared, seemingly out of nowhere.

Darcy removed his flat cap, fidgeting with it as he said, "Miss Hunter? What a surprise. I wasn't expecting you quite so soon."

She turned a shoulder toward him, bringing her chin down in a slow and deliberate movement. "I was getting anxious. I needed to come outside into the fresh air." She moved closer to him. "Do you like to dance?"

The very suggestion reminded Darcy of how he had danced with his family in Ireland. Special memories of his mother flooded through him; of how much she'd loved to dance before she fell ill. He stuttered a little as he replied, "W-w-well, yes. I love to dance!" He looked around and spread his arms. "But sadly, Miss Hunter, there's no music."

Hunter touched his cheek. "Listen, Darcy O'Sullivan, can you hear them? The cicadas, the crickets, and the frogs?"

"Well, yes, but—"

Hunter pulled away from him, spinning in pirouettes as she moved out of the stables. Violets sprang up wherever her feet touched the earth, causing Darcy to wonder if perhaps he were caught in a dream. She kept her head looking back at him, gesturing with her hands for him to follow.

Watching the gracefulness of her movements, Darcy shifted his weight from one foot to the other in an effort to build courage. Dream or not, he felt compelled by this young woman who was so full of the magic of life. It seemed only natural to him that one so beautiful should leave flowers in her wake.

As Hunter danced her way into the open, her movements brought the divergent sounds of nature into time with each other, as though she was conducting an orchestra. Crickets, frogs, flying foxes, all came together in harmony. The sounds made him want to move his own legs in time.

Unable to contain himself any longer, he threw the flat cap aside and took long strides out of the stables and into the night. Hunter was rim lit by the rising moon's soft light, appearing more beautiful than ever as she glanced over her shoulder and smiled at him. He didn't even notice that it was her thoughts he was hearing now rather than words: *Come, Darcy O'Sullivan. Come dance with me.*

He joined her in the moonlight, his legs rising and falling in time with the sounds of the night, sounds that filled his head and left no room for thoughts other than the need to dance and be close to this mysterious young woman.

Hunter spun around and laughed, her daisies freeing themselves from the constraints of the garland and dancing through the air in a circle around her.

As the tempo increased, Darcy became breathless.

Yet still, he danced.

The daisies grew larger, creating a wide circle around their host; a circle Darcy was now part of.

Faster and faster he moved, unable to breathe, yet unable to stop.

The violets from Hunter's footfalls had spread beyond the area of their dance, turning the paddock into a sea of colour.

Darcy looked around the circle as he continued his dance and saw that what had once been daisies were now fantastical creatures, the like of which he'd never seen.

One beast appeared as a tree with the facial features of a man that was somehow free of the ground, yet able to move its roots at will, like so many legs.

Another appeared similar to a human, but with a more slender appearance that lacked clothing or hair.

As best as he could tell there were eleven such creatures, each one different in appearance, and all consumed by the music of the night as the tempo increased still more.

He looked around the circle and noticed the disparate creatures had all joined hands, including himself.

Hunter laughed as she danced in the centre of it all, her whole body glowing in the light of the moon. Or was it something other than the moon that lit the dancers?

It was Hunter.

She had become the light.

She was chanting now: "Fusta abra-mouwn mouwn-be dis lessdee." To his surprise, Darcy could understand her unusual language as though it were English. *Dance for me, my little pets.*

The pace grew faster, and from out of nowhere, a single thought sprang into Darcy's mind. At first, he couldn't make out what it was until it grew enough to take over his consciousness.

Break free.

It was too late. The fantastical creatures had already begun to change. They were no longer dancing on the ground but moving through the air.

Hunter brought her hands down in a swift and sudden movement that caused the music to stop. In that instant, Darcy, and the other dancers from the circle were drawn in towards her as though she were a magnet. As they drew closer, Darcy watched the other creatures transform back to the daisies they'd been before. He was compelled to look outward, as were the others, then he felt the warmth of Hunter's hair against his back, a sensation that spread from head to toe.

Realising all too late what had become of him, Darcy tried to scream, his tiny daisy voice barely audible to even the others in the garland.

Hunter smiled as she walked to the house.

The mass of violets where she'd danced wilted and withered away to dust after she'd taken just a few steps.

*

Having no interest in joining the others for dinner, Talia remained in the library. She'd come to the McIntyre property with a specific purpose and could feel the echoes of what happened earlier in the day. There'd been an altercation with a mind thief, of that she was certain. She could almost taste it. But there was more. In all her lifetime, she'd only ever once felt the after-effects of a time freeze spell. And here, in this room, she could feel the evidence of three of them having occurred almost back-to-back, the last one having gone wrong. She could tell it all by the stench of the time leakage. Humans weren't inclined to pick up on such things.

Talia sat down on the chair where the Magistrate had suffered his heart attack. There was another echo she could feel, almost like it were a memory. She could feel its distress lingering all around her. Fear, abject horror of what some creature had faced. Her heartbeat quickened and she struggled to breathe. She stared at the space Hunter had filled just before reaching into the Magistrate. Pain tore through her chest until she pulled herself away and flew to the other side of the room.

She landed on top of a bookcase and lay on her back as she let her breathing return to normal. Having felt the echo of its pain, she could feel the presence of the mind thief still lingering, as though it were occupying the space within the room, but in a different crossworld. The more she dwelt on it, the stronger the feeling became. In the back of her mind, she heard the words, *Ellise-ar.* It was the language of the mind thieves… a language she rarely came across.

She knew that *ar* meant *I* or *me*.

But *ellise*… what did that mean?

She was sure she'd heard it before, but it must have been thousands of years ago.

Talia took her mind back to a world she'd dwelt in for a few centuries, just after she and Bandah had married. Then it came to her: *Ellise*, to *come*, or *follow*. There was a mind thief co-existing in this spot, but not within this crossworld, and it was asking her to follow.

There could be only one reason a mind thief would want anything to do with a pixie like her. It must have befriended Bandah. And if that were the case, they must both be trapped in the void between worlds. "Is Bandah with you?"

There were a few seconds of silence and then, *Ellise-ar*.

Talia bit her lower lip and looked down. "I can't believe I'm saying this… okay, I'll follow you."

Boe-esta.

Talia thought about the words then nodded. "You want me to stay low? That makes sense."

The mind thief led her out the front door, then down the side of the house and across the paddock to the stables. It was leading her toward where the other incident had taken place but paused before reaching the stables because of the conversation Darcy and his father were having nearby. When Jimmy O'Sullivan made his way to the servants' quarters, she expected Darcy would do the same.

Then Hunter appeared.

Talia hid behind a tuft of grass and watched the dance of the garland play out. She had to stay as quiet and still as possible to ensure she wasn't seen. For the first time she could remember, Talia felt scared—so scared she was worried the sound of her heartbeat might give her away.

She started to think it might be safe to draw a breath when Hunter started walking back up toward the house. Then, Hunter turned and looked straight at where she was hiding in the darkness. "Another pixie?"

Hunter reached out toward Talia, then pulled back, causing the pixie to be drawn straight to her. Unsure of what else she could do, Talia defiantly asked, "What have you done with my husband?"

Hunter feigned a coy expression. "Oh, how sweet! The two of you are married? And now you've come looking for him?" She smiled. "I so like it when I can help others find what they're looking for." She flicked a finger toward Talia and the pixie vanished.

•

Captain Taylor kicked Sean O'Malley's chest. "Wake up! We've word back from the Governor."

The gravedigger groaned. "I think you just broke a few of my ribs." His hand released its grip on the empty rum bottle it had clung to while unconscious.

"You make me sick. The way you let yourself sink into the embracing effects of drink and pain that your host experiences. You wonder why you haven't been entrusted with a host of higher station?"

O'Malley snarled at the Captain. "There's little else to get joy from when you're sent into the body of a gravedigger."

"Pitiful… truly pitiful."

"You criticise me, while you bathe in the glory of your status. I see so much hypocrisy in your words."

The Captain replied with another kick. This time his boot connected with O'Malley's face, knocking one of the gravedigger's few remaining teeth out as his head was flung back against the wall.

O'Malley wiped the blood and spittle away with a dirty sleeve. He glared at the Captain in the dull moonlight that shone through the room's one small window. "We could have this fun all night, but I'm curious as to what Governor Pritchard had to say."

Captain Taylor took a seat and put his feet up on his desk. He looked down at O'Malley and wondered why he'd allowed the man to sleep on the floor of his office in the first place. "He said we should act. He wants us there before dawn… before they have a chance to move the body. That way, we can make it look as though we were going in to protect the Magistrate. We can go in with force, eliminating McIntyre and making the seizure of his properties seem more reasonable to the good citizens of the Blue Mountains."

"What of our brethren?"

"That's none of our concern."

"Oh? Is it not true that without his call for help, we'd be none the wiser of what has already transpired at that property? And what of the under-god?"

"We will be going in there with twenty armed troops. Our target is McIntyre, not the under-god. The Governor believes she will ignore us if she knows we are only interested in the seizure of his land."

O'Malley shook his head as he thought to himself, *And you thought I was a fool.*

The Captain stood up and began walking to the door. "Sleep while you can. In a few hours, we'll be on the road to Blackheath and the McIntyre property."

•

Talia was winded when she hit the ground. She felt familiar hands lift her head and cradle it in a loving caress, then a voice she hadn't heard in decades said, "Oh, my poor—"

Bandah was cut off by Mrs Smith. "Well, that was some rescue. Did it ever occur to that wife of yours that she might want to take more care while watching that under-god thing?"

Talia, shocked by the interruption as much as by being forced into the void, looked at the aging fairy. "Who, or should I say *what*, are you? And who gives you the right to talk to me like that?"

Bandah's voice had a patronising tone. "Now, my—"

"Don't you start with that. I've barely seen you since that priest became your grundai." Talia sat up and looked at Mrs Smith, then turned back to Bandah.

Bandah looked at his wife and gestured toward the fairy. "Talia, meet Mrs Smith."

Talia got to her feet, staring at Mrs Smith. "Mrs Smith? Rather an odd name for a fairy, isn't it?"

Bandah shrugged his shoulders. "She's an odd fairy."

"I can see that." Talia made a small reflex jump as she caught a glimpse of the moving shadow to her right.

A sound almost like a voice came from the shadowy creature: *Ar-elliah*

Bandah nodded toward the mind thief as Talia pushed herself against him for safety. He put his hands on her shoulders, his cheek next to hers. "He says he's your friend."

"How do you know it's a he?"

"I don't, but the last body he inhabited was male, and I prefer 'he' to 'it.' Since he's been helping us, I've come to the conclusion that even a mind thief deserves a little dignity."

Mrs Smith folded her arms and rolled her eyes. "Here we go again. Are all you pixies such bleeding hearts?"

Talia glared at her. "Definitely not." She flicked a glance at Bandah. "Just him." She shifted her weight onto one foot, put a hand on her hip, and pointed at Mrs Smith. "I'm still puzzled as to how a fairy ends up looking so old and wrinkled. From my experience, fairies still look young after tens of thousands of years." She turned back to Bandah and took a step back. "And as for you… I want an explanation. What exactly is going on here? How can this girl, Hunter, be able to do this to us? Who is she?" She pointed toward the paddock. "You did see what she did to the stablehand?"

"Our friend calls her an under-god. The mind thieves, or Nasqa as they like to call themselves, they fear these under-gods more than any other creature."

The mind thief, being the combination of remnants from two such creatures, now rose high above its companions. It stretched out as though trying to listen to a distant voice, then let out a moan that sounded like wind whistling through trees. A sequence of sounds from what could have been considered a type of mouth followed. *Gak ye-ar-dat elka di-cun, fell-gosh os sess jai-bo-stae*

Talia asked Bandah, "Did you understand that?"

"He says that others of his kind are coming to help. That they'll be here before dawn."

Talia looked toward the shadow as she addressed Bandah. "You're not seriously going to trust them. Please, tell me you're not."

Mrs Smith approached her and placed a hand on her shoulder. "I never thought I'd live to hear it. A pixie making sense!"

Talia pushed Mrs Smith's hand away as Bandah replied, "I can't see we've any other choice. I've tried to reach Alfred with little success.

When you arrived, I had new hope, until you found yourself in the same predicament." He turned toward the shadow. "The Nasqa's plan is our only choice. And I, for one, trust him."

CHAPTER 10

Colin and the Reverend had already adjourned to the library, leaving Neridah, Meredith and Patsy at the dining table.

Meredith folded her napkin and placed it on the table then turned to Patsy. "I think it's time you retire for the night."

Patsy protested, "But what about Hunter? Can't I wait until she's back, so I can show her to her room?"

"Patricia, I'm more than capable of showing Hunter to her room. Mrs Banks has already prepared it for her. We all need a good sleep tonight, and your father will be leaving before the dawn. I've no idea how long Hunter will be gone while spreading her flowers, and to be quite honest, I don't really care." She stood up as she continued. "What I do care about is that you've had a long day and need your sleep."

Patsy crossed her arms in an act of defiance. "I think you're going to join Father and the Reverend in the library to talk about things you don't want me to hear. You want to talk about what worries you about Hunter, and you're glad to have the opportunity to send me to bed before she returns."

Neridah swallowed her last morsel of the apple pie Cook had served for dessert before suggesting to Meredith, "She's right on all counts, you know."

Meredith couldn't believe it. Why couldn't her mother offer a bit of support from time to time, rather than always taking Patricia's side? The girl wasn't even in her teen years.

It was as if Neridah had read her daughter's mind. "She's almost twelve… you do realise that?" Neridah pushed her plate away and stood up. "I think there could be much to be gained if the three of us consulted the Book of Wisdom together."

Patsy's jaw dropped. *Yes! Oh please,* she thought. She'd spent many hours going through the Book of Wisdom with her mother and grandmother, but never before when there was something particular to research. She liked Hunter, but for reasons she was struggling to remember, the garland bothered her.

"We can't. At least, not until Colin and the Reverend have retired."

Neridah waved a dismissive hand at Meredith. "Alfred's house burnt down today, and Colin's day has been filled with stress. If they're not both ready to retire within the hour, I'll be most—" She stopped mid-sentence when she noticed Hunter's silhouette in the doorway. She put a hand to her chest and asked, "Hunter, how long have you been standing there?"

"Long enough." She walked into the room and looked at Patsy. "I thought we were friends."

Patsy looked puzzled. “I want to be friends, but you do make it difficult.”

“Well, you don’t need to worry, I’ll be gone before sunrise. Can someone show me to my room? I’d like to get some rest now.”

Patsy thought she could hear a tiny voice calling to her… so tiny it was more a distant whimper than a voice.

Pats, help me.

Noticing Patsy’s distraction, Hunter stared at her. “Is something wrong?”

“No, I just thought I heard something.”

Meredith made her way toward the doorway. “Come on, Hunter, I’ll show you to your room.”

As Hunter and Meredith left the room, Patsy tried to remember what it was she’d heard a moment ago. It was lost.

Patsy and Neridah watched the backlit forms of Meredith and Hunter make their way to the stairs. Once they were out of earshot, Neridah asked, “Have you struggled to remember things today?”

“Yes… in fact, just now, I thought I heard something, but can’t remember what it was.”

“I fear it’s happened to all of us. It’s like parts of the day are shrouded in fog. Colin seems to have been particularly susceptible, to the point where he’s just not himself.”

“I want to like her, but she keeps making me angry. I made her fall in the creek earlier.”

Neridah smiled at the thought.

*

As they made their way up the stairs, Meredith said to Hunter, “Your plan will never work.”

"What plan?"

"It's not really your plan, it's your father's."

How can you dare presume to know what my plans are?

Meredith turned to her and smiled. "It's written into the future's history. You and Albiorix will fail."

You will forget!

"No, I won't forget. I'm prepared for you, Hunter. Or would you prefer I use your real name rather than your title?" Meredith opened the door to Hunter's room. "You'll find a chamber pot under the bed if you need it. I hope you sleep well. You'll need it."

Hunter stared at Meredith's sardonic smile as she entered the room. "Not as much as you will." She walked toward the bed, then turned and added, "By this time tomorrow, you will go to my father begging to join in his service."

Meredith smiled and said, "You underestimate us." She pulled the door shut and made her way back downstairs.

*

The Reverend rejected Colin's offer of a brandy. He looked down at some of the cuts and bruises on his exposed forearms. "It won't do much to repair the damage of today, and certainly won't help me in my search for what's become of Bandah."

"I understand. However, I think I might indulge in one more, if for no other reason than to help me sleep while there's a corpse in the house." Colin took a seat and said, "Come with me in the morning, Alfred. On the way back from Springwood, we can order you some new clothing. I'll happily pay for it on my account. There's not much here I can offer you. Your shoulders are so much broader than mine."

The Reverend raised an eyebrow, curious that Colin seemed to have forgotten his earlier assertion that the Reverend would be accompanying Hunter in the morning. He nodded in appreciation. “You’re a good man, Colin McIntyre. While I appreciate your welcome, I have much to attend to, and I’ve no intention of imposing on your hospitality longer than absolutely necessary.” He looked at the ceiling. “The longer I’m here, the harder it will be to convince Neridah that my place is elsewhere. I’ll be needing to organise a tent to see me through until my home is rebuilt.”

“Hmmm. I wonder. Is that concern about how Neridah will feel, or about how you might struggle to leave her?”

The Reverend made a sweeping and dismissive gesture with his arm. He was unconvincing as he retorted, “Nonsense man!” He was about to continue when he heard something like a muffled voice next to his chair. “Did you hear that?”

Colin looked puzzled. “Hear what?”

“It was like a voice, but I couldn’t make out a word.”

“Bandah?”

“Perhaps.” The Reverend looked around. “I would’ve expected the pixie woman to return by now.”

Colin rubbed his brow, as though he had a headache. “I have to say, I’m struggling to stay awake. Everything feels a little hazy.”

“Perhaps you’d do well to retire for the evening.”

Colin held a hand against his forehead. “I’ll be fine, really.” He sat up straight in his chair, as though he’d had a sudden surge of energy and inspiration. “It just occurred to me. If you want to find out what’s happened with Bandah, perhaps you should go with Hunter when she leaves tomorrow. Maybe her father can give you the answers you need.”

The Reverend stared at him. “Those aren’t words I’d expect to hear come from you, Colin McIntyre.”

Again, Colin found himself rubbing his forehead. “What? That I’m struggling to stay awake?”

“No, it’s what you said after.”

“I’ve… no recollection of saying other than that I’m tired. Things are a little hazy.” He looked up and saw Neridah standing behind Patsy in the doorway, her hands resting on the younger girl’s shoulders.

Neridah said, “We thought we might join you for a few moments before Patricia goes to bed and you retire.”

Colin looked at his daughter’s smiling face. “Yes, of course, come in… both of you.” He rose from his chair, far slower than Patsy was used to seeing him move. “I’m afraid, however, that I may have to leave you in Alfred’s care. The day seems to have caught up with me and I need to rise well before the dawn.”

Patsy and her grandmother stepped forward into the library, creating space for Colin to stagger past them. “Goodnight, Father. I hope you feel better in the morning.”

Colin gestured with his hand as he passed them. “Yes, of course. Goodnight, pumpkin.” It had been years since Colin had called her pumpkin. He paused at the bottom of the staircase and looked back at his daughter. Despite his extreme tiredness, her smile was infectious. The subtle grin that spread across his face helped him straighten as he made his way up the stairs.

The three remaining in the library waited until they heard the door to Colin’s bedroom close before they dared to speak. Then Neridah walked up to the Reverend and said, “Tell me, Alfred. Tell me you’re not going to do it.”

“How can I tell you such when I’ve still no idea myself of what I’ll be doing?”

Patsy asked, “Shouldn’t Talia be back by now?”

The Reverend said, “Aye, it troubles me greatly.” He turned back to Neridah. “That’s why I’m feeling such uncertainty. It may be that the only way to find answers is to follow Hunter back to her own world.”

Neridah grabbed his shoulder. “Then I’ll go with you. Together we’re so much stronger. Remember when we shut the portal?”

The Reverend shook his head. “No. That cannot happen. You cannot go breaking up the Trilogy at such a time. The power of you three women working together is far greater than the power you and I share.”

They all turned to the door when Meredith entered. “Do you really think it’s wise to have these discussions so openly when Hunter is upstairs? You do know she hears our thoughts?”

Patsy said, “I can read her thoughts too. And I made her fall into the creek when she made me angry.”

The Reverend raised an eyebrow.

Neridah was about to speak when she heard frantic knocking at the front door. Meredith said, “I’ll see who it is.” She walked through the library doorway and into the corridor calling out, “Who’s there?”

A panicked voice with a thick Irish accent replied from beyond the door. “It’s Jimmy O’Sullivan, Mrs McIntyre. I’m sorry to be troubling you at this hour.”

Meredith opened the door. The others were huddled in the library doorway, curious as to what the problem might be. “That’s okay, Jimmy. What’s wrong?”

As a sign of his respect, he took off his flat cap. His eyes were wide with desperation, and a tear ran down his cheek. He rubbed his chin as if it would help him find his words. “It’s my boy, Darcy, Mrs McIntyre. He went walking earlier this evening with your young guest and hasn’t returned. I saw through my window when your guest returned to the house, but when I went back to our shared quarters, Darcy was nowhere to be seen."

Neridah made her way to the front door. "And where were you while your young son went walking with our house guest? Do you think that's responsible, especially with a girl who appears so young?"

Jimmy stared at the ground. "I'm sorry to say that I was with Mrs Banks, sharing a wee rum before dinner." He looked up with eyes full of sorrow. "There was nothing more than a shared drink and some laughter, honest to God, ma'am." He looked directly at Neridah. "Honestly, Mrs Corrigan, I trust my son's good intentions. He rarely gets to see girls other than your granddaughter, so I was happy for him."

Neridah glared at Jimmy. Every time she heard the name Corrigan, it reminded her of the short-lived and loveless marriage she'd never wanted.

In contrast, Meredith smiled as she placed a reassuring hand on Jimmy's shoulder. "You're a good father, Jimmy. And I'm glad that you and Mrs Banks are spending time together." She looked over her shoulder and called to Patsy, "Did you know of this liaison between Hunter and Darcy, Patricia?"

Patsy looked down to hide a guilty smirk. It took great effort to feign a look of innocence as she looked up. "Well… sort of…"

The Reverend said, "Mr O'Sullivan deserves to know what you know." He gestured toward the front door. "Go on, lass."

She looked at Jimmy and said, "I don't know that there's more I can tell you other than what you already know. She asked if he thought she was pretty, and then Darcy asked if she'd like to go for a walk after dinner."

Jimmy choked back tears. "Darcy's dinner is still waiting on the table…"

Patsy tried to say something, but the sudden realisation of how serious the situation was left her speechless.

Neridah turned to Meredith. "I think we should go upstairs and ask Hunter what she knows."

Meredith nodded in ascent.

Patsy said, "I'll join you."

Neridah and Meredith replied in unison, "No!" Then Meredith put her hand on Patsy's shoulder. "It's better that you stay here with Jimmy and the Reverend."

"But I know her bet—"

Neridah interrupted her, "Patricia, you know better than to argue with your mother." She turned to the Reverend. "Perhaps Mr O'Sullivan would be more comfortable if you and Patricia sit with him in the parlour while we learn what Miss Hunter knows of Darcy's whereabouts?"

The Reverend nodded. "Aye, come on Jimmy, or you'll be catching a cold standing out there."

As the Reverend ushered Jimmy into the parlour, he glanced over his shoulder, sure that he'd heard something, yet unable to say what it was. He turned to Patsy and said, "Perhaps you can see if Cook is still in the kitchen, and if she is, you might ask her to prepare a pot of tea?"

Patsy turned and dragged her feet as she left the room. "Okay, if I must."

The Reverend glared at her. It never ceased to amaze him how much he could see Neridah's attitude as a young girl reflected in Patsy.

*

Neridah and her daughter lifted their dresses as they ascended the stairs, conscious of avoiding the risk of tripping on the hems. Their silence and grim expressions betrayed their shared understanding of the seriousness of the situation.

On reaching the top of the staircase they turned toward the guest room and walked toward it, yet with each step, the room seemed just as distant as before. Mother and daughter looked at each other and quickened their pace.

Again, they found themselves lifting the hems of their dresses, allowing them to break into a run. Still, the door at the end of the corridor remained distant.

Meredith grabbed Neridah's shoulder. "Mother, stop. We need a different approach."

Neridah complied and squatted with her dress pulled over her knees as she struggled to regain her breath. She looked at her daughter and asked, "Okay, so what would you suggest?"

Meredith bent her knees to bring herself closer to her mother's level. "The more we tried, the further away the door seemed to be. Perhaps we need to release that sense of purpose, and merely walk to the end of the corridor."

Neridah nodded. "It's worth a try."

The two women stood up, then looked at their surroundings in stunned amazement. Meredith wrapped her arms around her shoulders, steam coming from her lips with each breath. She looked up at the stars and asked her mother, "How did we end up out here?"

"Your guess is as good as mine, but I'm thinking our guest had something to do with it." She looked up the paddock to the lights shining from the windows of their home. "We'd best get back to the house."

Meredith nodded her agreement and the women started up the hill.

After a few steps, Neridah asked, "Earlier today, you looked back at me and placed a finger over your lips. I'd thought I must have been dreaming when I watched you walk through the room with me."

"Your time freeze went wrong."

"How did you know?"

"I can't tell you… not yet anyway."

"You did one too, didn't you? Only earlier… that's why mine failed."

Meredith stared at her mother but didn't reply.

They finished their walk back to the house in silence.

*

Jimmy stared out the parlour window. "Isn't that Mrs McIntyre and Mrs Corrigan approaching?"

The Reverend stood up and approached the window. "Aye, that it is."

"I thought they went upstairs to talk to their house guest?"

"You're not wrong, they did just that." He turned to Jimmy. "Perhaps they couldn't find her upstairs, so went outdoors to continue their search."

Patsy interrupted, "That's just silly."

The Reverend turned and glared at Patsy.

Jimmy's face betrayed the horror he felt at hearing Patsy speak that way. "Young lass, that's no way to speak to a man of the cloth."

"I don't care. I was in the kitchen with Cook. They would have had to go through there to end up in the garden without being seen by you."

The Reverend's words were calm but firm. "I've had a hard and trying day, and Jimmy is in distress. Under such circumstances, it's highly likely that we might miss your mother and grandmother slipping by and out the door."

Patsy's breathing was getting heavy. She knew he wasn't telling the truth.

The tension eased when Neridah and Meredith entered the room. Meredith sat down next to Jimmy and placed a hand on his knee. "I'm sorry, Jimmy. We've searched high and low, but we didn't come across Hunter or Darcy."

Jimmy bit his lower lip as he wiped a tear from his eye. "I understand what you're saying."

Neridah looked at him and said, "Surely, you don't think—"

Jimmy cut her off. "I thought I could trust my son to be better than that." He got up from his chair. "Thank you for your care and hospitality, Mrs McIntyre." He made his way toward the door, but Patsy lunged across and blocked his path.

"It's not what you're thinking, Mr O'Sullivan. Darcy's not like that."

Jimmy gently guided Patsy out of his path. "I appreciate that you think the best of the boy, but there's things a young man can be tempted by that I don't think you're ready to understand." He turned towards the others and tipped his cap. "Ladies, Reverend, I'll be bidding you a good night and my apologies for disturbing you. There'll be hell to pay for Darcy when I see him in the morning."

"Arrgh!" Patsy couldn't contain her frustration any longer. The others knew as well as she did that Hunter had to be behind whatever had happened to Darcy. She ran past them and stormed up the stairs.

Meredith called out, "Patricia! How dare you! Come back here, now!"

The Reverend placed a firm hand on her shoulder and said, "Let her go."

As Jimmy walked out the door, Neridah turned to Meredith. "I'll go after her." She leaned across and whispered in her daughter's ear, "Perhaps you should go with Jimmy to the servant quarters and see if you can work out what's happened to his boy."

Meredith nodded and set out after the Irishman. "Hold on, I'll go with you, Jimmy. Maybe I can find a clue you may have missed."

Jimmy stood at the bottom of the veranda steps waiting for her to catch up. "That's most kind of you, Mrs McIntyre."

•

Patsy stomped up the stairs, each footfall hitting hard enough to make the whole staircase vibrate. Her grandmother called out to her, "Patsy, please. Not on your own."

Patsy paused. It was rare that her grandmother would address her in front of the others as Patsy. But it lacked sincerity. Why couldn't they see it? Weren't they aware how few friends she had living so far out of town? Darcy was the only person even remotely near her own age that Patsy got to speak to on a daily basis… and no one seemed to really care about finding what had happened to him.

No one but Patsy.

She turned away from her grandmother and continued up the stairs. She reached the top and turned to face the door at the end of the corridor. She took brisk, confident strides as she approached, throwing her arms up when she was halfway and causing the door to fly open with such force it almost came off its hinges.

The room was empty.

Patsy ran into the room and straight to the open window. She felt sure she knew where to find Hunter. As she started to climb out the window, her grandmother called out from the doorway, "It's too dangerous."

Patsy replied, "Not for me it isn't." She ducked her head to get through the window, let her feet down onto the corrugated iron, then made her way to the latticework supporting the jasmine, just like she'd done the year before.

CHAPTER 11

Neridah raced downstairs and into the parlour. "She's going to the portal. We've got to stop her!"

The Reverend grabbed her shoulders. "Who? Patricia, or Hunter?"

His question was answered by the sound of Patsy's feet scampering across the corrugated iron of the veranda roof before they saw her through the windows as she climbed down the lattice. She was illuminated by the full moon when she paused after noticing the faces in the room staring at her. She pushed her feet against the lattice and thrust herself into the night. The air around her thickened as she drew masses of atmosphere from adjacent crossworlds into their own, increasing the air's density so she was able to swim through it as she would through water.

Neridah took the Reverend's hands in hers while they watched her granddaughter labouring to pull herself along. "Alfred, we need to stop her. She can't do this on her own."

"Aye." They both closed their eyes and allowed themselves to be elsewhere. Every part of their being connected to the myriad strings of energy spreading through the Crossworlds. Their recognition of where they were allowing themselves to be shifted the energy in several nearby crossworlds to the corresponding location, causing the space they occupied in this world to snap across to the position they wished to relocate to. There was no movement as such, just a change in the location they occupied.

A moment later, when they opened their eyes, they were immediately below Patsy as she flew over the paddock. Although she was above their heads, she was still low enough that they could reach out for her. Neridah grabbed her wrist, and the Reverend caught her ankle. She kicked against the Reverend's arm as he pulled her down and she clipped her grandmother's jaw with a wild swing of her free arm.

"Let me go!" She closed her eyes and tried to be elsewhere.

The Reverend's voice was firm. "That'll not work for you while you're struggling. Particularly not while we've got hold of you… unless you believe you've enough strength to move us all."

Patsy gave up the struggle. She allowed the thickened air to return to the neighbouring crossworlds and let herself fall. The hold the others had on the girl prevented her from hitting the ground. Instead, she ended up embraced by Neridah, who wrapped an arm around Patsy's shoulders. "You can't risk this on your own. Not with Hunter. She's too powerful."

"I just want to know what she's done to Darcy."

The Reverend's voice was soft and reassuring. "Aye, and I'd like to know what's become of Bandah and Talia. But I fear that we won't learn of their fate by direct confrontation."

"She said she's leaving before sunrise! We'll never find out what's happened to them once she's gone."

"And that's why I'll be going with her."

Neridah took a step back. "No! There has to be another way."

He turned to face her. "If there is, then I'd certainly like to hear it." He looked up to the house, then at Patsy. "Seeing Hunter has obviously left the house, for now, I suggest we make our way back and get some sleep. I believe the Trilogy will need to be ready for something we've yet to learn of come the morning."

They made their way up the hill, each of them feeling tired after using the power of the Crossworlds to transport themselves.

*

Mrs Banks rushed downstairs, wearing a dressing gown and a concerned expression, when Meredith and Jimmy entered the servants' quarters. "Did you find him?"

Jimmy shook his head. "I thought I could trust him." He wiped a tear from his eye. "He's always been better than this."

Meredith asked, "Perhaps you could make a pot of tea, Mrs Banks?"

"Yes, of course."

"In the meantime, I might have a look around, if that's okay with you, Jimmy?"

He nodded his approval. "Feel free, Mrs McIntyre."

"Can I ask where you saw him last?"

"He was waiting for the girl down by the stables. I believe that's where he'd arranged to meet her."

"Thank you. I'll start there in that case."

Mrs Banks said to Jimmy, "You just go through to the kitchen and make yourself comfortable while I get the kettle on. Cook should be back from the house soon, so we'll all be able to enjoy a relaxing cuppa together. I'm sure Darcy will be back by the time we're through."

As Jimmy made his way to the kitchen, Mrs Banks followed, looking over her shoulder at Meredith. "Honestly, children today. They have no respect."

Meredith turned and headed toward the stables, her bold stride conveying a sense of purpose. Her attention was momentarily distracted by movement near the house. From this angle, she could see the back door that opened onto the kitchen. Cook had finished for the night and Ferdinand had slipped out the door with her. Cook pulled her shawl tight around her shoulders and made her way to the servants' quarters while the big tom raced around the corner and down the paddock, heading toward the portal. As Meredith focused in that direction, she noticed a dull glow behind the trees.

On reaching the stables, she felt the blue chill of the time freeze. Not on her flesh, but on the outer surface of her mind. It had colour and texture that was familiar, and an aroma of jasmine that she felt rather than smelt. It was almost identical to the echo left behind by the time freeze she'd created earlier in the library, not long after Hunter's arrival. The colour of the echo in the library had changed after the subsequent time freezes from Hunter and her mother. Three time freezes in one space within just a few hours, little wonder her mother's had gone so wrong.

She walked through the space where the freeze had occurred. The area was clearly defined. Sometimes she wondered how people without the gifts her ancestral line possessed could fail to notice such things. Even her husband, who she'd successfully taught to listen to the animals and nature, would more than likely completely miss what to her was so obvious. In that moment she wondered if Hunter had noticed the echo of her time freeze when she'd entered the library earlier. Her mother had missed it, which surprised her.

Meredith cast her eyes on the paddock below the stables. A large area of grass that had been lush and green earlier in the day was dead. She walked out and stood in the middle of the area of withered and wilted grass. She closed her eyes and waited for stray echoes from memories of what had transpired here to flow through her mind.

To her surprise, the echoes remained clear. Hunter had done little in way of cleaning up after herself. As Meredith soaked up and digested them, it became obvious. This couldn't be left until the morning. Hunter had to be dealt with now.

She closed her eyes and allowed herself to join Hunter at the portal.

•

Hunter didn't take her eyes away from the glowing centre of the portal when Meredith appeared by her side. She was holding Ferdinand in her arms and stroking him behind the ears. "I was wondering when you'd appear."

"You were careless. You left memories behind."

Hunter smiled. She still hadn't made eye contact with Meredith. "Perhaps I left only what I wanted you to find?"

"What did you do to Darcy?"

Hunter's smile grew wider. "See, you know something of what happened, but the detail you long for is missing."

"He was just a boy."

"And now, he will live for thousands of years. His life will have far greater value and meaning than it ever would have had I not intervened."

"Who are you to judge the value of a life? What gives you the right?"

"I am my father's daughter. I have the right to do as I please."

"You are Kerridwen, daughter of Albiorix. My ancestors banished your father. And we'll banish you too."

Hunter turned to face her. "And you learned this from your pretty book in the library?"

"I learned of your father's name from my grandmother. She warned me of the god-like being called Albiorix who wore a dancing garland of flowers on his head, as her grandmother had warned her. The warning has been passed through the generations since he was banished."

"But you learned my name from your book?'

"Yes."

Hunter squatted and released the cat. At first, he looked confused, then he ran up the bank and into the paddock. "The cat won't be able to speak in ways you understand now. He'll understand only your intentions but not your words."

"Why would you do such a thing?"

"The cat said he wished to join me when I leave. He's not happy. He feels that being understood only makes his life harder."

"You behave as though you're a god. But I know you're not. The mind thieves call you and your father under-gods."

Hunter laughed. "My father was worshipped as a god in this world for thousands of years."

"My ancestors banished him. He can't return."

"And in return for what they did to him, I shall banish you from this pitiful world of yours too!" Hunter drew an arm back then thrust it forward. Meredith was swept off her feet, straight toward the swirling glow of the vortex within the now active portal that lay at the pool's centre.

•

Neridah stood in the doorway to Patsy's room. Her granddaughter had changed into her nightgown and was climbing into bed. "Can I trust that you won't climb out that window during the night? You need your sleep."

Patsy rolled her eyes and looked away. "Okay, if you insist."

Neridah planted her hands on her hips. "Honestly, Patsy, I shouldn't have to ask such a thing of you. You'll send me grey before my time."

Patsy smiled and laughed to herself. It was a private joke they often shared about how a woman of Neridah's age would normally be grey by now for sure. She also liked that when they were alone like this, her grandmother often referred to her as 'Patsy' rather than 'Patricia.' She pulled up the blankets and said, "Goodnight, Nana-Neri."

Neridah entered the room and walked over to the bedside. She leaned over, kissed Patsy on the cheek, and said, "Goodnight." She turned and left the room, pulling the door shut behind her.

Patsy waited patiently until she'd heard Neridah going down the stairs. Once she felt sure it was safe, she threw back the covers, tip-toed across the room, and grabbed her dressing gown from its hook on the back of the door.

She closed her eyes and allowed herself to be at the bottom of the pathway that led to the portal. Strings of energy in multiple crossworlds moved to the location she'd visualised and, a moment later, her physical being shifted from where she had been in her room to the spot where those strings demanded she should be.

Patsy opened her eyes as Hunter threw her arms forward to send Meredith hurtling toward the open portal. Without hesitation, she thrust her right hand towards her mother, then pulled back. The gesture pushed the air between herself and her mother into an adjacent crossworld, creating a vacuum. At the same time, air from a hundred worlds filled the space immediately behind the airborne woman, creating pressure that released itself by pushing Meredith toward the shore like she'd been fired by a slingshot. She landed so hard she was winded by the impact when she hit the ground next to Patsy.

Hunter glared at Patsy with eyes that betrayed the fire burning within. "How dare you!" The daisies in her garland turned to face Patsy, each in turn seeking to break free of their constraints and snap at her... all the daisies, that is, excepting one toward the back of the garland that appeared wilted and sad.

Patsy remained calm and stood her ground. "I'm not scared of you."

Hunter stood still as the wind began building around them. Her breathing was heavy, her words slow and deliberate. "Well, you should be. I am Kerridwen, daughter of Albiorix. I am the hunter, the under-god that the Nasqa fear." The wind had built to a howling gale. Lightning flashed and a crack of thunder shook the earth. "I am the one you should fear."

"Well, I don't"

Hunter raised her right hand and thrust it towards Patsy, releasing a burst of lightning from the palm of her hand. Before it reached the space Patsy occupied, she was gone. Hunter turned and saw Patsy was now behind her. Again, she thrust out her arm, releasing another lightning bolt, and again Patsy was gone. The lightning struck a tree and caused it to explode. Hunter turned again, just in time to see the ball of energy heading towards her from Meredith's outstretched arm. Taken by surprise, the under-god was sent backward, coming down hard on the sandstone of the path. She prepared to send a reprisal Meredith's way but was knocked over by another ball of energy, this one coming from Patsy. She raised herself on her elbow and said, "Attack. Show them no mercy!"

The daisies broke away from her garland and grew. They swirled through the air in different directions as they continued to grow and develop ferocious jaws filled with razor-sharp teeth that snapped open and shut in a constant and rapid pace. Meredith and Patsy held their hands low and drew energy from across a hundred crossworlds to create glowing shields of energy around themselves.

The snapping jaws of the daisies descended on them. Each time they made contact, they tore away part of the shields, only to then be repelled by the sting of the energy produced by what remained of the very shields they were attacking.

Each time they retreated, they would regroup and descend again to take another bite.

Among all the daisies, there was one that swirled in a panicked circle, unable to resist the need to snap its jaws, but unprepared to allow itself to swoop at Meredith or Patsy.

While struggling to maintain the strength of their shields, the witches were unable to strike back. Hunter took advantage of the opportunity her snapping daisies created and began hurling bolts of lightning at the shields, reducing their size further with each blast.

Patsy had to shift her hand to avoid it coming into contact with one of the attacking daisies and Meredith was dragged backwards when a strip of fabric was torn from behind the shoulder of her dress.

A voice thundered above the chilling noise of the attack. "Enough!"

The Reverend stood at the top of the path, silhouetted by the moon.

Hunter stood up and raised both hands, gesturing with a waving motion of her fingers for the daisies to return to the garland.

Neridah stood behind the Reverend Alfred Casey, remaining at the top of the path as he descended the sandstone stairs. He spoke in a calm voice. "I'll go with you to meet your father. But we leave now, or else not at all."

With the daisies back in place within the garland, Hunter said, "Very well then, Alfred Casey." Ferdinand ran to her and let out a loud meow as she turned to face the water. She bent down and picked him up. Stroking his chin, she began walking into the swirling pool with the Reverend close behind.

At the top of the stairs, Neridah buried her head in her hands and sobbed.

CHAPTER 12

As Patsy, Meredith and Neridah began their lonely ascent up the paddock towards the house, they were brought alert by the frantic calls of Jimmy O'Sullivan running toward them. "I saw the lightning! The thunder was near deafening! But I heard voices too. One of them I'm sure was the girl." He looked around, his eyes scanning all around, expecting one of the faces to be Hunter's. "Did you see her? Have you come across Darcy?"

Neridah looked away and burst into tears. Meredith looked at the ground, unsure whether the priority was to console Jimmy or her mother. Patsy, however, showed little hesitation. She walked up to Jimmy and said, "Don't worry, Mr O'Sullivan. If Darcy isn't back tonight, he'll certainly be back tomorrow. It seems Hunter had to leave at short notice. I daresay he's travelled part of the way with her to ensure her safety."

Jimmy looked at Neridah. With his eyes transfixed on her grandmother, he asked Patsy, "Then why is it she's bursting into tears?"

Patsy put her hands on her hips and let out a deep breath as she shook her head in surprise. "Mr O'Sullivan…" Jimmy turned to face her. "In case you've forgotten, the corpse of a magistrate who came to visit today is in the larder. You know she's a sensitive woman. Is it little wonder that her concern over the panic you're feeling over Darcy's whereabouts has sent her over the edge?"

Jimmy nodded his head. "Aye, I guess you'd be right there." He turned to Neridah and said, "I'm sorry for the extra burden I've placed on you ladies this evening. As Patsy here so rightly says, Darcy will more than likely be back tomorrow… and he'll have some explaining to do." He tipped his flat cap. "I'll bid you goodnight."

Meredith replied, "You've nothing to apologise for, Jimmy. I'd be surprised and concerned if you reacted in any other manner. I'm sure Patricia is right… that Darcy will be back at some stage tonight or tomorrow." As Jimmy walked back up the hill, Meredith looked at her daughter and spoke in a soft voice to ensure Jimmy couldn't overhear. "You did well, Patricia. He may well sleep tonight after all, thanks to your quick thinking."

Patsy stared into the space in front of her as she replied, "I just hope we can find a way to get Darcy back for him before the sun rises."

*

For a second time, Sean O'Malley was woken by Captain Taylor's boot connecting with his belly. He coughed and spluttered, feeling sure the Captain had damaged some vital organ.

"Come on, gravedigger. It's time to get yourself together. We ride out within the half hour."

Sean rolled over and clutched his belly. He lay there and watched the Captain's boots as he left the room, the sound of each step reverberating through his head like a hammer hitting an anvil. This was the price he paid for allowing himself to feel the effects of the alcohol on his host. He experienced the carefree abandon, but also the repercussions the following day. His back resisted as he pushed himself up from the floor. Once he had one knee up, he felt confident to reach for the top of the table next to him. His sweaty shirt clung to his grime-covered chest as he struggled to his feet.

A loud ruckus from outside drew his attention to the window. "Oh my…" He found himself lost for words when he realised what was going on. He'd come to the barracks expecting to take a small handful of men with him to the McIntyre property. Now, as he surveyed the scene outside, there were dozens of soldiers on horseback. Seeing Captain Taylor approach a dismounting officer, he shifted himself to the side of the window, to be able to hear what was taking place without being seen.

Captain Taylor's voice boomed loud. "Lieutenant Stewart, I trust your ride from Parramatta wasn't too difficult. At least you had the light of the full moon to guide you."

Lieutenant Stewart didn't bother to look at the Captain, nor accept the hand he'd extended. "Spare me the platitudes, Taylor. Technically, you may outrank me, but make no mistake, the Governor has made it clear that the McIntyre property is to be secured as soon after daybreak as is physically possible." As he spoke, he led his horse to the water trough. "And he has placed that burden squarely on my shoulders."

The Captain's eyes darted around to see how many of Lieutenant Stewart's troops had noticed the ignored offer of a handshake before lowering his arm. “In that case, I’ll have my men saddle up their horses immediately.”

The Lieutenant turned to face him, the features of his round face accented by his sunken eyes, waxed moustache, and meticulously groomed hair. “Where’s the gravedigger, the one who informed you of what was taking place?”

“He’s eavesdropping, just behind the window back there.”

“Splendid!” Lieutenant Stewart approached the window. “Come on, O’Malley, you’ll be riding up front with me, as an honorary member of the Parramatta Lancers.”

Sean O’Malley rolled his body against the wall until he was facing the Lieutenant. “That will indeed be an honour, sir.” A warm smile emerged on his face as his eyes drifted toward the humbled vestige of Captain Taylor.

*

The Reverend Alfred Casey looked around at the unfamiliar surroundings. Never had he seen so much colour. When he brought his eyes back to the shore, he saw dozens of men and women dressed much like Kerridwen. Many wore garlands like hers as they lazed about among flowering bushes. It appeared they were enjoying a mass picnic celebration.

The Reverend turned to Kerridwen and asked, “Are their garlands all like yours?”

Before Kerridwen had a chance to reply, one of those sitting on the shore turned his head toward them and pointed. “Look, the hunter has returned!” Others turned, then stood up and watched the pair. “It’s as the prophecy said. She has brought back with her a priest from another world.”

The Reverend maintained his original stance, unprepared to shift till Kerridwen gave him an answer. "Answer me, girl, or I'll turn around and go back."

Kerridwen laughed as she waded through the water. Her eyes were on Ferdinand who was snuggling into her shoulder and purring as she stroked the back of his neck. "There's no turning back."

"Answer me."

She turned to the Reverend and sneered. "You dare propose to tell me what to do? You are but a worthless priest. You are mortal. I am an under-god."

"Don't treat me like a fool, woman. I don't care what you want to call yourself. You may be long-lived, but you're still mortal, I sense that. I'm here because your father needs me. And with that being the case, you'll be wanting to tell me the truth, else things won't play out well for you in the long run."

A voice boomed out from behind them. "He deserves to know the truth."

The Reverend turned to see who the voice belonged to. A man with broad shoulders, around the same height as himself, was taking giant strides above the water. As each foot came down, a hefty chunk of solid earth materialised to take his weight, dripping with violets of every hue. They flowed off the newly created earth, like a stream rippling over rocks. The footfalls echoed through the shallow valley, demanding the attention of all who were there. The imposing figure's white tunic was held tight about his waist by a leather belt with a gold buckle shaped like a garland. A red cloak with elaborate trim billowed in his wake, making his long mane of grey hair and his majestic beard stand out. On top of his head rested a garland of daisies, somewhat like Kerridwen's, but more elaborate, like a crown. In addition to the flowers, there were dozens of dark berries that grew at a rapid pace, then burst like so many bubbles. When he made eye contact with the Reverend, a huge smile lit up his face. "Alfred!" He extended his arms in greeting as he came closer. "I can't begin to tell you how pleased I am to see you."

The Reverend narrowed his eyes. "I'd be curious to know why that might be."

Having come up level with the Reverend, Albiorix reached down and extended a hand to his guest. "Come on up from the water and join me. You've no need to be wet any longer."

The Reverend accepted his hand and took a step up, a piece of earth forming at the perfect spot to create a step. When he brought up the other foot, ground formed beneath it as well.

Kerridwen looked at Albiorix, but the hint of anger that dwelt in her father's eyes told her it was not the time to ask if she could join him. He threw a thought at her. *You brought him sooner than you'd proposed. You caught me unprepared.*

I had little choice. The witches came after me.

Excuses!

The Reverend looked from one to the other, making it clear he could hear at least part of their thoughts.

Albiorix laughed and slapped him on the back. "Hah! I knew you were the right one. I should know better than to think so loudly around one such as yourself." He turned to his daughter. "Come on up and join us, Kerridwen. Let the people see their great hunter as she approaches the shore!"

As Kerridwen stepped up to walk above the water with the others, the Reverend faced his host. "So, would I be right in thinking that I'm some kind of trophy to you?"

"You are far more than that, Alfred." He reached up and took a grape-sized berry from his garland. He examined it as he continued. "You are the key to our future prosperity." He closed his eyes then placed the berry in his mouth and savoured its flavour. He swallowed then said, "You wanted to know about the garlands?"

"Aye." The Reverend stared at his host as they walked.

"The people on the shore, they aspire to be like my daughter, to have the power that she wields. But the truth is, they have spent their lives in devout service, as will continue to be their lot. They wear their garlands as a symbol of their aspirations and respect."

"You give them false hope?"

"Hah! It's so long since we've had someone come to this land worthy of being called a priest. One who has so much power yet seeks to speak for the people!" He reached up and took another berry from his garland and offered it to the Reverend. "They have everything they could hope for. They want for nothing."

The Reverend took the fruit and examined it. "You contradict yourself. A moment ago, you said they have aspirations, and now you tell me they want for nothing?" He noticed out of the corner of his eye that Kerridwen's daisies were becoming agitated, as though they were snarling at him. What surprised him most was that the cat glared at him and hissed. Kerridwen herself remained silent and ensured she was looking away from him as she smiled and waved at the gathering crowd on the shore.

Albiorix let out a hearty laugh. "Yes, yes, yes! I do that all the time." He waved a hand dismissively. "There's a feast laid out for us under the marquee on the shore. You'll get all the answers you need in good time." The Reverend looked to where Albiorix was pointing and saw a massive marquee where none had been before. They were almost at the shore now, where the growing crowd had formed into a guard of honour. "First, we must join our flock for the ceilidh and celebrate your arrival!"

*

Meredith couldn't sleep. She tried, but it was no use. The storm brewing outside didn't help. Her grandmother had warned her this day might come. She'd done what she could, but it wasn't enough. Kerridwen had achieved her goal.

The Reverend Alfred Casey was gone.

But there was always hope, a distant one that lay somewhere in the pages of the Book of Wisdom.

Colin couldn't sleep either. The day had been long and hard for him. His tossing and turning contributed to Meredith's insomnia.

In the hours before dawn, Colin dragged himself out of bed to prepare for the arduous task of taking the Magistrate's corpse to the Springwood Barracks.

Meredith pretended to sleep. She half opened an eye to watch him as he dressed. It was sad for her to see the man she knew as being so forthright and strong looking sullen and unsure of himself. Yet she felt too overwhelmed to offer him the support he needed.

In the morning, she would have to work with her mother and daughter to find a way of somehow bringing the Reverend Casey back from Kerridwen's world. If she gave in to her desire to support the man she loved now, it might drain her of the emotional energy that she'd need as the day wore on. She had little choice but to believe in Colin's strength to navigate his way through what would no doubt be a difficult day without her support.

Still, a gnawing pain remained in her stomach.

She lay in bed listening for close to an hour after Colin had left the house before she felt sure he was on his way. Then she waited a few minutes longer.

She closed her eyes as tight as she could and pulled the blankets over her head.

The thunder was getting louder as the storm came closer. Colin would be caught in it for sure.

The pain in her stomach grew stronger.

She knew its origin. Would it really have changed anything if she'd got out of bed and given her husband a simple reassuring hug before he left? The only thing preventing her from doing so was the knowledge that he wouldn't approve of what she planned to do, and her paranoia that he would've seen her intentions writ large when he looked into her eyes.

Regardless, she knew what she had to do.

When she at last felt sure it was safe, she leapt out of bed, grabbed her robe from the back of the door, put on her slippers, and made her way to the corridor.

She heard Patsy's whisper as she passed the door to her room. "Mother?"

Patsy opened her door wider and stepped into the corridor. "What are you doing?"

Meredith looked over her shoulder to where her daughter's voice came from, only able to vaguely make out Patsy's silhouette. "I'm going to consult the Book of Wisdom. I won't sleep until I know more about what we're up against."

A flash of lightning illuminated the outline of Patsy's face. "Aren't you tired?"

"Yes, but I can't sleep." Meredith sighed. "We need to find Darcy and get Alfred back. But it's worse than that. I suspect more trouble's coming. I can feel it." Her statement was punctuated by another crack of thunder. "Your father left for Springwood an hour ago, so it's just us here now. I want to be as well prepared as we can be." She reached for her daughter in the darkness and kissed her forehead. "You should get more sleep. In the morning, I'll have a plan."

Patsy's eyes looked heavy as she turned to go back to her bed. Meredith reached out and grabbed her shoulder. "If anything should happen, meet me behind the shed in the garden."

Patsy nodded then slipped back into her room.

•

Jimmy pulled down hard on the rope that secured the Magistrate's corpse to the base of the cart, allowing Colin to tie it off with ease. "To be sure, Mr McIntyre, I'm more than confident that'll be safe. If you were travelling to Parramatta or Sydney I reckon you'd be wanting to tie it down some more, but this should easily be adequate to get you to Springwood. And it's covered well enough to keep it dry when that storm hits." He straightened up and put a hand on Colin's shoulder, a very forward gesture for a stablehand to make toward his employer. "Are you sure you want to do this journey now? Would you maybe be better off waiting for the storm to pass?"

Colin appreciated Jimmy's concern. He'd come to view the Irishman as one of his closest friends. "I'm very sure. It'll be daylight before long, and the sooner this man's body is off my property, the happier I'll be." Colin tugged at the finished knot to ensure it was indeed secure then turned to the Irishman. "Thank you, Jimmy. I can't tell you how much I appreciate you getting up so early to help me out."

"Think nothing of it. I've been awake all night anyway."

Colin's look of concern presented his question without the need for spoken words.

Jimmy shook his head. "No, he hasn't. But I'll tell you what, he'll be in a world of trouble when he does show his head." He looked at the lightning in the distance. His voice softened. "I'd be a lot happier though if he was back home before that storm hits."

Colin climbed aboard the cart and into the driver's seat. "You've raised him well. I'm sure all will be fine. If he is still out, he's sensible enough that he'll seek shelter, more than likely by coming home." As Colin finished his sentence, he felt that his words came across more as platitudes than the reassurance he'd wanted them to convey.

An awkward silence followed, then Jimmy looked to the ground as Colin rode off into the night.

The full moon was falling low in the sky but was still adequate to guide Colin along the road for the hour it would take before the sun crept over the horizon. As he rode the cart away from the property, he found himself wondering for the first time how the Captain at Springwood Barracks would react to him arriving with the corpse of a magistrate who'd come to his property to discuss such a difficult matter.

He felt haunted by an unfamiliar sensation… uncertainty.

The miles rolled by as Colin rocked back and forth, struggling to see in the fading light as the moon slipped ever lower in the sky and the clouds began closing in. If the sun didn't rise soon, he'd have to stop and wait for the darkness to pass.

His head was swaying. He needed more sleep. Rain had started falling and the light was almost gone.

He had to stop.

A flash of lightning illuminated a tree under which he could achieve at least some shelter from the rain. He pulled his coat tight around himself, burying his hands beneath his shoulders for warmth. It was now so dark that he could barely tell the difference between his eyes being open or closed. A moment later, he was asleep.

He was brought back to consciousness by the sound of horses pounding the road. Lots of horses. In the dull light of the approaching dawn, he managed to make out the silhouettes of half a dozen riders moving around him through the incessant drizzle of ice-cold rain.

A voice demanded, "Who are you?"

Colin was unsure which rider had delivered the question. "I might well ask the same question."

"I am Lieutenant Neil Stewart. In the name of the Governor, I demand that you identify yourself."

"Lieutenant, this is indeed fortunate. I was on my way to Springwood—"

"Your name!"

"Colin McIntyre."

"Captain Taylor, arrest this man. Clap him in irons and take him back to the barracks. I want him tried and hung by sunset."

Colin retorted, "How can you—?" He looked from the Lieutenant to the Captain. "Since when did lieutenants order around captains?"

Lieutenant Stewart rode up, so his silhouette was immediately next to Colin, then swung his arm so the back of his hand struck him, drawing blood and almost knocking him off the cart. "Speak to me like that again and I'll have you flogged until the hide falls off your back. You'll likely beg for the hangman to end your suffering."

*

Neridah went straight to her room when they returned to the house.

Overflowing with anguish, she lay her head down on the pillow, tears streaming down her cheeks.

Why?

Why was Alfred doing this to her?

Time and again he'd rejected her love, while at the same time feeling free to let her know how deep his true feelings for her ran.

Okay, he's a priest, she understood that. She could live with that.

But no, that was wrong. She couldn't.

More to the point, how could he do what he'd done? How could he go and take those stupid vows?

And to make it worse, time and again he rubbed salt in her wounds by telling her how he'd taken his vows for *her* sake… all in the hope it would help him rescue her from Sellemae's clutches.

Mission accomplished.

He'd rescued her.

And now, he's gone.

She buried her head as deep in her pillow as possible, hoping to drown out the sound of her sorrow. "Why, Alfred, why?"

She heard the distant rumble of thunder. A storm was coming. Good, it might distract her enough that she might still get some sleep.

As the rumbling continued, she realised it wasn't thunder at all.

It was music.

The crickets, flying foxes, and frogs—all were in tune, creating a symphony unlike anything she'd ever heard.

Curious, she got out of bed, wrapped a blanket around herself, and walked to the window. She put her hands against the window, shocked by what she saw. Kerridwen had returned and was dancing in the paddock, multi-coloured violets surrounding her as she danced.

But it wasn't just Kerridwen.

There were others.

She saw Darcy spinning wildly in time to the beat… her daughter was there… her granddaughter!

There were so many others, all dancing in a circle.

The rhythm and flow were hypnotic, compelling Neridah to join in.

No!

It was too cold outside.

Kerridwen couldn't be trusted.

This was all wrong.

Then realisation hit. She wasn't just witnessing the dance; she was part of it. Somehow, she'd shifted from the warmth of her room to the chilly outdoors.

And she was dancing.

She cast aside her blanket, no longer caring about the cold. The music and the movement felt so good.

There must have been a dozen others dancing with her in the circle, some were creatures the like of which she'd never seen before.

She tried to draw Meredith and Patsy's attention, but it was no use. They were so absorbed in the dance they were unaware of her presence.

But what did that matter?

She closed her eyes and let nature's symphony carry her, spinning wild and free like she'd never done before.

When at last she opened her eyes, she was soaring above the ground with the other dancers, violets cascading off her feet as she moved through the cold night air.

She couldn't help but laugh.

This past day had been wasted in the family's resistance to their exotic guest.

To what end?

Her laughter grew louder the more she danced.

She felt Kerridwen reaching out to her. “Come with me.”

“Why?” She wanted to keep dancing. “Why come with you?”

“Join me. There’s no time for other choices.”

“I want to dance.”

The voice changed. “Nana-Neri, there’s no time.”

As she danced, Neridah felt hands gripping her shoulders, trying to stop her. She looked to the centre where Kerridwen had been and instead saw Patsy.

“Nana-Neri, you need to wake up. We have to go!”

*

The horses thundered through the mist as they carried the soldiers from Springwood Barracks onto the McIntyre property, Lieutenant Stewart barking orders as he rode on past the stables and headed toward the homestead, oblivious to the pouring rain that had saturated his uniform. “Secure the servants’ quarters and the stables first, lest we end up watching some ill-conceived heroics play out.” He turned to Sean O’Malley as the first of his troops dismounted and burst through the door of the servants’ quarters. “Tell me, gravedigger, can you sense the one who called you?”

O’Malley was leaning forward in the saddle, oblivious to the rain, his arms crossed against the back of his horse’s neck as he contemplated his options. “Oh, yes. But he’s laying low till we secure the property. He doesn’t trust the witches.”

“Pathetic!” Lieutenant Stewart turned his horse and started toward the main house. “That’s one Nasqa that doesn’t deserve saving.”

*

Jimmy O'Sullivan was waiting inside the door, holding a blacksmith's hammer. He charged at the lead soldier and let out a frantic battle cry as he swung his arm back. He didn't have the chance to bring it forward. The hammer dropped to the ground as the soldier's rifle fired and found its mark.

Mrs Banks and Cook stood further back in the corridor, just outside the kitchen door. At first, their dropped jaws emitted no sound, but their silence was replaced by screams as the soldiers stepped over Jimmy's slumped form and approached them.

*

Sean O'Malley dismounted and walked his horse to the stables. He stopped and sniffed the air when he reached the area of Hunter's time freeze, then turned his head to survey the dead patches of grass further down in the paddock where Hunter had danced. He tied his horse to a post and stared at a spot in the corner of the stable. "I'll be back for you soon." The cold moist air triggered an arthritic pain in his left ankle that made him limp as he walked over to the house to join Lieutenant Stewart.

A dozen soldiers were gathered around the Lieutenant as he strode up the stairs to the veranda. The soldiers who'd gone to the servants' quarters were dragging the still screaming Mrs Banks and Cook through the mud and rain toward the house. They went silent after a loud crack of thunder shook the ground beneath them. Lieutenant Stewart smiled at them, then turned to one of his men. "Put them in the drawing room." He kicked in the front door. "As for the rest of you, go upstairs, find whatever women and children are still here."

While half a dozen of his men raced up the stairs, Lieutenant Stewart walked toward the closed door of the library. Intuition told him there was someone in there. *No doubt protecting their precious book.* He took slow and cautious steps so as not to alert anyone behind the door of his approach. A floorboard creaked under his weight. He paused for a few seconds, then took the final steps. Once at the door, he embraced it with his body, turned the handle, and pushed.

It was locked.

He placed his ear against the door's surface and called out, "I know you're in there. I can feel it. I can feel lots of things, like the chill of the time freezes that happened here today. Those tricks won't help you now." He stepped back and raised his boot in preparation, smiling at the thought of catching one of the witches trying to protect the ancient text.

He kicked hard, causing the doorjamb to splinter as the lock broke free of its constraints. The door flew open and Lieutenant Stewart stepped into the room.

It was empty.

So was the stand that was normally home to the Book of Wisdom.

*

Meredith reached the bottom of the stairs and entered the library. She locked the door behind her before tapping the side panel on the writing desk to retrieve the key to the book's ancient lock.

She sensed that her time was limited, not so much by the impending sunrise, but by something else.

Trouble was coming, she could feel it.

As she unlocked the massive volume, she considered the risks of trying another time freeze, like the one she'd done not long after Kerridwen's arrival. She pulled out the key and placed it carefully on the desk next to the book stand. Her mother's failed try at a time freeze had ruined any possibility of attempting another. The fabric that held time together in this space had been weakened by three people freezing time in the same place within the same day. Neridah had been thrown back along her own timeline, creating a dangerous overlap. Time in this space would likely take weeks or even months to heal.

Her grandmother's words echoed through her head: *Be wary of anyone who wears a garland of dancing daisies.* When she first saw Hunter, she couldn't help but feel concerned. But even after consulting the book, she wanted to be sure before sharing her fears. It was Darcy's disappearance that confirmed her suspicions.

She found the page she'd opened the book to earlier, the page where she'd read about Kerridwen the Hunter before the time freeze had collapsed. She needed to learn more; the time freeze had been so brief.

She wanted to learn about the garland.

She struggled to decipher the words, too tired to translate the language of the book as she read it.

She had to try, despite the heaviness of her eyelids.

Then, she jumped at the sound of horses arriving outside the house. She'd been slumped across the open book. She must have fallen asleep and had no idea how long she'd been there like that.

Horses… lots of horses. They had to be one of two things: soldiers or bushrangers.

Whichever they were, Colin more than likely would have encountered them.

As far as she knew, her mother and daughter were both still upstairs.

She heard heavy boots on the veranda and one of the invaders kicking the front door open.

There was no choice. She'd have to trust that Neridah and Patricia would find a way out.

She closed the book and used all her strength to lift and hold it against her chest as she closed her eyes and allowed herself to be behind the shed near the bottom of the garden, most importantly, to be somewhere safe.

She opened her eyes and tried to adjust to her new surroundings.

*

A crack of thunder from the storm outside dispelled the last remnants of her dream. Neridah sprang upright, struggling to get a decent breath. Her nightclothes were drenched in perspiration.

After she'd taken a few deep breaths, she held a hand to her chest and looked at Patsy. "I was dreaming?"

"You were reaching out and rambling. I was starting to worry if you'd ever wake up."

Neridah glanced out the window and saw the first rays of light revealing themselves over the horizon. "What's happening?" She turned to her granddaughter. "Why did you need to wake me?"

Patsy whispered, "There are soldiers. Father left for Springwood Barracks hours ago. The soldiers have only just arrived downstairs. We need to get out while we can."

"Where's your mother?"

"She's gone to the library to consult the Book of Wisdom. These soldiers, I think they're controlled by mind thieves… I can feel it."

They heard a voice call out, "Go upstairs, find whatever women and children are still here." The pounding of boots on the stairs told Neridah and Patsy their time was limited.

Neridah grabbed Patsy's arm as she leapt out of bed. "You're right. We need to leave, now!"

CHAPTER 13

Patsy was adamant. "We need to allow ourselves to be behind the shed at the bottom of the garden. That's where Mother said we should meet her if there was a problem."

Neridah held Patsy's shoulders. "No! If you can feel the mind thieves, then they can feel you. If we move that way, they'll be able to tell exactly where we are." She looked to the window.

With the adrenaline already pumping, Patsy walked to the window and opened it, taking care not to make any loud noises on the way. She looked over her shoulder as she lifted her leg up and over the windowsill. "I know it's cold outside, but you'll need to leave your slippers behind, else you'll slip on the roof for sure."

Neridah whispered as she followed Patsy through the window, "We'll worry about frostbite later." Once they were both outside, Neridah pulled the window shut, hoping it would take time for the soldiers to realise how they'd escaped.

They heard soldiers barging into Neridah's room as they crawled along the roof, keeping as close to the wall as possible in case the soldiers looked out the window. Patsy felt her heart beat faster when she heard their voices.

"No one in here."

More footsteps, then another voice. "The bed's been slept in." There was a pause. "Check the window, they might have tried to sneak out that way."

Patsy and Neridah scrambled when they heard the window open. Once the sound of its movement stopped, they froze. A soldier's head protruded from the window. They were fortunate the shadows protected them when he looked their way.

Neridah worried the chattering of her teeth might give them away. It was, without doubt, the wrong time of year to be outdoors in the rain with inadequate clothing. They both breathed a sigh of relief when the window closed. Now was their chance to work their way to the lattice supporting the jasmine outside of the drawing room.

As they climbed down, they were mindful of what was happening in the drawing room where Mrs Banks and Cook sat huddled together, watched over by a handful of disinterested soldiers. Patsy could see from the sinister shapes their shadows threw on the wall that they were indeed controlled by mind thieves… Nasqa. Fortunately, the soldiers had little interest in what was happening outside, so missed the moments where the two witches climbing down the lattice were illuminated by the occasional lightning flash. During one such flash, Cook's eyes widened at the sight of Patsy and Neridah. Patsy put a finger to her lips and Cook nodded before turning her head away.

One of the soldiers, noticing Cook's expression, looked up at the window.

The two escapees froze as they clung to the lattice, hoping they wouldn't be given away by another lightning flash.

The soldier turned his head away and they continued their descent.

When they'd reached the bottom, they huddled in the darkness below the veranda.

Neridah whispered, "Let's wait till after the next lightning flash."

Patsy nodded.

They waited.

The rain was easing.

Patsy asked, "Should we just go?"

"No, be patient."

A near-blinding flash of light was followed by a loud thunder crack.

Neridah nudged Patsy and whispered in her ear, "Now, Patricia, run!"

As they ran, the cold ground felt like daggers cutting into their feet.

But this was life or death.

They were close to the shed when lightning again lit up the paddock. Driven by an instinct for self-preservation, Neridah and Patsy dived to the ground.

A voice called from the distance, "Did you see that?"

"What?"

"Over there, I thought I saw movement."

A moment later, a pair of wallabies hopped across the paddock, well away from where Neridah and Patsy lay in a muddy puddle.

"Keep looking. We'll spread out and work our way through the paddock."

The rain started pouring down again, even heavier than before. Neridah and Patsy weren't prepared to risk getting to their feet. Instead, they slithered through the muddy paddock hoping they'd be hidden from view by the length of the grass around them.

Neridah said to Patsy, "When we get there, we can combine our strengths and work as the Trilogy. We'll beat them easily then."

Patsy didn't respond. She continued dragging herself along.

On reaching the shed, they got up and darted around the back to meet Meredith.

They turned the corner and came to an abrupt halt.

She wasn't there.

*

Meredith looked around at the dark stone walls.

There was no door and no windows.

At the far end, there was a small stone fireplace, stoked so well the flames danced in celebration of their good fortune.

She turned back to face the other end of the room. No more than half a dozen paces from her, a small white-haired man, not much taller than the height of Meredith's knee, sat perched on a stool at a writing desk. The large feather quill he held worked its way across the large sheet of vellum on his desk. He had long pointy ears and wore a green felt hat.

The most amazing thing about the little man was that he hadn't been there when Meredith first arrived in the room just a few seconds earlier. He reminded her of a picture her grandmother had once shown her in the Book of Wisdom, the book she now held tight against her chest.

"Hello," she said, "are you a wood-elf?"

The little man kept writing with his back turned to her.

She took a tentative step closer. "Can you even hear me?"

An exasperated sigh let her know that, yes, he could. He paused from his frantic efforts to control the quill and looked up. "Do you have any idea how long I've spent trying to write down this thought while I still had it in my head?"

"Well, no… how could I?"

He turned to face her and looked over the top of his wire-framed spectacles. They sat on his nose in a manner that left Meredith surprised they hadn't fallen. "How could you indeed. That's the trouble with humans, you have so little knowledge of what other folk are doing."

"You haven't answered my question. Are you a wood-elf?"

"Come now, Meredith McIntyre." He waved a hand at her as though her question were silly. "You do remember the drawing your grandmother showed you?"

Meredith responded with an icy stare, not unlike the way her daughter was apt to do when she felt patronised.

The wood-elf put down his quill.

This was going to take longer than he'd hoped for. "Yes, I'm a wood-elf." He jumped off his stool and approached her. "My name is Krinkle-myst, and this is where I come when I want to work in peace."

"Why am I here?" She pointed to his desk and asked, "And what is your work?"

"You are here because you allowed yourself to be somewhere safe. Somewhere the Nasqa can't get to you. Somewhere that is not a part of your Crossworlds."

"What do you mean?"

"The book brought you here. It's seeking to protect itself."

"So, you had no hand in that?"

Krinkle-myst laughed. "I come here to get away from distractions. Trust me, you being here is the last thing I would've wished for."

"How do I get out of here?"

"You wait for your mother and daughter. You won't be able to leave here without the power of the Trilogy."

"How do you know so much?"

"It's my job to know."

"That leads me back to my other question, the one you've yet to answer. What is your job?"

"I write the stories that weave the fabric of morality into all that exists."

Meredith frowned. "Books are wonderful for sharing knowledge, but—"

"You underestimate the power of the written word."

"What do you mean?"

He turned and started walking back to his desk. "It's no use trying to explain. You wouldn't understand."

"I beg your pardon!" She took a step toward him. "How dare you presume such a thing!"

He replied in a disinterested voice as he climbed back onto his stool. "I suggest you put down the book and make yourself comfortable by the fire while you wait for the others to get here."

"What, just place the book on the floor?" She grappled to find words. "This is a sacred book. And where do you expect me to sit?" As she finished her question, she turned to the fire and saw a sturdy oak table and a solid chair with elaborate carvings of fairies, butterflies and flowers. It was positioned by the fire as though it had always been there. And the room—it had grown since she'd last looked toward the fire, which was now a good twenty paces away.

Her first impulse once she'd placed the book on the table was to sit in the chair and sulk, but then she decided it may be better to spend her time exploring the wisdom within the book's pages. Krinkle-myst's voice interrupted her thoughts. "What a shame you left the key in the library."

Damn!

He was right.

She glared at the wood-elf and asked, "How can you know these things?"

He turned to face her and looked over his glasses once more. "Like I said, it's my job to know things. How could I possibly hope to write moral codes people will abide by if I don't know what's going on throughout all the worlds?"

"How do you write a moral code? Isn't that something people find within themselves?"

Again, the wood-elf put down his quill. "I can see I won't get any peace until you have your answers." Meredith blinked, and then found she was sitting in the elaborate chair, with Krinkle-myst sitting in a smaller but otherwise identical furniture piece on the other side of the fire. "I write the fairy tales that guide people to find that inner truth. The sad fact is, many people can't find that truth without some form of guidance. Written words are powerful things." He pointed to the Book of Wisdom on the table. "Just imagine, where would you be without the words within that volume?"

Something deep within Meredith awoke, an awareness of how important it was to listen to what the wood-elf had to say.

*

Neridah and Patsy shivered as they huddled together behind the garden shed. The building's eaves had provided some welcome respite from the driving rain. But their drenched nightclothes clung to them and their hair was so saturated that water from it ran down their backs, making them colder by the moment. Despite the sound of the rain belting down on the shed's roof, they could hear the chatter of the soldiers searching the paddock.

Neridah whispered to Patsy, "We need to make our way to the trees and hope we lose the soldiers in the darkness of the forest."

A flash of lightning, the brightest they'd seen since climbing out the window, illuminated the paddock, revealing a path neither had noticed before. The accompanying thunder crack was immediate and deafening.

They got up and raced for the trees, mud splashing over them as they went. It was at least fifty paces to the forest, and despite her legs moving faster than Patsy could remember, their destination seemed to remain ever more distant with each painful stride.

A soldier's voice called from the distance, "Someone's making a run for the trees!"

"There's two of them!"

"Stop them!"

They heard a loud blast like thunder, only different. It was followed by another, and then several more in quick succession.

Gunshots!

Patsy's chest hurt from the strain of breathing as they continued struggling to reach safety.

The sounds of the pursuit faded into the distance the moment they entered the forest.

The storm no longer persisted and, instead of running through the darkness of the morning downpour, their way was lit by beams of sunlight streaming through the trees.

Neridah grabbed Patsy's arm. "We need to stop for a moment."

Happy to oblige, Patsy stopped. She looked around. None of the trees looked familiar. "Nana-Neri, did you ever come across this path?" Before Neridah had a chance to reply, Patsy continued, "I thought I'd explored every inch of Father's property, but this looks totally unfamiliar to me."

"The trees are all wrong." Neridah turned and faced where they'd come from. "We've only run a short distance into the forest, but the house seems so far away." She turned back to Patsy. "And the storm… where'd that go?"

Before she had a chance to respond, Patsy noticed a small cloud of sparkles sweep past. She looked up at her grandmother and asked, "What's that?"

Neridah smiled, "It's pixie-dust!"

"Pixie-dust? What's that?"

"For us, a guiding light." She took Patsy's hand. "Come on, let's go after it."

The pixie-dust paused, as though waiting for them, then continued its merry dance through the trees. They ran on and on for close to an hour before the pixie-dust dispersed without warning and they found themselves staring at a small stone cabin with a roof of slate shingles.

The whole thing appeared from the outside to be too small for an adult to stand upright on the inside. There was a chimney at one end delivering a liberal quantity of white smoke that rose high before dissipating into the forest air.

Patsy asked, "Do you notice something strange about this?"

Neridah replied, "That's it's too small, and that it shouldn't be here?"

Patsy walked around to the other side. "There's no doors or windows." She looked across the roof at Neridah. "I want to see what's inside."

In the next instant, they found themselves sucked in toward the little cabin, then realised they were within the structure's walls. Patsy looked around in wide-eyed wonder when she saw how much bigger it was inside.

Meredith rose from her chair and raced across the now massive hall to embrace her mother and daughter. "Thank God, you made it!"

Patsy threw her arms around her mother.

Neridah joined them in a group hug, holding her daughter and granddaughter tight, then eased back when she noticed the small figure sitting by the fire. A goblet appeared in his hand that hadn't been there when Neridah had first noticed him.

Krinkle-myst remained in his chair. He took a sip from a goblet of spiced mead, savouring its soothing flavour. He turned to face Neridah and cut her off before she'd begun to ask a question. "In regard to your first question, the building is only ever as big as it needs to be. It has different needs outside and inside. And its internal needs change depending on how many people it's playing host to."

Patsy said, "The world doesn't work that way." She looked unconvinced and miserable as she stood shivering and dripping water on the stone floor.

The wood-elf got up from his chair and walked toward them. "Ah, Patricia McIntyre, or would you prefer I call you Patsy?"

Patsy's lips trembled as she asked, "How did you know that?"

Krinkle-myst ignored the question. "You are destined to be the most legendary of all the Witches of the Crossworlds. But what you need to understand is that, for all the vastness of the crossworlds you are destined to visit, there is still far more that exists beyond those realms." He sighed. "But we'll have to discuss that another time. You have more pressing concerns to deal with today. You and your grandmother need to warm yourselves by the fire. You won't be solving any problems if you catch a cold."

As if on cue, Patsy sneezed. She looked up and saw she had shifted from the far end of the room to be standing by the fire. Her legs collapsed under her and she fell into a chair that appeared at just the right time to catch her… a chair that she somehow knew would be there. She looked around and saw they were all seated by the fire and the room was smaller and cozier. The warmth of the flames was a welcome respite from what Patsy and Neridah had endured. Patsy extended her hands toward the flames. "We need to find out what Kerridwen did to Darcy."

Neridah was quick to respond, "We need to get Alfred back first."

Meredith followed up, "I want to ensure Colin's safe. He must surely have encountered the soldiers after he left for Springwood. And the servants, we need to protect them."

Neridah looked at her daughter and said, "You and Patsy should try to drive out the soldiers while I go through the portal and go after Alfred."

Krinkle-myst laughed. "And break up the Trilogy? You have many problems that require solving. And each one requires that you work together. The first thing you need to do is fetch the key for the Book of Wisdom. You won't solve your other problems without help from what's been written within its pages."

Patsy asked, "How can you know that?" She looked across at the wood-elf's writing desk that seemed closer now the room had shrunk. "The page you're working on… it's vellum, like in the Book—"

Krinkle-myst replied, "I've contributed to many books."

Patsy stared at him, enthralled. "You wrote the—"

"Parts of it, yes. As you have done, and many thousands of others."

"But I—"

"There is much that you have written in the future. Your contribution is greater than most have made."

Neridah said, "I don't understand."

Krinkle-myst turned to her. "And that's why your contribution is so small compared to that of your granddaughter. Despite all you've been through, you have so little understanding of how time works. It's small wonder you made such a mess of your time freeze." He stood up. "But I digress. There are many constraints of time that matter right now." He addressed Meredith, "Before the sun's last light today, you will need to place faith in someone who's intentions you distrust if your husband is to have any hope of being rescued from the gallows."

Meredith grasped her chest as her mouth hung open.

"If you attempt his rescue yourself, all hope of saving him, or bringing back Alfred or Darcy, will be lost."

Krinkle-myst turned to Neridah. "You will indeed travel to the world of Albiorix, but not on your own. Albiorix and his daughter are strong. Only the Trilogy of Crossworld Witches has a chance of defeating them in their own world. He has ways to influence Alfred to join his crusade. You will need to consult the Book of Wisdom and learn the power of written words to succeed. Your love for him is strong, and that is your greatest strength."

Neridah protested, "But what of his love for me? What power is there in my love if his is not equal?"

"Learn to look past your dreams and hopes and you'll see how deep his love for you truly is. You must trust in this, or else you'll surely fail." The wood-elf turned to Patsy. "And you, young lady, if you wish to see your friend Darcy again, must learn to think before you call on the science of magic."

Patsy crossed her arms in defiance. "My power is at its greatest when I'm angry."

"That's only because you don't understand the science of the magic."

Patsy's face contorted and her breaths grew shorter

Krinkle-myst stuck his arm out and dropped his now empty goblet. "See how that just fell to the floor? Was that not magic?"

Patsy's response was quick. "That's not magic, it's gravity. I've learned all about gravity. It's part of the science called physics."

Krinkle-myst smiled as he pointed his finger in the air. "Exactly! Yet the fact that you understand the science behind it doesn't reduce the magic of how something almost always falls when you drop it. All magic is driven by science, just not so much of it is well known or understood, even by some of its most accomplished practitioners. It's through gaining this understanding that you will reach your fullest potential."

He took a step back and addressed them all. "Now, it is time for you to retrieve the key and bring it back so you can learn what you must to defeat Albiorix and Kerridwen."

Her breathing having returned to normal, Patsy asked, "But how will we find our way?"

Krinkle-myst stepped toward the fire, reached in, and grabbed a handful of flame. He threw it in the air, and it became a dancing cloud of sparkling pixie-dust like the one Neridah and Patsy had followed through the forest. "Follow the dust. It will guide you there and back again whenever there is the need."

Neridah asked, "Will you be here when we return?"

"No, but the book will remain here till it is safe for it to return to your home. I've no doubt that we will meet again sometime soon." As soon as he'd finished his sentence, the wood-elf and his writing desk were gone.

*

Sean O'Malley stepped over Jimmy O'Sullivan's slumped body and made his way to the servants' kitchen. Sure enough, there was a bottle of rum on the sideboard. He pulled out the stopper with his few remaining teeth and spat it out as he made his way back down the corridor. This time, when he stepped over Jimmy's slumped form, he heard a moan escape the dying man's lips. Sean paused and splashed some rum over Jimmy's head. "You can have a drink on me." Satisfied with himself for what he saw as a noble gesture, he made his way out the door and ambled back to the stables.

On the other side of the bounds between reality and the void, Bandah, Talia, Mrs Smith and their Nasqa companion waited in anticipation, hoping that Sean O'Malley would be able to release them. The Nasqa turned its shadowy head to the others. *Ak-ney boe-jas pisa bo-opi bo-nassie-elphie gamoo. Bo-numma ja-dista ak-prac-nestwee ol-lie koop-boost-ast sess.*

Mrs Smith looked at Bandah. "Well?"

"He says we need to wait near where a time freeze has happened, that the bonds between worlds are weakened by a time freeze."

Sean O'Malley made it back to the stables, knelt down, and took a long swig from his stolen bottle of rum. He tossed the bottle aside. "Let's see what we've got here." He held his hands together and pushed them into the air in front of him before pulling them apart in a slow, deliberate action, then pushed his head into the gap and looked around. He smiled at the sight of Mrs Smith. "You're a funny looking fairy if ever I saw one."

"I was held captive in human form for just forty short years and this is what I'm stuck with now."

He looked toward Bandah and Talia. "Hmmph. Pixies! Well, *you* won't be leaving the void any time soon."

Bandah stepped forward to protest, but Talia held him back. "Don't bother, darling. Look at his eyes. You'll never get past hate like that."

Bandah looked at their shadowy friend. "But we—"

Again, Talia pulled him up and whispered in his ear. "At least if the fairy gets out, she may be able to get us help from elsewhere."

O'Malley said to the Nasqa, "Come on through. There's probably just enough of you there to take over my horse. It's a good healthy runner that one."

Without hesitation, the shadowy figure slipped through the hole O'Malley held open and was gone. O'Malley looked at the fairy and said, "Come on then, I'm not going to hold this open forever." He glanced at the pixies. "As for you, pixie vermin, you can rot forever in there for all I care." Mrs Smith flew out of the gap and was out of sight within seconds. Sean O'Malley released his grip on the hole into the void and let it snap shut. He picked up his bottle of rum, mounted his newly possessed horse, and rode off into the night.

Bandah squatted and buried his head in his hands. "I just can't believe it. I thought we could trust him."

Talia sat on the ground next to him. "Don't worry. Help will still come for us."

"Oh yeah? The options for where that might come from seem to be running out."

Talia stood slowly. "Honey, you need to see this."

Bandah turned to see what she was looking at. In all his years, he'd never seen something that surprised him quite so much. It was Mrs Smith, standing right where Sean O'Malley had been a minute earlier. She looked into the space around them. "I can't see you, but I trust you're still there. I'm going to get help. I'm going to find the witches and we'll get you out of there."

•

Colin groaned when Captain Taylor's boot connected with his belly. "You've caused me a good deal of anguish, McIntyre. I've a good mind to save the hangman the effort and finish you off myself before you face justice." He swung his boot again, pushing Colin up against the wall of his cell. "The only reason you'll live till sunset is because you killed a magistrate, so the Legislative Council will insist that justice is meted out in accordance with the law. If it were up to the Governor and myself, you'd be dead already."

Colin groaned. "I didn't kill anyone."

Another kick to the belly. "Liar!" The Captain departed the cell. He walked a few steps then turned and walked back. "By the way, the Justice of the Peace will be here in an hour for your trial. Try to make sure you're cleaned up and presentable by then." He grinned. "We do want you to look your best when you swing from the gallows."

*

The Reverend Alfred Casey sat next to Albiorix at the main table of the feast. There was an amazing variety of fruits, vegetables and breads. Alfred held up a yellow fruit with purple spikes protruding from its top. Albiorix leaned across and said, "That's an obellie. Tastes like an orange but has the texture of an apple. You need to peel it as you would a banana." He waved a hand across the table. "You'll not see any meat within this spread, Alfred. It's not that I've got anything against how many of the people on your world eat meat. Goodness no! I quite happily ate meat there, and while I travelled through many other worlds. But here, we have such an abundance of fruits and vegetables to choose from, there's no need to end another creature's life for the sake of simple sustenance. You know what, Alfred? During the centuries that I roamed your world, being treated as a god, your people would sacrifice all sorts of animals to me… even other people on occasion. It was all just part of their need to worship, and I took it as such. But I must stress, I never encouraged such behaviour. That was all due to the priests of the day. And that's what I like about you, Alfred! You're unique on your world! A priest who understands!"

A priest who understands? The Reverend was struggling to understand why Albiorix was so keen on him being there. He slowly peeled the fruit, almost oblivious to his host while he surveyed the scene around them.

All eyes were on him.

There were two dozen men and women who sat on the ground close by. Each of them reached out at some point to try to touch him. He turned to the closest and asked, "What's your name, boy?"

He came forward and knelt before the priest. "I've had many names over the centuries. Right now, I'm known as Felibrey the Humble. I've had the honour of serving in the garlands of both Kerridwen and Albiorix, and now I'm hoping you'll allow me to serve in yours."

"And how old would you be, Felibrey?" The Reverend took a bite of the obellie fruit as he waited for Felibrey's answer.

"I am past twenty thousand rounds of the seasons."

The Reverend turned his attention to Albiorix. "The boy, Felibrey, referred to serving in the garlands. What exactly does he mean by that?"

Albiorix slapped his hand on the table and laughed. "Hah! I was wondering when you'd ask about that." He gestured toward the crowd of devotees. "All of these beautiful men and women have served in the garlands. It's the ultimate training. They enter service as mere mortals, and they leave after a thousand years' service as immortals." He nudged the Reverend's shoulder and made a show of whispering in his ear. "And now, Alfred, they all long to serve you… to worship and protect you. As long as you are the bearer of a garland, you too will be immortal."

"And their garlands?"

"Some are merely floral decorations. Others are hosts for novices from a thousand worlds. They all aspire to live in what many on your world would refer to as heaven."

"Do these souls all enter service willingly?"

Albiorix spread his arms wide. "Look around you. Why wouldn't they? All of them have the opportunity to explore their full potential as artisans, as poets, philosophers, whatever their hearts desire."

The Reverend looked into the smiling faces of those who would be his disciples. "Be that as it may, I see little in the way of individualism among them." He turned back to Albiorix. "You still haven't told me the truth of why I was brought here."

Albiorix took on a more serious tone. "I've been unable to travel to your world for the past five thousand of your years. I very much miss the devotion and love of your world."

"What prevents you from travelling there? Why do you send your daughter in your place?"

"I am burdened by my own success as one who is worshipped. When so many look on you as a god, it becomes more difficult to travel through the portals. For thousands of years now, I have relied on priests of different faiths on your world to maintain the people's devotion. But, with time, the priests corrupted the faith of my followers to suit their own needs and desires."

"So, do you see yourself as a god?"

"No, not at all. I am a channel, a conduit for their worship to reach its intended destination. People see me as a god, as their god. But the truth is, gods are elusive. They rarely make their presence known or felt. Often, devotion that is meant for them becomes lost. Gods require devotion for strength, and I ensure they receive that devotion."

"But a part of it is withheld for your own gain?"

"A small percentage. It's a symbiotic relationship that all involved win from. I am an under-god. My service assists countless gods throughout what you would call the Crossworlds." He put his arm around Alfred's shoulder. "I know that your god insists his followers see him as the one true god, but can I tell you how many gods make the same claim? I have never shown favour to one god over another, but if you wish to continue to do so, that's fine with me. Just say you'll join me in my quest for all the gods to receive the devotion they deserve… that you'll become the under-god you were born to be, one who lives to focus the devotion of those who worship on your world."

CHAPTER 14

As the three witches struggled to keep up with the ball of pixie-dust, Patsy asked, "So, why haven't I heard about pixie-dust before?"

Meredith said, "It's the first I've heard of it as well."

Neridah smiled and looked over her shoulder toward the others. "It's one of my favourite memories from childhood. Mother used to ask me where I'd most like to go on the property, then she'd reach into the fire, throw a ball of pixie-dust, and I'd follow it."

Meredith frowned as she countered, "Well, that's something that was missing from my childhood." She couldn't help but feel disappointed. *Why did grandmother do that for my mother, but not for me?*

Patsy asked, "Why is it called pixie-dust?"

Neridah replied, "The pixies were the first to draw our attention to it." They ran on a bit further, then, between breaths, she added, "Ironically, it has nothing to do with the pixies. In fact, they rarely use it themselves."

The ball of pixie-dust came to an abrupt halt.

Taken by surprise, Meredith stumbled into her daughter, who'd been the only one to anticipate the stop. As they fell, Patsy threw an arm forward to cushion the impact, catching her grandmother's ankle in the process and causing her to also tumble to the ground. The three of them made for an interesting sight as they tried to disentangle themselves. Neridah and Patsy's nightclothes were already filthy and torn because of their earlier escape from the soldiers. Meredith, on the other hand, had transported herself to Krinkle-myst's cabin, so had mostly avoided exposure to the elements… until now. She landed face first in a generous mud puddle.

Meredith looked up and said, "It's raining." She pushed herself up, the front of her nightgown now covered in mud. "And it's freezing!"

Neridah, having also found her face in a puddle, pulled a strand of muddy hair from her mouth. "I noticed."

Patsy looked at the paddock and the house that stood in the distance then glanced over her shoulder to where they'd come from. The pixie-dust was gone, but the pathway they'd travelled along remained, with dappled sunlight sprinkled across the forest floor. "It's a portal." She got to her feet and took a step back onto the path, passing from the cold wet of Blackheath into the warmth of the other world. When she looked over her shoulder, she could barely even see the world she'd just stepped back from. It seemed somehow distant. "Can you hear me?"

Neridah and Meredith gave each other a puzzled look then Meredith said, "Of course we can. You're only a few paces away."

She walked backwards along the path. "I only need to take a few steps back and you disappear. I can't see you at all." She walked forward to what appeared to be a never-ending forest. The paddock, along with

Meredith and Neridah, reappeared, becoming clearer the closer Patsy got to them. She reached out and felt raindrops on her arm then took a tentative step from the sunlit forest into the rain-soaked paddock, rejoining her mother and grandmother.

Neridah looked toward the house. "We'd best keep quiet and stay out of sight. We can consider ourselves lucky we weren't seen." She glanced across at the garden shed. "If we stay low, we can make it to the shed without being seen. Then we can consider the best course of action from there."

Patsy was about to make a suggestion when she was distracted by something she saw out of the corner of her eye. She pointed to the low-flying fairy approaching them. "Look, it's Mrs Smith."

*

The Reverend took another bite of the obellie. He had to admit that it was probably the most delicious flavour he'd ever experienced. Kerridwen looked across at him. She picked up what looked like a green mandarin and began peeling it. "If you like the flavour of the obellie, then you'll likely love this even more." As the skin of the fruit fell away, she broke apart the segments of the red inner flesh and, leaning across her father, held one out for the Reverend. "It's called a phelare." Albiorix leaned back to make it easier for Kerridwen to reach across. The daisies in her garland turned toward the Reverend in expectation.

He looked at her smile and couldn't help but wonder about the wisdom of accepting anything the girl had to offer. The thoughts of one of those who would be a disciple ran through his head. *Oh, the phelare! You've never tasted it? I wish you wore a garland and I were in it now, so I could experience this with you.* He glanced around at the smiling faces that surrounded him. They looked full of innocence and awe, making it easy to ignore that these souls had lived for many thousands of years.

Albiorix's voice sounded distant. "Do you not trust my daughter?"

The Reverend looked back to Kerridwen. Where there had been a smile there was now a look of wistful sorrow, like that of a puppy seeking the affection of its master. Even the daisies within her garland seemed to wilt a little. Her smile returned when the Reverend reached across to take the fruit and said, "Thank you." Kerridwen's face glowed as her eyes followed the piece of fruit.

The Reverend felt the quiet expectation of all those around him. He took a bite from the small segment of fruit. The moment his teeth pierced its skin, the flavour began running through his mouth. It reminded him of a tender roasted lamb, but with the sweetness of fresh honey. The texture was like a runny jam. Tiny seeds rolled through his mouth and popped open, releasing small bursts of a subtle chilli-like bite that was immediately soothed by an aftertaste reminiscent of vanilla. When he swallowed, his mouth felt fresh, like it would after eating some mint leaves. He looked toward Kerridwen and said, "Delicious." Keen to savour more of the flavour, he took the rest of the segment into his mouth.

Kerridwen's eyes sparkled as she took a segment of the fruit for herself then offered the rest to the Reverend. She somehow looked older now that they were in her domain, more like a mature woman than the adolescent she'd appeared to be at the McIntyre property. He reached out and accepted the fruit, reminding himself that such perceptions were misleading when dealing with someone who'd lived for so long. He turned to Albiorix. "I can see why you wouldn't feel the need for meat when you have fruits with such abundant flavours."

Albiorix slapped him on the back, as he seemed so fond of doing. He plucked a berry from his garland and popped it into his mouth. "Hah! Wait until you try the fruits that will one day grow from your garland. The tastes you most enjoy, extracted from across a thousand worlds, their raw essence packaged in bubbles of strength."

"I've no desire to wear such a thing."

"Of course not! I wouldn't expect you to when you've just arrived. It wouldn't be in your nature."

The Reverend asked, "Why is it that yours is the only garland I see that bears fruit?"

Albiorix extended his hands by his side in a gesture that showed surprise, as though the answer should be obvious to all. "It is one of the privileges of an under-god."

The Reverend broke away another segment of the phelare then gestured toward Kerridwen. "Is not your daughter an under-god?"

Albiorix put his enormous arm around Kerridwen's shoulders and pulled her close to him as proud fathers are wont to do with their children when boasting of their achievements. Kerridwen wore a wry smile and looked away. Her father held his right hand over his heart. "Ah yes, but she is also a hunter! While she has the right to bear fruit as an under-god, such a thing would be a distraction from the importance of her role and could place her success in jeopardy."

The Reverend asked, "And what would that role be?"

"That, my friend, shall become clearer with time." He released his grip on Kerridwen's shoulder and placed a hand on the back of the Reverend's neck. "I want you to relax, Alfred. Your muscles are all tight and twisted… I can feel it." He glanced toward those who would be disciples. "The man needs a massage, across his shoulders and down his back." He clapped his hands. "Help the poor man relax. He's had little sleep and requires the attention of those who would serve him." He looked back to the Reverend. "Trust me, Alfred, you'll feel much better for it."

Before the Reverend had a chance to raise an objection, half a dozen hands had begun working at the knots in the muscles of his back and shoulders. He had to admit it felt good, and it seemed to protest would be seen by his host as provocation. He took another segment of the phelare fruit into his mouth. He hadn't even realised that he'd closed his eyes until Albiorix's voice snapped him back to reality.

The under-god held aloft a polished stone goblet encrusted with sparkling gems of every hue imaginable. A ring of blue stones, like gigantic sapphires, stood out just below the rim. "Some wine?" The offer made Alfred aware of his thirst. He took the goblet and drained it in one draught. He could hear the thoughts of his masseurs. *It's such joy to bring you relief... I look so forward to learning from you, the priest the hunter had promised to bring back for so long... We will be envied by all when we are in your service... The hunter was wise to choose you.*

The Reverend wondered about the last thought. *The hunter was wise to choose you.* Again, he realised only on opening them that he'd let his eyes fall shut. Kerridwen was now seated next to him, filling the goblet with more wine. She held it to his lips and said, "Drink of the wine, Alfred Casey, and let it help you rest as you prepare for your destiny."

He wanted to resist, but he found himself taking hold of the goblet and draining it once more. He moved back and forth, then became aware he was lying on a bed under the bough of a tree with sunlight streaming through. He felt his muscles relax more than they had in a long time. A dozen hands continued working on his back, legs and shoulders.

The hunter was wise to choose you.

What did it mean?

The last thing he saw before drifting off into a deep sleep was

Kerridwen's face as she leaned forward and whispered in his ear, "Sleep well and prepare."

•

Mrs Smith was frantic. "It's a good thing you're back. The pixies, they're trapped in the void between worlds… I was stuck there with them but was freed by a mind-thief-possessed gravedigger. He reached in and opened a hole in the membrane separating the void from existence. And Jimmy… he's barely clinging to life after a gunshot wound to his chest. The poor fellow's slumped in the hallway, just inside the door to the servants' quarters." She burst into tears. "I can't begin to tell you what a relief it is to see you three."

Neridah turned to the others. "We'll need to get to Jimmy before we worry about anything else."

Patsy added, "Going through the stables is probably the safest way for us to get to the servants' quarters. While we're there, we might as well try and rescue the pixies on our way."

Neridah replied, "And what do you suggest? Are we going to try to just reach in and open a hole like the mind thief?"

Meredith cut in, "Why not? If a mind thief could do it, then why can't we?"

Neridah screwed up her face and threw her hands in the air. "What are you thinking? We can't even consult the book for how to approach such a thing!"

Patsy said, "If the Nasqa could do it so easily, then maybe it's simple, like when we swim through the air or let ourselves be elsewhere. Maybe it's not a matter of trying, but of letting it happen."

Meredith looked at her mother and said, "It's worth a try."

Neridah asked, "What about soldiers? They're bound to have someone on guard."

Mrs Smith said, "I can round up the fairies from down near the creek and create a diversion."

Neridah felt the weight of Meredith and Patsy's expectation. She threw her hands in the air once more, looked to the sky, and said, "Okay, I give up. It's obvious you won't let up on this, so we might as well give it a try."

•

Bandah stared into space.

Talia ran a hand across the back of his shoulders. "Don't worry, baby, we'll get out of here sooner or later."

"I know that, but when? Will it be all too late by then?" He rubbed a hand against his forehead. "I can feel that Alfred's in trouble… big trouble." He looked up at Talia. "He's my grundai, and I've let him down."

"Oh, Alfred's in trouble! And we're not?"

"Are you even listening? There's a point to the commitment. Humans don't live for long. The ones who can make a difference deserve to be protected." Bandah looked to the ground. "I should have done better. He shouldn't be in the danger he's in."

Talia felt the blood pulsing through her temples. "An under-god flicked a finger and you were thrown into the void. How is that letting him down? And while we're at it, if you want to talk about promises and commitments, I'm your wife. Do you even remember the promises and commitments you made to me way back when?"

"And I've stuck to them."

She stood back and put her hands on her hips. "I beg your pardon!"

"What do you mean?"

"How many years has it been since you even bothered to contact me?"

"That's not a fair comparison you're making."

"It is from where I sit."

"I love you, surely you know that."

"It helps to get a reminder sometimes."

Bandah's attention seemed to stray.

"Hello?"

He pointed toward the trees. "Look, there. It's Mrs Smith." He turned to face his wife with a huge grin on his face. "She's been true to her word."

Talia's anger dissipated. "She must have found the witches!"

Mrs Smith said, "I don't know if you can hear me, but we've got a plan. Whatever you do, stay close to here. I promise you, I'll be back soon."

*

Vincent Donaldson pulled his coat tight. The rain was getting heavier. Today was Cook's day off, and he'd promised to take her into town for lunch. With luck, the rain would soon ease enough that they could still follow through on their plan. If not, he'd just have to settle for spending some time sitting with her by the fire at the McIntyres'.

He reached the turnoff that led to the property and noticed the road had been carved up by heavy traffic.

That could only mean one thing.

Soldiers.

He brought his sulky to a stop and ran his fingers along his waxed moustache, as he was wont to do when he was thinking. *I don't like this. I don't like it at all.*

He'd had dealings with Captain Taylor from the Springwood barracks before. And the last time he'd met up with Cook, she'd told of how Colin was feeling stressed because of attempts being made by a Sydney based magistrate to take over the property. If soldiers really were there, it more than likely had something to do with the magistrate she'd spoken of.

Vincent leaned back and opened the gun box that sat behind the driver's seat. He looked at the rifle and the loaded revolver, feeling glad that he'd followed his gut instincts and brought them with him today. His original concern regarded bushrangers. But with the reputation Captain Taylor's soldiers had built for themselves, he felt this was a far greater concern.

He closed the case and continued on his way.

*

The Reverend looked around as he rose from the bed. It was night, and the sky seemed unfamiliar. What had been a crowded and fertile landscape was now barren and dry.

The hunter was wise to choose you.

The thought continued to run through his head.

He moved toward the dry lakebed, then walked through an ancient market that appeared the moment his foot touched the cracked clay. The people wore long woollen robes and elaborate headdresses adorned with colourful feathers. Their skin was covered in dense fur, so short that it appeared like velvet. The faces had a feline quality, particularly around the nose and eyes. One of them was holding a decorated pot, inspecting the story illustrated on its surface. His fingers were longer than one would expect and, instead of fingernails, he had short claws. In the distance, a stepped pyramid towered over the landscape. At first, the Reverend couldn't make out what the people in the market were saying to one another, but it didn't take long before the language moulded into his own.

"Will you be going to the offering at sundown?"

"I wouldn't miss it. It'll be my son's first sacrifice."

"You must feel proud."

He walked on further and heard another conversation.

"That's a lot to pay for such small fruit."

"What do you expect? It's been almost a year since the last sacrifice."

"You blame the gods for a poorly tended crop?"

"Hey, there was no sacrifice last year. What do you expect? The gods punished us. They made us wait for the rains."

"We went almost a year without a sacrifice the season before, but there was plenty of rain."

"Don't expect me to know what the gods are thinking. That's the job of a priest, not a merchant."

He walked on but was pushed to the side as warriors came through, forcing a pathway through the crowd.

"Look, here he comes!"

"It's the priest!"

A muscular figure with a long dark mane of hair and a stern expression walked through the newly created passage. As he walked, the Reverend noticed the man's shadow reaching out and making threatening gestures to the crowd.

The Reverend turned at the sound of Kerridwen's voice. She was behind him, but unseen. "He's betrayed us! He's allowed himself to be taken by Nasqa! How could you let this happen?"

Albiorix's voice responded, "Don't worry, this will not go unpunished." As he spoke, the people disappeared. Within seconds, the city became desolate and overgrown by weeds.

The images dissolved away and a thick fog descended. The Reverend sensed a sentience within it as a deep voice echoed through the mist, "What do you have to offer?"

The response came from behind him. "The devotion of billions who would not know of you without my guidance." It was Albiorix, his voice carrying a humility that was unfamiliar to the Reverend.

The god's voice came not from a specific point, but from everywhere. "So, he who would be under a god, what would you seek in return?"

"Nothing more than to be the conduit for your devotion."

"I have dealt with your kind before. While it's true that without regular devotion, a god cannot exist, your kind are parasites. But you are a parasite that a god needs to survive in these times of change."

"All times are times of change."

There was a brief pause. "How many other gods do you now work under?"

"Not more than one hundred and fifty-two at last count."

"And how many of those would be darker gods?"

Albiorix stuttered for a moment then went quiet.

"Don't test my patience, Albiorix, or you may regret it."

There was an uncomfortable silence before Albiorix replied. "There had been some among those I served who were darker than I had imagined."

"There is dark or there is light."

Albiorix's voice betrayed a great pain underlying his words. "It is not always that clear when one works under a god."

"How can I be expected to trust one who is so uncertain?"

"I am certain now that I will serve only those where the light is clear."

"And what led you to this wiser path?" There was a long pause. "ANSWER ME!"

Albiorix whispered, "They... they took my wife."

The fog cleared to reveal a star-filled sky. The Reverend was surrounded by a ring of roughly cut stones set up to form a circle.

"Alfred!" It was Kerridwen's voice, coming from behind him.

He turned and saw her silhouette approaching. "Where are we?"

"A place that will be known as the Drombeg stone circle. My father had the people of your world construct this circle of standing stones not long before your ancestors banished him. He had them build many stone circles over thousands of years. They were built around portals, like the one on the McIntyre property. Whenever the portal shifted, he had a new circle built around the new location. They helped to channel the devotion to where my father and the druid priests directed it."

"My ancestors?"

"Your ancestors, and Neridah's ancestors. Did you not know? You come from the same bloodline. That's why you were able to absorb her father's power. You were born to be a druid priest."

Alfred was speechless.

Kerridwen came up to him and placed a hand on his shoulder. The Reverend could feel the warmth of her breath as mist rose from her lips before dissipating into the cold night air. "We need you. Your god needs you. All the gods that the people of your world worship need you. Without someone to channel their devotion, many of their prayers go unheard. We, the under-gods, are the brokers who ensure the prayers get heard by the gods they were intended for. People will follow you. Accept what we offer, and you will be a leader on your world. You'll bring change. You'll make your world a better place."

The Reverend looked around. The darkness had been replaced by the paddock outside his church. It was filled with a vast crowd, all eyes looking to the Reverend and Kerridwen. There must have been tens of thousands of people. They were all bowing toward him and chanting: "The hunter was wise to choose you."

"Together, Alfred, we will bring the people of your world to a spiritual enlightenment. It is not so much which god they worship, but that they must worship. It will make them stronger and more resilient, as it will the gods their devotion is channelled to."

An image rose up in the back of the Reverend's mind. It distracted him. It was a memory of a thought… of an emotion… of love.

Neridah.

Kerridwen grabbed hold of his shoulders and turned him to face her. "Don't let outside thoughts distract you and destroy the potential of our mission and what we can build together." The crowd was gone, as was his church. "The future of a thousand worlds relies on you."

The Reverend's eyes narrowed.

Kerridwen stamped her foot and clenched her fists. "You need to restore the balance." As Kerridwen's anger rose, the daisies of her garland began to lurch out and snap at the Reverend, never moving more than a hand's width from Kerridwen's head, but still enough to be intimidating. "The balance that was lost when the ancestors of those witches you're so fond of banished my father at Drombeg." She looked deep into his eyes. "We need you to help us right the wrongs."

The Reverend could feel movement around his scalp. He reached up and confirmed his suspicion. There were flowers coming together in a garland. The thoughts of his would-be disciples echoed through his head… a dozen voices all repeating the same thought. *The hunter was wise to choose you. The hunter…*

"Listen to them."

The Reverend stared at her as he tore the garland from his head and examined it, searching for signs of the personalities within.

Kerridwen fell to her knees, tears streaming down her cheeks. She buried her head in her hands.

The Reverend turned his gaze back to her, his eyes cold with brewing rage.

She looked up and said, "Do you have any concept of what it's like for an under-god to be banished? The humiliation?" Her own daisies had withdrawn and appeared to be wilting. "He didn't just lose the gods he worked under for your world. When news of his humiliation at the hands of a few human witches spread, other gods lost faith in his ability to hold the devotion of their followers. He had no choice." She looked up into the Reverend's unmoving eyes. "He took on work for darker gods. They took my mother, Alfred. And it was all because of three pathetic little witches."

The Reverend looked at the garland then tossed it aside. "This is just a dream." He turned and walked off into the darkness. "I'll not be drawn in by such mind games."

He walked on.

Again, he found himself approaching Drombeg.

There were three women in flowing white robes. The moon was full, its light making their flesh glow. They were talking to a small elf-like creature. As the Reverend approached, the women seemed unaware of him. They concluded their discussion with the wood-elf then started to dance around the circle.

As the wood-elf approached, the Reverend squatted low to look him in the eye. "I've not seen a creature like yourself before. Would you have a name, or a title, that you go by?"

"The name's Krinkle-myst. And I must say, Alfred, it's a pleasure to meet you." The wood-elf extended a hand.

The Reverend looked at the little hand, but instead of extending his own, he asked, "Would you be in league with the under-god and his hunter?"

Krinkle-myst laughed. "Heaven forbid! Goodness, no. I've far more important things to deal with than helping the likes of them." He raised a finger to emphasise the point he was preparing to make. "And I can assure you. They won't know you and I have had discussions." He turned and watched the witches dance. "They move beautifully, don't you think?"

The Reverend watched in awe. Their movements were fluid and graceful. As their pace quickened, a small fire flickered into life at the circle's centre. It was a fire that burned without fuel. The flames grew higher with each footfall of the witches' dance, with each pirouette, each turn or leap. The fire seemed to be in sync with them.

"This is the ritual to banish Albiorix, just as it happened," Krinkle-myst explained.

"Are the under-gods aware I'm witnessing this?" the Reverend asked, as he continued watching the dance.

"Oh yes, they intended that you would."

The witches picked up torches and lit them from the central flame, making that part of the ritual appear as a natural component of their performance.

The Reverend took a small step forward as the torches illuminated the dancers' faces.

Each one was familiar.

Krinkle-myst looked up at the Reverend's shocked expression. "This is what they wanted you to see. They want you to associate the witches you know with those who banished Albiorix."

"Did he deserve it?"

"He was playing favourites… taking devotion meant for one god, and sending it to another, all for the sake of his own gain."

"So, you intervened?"

"No, that's not my job. But I did let those who could intervene know what was happening. I also helped them find the pages in the Book of Wisdom that would help them do what they had to do." He turned from watching the dance to face the Reverend. "Misdirected devotion is a dangerous thing. It tears at the moral fabric that holds all of everything together. And that makes my job so much harder." He sighed. "And it also makes Mrs Krinkle-myst unhappy. She'd much prefer that I spend time with her, helping untangle people's sad thoughts and turning them into happy ones."

"What would you have me do?"

"Trust in the one who loves you." As he spoke the words, Krinkle-myst began fading away.

"Alfred!" There was a hand shaking his shoulder. "You need to wake up." There was an urgency in Kerridwen's voice.

The Reverend opened his eyes and saw those who would be his disciples gathered around as he lay on the bed with Kerridwen standing over him. Her smile triggered an identical reaction from the Reverend's devotees.

Alfred rubbed his eyes and said, "As far as dreams go, that was one of the more memorable." He looked at Kerridwen. "The visions in my dream, they were your doing?"

Kerridwen threw her head back and laughed. "Oh, my poor Alfred." She leaned in close, ran a finger down his cheek, and whispered. "This is all about helping you find your destiny."

He grabbed hold of her hand and pushed it away. "Then why was the need to wake me so urgent?"

Kerridwen's expression softened. She almost looked sad. "There was a moment where I lost sight of you. You were hidden from me like there was someone else steering you away from your purpose." She took on a serious tone. "You cannot do this without my guidance."

He felt himself drifting back to sleep as the would-be disciples began chanting: "The hunter was wise to choose you."

CHAPTER 15

"You must be crazy," said Elpheen. The fairy's iridescent emerald eyes glared at Mrs Smith. "Why would we want to help you?" Waves of blonde hair flowed over her shoulders and down to her waist. A frown was etched into her face as she hovered in front of Mrs Smith.

Mrs Smith replied, "I'm still one of you. And it's not me you'd be helping. This is about the witches."

"Hah! You don't even go by a fairy name anymore. You gave that up years ago." Her eyes narrowed, "And you can never change that."

Another fairy, Eldah, flew forward. "Of course we'll help." She turned to the others gathered by the creek, well upstream from where the Nasqa-possessed soldiers were patrolling. "What do you say?"

One by one, they flew forward.

"You can count me in."

"How could we not?"

"I think it goes without saying."

"We'll never forget what they did."

Elpheen protested, "You are joking, aren't you? They went in there to rescue one of their own!"

Mrs Smith turned to her and said, "And they could have left you there. They could have left me there. They could have left us all behind."

Elpheen glared at the others. "I guess I don't have much choice in the matter." She sarcastically threw her hands in the air. "I was so obviously wrong."

Mrs Smith took to the air. "Come on then, let's work some fairy magic on them."

As they flew off, Elpheen trailed behind the others. *How dare that freak make a fool of me*, she thought to herself. *One day I'll make her pay for this. She'll end up wishing she'd stayed in human form.*

*

Within the Reverend's dream, Kerridwen's voice was distant but forceful. "It's time to choose the disciples that will make up your garland."

A hundred voices echoed through his head.

The hunter was wise to choose you.

"You'd have me choose from these voices running through my head?"

He could see her now, standing before him, the would-be disciples standing behind her. "Every one of them would die for you."

He watched the movement of the daisies in her garland. "I'll not wear one of those things around my head."

"You don't need to. And I wouldn't want you to… at least, not while in your world. Once they are chosen, they will follow you. They'll be your garland whether they be flowers you wear as a crown or whether they be followers who walk with you. There have been many under-gods who have walked through your world with garlands of twelve disciples. Some have even been mistaken for gods or prophets." She looked at the anger in the Reverend's eyes. "Oh, don't worry, true gods and prophets have also had garlands of twelve, but only when they chose to walk through a world in mortal form. It's part of the natural order. We just use ours more proactively than they tend to."

"Why twelve?"

She shrugged her shoulders. "No one really knows. Some things just have to be accepted for what they are, as part of the natural order."

He turned away and shook his head. "I've no wish to do this. I'll not be seen to have disciples."

"Just do it, Alfred. The longer you put this off, the harder it becomes for everyone concerned."

The hunter was wise to choose you.

The Reverend looked around at the faces. "Why do they say that?"

"Perhaps, it's because they believe in you. And I do too, despite your persistent recalcitrance."

The hunter was wise to choose you.

They were getting louder. He stared at the ground near his feet.

"It's time for you to choose, Alfred." She placed a hand on his shoulder and lifted his chin with her other hand, forcing him to look her in the eye. "Time for you to make wise choices."

He tried to hold on to his memories of those he loved, but they were slipping away, leaving a dark void that he felt in the depths of his soul.

There was one person in particular, but her name eluded him.

The darkness was replaced by images from his future. Huge crowds gathered to listen to him preach. Kerridwen and his disciples by his side.

He walked through streets with throngs of people reaching out to touch him, their faces glowing with adulation.

It felt like years had passed when he heard Kerridwen's voice work its way into the dream he was having within his dream. "Choose, Alfred." She softened her tone. "They won't leave you to sleep in peace until you do."

The hunter was wise to choose you.

He looked around once more at the souls who would be his disciples. "My first choice is Felibrey the Humble."

•

The fairies flew up through the rain. They approached the stables from the high end of the paddock. When they felt they were close enough to be heard by the soldiers inside, they began singing.

Est nar-deh ace lief eft-lei bre kay,
Eft-lei kay maelief est ses-deh teal.

The words loosely translated as, "You don't know where we'll all be, we'll be somewhere you can't see." They sang in counterpoint harmonies that contrasted against the sound of the ongoing downpour. Despite the sweetness of the melody, the rain thundered so loudly that the handful of soldiers stationed in the stables were barely able to hear the fairies' voices.

The soldier closest to the upper end of the stables asked, "Did you hear that?"

His nearest colleague raised an eyebrow as he focused on the song. He looked up and said, "Fairies!" He turned to the other soldiers in the stables who were gathered around an upturned wheelbarrow they were using as a card table.

One of them looked up and asked, "Should we check it out?"

"Aye," replied the first soldier.

They picked up their rifles. Some made their way to the lower end while the rest went in the opposite direction, with the idea that they'd be able to surround the fairies behind the stables.

The first soldier to look around the corner of the building pointed. "There they are." The group of fairies flew away from the building toward the top of the paddock. Without a second thought, the soldiers ran after them.

Once the fairies had led the soldiers over the crest of the hill, the mud-soaked witches moved out from the cover of the trees. As they dragged themselves forward, it would have been hard to distinguish them from the dull background.

Unknown to the witches, there was one soldier who had stayed behind. They had almost reached the stables when he looked their way.

"Halt! Who goes there?"

Neridah and Meredith came to a stop, but Patsy was undeterred. Breaking into a run, she continued moving forward. Meredith reached out to grab her, but it was too late.

Patsy thought to herself, *If Kerridwen can rip out a mind thief. Why can't I?*

The soldier lowered his rifle so its bayonet was directed at her.

Patsy's momentum was carrying her toward it. There was no way she could stop in time to save herself.

"Hey! You should be ashamed of yourself, pointing that thing at a child." The voice next to his ear took the soldier by surprise. He turned his rifle toward the source of the sound as Mrs Smith disappeared into the darkness.

Patsy crashed into the soldier and did as she'd seen Kerridwen do before.

Don't think about it. It's like everything else. Let it happen.

She reached into his chest with ease and pulled out the Nasqa, throwing it as far away as she could.

The soldier fell to the ground.

She grabbed hold of his shoulders. "What's your name?"

He blinked, then said, "William Daniels." He looked at her, surprised by the young girl's confidence. "Who are you?"

"Listen to me, William. You need to shut your mind, and you need to shut it now! You need to make sure that thing can't re-enter you."

Neridah came up from behind. She grabbed Patsy's shoulder and swung her around to face her. "How could you be so foolish?"

Patsy frowned. "What do you mean? I just saved him."

"And probably ruined any chance we had of surviving this."

The soldier asked, "Who are you people?"

A distant voice called out from the front veranda of the main house, "They're at the stables!"

Neridah struggled to contain her anger. "You ripped it out without a thought of what it might do afterward."

Meredith stood in the spot where she could feel the time freeze had happened. "But we're here now. Can't we at least try to get Bandah and Talia out of the void."

"There's no time, we need to go."

Patsy ignored her grandmother. She went down on her knees next to her mother and did exactly as Mrs Smith had described the gravedigger doing. When she pulled her hands apart the two pixies flew out of the void before she'd even had a chance to see them.

Talia landed on her shoulder and hugged her around the neck.

"Thank you."

Bandah was already flying toward the servants' quarters. "Let's save the gratitude for later. These three ladies need to make a run for cover while we tend to Jimmy."

Talia lifted into the air. "He's right. They won't even notice us while they're going after you. This is the best chance there's going to be to save him." She was already flying after Bandah. "His wounds are easy enough to heal, but there's little time."

Neridah said. "This isn't good. We need that key." She glared at Patsy. "That was supposed to be why we're here."

"And what key would that be?" They all turned to see a soldier approaching with his rifle fixed on them. "Get on the ground, with your hands behind your head. You too, Daniels."

The soldier felt the coldness of gunmetal on the back of his neck. "I'd drop that rifle if I were you." It was Vincent Donaldson with his revolver.

The soldier let his rifle fall.

Patsy casually stood up and walked toward him.

Neridah called after her, "Patricia, we don't have time for this!"

Meredith grabbed her mother's arm and said, "Let her do it, Mother. We need all the allies we can get."

Neridah looked toward the soldiers approaching from the house. "We don't have time."

Patsy ignored them both. She reached forward, but the soldier slumped to the ground before she'd even touched him. The mind thief, or Nasqa, had preferred to flee the host of its own accord than suffer the humiliation of being torn out by a young girl.

Vincent raised an eyebrow as he watched Patsy reach down to help her fallen adversary.

A gunshot rang out.

William helped Patsy raise his comrade to his feet. "Come on, we need to go."

Vincent stood his ground and returned fire, sending off three shots in quick succession before he turned and joined the others in their dash for the trees.

•

The Reverend groaned, tossing and turning in his induced sleep.

"You've chosen one." Kerridwen stood over him, both inside and outside of his dream. "Now, who will be the next?"

The Reverend's head was buried in his hands. "I don't know them."

Felibrey sat next to him. "If it's your wish, I'm happy to help you. I've known them all for a long time. I can tell you of their strengths and weaknesses."

"That's interesting, lad. You call yourself humble, yet you offer judgement on others?"

Kerridwen was fed up with taking the gentle approach. She looked up and shook her head in exasperation. "Can we *please* just get on with it?" She glared at the Reverend while gesturing to Felibrey. "He absolutely reeks of humility. Can you just go with his offer? Otherwise, we'll be here forever while you procrastinate over your choices."

The Reverend lifted his head and surveyed the dreamscape. Within this phase of his dream, the disciples looked as they were to born to be, as opposed to the masking of reality within Albiorix's celebration. There were lifeforms that defied description and those that seemed familiar. He looked across at a soul far off in the distance who seemed more concerned with reading his scroll than what was happening around him. He had pale blue flesh and deep black eyes. "You, the lad with the scroll, what's your name?"

Kerridwen interjected, "No, you can't choose him. He is not one who would choose to be your disciple. He is here as an observer. His interest lies only in learning rather than service." She stared at the creature who continued reading from his scroll, oblivious to the unwanted attention he was garnering.

"Nevertheless, he interests me."

Feeling the intensity of the Reverend's eyes on him, the creature glanced up from his scroll. "They call me Bordauex the Learned." He turned back to his scroll and continued reading.

Felibrey whispered into the Reverend's ear. "He is from a world where learning is not valued. Since his arrival here two thousand years ago, he has rejected the quick path to knowledge and the grace that comes from service in the garlands, preferring to spend his days buried in the slow learning that comes from reading books and scrolls."

"I like those who seek knowledge in the pages of books." He looked across at Bordauex. "You are welcome to join me, Bordauex the Learned."

Kerridwen's knuckles whitened as she clenched her fists. "Alfred, you need to choose from those who would follow you. Urgh, you can be so frustrating."

Bordauex looked up from his scrolls. "Are books and learning valued in your world?"

"Aye. I have learned much from books, and those who I care to spend time with have done the same."

Bordauex stood up from his desk and said, "Very well then. I shall join with the others in their desire to follow you and say that the hunter was wise to choose you."

Kerridwen said, "Alfred, these choices are supposed to be about building your power, about making you stronger."

The Reverend's voice was calm. "Your understanding of power is obviously very different to my own."

*

"We need to do it."

Meredith put a hand on Patsy's shoulder. "No, it's far too big a risk."

Neridah said, "Patricia's right. I have to agree with her on this one."

Meredith sighed and shook her head. "I'm not happy about it."

"What are you talking about?" asked Vincent as he continued watching the paddock.

"I need to ask something of you, Vincent," said Meredith. "I need you to trust that Patricia, my mother, and myself are able to secure Cook's safety."

He stared at her for a few seconds without responding before turning his attention back to the soldiers. "I'm listening."

"But there's more than that." She paused to compose herself. "Captain Taylor has taken Colin to Springwood, with the intention of taking him to the gallows before day's end." She looked at the two soldiers who had joined them, then back to Vincent. "You and these two soldiers are his only hope."

"I'm not leaving this property till I know that Cook's out of harm's way."

Patsy said, "Don't worry, Mister Donaldson, we'll make sure she's safe."

"All these soldiers, against two women and a child? No." He was looking at Patsy, then turned to Meredith. "Don't get me wrong, I care about your husband as though he was a brother. But my first concern has to be Cook."

Daniel Williams stepped forward. "Forgive me if I'm speaking out of turn, but I really think you should listen to them." He looked at Patsy then back to Vincent. "I swear to you; your friend is safe in their hands. And they're right. If Mister McIntyre is to be saved from the gallows, he'll need the three of us to leave now to ride into Springwood and do what we can to intervene."

Neridah approached Vincent. He looked perplexed as she placed a hand on the side of his head and said, "You need to remember." She closed her eyes and began whispering, "Nelkar cane phay-tamullah ma-bel dae predae." She opened her eyes and pulled her hand away.

Memories of extraordinary events that had taken place the year before flooded through Vincent's head. He lowered his rifle and looked at the witches, studying each of them. When his gaze reached Patsy he said, "Are you sure of this?"

"I promise, Mr Donaldson, Cook will be safe when you get back. Just please, can you promise me you'll bring Father back with you?"

He bent over, placing a firm hand on Patsy's shoulder. "I can't make any promises. We'll be greatly outnumbered, and I've no idea how many soldiers we'll be up against."

Williams said, "Most of the soldiers still at the barracks aren't possessed as yet by these things that take over the mind. Those that are won't want to have the truth revealed. They'll need to take him before a Justice of the Peace for a sentence to be passed before they can lead him to the gallows. He's accused of the murder of a magistrate, and Captain Taylor will claim that he's too dangerous to risk transporting him to Sydney for a proper trial."

Vincent replied, "But surely if the crime is that serious, there's no choice but to take him to Sydney."

Williams shook his head, "The Governor himself is possessed by one of these things, and he is desperate to take control of this property. There will be tremendous pressure on the Justice to pass sentence swiftly. And if he does declare that Mr McIntyre should be tried in Sydney, Captain Taylor will ensure he dies en route. One way or the other, without our intervention, he'll be dead by sundown."

Meredith took both of Vincent's hands in hers. "Please, bring him back to me."

Vincent looked down at her hands, then brought his gaze up to meet her eyes. "I'll do what I can."

She threw her arms around him, burying her face in his shoulder. "Thank you."

Vincent returned the embrace then turned to the soldiers. "Do you two have horses up there in the stables?"

William replied, "We'd never get them out of there without getting caught."

Patsy said, "I've got an idea."

They all turned to hear what she had to say, but in that instant, she was gone.

•

Lieutenant Neil Stewart didn't appear surprised when Patsy materialised in the library. "I was wondering when you'd turn up." He held up the key as he leaned back in the leather-lined chair and put his feet up on Colin's desk. "Are you looking for this?" She watched the hideous shape of his shadow through the matted hair that draped over her eyes. Its talon-like fingers dangled a silhouette of the key near the muddy puddle at her feet.

"Oh, yes," said Patsy. "And I'll be taking it with me when I leave here."

"You really should be more careful of the situations you transport yourself into."

Hearing boots on the floorboards behind her, Patsy turned around and saw three soldiers just inside the door to the library pointing guns at her. Another walked toward her with a rope.

"Oh, and you'll have fun trying to reach into our souls with your hands tied behind your back."

Patsy closed her eyes, preparing to let herself be elsewhere.

The Lieutenant laughed, "Hah!" He took his feet off the desk and pointed her way. The soldier with the rope was tying Patsy's hands as the Lieutenant continued, "I knew you'd try that. But all those little time freezes that were happening in here today… oh my, how they play havoc with how the fabric between crossworlds reacts." He put the key down next to the inkwell and made a show of holding his hands out then brought them closer together as he walked around to the front of the desk. "The space around where the freeze happened slowly closes in, making it easy to pop in… but when you try to pop out? Why, it's a bit like having your feet stuck in a bucket of molasses. When your mother managed to get out with the book, the ability to leave that way from here pretty much snapped shut behind her." He leaned back against the desk and crossed his arms. "Now, I wonder how long it'll take before your mother and grandmother make the same mistake as you."

CHAPTER 16

"Oh, Patricia." Meredith beat a hand against her brow. "Why? Why can't she be more patient?"

Neridah said, "Probably because she didn't believe we'd let her do it."

Meredith looked up. "And for good reason."

Neridah looked out at the paddock. "Maybe not. Look, the soldiers, some of them are heading up to the house." She turned to Vincent and the soldiers. "This could be your chance to get the extra horses you need from the stables."

Vincent shook his head. "There's still more of them out there looking for you."

"That's just it, they're looking for us. They'll be assuming that you and the soldiers made a run for it as soon as they were set free."

"I think my mother might be right," said Meredith.

Vincent wasn't convinced. "They know I'm trying to help you."

Neridah said, "Think about it, Vincent. Think about what happened last year. They know how powerful we are together. If they think the three of us are in the house together, they'll want every mind thief they can muster up there. We just need to keep them distracted long enough for you to get to the stables undetected."

"And you'll be able to get Cook out of there?"

"Not yet, there's too many of them for us to defeat them straight away. We need to get a few things from inside and get out of there while we put our plan together."

Meredith said, "She's right, Vincent. They can feel where we go to when we travel the way Patricia did just now. They'll follow us."

Vincent looked at a group of soldiers who were heading toward the bushes they were hiding in. "Then, doesn't that mean they can tell where she came from as well?"

There was no answer. He turned around and both women had vanished.

•

Neridah appeared in the room Alfred was using as his temporary accommodation. The box he'd retrieved from his house when it burnt down was on the bedside table. She picked it up, then allowed herself to be in her own room. She went straight to the wardrobe and grabbed some clean clothes and shoes, then heard soldiers running up the stairs as she allowed herself to be in Meredith's room. Meredith appeared just after her, holding a bundle of clothes from Patsy's room. She dropped them on her bed then grabbed a suitcase from the top of the wardrobe. The soldiers had reached the top of the stairs.

Neridah whispered, “I grabbed enough for both of us.”

Meredith nodded. Once she’d opened the suitcase, they threw the clothing and the Reverend’s box in.

Neridah said, “We need to send it to the shed.”

“Can we do that without going there ourselves?”

“We have to try.”

Meredith slammed the case shut, closed her eyes, and thought of the garden shed, allowing the suitcase to be there. She opened her eyes as the soldiers kicked the door open.

The suitcase was still there.

A soldier raised his rifle and said, “Put your hands up.”

Neridah grabbed the suitcase and said, “My room.”

A shot rang out as the witches disappeared.

When they materialised in Neridah’s room she said, “We need to see it. Look, through the window.” They both closed their eyes, visualised the suitcase in the shed, and allowed it to be there. They opened their eyes as the soldiers kicked the door in. The suitcase was gone. Neridah looked at Meredith and said, “Library.” The next instant, they were gone.

*

Vincent let out a breath he'd held for over a minute when the soldiers turned away. He said to his companions, “That was close.” They looked across the paddock. The witches were right in their assumptions. All the soldiers were making their way up to the house. Once they were more than halfway, Vincent said, “We won’t have much time. Let’s go.”

The rain eased as they worked their way up the hill toward the stables. They froze at the sound of a kookaburra bursting into laughter in a tree not far from them. When it was clear the soldiers had ignored the bird, they continued walking.

Having reached the back of the stables, they clung to its walls and shimmied around to the lower entrance then, one by one, slipped inside. Williams remained silent as he pointed out the saddled horses not controlled by mind thieves.

There were just two of them.

Vincent was fine with that. He knew his own horse well enough that he felt comfortable with the idea of unhitching it from the sulky and riding it bareback if he had to.

"Hey, what are you up to?"

They turned around to see a soldier raising his rifle at them. Vincent pulled out his hunting knife and threw it as the soldier prepared to pull the trigger. The soldier let out a dull scream when the knife lodged in his shoulder. As he fell to the ground, he fired his rifle into the air, drawing the attention of other soldiers nearby.

Vincent said, "Now or never." They ran for the horses, Vincent leaping into the saddle of one while Williams jumped onto the other. Vincent lifted the other soldier to join him on the back of his mount then kicked his heels into the beast, causing it to rear up before it hit the ground running for the road.

"Stop them!"

They rode away from the stables, surrounded by the sound of gunfire. They were on the road out of the property when Vincent heard a bullet whiz past his ear then felt a jolt from behind. The soldier he was carrying had taken a bullet in the back. His arms fell away, then he fell off the back of the horse. Williams looked over his shoulder and called out, "We can't go back for him." Vincent turned his head and saw that Williams was right. The soldier was already dead.

He caught up to Williams and said, "I don't see anyone riding after us."

"No, the Lieutenant wants to keep everyone he has left there to fight against the witches. He'll likely send word somehow to the Barracks about us. We'd best keep our heads low. That soldier they shot as we were leaving will be blamed on us. We'll be wanted for his murder now."

*

Meredith and her mother appeared in the library on either side of Patsy.

Lieutenant Stewart smiled while he picked at his fingernails. "Well, that took a while. I was starting to wonder whether you even care about the girl."

Patsy looked at her mother and said, "The key. It's on the desk."

Neridah reached toward the desk and pulled back. The key flew toward her as though they were connected by a rubber-band. As her hand snapped shut around it, she said, "The shed."

Patsy looked up at her grandmother. "I tried it before. It doesn't work now. The time freezes have left us stuck here."

Meredith said, "Don't underestimate the power of the Trilogy."

The Lieutenant addressed his troops. "Shoot them."

The three witches closed their eyes as the gunshots rang out. They opened them a moment later in the shed, staring straight into the face of the Lieutenant. He grinned. "Well, that was a fun ride. I must say, I am impressed by what you three can achieve together." He took a step toward them. "But it won't help you now."

Neridah leaped forward and reached for his chest, as she'd seen Patsy do earlier.

Lieutenant Stewart laughed as he swung his arm across, the back of his hand connecting with Neridah's cheek and sending her to the floor.

Meredith looked around and saw the suitcase she'd transported to the shed before and stretched out to place a hand on it. She turned to her mother and said, "The pathway."

They closed their eyes and could feel the rain on their backs before they'd even opened their eyes.

Once again, they saw the Lieutenant's sardonic smirk. "We can play this game all day. Wherever you go, I will follow."

Meredith's jaw dropped when she looked past the Lieutenant. Where before there had been dense bushes, a pathway had revealed itself, a potential portal to safety via an altogether different world. Golden sunshine beamed through the trees. There was no doubt in her mind. It was the pathway to Krinkle-myst's cabin, where the Book of Wisdom was waiting for them to return. It had to be.

Meredith looked at the beckoning pathway behind the Lieutenant. "Maybe not." She lifted the suitcase and swung it by the handle so it connected with the Lieutenant's head, sending him to his knees. She turned to Patsy and Neridah, "Run!"

The path was just a few strides away.

Patsy wanted to take her grandmother's hand, but her own were still bound behind her back. As she followed her mother across the threshold between worlds, she looked over her shoulder and called out, "Come on, Nana-Neri."

Neridah was almost across the threshold herself when she felt a hand grip onto her ankle, pulling her to the ground. She turned just in time to see the humour had drained from Lieutenant Stewart's face.

"Where are they? How could they just vanish like that without me feeling where they'd gone?"

Beyond the threshold, Patsy said, "He can't see us!" She turned to her mother. "Cut me free, so we can help her."

"No time." Meredith stepped back through the threshold and into the rain. She pulled her hand back and drew power from across a hundred worlds.

Lieutenant Stewart looked up at the woman with the matted hair and mud-covered nightclothes. His expression betrayed his fear. He let go of Neridah and started to back away.

Meredith threw her hand forward, releasing the energy burst. Lieutenant Stewart was lifted off the ground by the impact, landing on his back several paces away.

The strain of drawing up energy from the Crossworlds after so many transportations left Meredith drained. She swayed back and forth and watched the world around her fall out of focus as she collapsed.

Neridah grabbed her daughter under the shoulders and began dragging her the short distance to the threshold between worlds. She looked toward the Lieutenant just in time to see him aim his pistol toward them, ready to fire.

•

The Reverend sat up and rubbed his eyes. He was on a bed in the middle of a grand garden. Creatures he'd not seen until experiencing the visions in his dreams wandered about enjoying casual conversation.

A male with feline characteristics, like he'd seen in his first vision, approached him. He wore a Roman-style toga with red trim. When the Reverend glanced down at himself, he noticed he was now wearing the same. The feline-like creature extended his arms. "Ah, the Reverend Alfred Casey. At last, we can speak on a more honest level." The voice sounded oddly familiar.

"What do you mean?"

"Do you not recognise me?"

The Reverend shook his head. "No, I don't believe we've met."

"Perhaps my name will help you. I am known as Ferdinand, Seeker of Knowledge."

"Ferdinand? You're the McIntyres' cat?"

"Oh please, must you insult me by inferring I was their property? Did you never see the absurdity of it? It's one thing to hear the gossip of the cicadas, but didn't the idea of having philosophical conversations with a cat ever strike you as being somewhat strange? I was sent to your world by my mistress."

Kerridwen walked up behind Ferdinand and stroked his neck. "Isn't he a lovely pussy cat?"

"You sent him to the McIntyres' property to spy on them?"

"I'd say it was more of a fact-finding mission. He is the Seeker of Knowledge." She extended her hand to Alfred. "Come. It's time you join us for breakfast. There is much you must do today. Father is eager to plan his return to your world."

Alfred rose and took Kerridwen's hand. "I'm struggling to remember much about the McIntyres'. The memories seem so distant, like they're fading away. Names and faces, they are all gone."

Kerridwen put her arm through his as they walked through the golden, dappled sunlight streaming through the trees, Alfred's chosen twelve just a few steps behind. "That's of no great surprise. It was quite an ordeal for you to choose your garland."

"Aye, it took a good deal of consideration."

Kerridwen smiled. "I was frustrated at how long you took, and I questioned your early choices. But now, when I look at your garland holistically, I see the wisdom in your selection. They are not who I would have chosen, but I'm a hunter, not a priest."

"Aye, that's true."

She looked up at him as they continued their walk. "Is there anything you feel you're missing from your world?"

He looked at her as he replied, "Aye, I feel a sense of loss, but what that sense relates to eludes me."

She leaned in close to him. "Don't worry, Alfred. That will pass."

*

"Nana-Neri!" Patsy yelled as loud as she could, hoping that somehow her voice may stop the bullet from reaching its intended target.

Neridah watched in horror as fire flared out from the barrel of the pistol that pointed her way. She could see the aim was accurate.

The sound of the gunshot thundered in her ears.

Instinctively, she went to her knees and released her grip on Meredith, then felt around her chest for where the bullet should have found its mark. She looked down but couldn't see any signs of a wound.

Lieutenant Stewart stood up and looked around, his gun dangling by his side. "Where are you, witch?" He screamed, "SHOW YOURSELF!"

Patsy went down on her knees next to Neridah. "You made it!"

Neridah struggled to get a decent breath as her heart raced. She stared through the portal at the Lieutenant. "He can't see or hear us."

Lieutenant Stewart walked along the tree line, yelling at the troops running down the hill. "Find them! They must be here somewhere. Reach out through the Crossworlds. Do whatever it takes! Just find those damned witches!"

Neridah turned Patsy's shoulders so she could untie her granddaughter's hands. "We'll get you free, and then see about waking your mother."

Meredith stirred and began to moan. "What happened? Did we make it?"

Neridah breathed a sigh of relief then hugged her daughter. "Yes, thanks to you. You were amazing." She took a breath before continuing, "We still need to get to the wood-elf's cabin."

Meredith replied, "Do you know the way?"

Neridah finished untying the knots in Patsy's bonds then shook her head. "We walked for an hour last time. I can't remember how we got there."

Patsy smiled. "The pixie-dust! Krinkle-myst told us it would lead us there whenever we needed it to."

Neridah put a hand on Patsy's shoulder. "I wouldn't be so quick to place my faith in promises made by a wood-elf if I were you." The moment she finished speaking a ball of pixie-dust sprang up behind her. There was a moment's silence while Neridah looked at the stunned expressions on Patsy and Meredith's faces. "It's behind me, isn't it?'

Patsy and Meredith nodded.

Neridah slowly turned around, then allowed herself to smile when she saw the dancing ball of pixie-dust.

*

"Alfred!" Albiorix threw his arms around the Reverend as Kerridwen took her seat. "I'm so pleased you've chosen your twelve."

"Aye. But tell me, why was it that I had to choose while in a dream? Are not sober choices in a wakeful state more valid?"

"You would question the validity of your choices? Trust me, my friend, you should never underestimate the power of decisions made within dreams."

The Reverend thought about his conversation with Ferdinand. He was struggling now to remember where he knew the feline from. There was a name, McIntyre, but he couldn't associate it with faces or places. He swayed back and forth and had to grab the back of a chair to steady himself before he took a step back and asked, "Why? Why am I here? What is this really about? Tell me, Albiorix, what do you want of me?"

Kerridwen looked up with a stern expression. "Alfred, I thought we'd been over this."

"Aye, but that was in a dream."

Albiorix looked to the sky, rocking his head from side to side. "Why, why, why?" He turned back to the Reverend and, for the first time, looked angry. "You dare to ask me why? I'll tell you why. Because the ancestors of your beloved witches banished me. They were jealous of the devotion I channelled to the gods and they shut me out." He moved closer to the Reverend, so much so that their noses almost touched. "Did it make your world a better place? Do people feel that their gods hear them better now? Too many prayers go unheard without an under-god to channel them. Or, do you feel that everyone's prayers in your world are answered?" He leaned back and gestured toward the multitude of creatures calmly going about their business. "Look at them, Alfred. Are the people on your world this content?"

Witches? Alfred remembered the witches in his dream, dancing among the standing stones at Drombeg. They were familiar, but he couldn't remember why. Again, he felt unsteady. He sat down in his chair and looked at the scene before him. "A small moment like this is barely adequate to determine the full extent of anyone's happiness." A thought rose up in the back of the Reverend's mind. *The hunter was wise to choose you.* "Tell me, if you will, why does this singular thought keep invading my mind? You surely know the one I mean."

"Hah!" The Reverend grimaced when Albiorix slapped him on the back as he too took his place at the table. It was a habit he was growing weary of. "This is just the beginning, Alfred. This is how you will learn to channel devotion. They who would follow you love and adore you. They have been trained in how to focus that devotion, so it opens the pathways within your own mind to accept devotion of any kind, no matter where it be directed. You have chosen twelve, and they will keep your mind open to devotion, wherever you may go."

A plate of fruit was placed in front of the Reverend. Despite his hunger, he resisted the temptation. His thirst and hunger were blurring his vision and his mind as he whispered, "I'll not be your puppet."

Albiorix threw an arm around the Reverend's shoulder. "Oh, Alfred. Tell me, do you think you really have a choice? You are going through changes. As this day progresses, your resistance will falter. You have chosen your twelve. Later today you will be ready to cross back to your world. You will meet your destiny and you will pave the way."

Kerridwen grabbed her father's arm. "It's too early for this discussion."

Albiorix pulled his arm away from his daughter. "Nonsense!"

The Reverend lowered his head, hoping it may help to stop his head spinning. "What would you have me pave the way for?"

Albiorix stood up and threw his arms out wide. "For my triumphant return."

The Reverend looked at the goblet set before him on the table. "I thirst."

Kerridwen smiled as she poured him a wine. "Don't worry, Alfred. Once you've eaten your fill and sated your thirst, you'll see things in a different light."

•

Bandah and Talia stood on Jimmy O'Sullivan's chest. They pulled their wings fully closed, turning them into heavy shields on their backs and making them resemble cockroaches. Talia looked at Jimmy's wound. "It's a nasty one. He's lost a lot of blood."

Bandah followed Talia into the wound. "Yes, but he's still alive. If we can pinch the damage together, he should be able to recover after a few days of induced sleep." They continued through the bloody mess created by the gunshot. "We'll have to get the bullet out first."

"What fun that'll be." Talia turned to Bandah. "He's lucky it didn't lodge somewhere worse." She wrapped an arm around the lead ball and tried to dislodge it. "Can you lend me a bit of muscle, Big Boy?"

"Maybe we can save ourselves some trouble if we push it into the void, rather than trying to drag it out."

"I like the way you think." She allowed herself a smile. "I knew there was a good reason why I'd married you."

Bandah worked his way in behind the bullet and readied himself to push. "We just need to make sure we don't slip across with it."

Talia squeezed in next to him, leaning against Jimmy's heart. "We can use his heartbeat to help us push. On the count of three." She made sure her count was in time with the beats and closed her eyes. "One… two… three!"

They pushed forward, creating a momentary break in the membrane that separates this world from the void. The lead pellet slipped through. Then Talia fell forward, starting to slip through with it. Bandah held her tight around the waist with one arm while hooking the other around Jimmy's aorta. The membrane closed tight around her, trying to suck her through, but Bandah's grip persisted. The membrane felt like icy water cutting through her as it slid along her body, leaving behind a trail of gooey mucus as it sought to close itself. Once it had passed over her fingertips and snapped shut, she fell back against Bandah and gasped for breath. She wiped the goo away from her eyes before daring to open them. “That stuff is disgusting.”

CHAPTER 17

Within minutes of arriving at Krinkle-myst's cabin, the witches had changed into dry clothes and were seated by the fire.

"It's so good to be warm and dry again." Patsy turned to her mother. "Thank you."

Meredith put an arm around her daughter's shoulder. "I'm the one who should be thanking you. I'm so sorry, Patricia."

"What for?"

"For decisions being forced on you that a girl your age shouldn't have to make."

Patsy embraced her mother in a warm hug.

Neridah walked over to the table where the Book of Wisdom lay defiantly shut. "Cosy as it may be sitting by the fire, we have urgent matters to attend to."

Meredith stood up and said. "Of course." She held up the key. "What's the main word we should focus on?"

"Kerridwen," said Patsy.

"Albiorix," said Neridah.

Meredith opened the book and said, "Under-gods."

The book opened to the page that best met their combined needs. There were drawings of Albiorix, Kerridwen, and a close-up image of a daisy baring its teeth. It took a few seconds for the witches to be able to decipher the language of the text and read it as they would English.

As they worked their way through, Meredith said, "This is worse than I thought."

Patsy said, "Going by what it says here, Darcy's trapped in her garland."

Neridah said, "Albiorix was banished by our ancestors. They sent him back to his own world, Dellakaran. Kerridwen, her coming here and taking Alfred back with her, it's all about him trying to come back."

Meredith continued reading for a while then looked at her mother, "You're right. They're going to manipulate Alfred to end the banishment by creating a new following. They want to make Alfred an under-god and have him channel devotion directly to Albiorix."

Neridah looked at her daughter. "Albiorix wants to become a god?"

Patsy asked, "How can he do that? I thought gods always were what they are."

Meredith shook her head, "No, most gods are created by people's belief in them. You should never underestimate the power of belief. If he is seen to be a god by enough people, then he'll be able to return. He was banished as an under-god, but if he comes back as a god, then no banishment will likely stop him."

Patsy said, "I'm a little confused. Doesn't it say that he was worshipped as a god while he was here before?"

Neridah replied, "Yes, but he was here acting as an under-god, channelling the devotion to others who were elsewhere. It's when power is channelled to those who are unseen that it is most powerful. To become a god, one has to be unseen."

"So, why would he want to come back? If he intends to use the Reverend that way, wouldn't he be better off staying in Dellakaran?"

Neridah put a hand on Patsy's shoulder. "He wants revenge, and he wants to take his revenge out on us."

Meredith said, "From what it says here, once Alfred has selected twelve disciples to make up his garland, the pathway is inevitable. His followers will be chosen from those who have served Albiorix, and they will likely control him more than he controls them."

Patsy turned the page, keen to learn more about Dellakaran. "It says here that Dellakaran isn't even real. It's an artificial world created by Albiorix and his garland." She looked up. "If we can destroy his garland, it will destroy his world." She turned to her mother and grandmother. "All the souls there would be sucked back through the Crossworlds to where they originated from."

Neridah said, "We need to go there, now. We need to bring Alfred and Darcy back. We need to let Albiorix and his daughter know we won't be beaten."

"I agree," said Meredith.

Patsy said, "Wait. Before we go, I want to look up a spell." She closed her eyes and turned to another page. "We need to be ready to banish Kerridwen, in case she tries to follow us back through the portal once we've rescued Alfred."

*

Talia and Bandah worked their way backwards as they pulled together torn tissue and fused it like they were pushing pieces of playdough together. Where they could see signs of potential infection, they tore out the offending pieces of flesh and put them in a sack they'd made from some damaged tissue.

It was difficult and tedious.

After several minutes working together in silence fixing the unfixable wound, Talia asked, "Have you missed me?"

"Yes."

"Then why did you leave?"

Bandah replied, "I needed to remember how it feels to miss you."

"We've been married for thousands of years. Don't you think we could have talked about it instead?"

Silence

"Hello?"

"We'd become so accustomed to it," said Bandah

"So accustomed to what?"

"To talking about it. We both knew what to say to every question, every thought or reaction."

A tear formed in Talia's eye. "I like to think that we respected each other enough that we were always honest in our responses."

"I wanted to think that too, but it felt like we became so close that we were losing what brought us together… that desire to want to know each other better…"

"So, you thought leaving me without saying a word would help?"

Bandah looked away from her. "You don't understand."

"No, I don't."

They continued patching Jimmy O'Sullivan back together in silence.

*

Kerridwen refilled the Reverend's wine as she spoke. "When we get there, they'll be so pleased to see you."

The Reverend ate a piece of a phelare then picked up the replenished goblet. "Who is it that you're talking about?"

Kerridwen said, "The witches who tried to stop you coming here."

Albiorix threw an arm around the Reverend's shoulders. "You need to jog your memory, Alfred. They were like family to you."

"Be that as it may, I don't remember them."

Kerridwen reached across in front of her father and placed a reassuring hand on the Reverend's wrist. "It's okay, Alfred. It's normal to lose memories when preparing for a garland. I'm just glad that you're past the mood swings and the anger. You had me worried."

The hunter was wise to choose you.

"The voices of my disciples, they seem to help dispel the confusion. I just wish I could remember more."

Kerridwen's voice was soothing. "Do you remember the witches dancing in the circle of stones in your dream?"

"Aye."

"The witches who would betray you, who tried to keep you from coming here, they appear the same as their ancestors. You will recognise them from your dream. It's crucial, Alfred. You cannot trust them, especially not the one who calls herself Neridah. You need to prepare to protect yourself from their deceptions."

Albiorix held up his goblet, spilling wine across the table as he raised it to the sky. "But first, we will feast! Soon, you and my daughter will return to your world, and that is as good a reason as any I've known to celebrate!"

The Reverend ate hungrily from the fresh bowl of fruit placed before him to replace the one he'd already finished.

Kerridwen whispered in her father's ear, "I'm not sure now that I want this."

Albiorix raised an eyebrow as he turned to his daughter.

"Oh, Father! Why do you never understand me? You may like his world, but I hate it. Now, I have to go back there with someone I absolutely detest and pretend to care about both him and the people of his loathsome world?" She looked across to make sure the Reverend wasn't aware of their discussion. The juice of the phelare was doing its job, reducing the Reverend's anxiety and rendering him unaware of most of what was taking place around him. Meanwhile, his chosen twelve worked through his mind, shielding his consciousness from memories that might create conflict with the desired outcome of their true masters. There was spite in Kerridwen's words as she whispered, "This is all because of your petty vendetta against that pitiful bunch of witches."

Albiorix whispered back, "You forget our purpose. Aren't you fed up with having to kowtow to the whims of the gods we serve? Don't you want to see your own father become a god, and maybe even become one yourself?"

"Why can't I just go back and kill off those stupid witches before we send the priest back? With them out of the way, we could rely on the garland to guide him, and I could stay here, where life is more civilised."

"No, I want the witches kept alive till I return, so I can have the joy of banishing them to a place where I know they'll suffer for eternity."

Albiorix placed a hand on his daughter's knee. "As for the priest, don't worry, my little dove. Once his role is fulfilled, you can discard him any way you wish."

*

Neridah held the Reverend's box and wondered what special treasure was concealed by its puzzle lock. Although she had no idea what it contained, she felt sure that it was important that they take it with them if they were to have any hope of bringing Alfred back.

"Nana-Neri, are you ready?"

"Yes, of course."

Patsy reached into the fire and, in one sweeping action, grabbed a handful of flame and threw it into the air. They watched the pixie-dust dance about the room for a few seconds then Patsy said, "I've got an idea. Let's close our eyes and allow ourselves to follow the dust this time. Maybe it'll be quicker."

Meredith said, "That's an interesting idea. I'm happy to give it a try." She looked across at her mother.

Neridah tucked the box under her arm and nodded agreement. The three witches held hands and closed their eyes. A moment later, they could feel the wind against their faces. They opened their eyes and watched the trees rushing past as they flew through the air behind the ball of pixie-dust, tumbling and turning as they went.

"Woo-hoo!" An enormous grin spread across Patsy's face. "This is so much easier than swimming through the air."

Meredith spread her arms out, imagining how a bird might feel. "We'll have to learn more about pixie-dust the next time we consult the Book of Wisdom."

Neridah pointed ahead. "Look, we're almost there." They could see a few soldiers gathered near the entrance to the pathway. "Let's walk the rest of the way."

Their momentum made them roll and tumble as they dropped to the ground and the pixie-dust vanished. Neridah pulled her hair back from her eyes. "So much for the clean clothes."

Meredith got up and brushed herself off. "At least they're still dry."

Patsy walked to the edge of the pathway. The rain beyond the portal to the paddock had eased to a fine drizzle. "The soldiers, they can't hear or see us." She turned to the others. "Do you think we might be able to sneak down to the portal without them seeing us once we've left the pathway?"

Neridah said, "It's worth a try. If we can keep ourselves mostly concealed by the tree line, we might pull it off."

Meredith put a hand on her daughter's shoulder. "I'm relieved you're not wanting to go out there and face them head-on."

Patsy looked up at her mother. "We need to save our energy. We're going to need it when we get to Dellakaran."

"I'm proud of you, you're learning."

Neridah looked up toward the house. "Oh, oh. This isn't good."

Lieutenant Stewart was leading Cook down the paddock with a gun pointed at her temple. He was halfway to the bottom when he yelled out, "HEY! WITCHES! I don't know where you are, but I'm sure you can hear me." His voice echoed through the valley. "You have one hour to show yourselves, or the servant dies, and it'll be on your conscience, not mine. Do you hear me, witches? I SAID, DO YOU HEAR ME! ONE HOUR!" Cook stood trembling with her hands on her head.

Neridah turned to the others. "We have to go, now!"

The three of them lifted the hems of their skirts and started toward the creek. Patsy asked her mother, “Do you think we can do this in an hour?”

Meredith replied, “We don’t have a choice, we’ll just have to.”

“But, shouldn’t we do something to rescue Cook before we cross over? We promised Mr Donaldson.”

Neridah said, “Not while there’s someone holding a gun at her head in the middle of the paddock.”

Patsy came to a stop. “No. I’m not running.” She disappeared, then, a moment later, reappeared a few paces behind the Lieutenant. She reached forward then pulled back, ripping the pistol out of the Lieutenant’s hands.

He turned to face Patsy. “Do you think you’ve saved her?” He sneered. “You’ve just sealed her fate.”

“I don’t think so.” She closed her eyes and reached into the Crossworlds with both hands to draw power. Glowing balls of energy grew around them.

She was ready to unleash the energy when she was knocked to the ground. She looked up and saw the Lieutenant. “Did you seriously expect that I’d sit there and just wait idly by while you drew up the energy to kill me? You really are quite stupid.” He pulled back his fist then felt Meredith and Neridah shift.

“Not as stupid as some.” Meredith’s arm went forward, hurling a ball of energy at the Lieutenant, closely followed by one from her mother. He managed to evade the first but was hit square in the chest by the second. It pushed him onto his back. As he lay there winded, Patsy sprang up and lurched across his chest, ripping out the Nasqa in one smooth motion. She threw it aside and called to her mother, “Time freeze!”

Meredith lifted her arms and pointed them toward where Patsy had hurled the Nasqa. "Ka dae marsie karn, com-ba swa-ba keb vog." She turned to her daughter. "That won't hold it for long."

"But it'll give us a chance to make a start."

Neridah helped Lieutenant Stewart to his feet. He rubbed his eyes. "None of this could possibly be happening. The past year of my life… it's a nightmare."

Neridah helped him down the paddock to where Patsy and Meredith were gathering around Cook. "Trust me, it's all real. And the time freeze my daughter captured that thing in will last a minute at most. We need to get you out of here, or it'll try to take you back. If it follows you when you leave here, you must shut it out. Do you understand?"

He nodded. "What would you have me do now?"

Meredith said, "You need to get Cook to safety, then do what you can to help the others who are already riding to Springwood to try and stop my husband being sent to the gallows."

"Yes, of course. What of the other servant, the one still held in the drawing room?"

"We'll look after her."

Patsy looked at her mother. "Mr Donaldson, he left his sulky at the side of the road near the entrance to the property. Maybe it's still there."

Neridah said, "Good thinking." She looked over her shoulder and saw the shadow within the time freeze was starting to show subtle signs of movement returning. "We need to go, now."

The three witches created a circle around Cook and the Lieutenant. They held hands, closed their eyes, and allowed themselves to be at the sulky.

•

The Nasqa that had possessed Lieutenant Stewart slipped out of the time freeze. It was too late to go after the witches, and it was powerless without a host body to control. It drifted up to the homestead in search of a possible new vessel.

Mrs Banks shivered as the cold shadow swirled around her. She was so petrified that her mind had erected barriers, leaving nowhere for the Nasqa to enter. Anyhow, the thought of inhabiting the body of someone who was so emotionally frail held little appeal. The Nasqa struggled to see how the troops would respect it if it spoke from within such a body. But then what choice did it have? Would it have to lower itself to inhabiting an animal?

The Nasqa drifted about the property, searching every room in the hope there was something it had missed.

It made its way to the servants' quarters. There, in the hallway, it came across the unconscious body of Jimmy O'Sullivan, with the pixies still working their way out of his chest wound.

The Nasqa watched as the pixies pulled the flesh of the stablehand's chest together. The moment the last of the wound was sealed, it flew into Jimmy's head, snapping him out of his induced coma and slapping the Irishman's hand to his chest.

Bandah and Talia were caught by surprise, the big hand leaving them breathless as it squeezed down on them. They looked up at the sinister grin spreading across Jimmy's face.

"Hah, I always wanted to catch me a pixie or two."

Bandah struggled to get air as he protested. "You can't do this to him. It's too soon. His body needs time to heal properly."

Talia followed up with a desperate plea. "You'll kill him."

Jimmy shrugged his shoulders. "What do I care? It'll do for now." Jimmy got to his feet. "Now, where would I find a nice, big jar, I wonder?"

*

Lieutenant Neil Stewart helped Cook into the sulky then turned to the three witches. "Thank you, for everything. I wish you luck."

Meredith spoke for the three of them. "And we wish you luck as well. You'll need every bit you can get."

"I'll see to it that Cook is comfortable at Mr Donaldson's property and then I'll ride with haste to Springwood."

A tear ran down Meredith's cheek as she threw her arms around the Lieutenant and said, "Thank you."

Patsy looked up at him as her mother stepped back. "Please, please bring Father back safely."

He put a reassuring hand on her shoulder. "I'll do everything I possibly can to see justice is served."

The witches held hands and allowed themselves to be at the pool that housed the portal.

*

The Justice Callum Sessions dismounted his horse and tied it to the hitching post outside the Captain's office. He took a handkerchief from his pocket and blew his nose as he stared at the gallows. The wood looked weathered, as though the structure had been there a long time, but the rope was new.

Captain Taylor opened the door to his office and stepped out into the light as the sun struggled to break through the clouds. "Ah, Justice Sessions. I'm so glad you could make it at such short notice."

"It would seem to me from the readiness of the gallows that you've already made up your mind how I'll be ruling in this case."

"The evidence is overwhelming, and the murderer is a dangerous man. Ordinarily, I would have transported him to Sydney for trial, but the risk of him escaping and causing further deaths was too great to ignore."

"I'll be the judge of whether he should be referred to as a murderer."

"Yes, of course." The Captain gestured toward his office. "You must be thirsty after your ride. Can I offer you a brandy?"

The Justice looked the Captain up and down, as though insulted by his very presence. "I never touch the stuff." He surveyed the barracks and asked, "Where will we be holding court?"

Captain Taylor pointed to a stone building across the courtyard. "Over there, in the mess hall."

"And the victim's body?"

"On its way to Sydney for burial."

"Good God, man. How do you expect me to conduct a fair trial if I can't inspect the body?"

"We have the testimony of several soldiers from the Parramatta Lancers who were with me when I took the accused's confession."

The Justice fanned himself with his handkerchief before returning it to his pocket. "Very well then, let's get on with it."

*

When the witches appeared at the pool housing the portal, a dozen soldiers raised their rifles. One of them said, "We've been waiting for you."

Elpheen rose up behind him and covered his eyes. "So have we." The soldier reached up, grabbed the fairy, and tossed her aside.

There were several fairies for every soldier, each of them focused on creating a distraction.

Patsy reached toward a soldier's gun and pulled back, causing it to go hurtling into the pool. Neridah and Meredith followed suit. One weapon after another was made useless as they hit the water. Mrs Smith flew up to Patsy. "You should go and do what you have to. We can't hold them back forever. Elpheen's wings are broken now, and the same will happen to the others. More soldiers will likely come down from the house."

Meredith said, "She's right." She looked up at Mrs Smith. "Thank you."

The three witches joined hands and started chanting as they walked toward the water while the fairies continued to distract their assailants.

Emblae ka pista lu Dellakaran,
Emblae ka pista lu Dellakaran...

The water pushed away from them as they approached, as though each drop was in a hurry to crawl over the others to get away from the approaching witches. A glowing ball of energy formed around them, and their eyes flared in an electric blue dance of raw power.

The soldiers who still held guns fired in desperation but were unable to aim as they were kept blinded by the persistent fairies.

Injured fairies started to pile up on the bank of the creek. Some had broken wings, others broken limbs.

The witches were nearing the centre of the pool. The water had become a swirling vortex around them.

But the soldiers now outnumbered the fairies as they continued throwing them aside. The first one to feel free of them lowered his rifle and took careful aim for the centre of the vortex that now hid the witches. As he squeezed the trigger, Mrs Smith threw herself at his face and bit down hard on the tip of his nose.

Patsy felt the wind from the bullet whistle past her ear before a blinding flash indicated their transition from one world to another.

CHAPTER 18

Neither Cook nor Lieutenant Stewart said a word until they reached the turn-off leading to Vincent Donaldson's property.

Cook pointed to the turn-off and said, "You'll be needing to head up there."

The Lieutenant turned the sulky and chewed on his lower lip as he weighed up what he wanted to say. He had crystal clear memories of what he'd done to Cook while possessed by the Nasqa. After a long and uncomfortable silence, he said, "I'm sorry."

Cook waited as she collected her own thoughts. For the past year, she'd managed to shut out the memories of what had happened before, but it had all come flooding back the moment Lieutenant Stewart and his soldiers arrived. She turned to face him and saw his humanity in the tear that was running down his cheek. "Don't worry yourself… it wasn't you."

Ten minutes later, they arrived at Vincent's property. His stablehand greeted them as they neared the homestead. "Hello, Cook." He looked at the Lieutenant then shifted his gaze back to Cook.

"Don't worry yourself too much, Toby. Mr Donaldson's heading into Springwood on some urgent business. There's trouble at the McIntyres' and Lieutenant Stewart has been good enough to escort me here so that Mr Donaldson can know I'm safe. He is just dropping me here now, for my safety, and will be back with Mr Donaldson either tonight or in the morning."

Toby nodded in acknowledgment, then helped Cook out of the sulky.

The Lieutenant thought that he saw something strange in the movement of Toby's shadow.

*

Albiorix turned when he heard the waters erupt at the centre of the lake. Large waves formed as space was made for the Witches of the Crossworlds to enter Dellakaran. They walked forward with their protective cocoon of energy, the waters parting before them, causing a tidal surge at the shore that pushed water right up to where Albiorix, Kerridwen and Alfred were sharing in their morning feast. The three witches continued walking, unblinking as they fixed their electric blue gazes on the Reverend.

Kerridwen rose to her feet, the daisies from her garland snapping violently in their desperation to break free and deal with the intruders.

Albiorix reached across to restrain her. "No! This is for Alfred to deal with. He is an under-god now, one of us. Let him prove his worth."

Kerridwen's eyes narrowed as she turned to the Reverend who was staring at the table and mumbling incoherently. She nudged his shoulder with her elbow. "Alfred, don't disappoint me."

The Reverend raised his head as though waking from a deep sleep. As the witches approached, he noticed an oddly familiar silky oak box tucked under the arm of one of the women. He looked around at his disciples who were bunched in close to him.

The waters receded as the witches neared the table. The Reverend asked, "Why have you come here?"

The ball of energy around the witches dissipated when they released each other's hands. Neridah stepped forward, extending her arms to present the Reverend with his box. "I bring you a gift. A token of my devotion. It is our hope that in return you will see it in your wisdom to assist us in our search for our friend, Darcy O'Sullivan, that he may join us when we leave Dellakaran."

"I know nothing of your friend, but I must say, this box… it appears familiar."

Kerridwen sneered. "Don't trust her, or anything she has to offer. This is the one they call Neridah, the most deceitful of them all."

Albiorix grabbed his daughter's shoulder. "This is for Alfred to deal with."

Felibrey the Humble stepped in front of the table to stand between the witches and the Reverend. "Be warned, she who has cheated age, I may be but a humble servant to a newly born under-god, but I will defend him to my death, as will the others of his garland. Be aware, we have all lived more than a hundred times longer than yourselves. We have spent our time learning to be strong for those we serve."

Neridah was unmoved. "Be that as it may, I have a gift that symbolises my devotion to the one you would call an under-god. Is it not fitting that I should be the first to present him with such a token?"

The Reverend asked, "Why? Why is it fitting?"

"Perhaps, when you inspect the gift, you will find out."

Kerridwen snapped, "Alfred! This is ridiculous!"

The Reverend turned to her. There was something in her spite toward this woman that made him angry. "Quiet, woman! As your father said, this is my business to deal with." He took a moment to compose himself, then addressed Felibrey. "Step aside, that the witch can come forward and present me with her supposed gift of devotion."

Felibrey looked to the other disciples. They moved away from the Reverend and walked down to create a semi-circle around the witches to block their retreat. Felibrey stepped back to join the others and bowed as he said, "As you wish, oh Chosen One."

Neridah stepped up to the table and handed the puzzle-box to the Reverend.

He stared deep into her eyes as he accepted the gift. There was a sensation he felt in his stomach that defied description when their hands briefly touched. She stepped back, looked to the ground, and burst into tears.

The Reverend was oblivious to her as he turned the box over in his hands. There were scorch marks on its surface, exactly where he expected them to be. He pushed back on the right-hand panel, down on the back, then slid the top to the left. The lid lifted slightly of its own accord. He glanced down at Neridah, who had now fallen to her knees as she continued crying. Meredith and Patsy had gathered around and embraced her to try to console the woman's anguish. The Reverend felt anxiety wash over him as he looked down at the box and lifted the lid.

•

Mrs Smith groaned in agony as she was tossed onto the sandstone rock with the other fairies. The exploding pain in her ankle told her it must be broken. She had no feeling at all in her wings or left arm. Elpheen glanced across at her. "We should never have given up our wands when we came here."

"What wands? You didn't have wands when you came here. Surely, you'd remember that? It was Sellemae who took them from you, not the McIntyres."

Elpheen had a minor convulsion, coughing and spluttering bile down the side of her mouth.

Mrs Smith asked, "How badly are you hurt?"

"I can't feel anything from the neck down."

Mrs Smith found herself thinking how insignificant her own injuries were.

"Hey, Smith. Do you think we've repaid our debt to the humans now?"

"Aye, I think we have."

"Good." Again, Elpheen found herself convulsing. Once she'd settled, she said, "The way I see it, they owe us now."

"Well, that's good to hear." It was Jimmy O'Sullivan's voice. He leaned down so he was at eye level with the wounded fairies. "I think I can help you get back some of what they owe you." He placed a jar on the rock. Bandah and Talia held their hands against the glass as they looked out at the fairies. Jimmy smiled. "And, I think I can help you with mending your wounds."

On the other side of the creek, Eldah, the one fairy to avoid injury and capture, watched through the bushes. "Please, Elpheen, please don't sell us out," she whispered.

Elpheen coughed and spluttered some more, then took a few deep breaths. She turned her eyes up toward Jimmy. "If you can help us, we'll help you."

Mrs Smith looked at Elpheen. "That's not what I meant when I agreed our debt was paid."

Elpheen coughed again before replying, "Hey, I can't move, and I can barely breathe. This is about survival."

Mrs Smith frowned at her. "Then tell me, what was this for?"

"To free us from the burden of our debt."

•

The Reverend Alfred Casey looked down into the box, the one thing he'd felt the need to rescue from the charred remains of his house at Pulpit's Hill.

There were letters.

Dozens of letters, all carefully stored in the envelopes they were delivered in.

Each one treated as an individual treasure.

He pulled one from the stack at random.

> *Dearest Alfred,*
>
> *This is, without doubt, the most difficult letter I have ever written, and probably ever will.*
>
> *My father has found a suitor whom he believes is appropriate for me to marry. I do not love him. I don't even care for him. But, I am with child, and as such, I must be wed before it becomes obvious and brings shame on the family.*
>
> *I wish with all my heart there was another way. But it is not my choice to make.*
>
> *Maybe, in a future time, people who love each other will be free to make their own choices.*

It still grieves me that Father banished you from my life. You are, and forever will be, the only man I've loved.

I just pray that you will one day meet someone and find the happiness you deserve.

I will forever carry you in my heart,

Neridah.

Tears welled up in his eyes, blurring his vision. He wiped them away before looking over the top of the letter and down at Neridah. She pushed Patsy and Meredith away as she rose to her feet and moved forward, toward the man she loved. The Reverend gazed into her eyes. "How is it that I'd somehow let the madness of this world steal away the memories of all in this life that has ever mattered to me?" He put down the letter. "You will always be the most powerful magic in my life."

Kerridwen slammed her fists on the table. "NO!" She glared at Neridah. Her daisies were breaking away from her garland and snapping in Neridah's direction before withdrawing. They were anxious to be set free to attack those who would invade Dellakaran.

Albiorix turned to the Reverend. "See the power of devotion, Alfred?" He gestured toward Neridah. "This woman has travelled across worlds because of her devotion. And that is where the true power she gives you comes from."

The Reverend replied, "These analyses you make are nothing but an illusion. You twist everything that you or others experience to suit your purposes. You and your daughter delude yourselves when you suggest you have a mastery of magical powers. You are merely masters of the deception of others… and of yourselves."

Albiorix rose to his feet, sending the table, and all that was on it, flying forward. The witches were forced to duck, lest they be hit by flying trays, platters, and foodstuffs. "How dare you!" Albiorix appeared to be three times the Reverend's height. "You will do as I command!"

The Reverend looked up at the towering figure. The daisies in Albiorix's garland were now as agitated as those in Kerridwen's. The Reverend's reply was soft and filled with humility. "No, I won't." He turned back to Neridah.

Kerridwen sneered at him. "Then, you will watch as your pitiful witches die!" She turned to Alfred's disciples. "Don't let any of them flee." She glared at Patsy. "We'll start with this irritable little pest."

Patsy's eyes narrowed as she prepared to defend herself. She reached back and drew power from across a hundred worlds.

Burning with resentment at the memory of Patsy humiliating her by the creek, Kerridwen threw her right arm forward. "I owe you this one." A bolt of lightning flew out from her hand. It hit Patsy square in her chest and sent her flying back at least twenty paces. Kerridwen prepared to follow through with her other arm.

Seeing what Kerridwen was doing, Meredith lunged forward in a reflex to protect her daughter. She hurled a ball of energy at the hunter. Its impact was minimal, but still enough to break Kerridwen's momentum. Kerridwen turned her attention to Meredith and screamed at the daisies in her garland, "Attack them, my pets! Show no mercy! Tear them apart and scatter their remains through the void."

The daisies broke free from Kerridwen's garland, growing in size as their razor-sharp teeth snapped again and again. It was as though the snapping motion was how they propelled, or rather dragged, themselves through the air.

The Reverend reached up at the nearest daisy, grabbing it from behind and pulling it from the air. He threw it to the ground, brought his foot down hard, and crushed it. A shrill scream rang out that drew

Albiorix's ire. "You could have one day been a god! Now I will crush you as you have crushed my daughter's disciple. Then my garland's souls will devour your remains."

"You talk too much." The Reverend pushed his hand toward Albiorix's face, hitting him in the jaw with a burst of energy. The under-god stumbled backward while the Reverend swung his other arm around, releasing another burst that hit Albiorix square in the back. The Reverend called out, "Hah," mimicking Albiorix. The under-god fell forward and landed face first among the scattered paraphernalia from the breakfast table. One of Kerridwen's daisies closed in on the Reverend. It was about to snap down on his shoulder when it was snatched from behind. Bordauex the Learned pulled it back and tore the creature in two, causing another scream to ring out.

He turned to the Reverend. "I chose to follow you to the end. The only wise thing the hunter has done was to choose you."

Kerridwen looked at the Reverend's disciple and said, "You idiot." She pushed a hand forward, sending a bolt of energy toward Bordauex that knocked him to the ground. She pulled her arm back to prepare for another attack but felt a hand grip it tight. She turned and saw Felibrey.

The disciple turned to the Reverend. "Leave now." He grabbed hold of Kerridwen's other arm. "We'll distract them as long as we can."

"What of your own well-being?" replied the Reverend.

Kerridwen was struggling to break free. But Felibrey's grip was strong. "We swore an oath to protect you to the death. The hunter was wise to choose you."

Kerridwen vanished.

Felibrey continued, "And you were wise to choose us."

Albiorix rose to his feet. His voice roared across the landscape. "Disciples of Dellakaran, I call on you all to defend our realm." Disciples wearing garlands began appearing around Albiorix.

Kerridwen reappeared behind Felibrey. He looked at the Reverend and said, "You need to go."

Kerridwen struck Felibrey in the back, causing him to lurch forward in pain. The Reverend thrust a hand toward Kerridwen and again she disappeared.

Meredith called out, "Patricia!"

The Reverend turned and saw a daisy preparing to bite down on Patsy's face as she struggled to sit up. It was too close for the Reverend to stop it, but he drew his arm back anyway. The daisy's jaws were open wide as it positioned itself. Then a shrill scream rang out as it was bitten from behind by another of the daisies.

"Darcy?" the Reverend whispered.

The battle intensified.

Meredith saw Albiorix prepare to thrust his hand toward her. She reached for a gleaming silver tray that had come from the upturned table and held it in front of her as a protective shield. The power unleashed when Albiorix extended his arm pushed her to the ground, but the bulk of it was reflected by the tray's shining surface. It scattered in several directions and knocked down one of Albiorix's followers who'd been racing toward her with a knife.

Kerridwen was walking slowly toward Patsy, drawing her arm back. Her hand glowed with the lightning that danced around it. She addressed her remaining daisies, "Leave the girl to me and don't fret about your wayward brother, Darcy. I'll replace him with a more worthy follower when we're through."

Neridah swung a wine jug and smashed it into a daisy that was descending upon her, sending it flying as it squealed in pain. She thrust her arm forward and hit another that was approaching Meredith.

The Reverend's disciples were doing their best to distract the other daisies, hurling whatever items they could find at them. The Reverend ran to Patsy's aid but was stopped by one of Albiorix's minions who appeared next to him and tackled him to the ground. He quickly rose to his feet again, drew back his arm, and summoned power, but was brought down again by another minion who'd appeared from nowhere.

Neridah watched from the distance as Kerridwen prepared to unleash the crackling energy she'd called up. There was no other choice. She closed her eyes and allowed herself to be between Kerridwen and Patsy, taking the full force of the blinding surge of power unleashed when Kerridwen's arm went forward.

The world stood still for the Reverend as he watched Neridah fall. The blood pulsing through his temples seemed deafening as he cried out, "No!"

Patsy sat bolt upright. "Nana-Neri!"

Meredith turned her attention from a ring of attackers that had her surrounded. "Mother!"

Patsy was brought back to the reality of the battle when Kerridwen laughed at her. "Your precious Nana-Neri is finished, as will you be soon." Again, Kerridwen drew her arm back with dancing lightning building around her hand.

Patsy rose to her feet wearing an expression of grim determination. She held her hands in front of her, burning energy coalescing between them and building a dazzling ball of light in the centre that blazed as bright as a sun. "You really shouldn't make me angry," she said.

Kerridwen shielded her eyes with her left hand as she thrust forward with her right. Patsy pushed both hands forward to release her miniature sun. A deafening crack of thunder drew the attention of everyone as the two energy sources collided. Patsy's sun had the greater momentum.

It flared so bright that all who watched were forced to cover their eyes. Kerridwen began backing away as it approached. She threw her arms forward again, releasing more lightning bolts, but they did little to hinder the burning ball of light's progression toward her.

Albiorix thrust an arm at the miniature sun, sending forth a power surge that caused the ball to explode. Everyone, Albiorix included, was knocked off their feet and sent backwards.

Everyone except Patsy.

She maintained the stance that she'd struck when defiantly bracing herself against the power of the blast. She called to her mother, "The garland!" She pointed to Albiorix. "We need to attack his garland."

Albiorix rose to his feet. "How dare you! You should be grovelling at my feet, begging forgiveness."

Patsy said, "I think not." She disappeared and reappeared a few paces behind Albiorix. She was about to thrust her arm forward when Kerridwen appeared in front of her, thrusting out her hand and hitting Patsy with a bolt of lightning from her outstretched hand.

Patsy flew back and hit the ground. Kerridwen looked down on her and prepared to make another strike when Meredith appeared between them, pushing her tray forward to intercept the blast. The tray reflected the lightning back at the hunter, forcing her to stumble and almost knocking her to the ground.

The Reverend reached the spot where Neridah lay. He felt for a pulse, but there was nothing. He turned and extended his arm toward Albiorix, hitting him in the shoulder. The under-god looked at where he'd been hit and laughed. "You'll have to do better than that, Alfred." He leaped up and started running through the air toward the Reverend, large blocks of earth appearing under each footfall. Again and again, the Reverend thrust forward, each blast of energy hitting its mark but making little if any impact on the approaching figure.

The Reverend's disciples continued to battle the daisies of Kerridwen's garland, but almost all were now surrounded by the under-god's followers.

Patsy said to her mother. "We need to stop Albiorix."

In the split second that Meredith was distracted by her daughter, Kerridwen unleashed a bolt of energy that knocked her to the ground. She turned to face Patsy again, but the girl was gone.

Patsy struggled to balance when she appeared on Albiorix's shoulders. She lost her footing and slipped down his back. Hooking an arm around his neck, she tilted her head back as far as she could to avoid his snapping daisies.

Albiorix grabbed the arm she'd placed around him and pulled her up. He held her high, ready to hurl her to the ground. "You dare to touch me? Foolish—"

His mouth hung open in disbelief. With her free hand, Patsy had ripped the garland from his head. The daisies were attacking her hand and wrist, but she held tight, grimacing in pain with each snap from the daisies' jaws. Unlike Kerridwen's garland, none of the daisies had been prepared to leave the all-important garland that held Dellakaran together. Patsy swung her arm and hurled it as far as she could. It landed just where she'd intended it to… at the Reverend's feet. He looked at the fear in Albiorix's eyes as he stomped down hard on one of the daisies. The most ear-piercing screech any of them had heard rang out, and the ground beneath them began to rumble. Shocked by what he was witnessing, Albiorix let go of Patsy's arm. Her ankle twisted when she hit the ground. When she tried to get up, it collapsed beneath her.

Kerridwen stared in shock at her father, distressed that he seemed to have given up.

She failed to notice Meredith had disappeared, reappearing the next instant next to Patsy. They held hands then both closed their eyes and allowed themselves to be next to the Reverend.

Felibrey ran up to the Reverend as he stomped on another of the daisies. "You and your witches really must go now. Go to the lake, and you'll get safely back to your world as this illusion decays." As a second screech rang out, rocks and trees exploded.

"Aye, it's time we go." The Reverend carefully picked up Neridah's limp form. Meredith had an arm around Patsy's shoulder as the girl supported herself on one foot. They were about to allow themselves to be in the middle of the lake when Patsy was distracted by an urgent meowing and the feel of a cat rubbing against her shins.

"Ferdinand!" She reached down with her free arm and picked up the cat. "We can't leave you behind."

The Reverend glared at the cat. "You don't want to be taking that thing back with you."

The cat snuggled into Patsy's shoulder as she held it tight. "Nonsense. He deserves to be safe as much as the rest of us." The ground was shaking, and huge chunks were exploding into dust.

Albiorix dropped to his knees.

Kerridwen screamed at him as she struggled to balance on the shaking ground. "Father! Do something!" When he ignored her, she called out to her remaining daisies. "Come back to me, my pets!"

Meredith said, "We need to go, now!"

Patsy said, "No, wait." There was a daisy circling around them, trying to resist being pulled back to Kerridwen. "It's Darcy! I just know it is! We need to save him!"

Meredith saw that, unlike the other daisies, this one wasn't snapping. She reached out to snatch it from the air.

Then Kerridwen appeared between them.

The Reverend stamped on another of Albiorix's daisies. Kerridwen covered her ears at the sound it emitted as the creature imprisoned within the flower perished.

The ground beneath them slipped away.

Kerridwen lost her balance and fell backwards.

Meredith reached again for the daisy. Her fingers wrapped around it and she said, "Now."

They closed their eyes and were gone.

CHAPTER 19

Colin's face was covered in bruises. His left eye was blackened and almost fully closed. His jaw was so swollen it was barely possible for him to talk. He shuffled across the courtyard in his handcuffs and leg irons, trying to ignore the presence of the gallows to his right.

Once he'd reached the mess hall, the Justice looked him up and down. "For God's sake, will someone give this poor wretch some water?" The Captain nodded to one of the soldiers who dutifully left the room. "Colin McIntyre, do you understand the charges that have been brought against you today?"

A dry whisper cracked through Colin's parched and swollen lips. "I'm innocent, Your Honour."

"Hmmph! I've heard that before."

The soldier returned with a cup of water he'd filled at the horses' trough. Despite the foul taste, Colin drank thirstily.

The Justice looked over his spectacles toward Captain Taylor. "What evidence do you have?"

"As I told you before, there are several of my men who witnessed his confession."

The Justice looked at Colin then back to the Captain. "We're talking about a man's life here, a man you'd have swinging from those gallows out there before sunset. You'll have to do better than that."

Captain Taylor stepped forward. "Your Honour, this is a man who killed a stipendiary magistrate in cold blood. The Magistrate was acting on orders from the Governor to take possession of Mr McIntyre's land after he'd been found to have defrauded the crown. There is evidence, motive, and guilt."

"In my court, I will decide who is innocent or guilty."

A soldier entered through the back of the room and whispered in the Captain's ear. "Sir, the gravedigger's back. He says he wants to give testimony."

The Captain nodded his approval then turned to the Justice. "Your Honour, it seems another witness has just arrived. The local gravedigger in the area where the accused resides, one Sean O'Malley, a fine and respected member of the community."

"Very well then, have him come in."

Sean O'Malley sauntered into the room. He reeked of every foul smell imaginable, causing each soldier he passed to gag as they tried to hold their breath till he'd passed them by. He smirked when he made eye contact with the Captain. He turned to the Justice and rubbed a hand across his belly, still tender from the impact of the Captain's boot. Well, he was about to kick the Captain back, inflicting an even greater pain. "McIntyre's innocent. The Magistrate died of a heart attack."

Captain Taylor was outraged. "How dare you come in here and—"

The justice banged his wooden gable. "Order! Let the man continue."

O'Malley smiled at the Captain then turned back to face the Justice. "The Captain had the body sent to Sydney knowing that if it were left here while the trial took place, you'd want the body examined and that any doctor worth a pinch of salt would tell it was a heart attack that killed him."

The Justice looked at Colin. "Do you know this man?"

Colin said, "No, I've never seen him before. But he speaks the truth."

"So, Captain Taylor, you say O'Malley's a well-respected member of the community, yet this long-time resident, the defendant, says he's never met the man."

"They're both liars."

"Hogwash! It's my opinion that you are somewhat overzealous in your desire to see this man swing from the gallows."

"The Governor himself considers this man guilty."

"What? While he sits behind his desk in Sydney? If your intent with such comments is to intimidate me, then, may I remind you, I answer to the Legislative Council, not your precious Governor."

"He represents Her Majesty, Queen Victoria!"

"That has no bearing on this man's guilt or innocence under the law." He banged his gable on the table. "Court is adjourned. I shall have a cup of tea while you see if you can provide some decent evidence of this man's guilt."

*

The centre of the lake became a swirling vortex. The witches and the Reverend had no choice but to let themselves be swept along as they slipped down the spiralling funnel of water.

Patsy felt Ferdinand's claws dig into the back of her shoulder as he clung tight.

Meredith couldn't maintain her grip on Patsy but managed to continue holding the daisy they hoped was Darcy.

The Reverend clung to Neridah's limp form. He made sure to keep a hand behind her neck and her head above water, often having his own head submerge for extended periods as a result.

The sky erupted in an explosion of thunder and lightning, the clouds rolling and tumbling as though they too were attempting to escape the dying world of Dellakaran.

The walls of the vortex steepened, creating a turbulent tunnel to darkness.

The Reverend and the witches fell, wind rushing past as they continued to plummet.

Patsy strained to look over her shoulder at where they'd come from and saw only darkness. When she turned her head back to face the wind, she saw the same.

They continued falling. The roar of the water swirling around them made it pointless to attempt communicating with one another.

Then Patsy saw dull, watery light ahead, like being underwater and looking up at the surface, only more distant.

They hit the water and Patsy felt its cold embrace as their momentum pulled them deep below the surface.

•

Justice Callum Sessions was walking back to the mess hall when two horses rode into the barracks. The horses carried a soldier and an older gentleman wearing a full-length coat and broad-rimmed hat, sporting a waxed moustache. Because he was accompanied by a soldier, he rode past the guards at the gate without being questioned.

Vincent looked at the noose swinging in the breeze as it dangled from the gallows.

Once they'd dismounted, Daniel Williams approached the Justice. "Gunner Daniel Williams, at your service, Your Honour."

The Justice looked at the young soldier then across to Captain Taylor. He turned back to Daniel and asked, "Why would you be reporting to me and not your superior officer?"

"Because he's corrupt and would see you condemn an innocent man to be hanged."

Captain Taylor looked at a pair of soldiers he knew were possessed by Nasqa, and thus loyal to him. "Arrest this soldier and clap him in irons. He was under strict orders to remain with Lieutenant Stewart." He looked at Daniel. "You'll be court-martialled for this."

Vincent glared at the Captain with an intensity that was hard to look away from. He put out a hand to stop one of the arresting soldiers from grabbing Daniel. "Now you hold on for just one minute. There's a bigger story to this, and I think you boys know it."

Captain Taylor smiled. Something in his gut told him he held an advantage over this man, that he had a lot more to lose than the Captain this day. "He deserted his post. He'll have ample opportunity to explain why at his court-martial."

Vincent turned to the Justice. "Are you going to just let this happen?"

The Justice shrugged. "It's a military matter. There's nothing I can do in that regard."

"An innocent man's life is at stake."

"Then we'd best get to the mess hall and resume the court proceedings, so you can testify to his innocence."

•

Jimmy wore a cheeky grin as he peered into the jar at Bandah and Talia. "What a shame for you two that pixies have to be on the move to jump between the Crossworlds." He laughed. "I've always wanted to have a pixie as a pet. Now I've got two of you!"

Bandah sat at the bottom of the jar with his head slumped between his knees. Talia stood and started to let fly, telling Jimmy what she thought.

Again, he laughed. "Oh, I'm so sorry. Can't hear you through the glass. Maybe that's because I forgot to put the air holes in. Might be wise to calm down and conserve your air. I've got things to attend to. Don't run away now, will you?"

He stood up and walked away from where the glass sat next to the injured fairies on the large rock downstream from the pool. The soldiers were sitting around, relaxing and soaking up the sun that had broken through the clouds not long before. A couple of them stood by the water's edge skipping stones. "Hey! Snap to it. We don't know when the witches are going to come back through that portal. When they do, we need to be ready."

One of the soldiers turned and asked, "Should we even pay attention to what you've got to say now you're in a civilian body?"

Jimmy walked up to the man and swung his fist, sending him flying onto his back in the pool's shallows with a broken nose. "You can get the pixies to fix that for you after we're done here." He turned and faced the others. "Any more questions or suggestions?"

They shook their heads, grabbed their rifles, and got to their feet.

Then the cicadas started. Jimmy looked around the trees. "Cicadas, at this time of year?" The birds joined in: magpies, bellbirds, whipbirds, and kookaburras.

The soldiers could barely hear Jimmy over the cacophony. "They must be coming."

The cicadas grew louder, starting to sound more like words as the deafening noise reverberated in the soldiers' ears. *They are coming, they are coming...*

With Jimmy and the soldiers focusing their rifles on the centre of the pool, Eldar took the opportunity to come out of hiding, flying across the creek and landing by the jar. She wrapped her knees around the base, to keep it steady, with her arms around the lid. Satisfied that she had a good grip, she tensed the muscles in her arms and shoulders, putting everything she had into trying to twist the lid. It was no good. She relaxed, took a breath, then clenched her teeth as she tried again. Still no good. She looked at her broken and injured sisters lying on the rock. If she was going to have any chance of getting them to safety, she'd just have to get the pixies out first.

Inside the jar, the pixies watched. Talia said, "She'll never do it. She doesn't have the strength."

Bandah got to his feet. "I've got an idea. What if she pushes the jar off the rock, letting it break when it falls. If we huddle together in a ball, we can use our wings as shields to protect us when the glass breaks."

Talia smiled. "And again, I like your thinking." She tapped on the glass to get Eldar's attention, then they started gesturing with their hands, as though playing charades, to communicate their idea.

Eldar smiled once she understood what they were suggesting. She braced herself behind the jar and rocked it back and forth while indicating with her fingers that she would do it three times then push it all the way. Bandah and Talia embraced each other and covered themselves as much as they could with their wings. They felt a moment of free-fall when the jar toppled over, then had the wind knocked out of them when it hit the ground and shattered.

In the instant before the jar hit the ground, the cicadas and the birds stopped. Jimmy and his soldiers turned as one at the sound of the jar shattering. He raised his rifle and aimed at Eldar.

His finger was about to squeeze the trigger when the water at the pool's centre erupted. An impossible wall of water, holding more than what the whole pool contained, rushed from the pool's centre to the shoreline. The soldiers turned to flee, some of them casting their guns aside in panic. It was to no avail. The wave crashed over them, knocking them to ground and sending them tumbling against rocks and trees.

The surging water left the centre of the pool dry, revealing the Reverend, the witches, Ferdinand and Darcy. Having broken away from Kerridwen's influence when crossing between worlds, Darcy O'Sullivan had reverted to human form.

They were all hunched over and coughing up water when they heard Jimmy's voice. "Who's first?" He stood in a knee-high muddy torrent that was rushing back down the hill. Still holding his rifle, Jimmy once more prepared to fire.

"Dad!" yelled Darcy as he started toward the shore.

The possessed Jimmy O'Sullivan smiled. He looked at the boy and said, "You'll do," as he squeezed the trigger.

Nothing happened.

The flintlock rifle was waterlogged.

Meredith reached out then pulled back, ripping the gun from his hands. She held her hand low to draw power from the Crossworlds.

"No!" yelled Patsy. She got up and ran toward Jimmy, blood still pouring out from the torn flesh of her left hand. The water running back to the pool knocked her from her feet. With grim determination, she got up and continued.

Jimmy yelled at his soldiers, "Get them." He pointed at Patsy. "She's the danger, stop her!"

Those who didn't have broken bones from the crushing of the wave stood up and ignored him. They'd had enough.

As Patsy approached, two of the soldiers turned to each other and nodded in agreement.

It was time to bring this madness to an end, time to cut their losses.

The only way to do that was to stop the Nasqa possessing Jimmy O'Sullivan… to force him to face his reckoning with the young witch.

They grabbed him and held his arms back.

"No, this is treachery!" Jimmy struggled to break free as Patsy approached. He looked into her eyes and saw emotionless determination.

Throughout the ages, the Nasqa had always feared the under-gods, but never witches or wizards.

But this girl was different.

She was someone to fear.

Patsy stood before him and for a moment did nothing. Then she reached inside and tore the Nasqa from Jimmy's body.

Instead of flinging it into the void or another crossworld, she held it high and addressed the remaining soldiers. "If you agree to leave now, I will let you go back to your own world rather than cast you into the void. But hear this…" She climbed onto a rock so all could see her. "It is on the understanding that you will all vow never to come back and that you will spread the word. For countless centuries my family's bloodline has fulfilled the sacred task of protecting this world from that which would come across worlds to do us harm. We have defeated Sellemae and now, we have defeated the under-gods. Take us on at your peril."

She opened her hand, releasing her grip on the Nasqa. It slipped away, grateful to be still in one piece and not trapped in the void.

The soldiers holding Jimmy's slumped form eased him to the ground while the last of the water ran down the hill, then they collapsed as the Nasqa controlling them departed. The same happened with the other soldiers gathered by the creek.

Darcy O'Sullivan ran up the bank and threw himself to his knees next to his father's unconscious body. He turned to Patsy and asked through his tears, "Will he be alright?"

A small voice behind him said, "He'll be fine. He just needs a day or two to sleep and recover."

Darcy turned. "Who, or should I say what, are you?"

Patsy said, "May I introduce you to Bandah? He's a pixie… and he does a wonderful impersonation of a cockroach when he wants to."

Bandah wanted to respond, but his eyes were drawn to the pain etched across his grundai's face as the Reverend carried Neridah's limp form from the pool, Meredith walking alongside him with her head bowed in sorrow.

The Reverend carried Neridah up the path until he reached a dry section where he could lower her to the ground. Bandah sought to console him while Talia inspected her body. She ran a finger along the side of Neridah's neck then looked up and declared, "There's still life!"

The Reverend raised his eyebrows as hope returned.

Talia reached into Neridah's chest and began massaging her heart, coaxing it to beat again. She looked up at the Reverend. "She needs your heart to help hers."

"How would I do that?"

"Sing to her," said Talia. "Sing from your heart to hers."

"What should I sing?"

"Whatever is deep within you. It doesn't need to be words, and it doesn't need to be heard. Her heart needs to feel yours. She needs to feel your love."

The Reverend took hold of Neridah's hand. He took solace from the lingering feeling of life's warmth in her soft fingers. Looking down at her closed eyes, he marvelled at the simplicity of a beauty that couldn't hide behind scratches, bruises, or any of the other evidence of the battle she'd been through these past hours... a battle she'd fought because of her love for him. If his heart had limbs, he felt it would reach out from within and embrace her.

He let his face hover over hers, inspecting every detail of the face he knew so well.

The only woman he'd ever loved.

He heard a gentle sound that soothed his anguish. It took several seconds before the truth dawned on him. The melody was his own voice, a tune that unfolded of its own volition as he explored the depth of his feelings. It was only then that he realised something had changed. Neridah's hand was gripping his as he was hers. The next instant, Neridah's eyes sprang open. Her chest heaved violently, sending Talia flying back. She sat bolt upright and coughed up copious amounts of water.

Once the coughing subsided, she turned to the Reverend and buried her face in the warmth of his chest, wrapping her arms around him and holding him tight. "You made it. You came back."

"Aye. And it's your doing more than anyone else's. I don't know that anything other than those letters would have been able to break me out of the bewitching spell Kerridwen and Albiorix had me under." He stroked her hair, tilting her head back slightly so she was looking in his eyes. "How did you know the box contained those letters?"

"I didn't. I just trusted that if the box meant enough to you that it was all you had bothered to save from your house, then it must somehow relate to us." She smiled. "I placed my hope in trusting that your love for me was equal to my love for you."

•

"So, Vincent Donaldson, you claim this man to be innocent on the basis of his good character and the assurances of a soldier who is now awaiting court-martial?"

Vincent looked the Justice in the eye. "Absolutely, Your Honour. And I believe the soldier to be innocent as well. The guilty parties here are Captain Taylor and his lackey, Lieutenant Stewart, who he sent to terrorise Mr McIntyre's family."

"Hmmph." The justice looked at the witness, then to the defendant who stood with his head bowed as he struggled to remain standing in his chains, then to the Captain with his bushy sideburns, medals of honour, and full ceremonial uniform. "Captain Taylor, while I see the possibility of the truth in your accusations against this poor soul, you have yet to convince me of his guilt."

A soldier rushed in through the back of the mess hall and approached the Captain. Everyone watched in anticipation when the soldier whispered in the captain's ear. The Captain smiled as he looked up to the Justice. "Your Honour, I have just received word that Lieutenant Stewart has arrived and wishes to give evidence."

The Justice leaned back in his chair. "By all means, send him in."

As soon as Lieutenant Stewart entered the room, Captain Taylor sensed something was wrong. His smile disappeared as the impeccably groomed Lieutenant approached the bench.

The Justice looked at him. “Lieutenant Stewart, do you swear to tell the truth, the whole truth, and nothing but the truth, so help you God?”

“I do, Your Honour.”

The Justice gestured toward Colin. “Do you know this man?”

“I have met him only once, Your Honour. Captain Taylor and I encountered him on our way to his property. He was on the road himself, setting out to bring the body of a magistrate, the Justice Albert Johnson, to the barracks, here, at Springwood. He told us the man had died from what he believed to be a heart attack the day before during a meeting at his property. He wanted to be sure that the truth of his death was known and that he could be examined by a doctor to determine the true cause of his death. He was setting out to carry out his duty as all good citizens should.”

“Do you believe him innocent?”

“Yes, Your Honour, I do.”

The Justice turned to face Captain Taylor. “It would seem to me that the only case you have against this man is your own personal vendetta.” He banged his gable. “I declare Colin McIntyre to be innocent of all charges.”

Captain Taylor’s eyes bulged as he protested. “Your Honour, we were heading to his property for a reason, under the orders of the Governor himself!”

“You will shut your mouth, Captain, or I will hold you in contempt of court. If the Governor has a problem with my release of Mr McIntyre, then he can follow due process under the laws of New South Wales. Case dismissed.” He got up from the table and prepared to leave, then stopped and looked at the Captain. “I’ll be sending a report of this trial to the

Legislative Council and, I can assure you, it will not be favourable to you personally. I would suggest you keep your head low." He turned to Colin. "I believe you to be a good man. The injuries I see upon your body tell me more about the Captain than about you." He then cast his gaze on the Lieutenant. "Will you see that this man reaches his home in safety?"

The Lieutenant nodded. "Absolutely, Your Honour."

The Justice walked to the door then paused in the doorway. He looked over his shoulder. "One more thing, Captain. If I hear of any harm coming to the gravedigger or that soldier you intend to court-martial, I'll personally see to it that you're tried on charges of perjury. Good day, sir."

*

Patsy was sitting on a rock with Bandah inspecting her wounds. Ferdinand sat on her lap purring while Patsy stroked him under the chin with her good hand. Meredith sat next to her and put an arm around her shoulder. "I was so proud of you when you made that speech. You're learning."

Patsy allowed herself a half smile. "I'm still angry with myself about Kerridwen. I trusted her."

"And it's good that you did."

"You didn't. But you pretended you did."

"Yes, but I'd been warned as a child by my grandmother about the under-gods. Despite that, I wanted to be sure before I cast judgment and influenced the opinion of others."

"She played with our minds. She had me convinced… and Father too." Patsy looked down at the cat. "The Reverend says that I shouldn't trust Ferdinand."

"Well, that's your decision to make."

Bandah looked up and asked, "Can I offer an opinion?"

Patsy and her mother looked at each other, then Meredith replied, "Maybe later. With everything else we're dealing with, the last thing I want to worry about is whether or not to trust a cat."

Bandah went back to tending Patsy's wound. He'd never liked the cat.

Meredith looked around at the soldiers. Some were on their feet, but many of them had injuries that prevented them from moving. Their moaning made it feel as though they were in the aftermath of some great military campaign. She looked downstream to the rock where Eldar was doing her best to comfort the wounded fairies. Then, she allowed herself to wonder about Colin's fate. She wanted to believe those who had gone to his rescue had been successful, but it was hard while surrounded by such suffering.

She'd become lost in her thoughts about Colin when her attention was drawn to a soldier coming down the hill with his hands in the air. He was waving a white handkerchief and was followed by another three holding their hands in the air. "We surrender, your surviving servant is free… as we are free from the creatures that stole our minds."

Patsy and Meredith smiled, then hugged each other. Maybe they'd be able to relax now.

Patsy lifted her head from her mother's shoulder. "Did you hear that?"

The cicadas.

Meredith said, "This isn't good."

She is here, she is here…

Neridah walked across to join them, drawing the Reverend

behind her by the hand. She looked at Patsy. "I'm glad now that you looked up the spell."

Patsy and Meredith stood up and the three witches held hands in preparation.

The noise of the cicadas rose to a deafening roar, then the pool exploded, every drop within it flying into the surrounding trees. Standing in the centre, shrouded in an electric dance of energy, stood Kerridwen. Her youthful appearance was gone. Rotting flesh dripped from her bones like wax dripping from a candle.

The Reverend leaned in toward the witches and whispered, "Whatever she does, whatever she throws at you, don't fight back."

Kerridwen sneered, "Why would that be, Alfred?" She thrust an arm at one of the injured soldiers, causing him to scream out in pain.

The Reverend continued, "If you attack her, she'll use what's left of her garland to absorb the power. She's weak, too weak to fight you head on."

Kerridwen glared at the Reverend. "How dare you accuse me of weakness." She threw an arm forward, sending a bolt of lightning at him. He flew back ten paces, landing on his back unconscious.

Neridah put her hands to her lips and screamed, "Alfred!"

Kerridwen turned her attention back to the witches. "Come on, take me on."

Patsy said, "The Reverend was right. She needs us to fight. She knows she can't beat us unless she draws from our power."

Kerridwen locked her gaze on Patsy. "You recalcitrant pest! Kneel before me or taste my wrath."

Patsy said, "No."

Kerridwen disappeared and reappeared directly in front of Patsy, then physically pushed back against her with her hand engulfed in the dancing lightning.

Patsy hit the ground laughing. "That didn't even hurt. You used the last of your real power trying to scare us when you hit the Reverend." She got to her feet. "You probably can't even go back to where you came from now without our help." She smiled. "Which we're more than happy to give." She started chanting. *Kerridwen le cana dis-tarah…*

Kerridwen said, "No, don't… there's nothing left for me there. We can work together. I can give you power beyond your dreams."

"And that's what you don't understand about me. I don't dream of power."

The three witches picked up the chant together: *Kerridwen le cana dis-tarah, Kerridwen le cana dis-tarah…*

It was hard to distinguish between the moment Kerridwen was there, and when she was gone. The witches didn't care one way or the other. All that mattered was that Kerridwen was gone… banished from their world forever.

CHAPTER 20

Neridah couldn't believe it. "You're doing this to me again?"

The Reverend continued packing his saddle bags. "I have a house to rebuild and a church that is my responsibility. It doesn't mean I love you any less."

"How so? You can actually recant your vows, you know. Other priests have done it."

"I believe we've had this discussion before."

"I don't see how you can call it a discussion when you avoid giving a decent answer every time."

The Reverend took a deep breath and looked to the ground as he composed his thoughts. "I followed the path I chose so as to find the strength to rescue you from Sellemae's lair. Without having done that, we wouldn't be sharing this discussion now." He looked into her eyes. "I love you more than I imagine it's possible for any man to love a woman. But I did take those vows, so we have little choice but to content ourselves with sharing what we can of our lives. In all honesty, Neridah, my life would be meaningless without you."

She started crying. "You just don't get it, do you?" She turned away and ran back to the house.

The Reverend looked up as she disappeared inside. He'd have to make a point of coming by to visit more often than he had in the past year. He secured the last of the saddlebags, then mounted Elsa and rode away.

*

The Reverend Alfred Casey could feel a presence as he rode up to his church and the burnt out remains of his home. He dismounted and walked Elsa to her stall in the stables.

A pair of wallabies watched him walk from the stables and up the paddock to the steps of his church.

There was something in there, he could feel it. Something that tried to reach into his mind. The wooden steps creaked under his weight. He put his ear to the door and wrapped his fingers around the handle. He couldn't hear a thing inside.

A magpie warbled in the distance as he pulled down on the handle. He leaned in, the door creaking on rusty hinges as it opened.

His foot echoed through the church as he stepped inside. The silhouettes of twelve heads sat motionless in the front pews.

He walked up to the end of the aisle then turned to face the one who sat closest. "Felibrey?"

Felibrey stood up and held out the Reverend's silky oak box. "We brought this for you. We have seen the power it gives you."

The Reverend took the box. "Thank you." He surveyed the faces of the twelve he'd chosen while his mind was held captive in Dellakaran. "Why are you here?"

Felibrey spoke for them all. "Because the hunter was wise to choose you. We feel privileged to have sworn an oath to serve you."

"But, with the collapse of Dellakaran, would you not have been free to return to your own worlds?"

"We have served in the garlands for many thousands of years. Those we knew in our own worlds have long since passed away. Our worlds have changed, and so have we. They are no longer our homes. In serving you, we found a purpose. You have a wisdom that the under-god did not."

The Reverend felt humbled. "It is I who feels that I should be learning from you."

Bordauex the Learned stood up. "No, we are not teachers. Short though your life has been, you have used it well. We have all learned much from you already. We will follow you, that we may learn more."

Destellie the Devout stood up next to Bordauex. "And we will help you rebuild your home."

The Reverend placed a hand on her shoulder. "Well then, we may need to add a few rooms."

*

Patsy walked down the stairs and heard her parents talking to someone in the sitting room. As Patsy tentatively looked through the door, her mother gestured to her and said, "Patricia, this is Miss Jenkins. She'll be your new tutor as of next week."

Miss Jenkins turned and looked at Patsy. "I'm so looking forward to spending time with you. Are there any subjects that you like more than others?"

Patsy smiled as she took a tentative step into the room. "Do you know much about science?"

"It's my favourite subject… especially when it comes to what's being learned today about physics."

Patsy clapped her hands, giggled, then raced out of the room and down the passage to the kitchen. "Cook, you simply must meet the new tutor. She likes science."

Cook leaned back and looked Patsy up and down. "And what would you be wanting to learn about science for?" She placed a bowl of porridge on the kitchen table where Patsy had taken a seat and continued talking before Patsy had a chance to answer. "A young girl like you should be focused on learning about manners and needlework—things that will help you find a good husband." Patsy smiled, she knew Cook meant well and that there was no point trying to convince her the world was changing, that men and women would one day be seen as equals.

She ate her breakfast then said, "I'm going for a walk in the paddock."

"Okay then. Just make sure you're back in time for lunch."

The pathway to Krinkle-myst's cabin appeared as Patsy approached the bottom of the paddock. As soon as she saw the ball of pixie-dust she closed her eyes and allowed herself to travel the winding pathway through the forest in its sparkling wake. A minute later, she was in the stone cabin. The Book of Wisdom still sat on a table by the fire. Krinkle-myst was sitting in his corner writing on sheets of vellum.

"Hello, Mr Krinkle-myst."

The wood-elf turned and looked at Patsy over the top of his glasses. "Hello, you've had quite an adventure."

"Would you like me to tell you about it?"

"Oh, there's no need for that. I've just about finished writing your story, that others might know of your recent exploits."

"Who would want to know about that?"

"Lots of people, like the one who's reading about our discussion right now."

Patsy looked around. "Can I see them?"

"No, but they can see you."

"How can that be?"

"Never underestimate the power of words and the imagination. Think of all the times you've seen something in your mind's eye that has turned out to be real."

The wood-elf turned back to his manuscript.

Patsy walked over to the fire and warmed her hands. She looked at the Book of Wisdom and asked, "Is it safe for the Book of Wisdom to return to the library now?"

Krinkle-myst sat back and turned to face her with an expression that suggested the answer was obvious. "Of course it is."

"Then, why is it still here?"

"Because it's been waiting."

"For what?"

"Open the book and you might find out."

Patsy turned the key to unlock the book, then opened it to a page in the middle. She turned to face Krinkle-myst. "The page… it's blank!"

Krinkle-myst opened the drawer of his writing desk. He pulled out a bottle of ink and a quill then walked over to Patsy. "Well, I guess the book must be waiting for you to share the wisdom you've learned during your latest escapade."

THE WITCHES OF THE CROSSWORLDS

BOOK III

FUTURE HISTORY

… the correct way to view time is like this, with all points co-existing together. There is little relevance as to what is future or past unless you are sitting somewhere within that line. From outside the line, it's all one and the same moment.

Krinkle-myst

PROLOGUE

Captain Taylor closed his eyes and took a deep breath before he entered Governor Pritchard's office. The Nasqa, or mind thief, possessing the captain's body was unaccustomed to feeling such emotions. He'd never experienced anything like anxiety until his humiliation before a justice of the peace at Colin McIntyre's trial twelve months earlier.

Nothing could have prepared him for this, though. The gravedigger, Sean O'Malley, sat in a chair across from the Governor. He was well groomed, wearing new clothing, smoking a cigar, and drinking a brandy. He stood up and extended his hand to the Captain. "What a wonderful day it is, made all the better for us being re-united."

Captain Taylor feigned a smile as he accepted O'Malley's limp and clammy hand for the briefest of moments before turning his attention back to his host. "Governor, it's a great honour to be summoned here today."

Governor Pritchard took a generous drag on his cigar, then gestured toward an empty chair. "Angus, my dear friend, take a seat. And for God's sake man, can we dispense with the formalities? Please, call me Charles." He grabbed the brandy decanter and poured a generous glass, which he handed to the Captain. Then he opened the cigar box on his desk. "Cigar?"

"No, thank you."

The Governor brought his hands together and cracked his knuckles before placing his feet up on his desk. "I can't begin to tell you how pleased I am that you could both make it today." He grinned as he watched the two men before him cast a nervous glance toward each other. He leaned back, looked toward the door to an adjoining office, and called out, "Gladys, you can come in now."

Mrs Gladys Bradshaw shuffled into the room with her eyes cast down. Her clothing was soiled, the flesh on her face and arms covered in grime.

The governor stood up and walked around the desk. "Gentlemen, I'd like you to meet Gladys Bradshaw." He put his arm around Gladys's shoulder and hugged her tight. "Widow, and former host to one of our kind." He brushed a lock of hair from in front of her eye. "One who fell victim to the pixies while performing her duty on our behalf at the McIntyre property." He looked down at the two men seated before him. "That was just on two years ago." He rested his forehead against the side of the widow's head. "The poor woman, losing all the power that went with her symbiotic relationship to our kin. The whole ordeal sent her quite mad." He took hold of her chin and turned her face to his. "You'd love to feel that power and security again, wouldn't you Gladys?"

The woman nodded then cast her eyes downward once more.

Governor Pritchard clapped his hands together as he moved away from her. "And this, gentlemen, is where you two can be of great help." He pointed to O'Malley. "You, Sean, have made no secret of your desire, your desperation even, for a host of higher station."

O'Malley looked to his feet as he shook his head, then, with a grim expression and a tear welling in his eye, he looked at the Governor. "I'm sorry, Your Governance, sir…" He looked away and his lower jaw trembled with no words coming out. *I have to say it*, he thought. *It won't change anything, but I have to say it.* He closed his eyes and shook his head. "It's just that I'm struggling… I'm struggling to see how there is much of a betterment in going from a gravedigger"—his eyes betrayed his dread when he opened them and stared at Gladys—"to a mentally deranged widow."

The governor smiled and stepped forward to be between the two men in their chairs. He squatted and put his arms around their shoulders. "Ah, but this is where it gets really good for you, Sean. You see, Mrs Bradshaw's station will soon be much higher." He turned to the Captain to make sure he was paying attention, then back to O'Malley, "That is, once she's married to the Captain, to the Captain of Springwood Barracks." His eyes sparkled with joy as he grinned at O'Malley. "By this time tomorrow, you'll be known as Mrs Gladys Taylor." He gave O'Malley a gentle punch in the shoulder. "You lucky old dog, you."

O'Malley cast his eyes toward Gladys, then glared at the Captain before turning his gaze back to the Governor. "And what's the benefit for yourself in this?"

The Governor straightened up. "You men are both familiar with the McIntyre property?"

The two men nodded in grim silence.

The Governor looked at the Captain. "Wouldn't you just love to have the sweet taste of revenge against the father of that family? What was his name?" He looked up snapping his fingers. "Ah, that's it." He turned back to the Captain. "Colin, Colin McIntyre. I know I certainly want revenge. There were a great many Nasqa who gave up on this world thanks to that family… not to mention our kin who ended up lost in the void."

Captain Taylor grimaced, his fingers massaging his forehead as the proposition the Governor had put forward swirled around his head. "Begging your pardon, Governor—"

"It's Charles. Just call me Charles."

"Begging your pardon, Charles, but there wouldn't be any need for me to get my revenge if it weren't for this lying scumbag here that you want to marry me off to."

The Governor leaned back and spread out his hands. "But don't you see? That's why this plan is such a good one. It was no secret that you two had a bit of trouble getting on with each other during all that kerfuffle last year. And the way I see it, you both bear some of the responsibility. I mean, really Angus, you did get a little bit nasty toward Sean. And Sean, you could've shown Angus here a tad more respect. After all, he is a captain and all. You can both see this as your chance to make amends. A fresh start."

A grin spread across the Governor's face as he tried to pick which of the two appeared more horrified. It was days like this when he derived the most pleasure from inhabiting this particular host.

O'Malley asked, "I'm just wondering what might be the rest of your plan. Do you have something specific in mind that you wish us to do to them?"

The governor snapped his fingers and pointed at O'Malley. "Very good question, Sean." He glanced across to the Captain. "See, Angus, Sean's already taking up the initiative. You'll make a wonderful team."

Captain Taylor closed his eyes in the hope it might somehow take him away from the situation. The Governor said, "I do indeed have a plan."

He opened a draw in his desk, pulled out a glass jar, and placed it in the middle of his desk. On first glance, it appeared empty. But when the Captain and O'Malley leaned forward for a closer look, they noticed some movement. There was a type of worm at the bottom of the jar that had the shape of a large leech, but refracted the light so it appeared transparent as though it were made of glass. The Captain looked up at the Governor. "Is that what I think it is?"

The Governor sat in his chair, leaned back, and put his feet up on the desk while having a quiet chuckle to himself.

O'Malley focused his attention on the jar as he whispered, "Tickle me pink if that isn't a stringworm."

CHAPTER 1

A magpie warbled. Miss Clara Jenkins smiled and looked around the treetops for where the bird might be as she and Patsy continued down the sandstone path. They descended further, then wound past an old fig tree that revealed the first glimpse of their destination. A pool expanded out from a bend in the otherwise narrow and fast flowing stream weaving through the southern end of the McIntyre property. A gentle mist rose from the icy water as its surface was caressed by the morning sunshine streaming through the tallest of the eucalyptus trees. It was a warm day, unusual for the middle of winter, made all the more magical by the sweet melody of the magpie and the myriad bellbird calls from the surrounding forest.

Patsy asked, "Please, please, Miss Jenkins, do tell me what the surprise is?"

Clara released a little giggle before replying, "It wouldn't be a surprise if I tell you."

"Is it a new book?" Patsy's question was punctuated by a nearby whipbird.

The broad grin expanding across Clara's face gave her away as she turned to face Patsy.

Infected by the contagion of Clara's smile, Patsy stopped walking and clapped her hands together. "I knew it! Please, just tell me what it is." In search of some kind of clue, Patsy's eyes darted around the woven wicker picnic hamper her tutor carried. "Is it about physics?" She jumped the next two steps and adopted a quicker stride than before to try and catch up to Clara who was now several paces ahead.

Clara raised a finger, a symbol of partial surrender to Patsy's wishes. "Ah, now that's something I am prepared to answer." She slowed her descent down the pathway so Patsy could catch up. "No, it's not about physics. It's more to do with biology."

Patsy came to an abrupt halt. Her eyes cast downward as far as they could go. "Biology? I thought it might be something exciting."

Clara's smile faded and she raised a hand to her brow as she took a deep breath to help compose herself. *It's okay, Clara. After all, while she may be gifted, she is still so young. Don't expect too much of her.* She exhaled and turned her attention back to Patsy, then placed a hand on the girl's shoulder. "Trust me, you'll be amazed." Patsy raised her eyes to look into Clara's as her tutor continued. "It's about a whole new field in science called 'Natural Selection.' It's all about how different types of animals came to be. Some scientists call it 'evolution.'"

Patsy moved past Clara and down the last few stairs that led to a small beach lining one side of the pool. She made a show of dragging her feet as she started across the sand. "How could that be as interesting as physics?"

Clara strode ahead and chose not to notice Patsy's displeasure as she took a seat on their favourite rock by the water's edge. "It's caused a lot of controversy." She pulled the book out of the hamper and handed it to Patsy. "It's called *On the Origin of Species*, and it's by a man called Charles Darwin."

Patsy took the book, but didn't look at it, preferring to continue staring at the ground. "It's a book about biology."

Clara's face screwed up in a frown. "I thought better of you than this, Patricia. We've spent almost a year together now learning about all sorts of interesting things." She stood up and walked a few paces away from her student, then turned to face her once more. Her lower lip quivered a little as she said, "This is the first time I've seen you shy away from something new."

An uneasy silence ensued.

It remained that way as Patsy sat down next to Clara on the rock, the place where they most liked to read together. After several uncomfortable seconds had passed, Patsy looked up. "Did you hear that?"

Clara looked from side to side, then said, "I don't hear anything."

"That's what I mean. The birds, the insects, they've all stopped."

The quiet was broken by a rustling sound in the bushes near the path, causing them to jump a little before turning their heads toward where they'd come from. A ginger tomcat emerged from behind and ran toward Patsy. Her face lit up as the cat approached. "Ferdinand! Do you know what's going on?"

Clara laughed as she rolled her eyes skyward. "Oh, but wouldn't it be nice if he could tell you."

Ferdinand purred and rubbed himself against Patsy as she stroked the back of his neck. "He used to tell me all sorts of things." She turned her focus back to Clara. "But he keeps his thoughts to himself these days."

Clara watched while Ferdinand looked at Patsy and let out a big meow. Then the cat turned toward the pool. "You know what? I think he actually is trying to tell you something, like he wants you to look at the water."

They both shifted their gaze toward the pool as a swirling vortex began stirring in its centre. Seeing Clara's wide-eyed expression, Patsy placed a hand on the woman's knee. "It's okay, Miss Jenkins, this happened last year, and the year before that."

Clara was speechless as she stood and took Patsy's hand in hers. "I think we should go up to the house now."

Patsy pulled her hand away as she rose to her feet and moved toward the water's edge. "You can go if you like. I want to stay and see what's coming."

"Coming? What do mean by coming?" asked Clara.

"It's a long story, and we usually keep it a secret. But I trust that you won't tell anybody about it."

The air above the pond began spinning, creating a whistling noise that held their attention on the vortex. It had grown wider, creating a hollow in its centre, a hollow that started moving toward the shore. There was something Patsy could see within its core. It was hard to focus on it at first, but as it came closer, it became clearer. The face of a boy.

Clara said, "I can't believe I'm seeing this. It must be a dream."

Patsy looked back over her shoulder to where Clara still stood, her arms wrapped tight about her chest. "It's okay, Miss Jenkins, I've witnessed this before. I can assure you it's quite real."

"That doesn't make me feel any better about it."

The vortex spread wider, allowing the boy to be seen from head to toe. He was lanky, with dark wavy hair and freckles on his cheeks. It looked to Patsy that he was around fourteen or fifteen years of age. He was staring at a small metal rectangular object that he held in his right hand. As far as Patsy could tell, he seemed to be talking to it. And his clothes, they were so unusual. He wore a shirt that had no collar or buttons. But most bizarre of all, it had a colourful picture on it of a screaming man with long hair holding what looked to be a disfigured violin against his waist. A strange kind of knapsack was on his back, and he wore blue trousers. As he came closer, she looked at his shoes. They were like no shoes she'd seen before, made of the brightest coloured fabric Patsy had ever seen. He lowered his small metal box then looked up at Patsy and said, "You must be Patsy. Patsy McIntyre." He glanced across at Clara. "And you must be her tutor, Clara Jenkins."

Clara swallowed hard, took a deep breath, and found the courage to step forward. She placed her hands on her hips and asked, "Who are you?" She took another step forward. "And how do you know our names?"

The boy's face lit up when he looked at the book Patsy was holding. "Oh wow! An original edition of Darwin."

"Answer me!" demanded Clara, her jaw trembling as she leaned forward. Her breathing had become short and loud.

The boy raised his eyebrows and leaned back in response to Clara's act of defiance. He recomposed himself, then stepped up to the riverbank and extended his hand. "Oh, sorry. I'm Jai, Jai Williams. I'm Patsy's great-great-great-great-grandson."

Clara ignored his gesture. "That's preposterous."

With Jai having cleared the water, the vortex had subsided. There was no sign of moisture anywhere on him or his strange clothing. Patsy giggled. "What a curious name you've got. It's almost as strange and funny as your clothes."

Clara spoke through clenched teeth. "Answer me." Her hands had screwed up into such tight fists that her nails were cutting into her palms. "How do you know our names?"

Jai smiled at Patsy then looked toward Clara. "How could I not?" He extended his arms as though the answer should be obvious. "You two are legends!"

Before Clara could reply, Colin's voice rang out from the top of the path. "Drop whatever you're holding and move away from my daughter."

Jai looked up and saw Colin's silhouette, the barrel of a flintlock directed toward him. Without taking his eyes off Colin he lowered the rectangular box to the ground, raised his hands above his head, and took two paces away from Patsy and Clara before asking, "Are you Colin McIntyre?"

"I'll be asking the questions. Why are you here?"

"Your ancestors, my mother and grandmother, they sent me to seek your help."

Colin began working his way down the steps, the flintlock still fixed on the boy. "What kind of help?"

"My little sister and the Book of Wisdom—" Jai struggled to get the words out as a tear ran down his cheek. "They've been taken." He wiped the tear away with the back of his hand. "The Nasqa, they took both of them."

•

Sean O'Malley left the chapel and took a deep breath. It was the first time he'd been in control of such a simple function in as long as he could remember. No more feeling like a passenger in his own body. Now, he was free of the Nasqa, free of the thief that had stolen his body and soul, using his mind the way a puppeteer uses strings. He pulled Governor Pritchard's letter of recommendation from his pocket. The very presence of the letter made him wonder if his freedom was an illusion. He looked down Macquarie Street toward Circular Quay and the Rocks. The undertakers the Governor had referred him to were located in Argyle Street. There were plenty of pubs between where he stood and his destination. Sean couldn't help but think that was part of the governor's reckoning. He reached into his pocket and pulled out his purse. He peered inside at the five gold sovereigns and ten shillings.

He was now the one in control.

No publican was going to get their hands on this accidental wealth.

He turned toward Hyde Park and looked to the distant spires of Saint Mary's Cathedral.

Confession, that's what he needed.

Sean started walking south toward the cathedral, determined to cleanse his soul of the corruption that had been so entrenched while the Nasqa had controlled him.

He looked around as he made his way along the busy thoroughfare, bumping into passers-by and offering cheerful apologies on each occasion. "Begging your pardon, sir." "My humblest apologies." "Sorry, sir. I'll try to take care to watch where I'm going."

On reaching the stairs to the cathedral he straightened his jacket and tried to appear taller. He couldn't remember the last time he'd ventured into a church. This would be the beginning of a new path for him, the path of righteousness. *Maybe I'd have taken vows had that dreadful thing not taken control of my mind.*

The scale of the building took his breath away. As he passed from the hot sun into its welcoming shelter, the aromas of soot and incense replaced the smell of the street in his nostrils. He glanced to his right and noticed a marble font containing what he assumed to be holy water. He dipped his fingertips in, then crossed himself before he made his way toward the altar, all the while marvelling at how the sunlight danced in the stained-glass window that dominated the towering back wall.

"Bless you, my son."

Sean turned and saw a priest wearing a black robe. There was a purple sash around his waist, and he wore a skull cap of the same colour. The priest looked to be in his sixties and wore a ring characterised by a large ruby. "Good morning, Your Holiness, sir. I've come looking to make a confession."

The priest raised an eyebrow. "Well, you timed it well. I was just making my way to the confessional." He gestured toward a group of three doors to the left of the cathedral. "Come, you can be the first to repent your sins."

Sean knelt in the dark confessional and waited for the priest to open the panel that would allow him to confess all that had happened. After what seemed an eternity, the wooden panel slid across. The priest on the other side of the heavy wire mesh seemed oblivious to his existence. Sean O'Malley initially fumbled with his words. "Bless me, Your Holiness, sir, for I am a sinner. That is to say, bless me, Father, for I have sinned. It is, by my reckoning, so many years since my last confession that I've now lost count."

"The Lord is forgiving of sins to those who repent, my son, regardless of how many years it may have been between confessions."

"There are a great many terrible things that I have done, but all of them occurred while I was possessed by evil."

"As long as you confess in full the Lord will forgive you."

"Well then, perhaps I should start with what I think the Lord would take the greatest affront to. That'd be the terrible things I've done to a man of the cloth."

"Did this man of God have a name that you knew of?"

"Oh, yes, Your Holiness. They call him the Reverend Alfred Casey. A man who fights evil like no other man I know."

The priest looked up at Sean for the first time. "I'd like to know about this priest, and how he fights evil. I'd like to know all that you can tell me."

*

Felibrey looked around, stunned by the enormous and diverse range of goods on the multitude of shelves. He stood silhouetted in the doorway of the Blackheath General Store. Specks of dust danced in the golden morning sunlight that streamed in through the shopfront's windows. Entering the shop, he tried to ignore the sensory overload of the new experience and focused instead on his goal of approaching the main counter. Once he'd reached his destination, Felibrey turned his eyes to meet those of the shop's attendant, a man in his sixties with bushes of white hair where he wasn't already balding. He had a meticulously waxed moustache and large sideburns. A stretch of silver chain revealed that he had a fob watch in the left pocket of his simple, grey waistcoat. Felibrey pulled a small purse from the pocket of his trousers as he said, "Hello."

The attendant placed his hands on the counter and leaned forward. He looked deep into Felibrey's eyes. "And good day to you, sir." He twisted his head a little and raised an eyebrow as he studied his customer's face. "I don't recall that I've seen you in here before."

Felibrey released an awkward smile. "This is the first time I've been to a shop. The Reverend Casey said that if I give you some coins, in exchange you'll give me the building materials I need. He said that you're a man who can be trusted."

"Aye, that's how it generally works. Tell me, what would your name be? I like to be aware of who I'm dealing with."

"My name is Felibrey."

"Well, Mr. Felibrey, I'm pleased to make your acquaintance." He extended a hand toward the Reverend's disciple. "My name is Lord, Jonathan Lord, but you're welcome to call me Jon. What would be your Christian name?"

Felibrey felt unsure how to respond. He stood with his mouth open but was unable to find any words.

"That's okay, Mr. Felibrey. I've met people before who are shy about such things on first meeting someone. I cannot help but wonder though, how does it come to pass that someone of your age has never before visited a general store?"

"I come from far away."

Jon nodded in acknowledgment. "That would explain the accent. You speak the language well, considering."

Felibrey smiled. "The Reverend is a good teacher."

"Aye, he's a good man in general. I'm guessing you'd be one of the twelve immigrants who offered to help him rebuild his house?"

"Yes, that's correct."

"So, did you come from the goldfields?"

"No, I come from far away. I have no interest in gold."

"Well, Mr. Felibrey, I must say, I like a man who'll travel a good distance to help another, especially one who has little interest in gold. What exactly would you be needing? Is it for the Reverend's house?"

"No, his house is finished. It's for the cottage I'm building for my fiancé and myself." Felibrey pulled a piece of paper from his pocket. "I have a list."

*

"Why should we believe you?" asked Colin, still pointing his flintlock at Jai.

The boy stood with his hands raised. He looked at his rectangular box then back to Colin. "I have pictures, photographs on my phone that will prove it."

"Phone?" Colin looked to Clara, who shrugged her shoulders.

"That's what the box you asked me to put down is called. It has lots of photographs in it, and other things as well." Jai bent his knees and started lowering his arms to reach for the phone.

"Get your hands back up. I've no desire to shoot a mere boy, but so help me, if you don't do as I say, then I'll have little choice." Colin glanced across to Patsy. "Patricia, would you be so kind as to retrieve our friend's little box, his 'phone' as he calls it?"

Patsy darted across and retrieved the phone from the ground and then raced back to be by Clara's side. They inspected it together, turning it over and looking for how they might open the box. Clara looked at Jai. "How do we open it?"

Jai kept his eyes on Colin and the barrel of the flintlock. "You don't open it. You just need to wake it from sleep mode then open the gallery app."

Clara raised her voice. "That makes no sense at all. Are you trying to make fun of us?"

Patsy took the phone from Clara. "Maybe I can open it. I've always been good at puzzles."

Jai said, "I can take you through it step by step. But you have to promise that you won't drop it when the screen lights up."

"My daughter doesn't have to promise you anything." Colin was working his way down the pathway, one measured step at a time.

"Please, Mr. McIntyre. It cost a lot of money. Mum will kill me if I go back with a cracked screen on it."

Patsy turned the phone over. "I don't see anything that looks like a screen."

"The side that's black, that's the screen," said Jai.

"It's so smooth. It's like black glass." Patsy stared at her reflection and ran a finger from top to bottom of the screen.

"There's a small button just below where your finger is. You need to press that, just gently."

Clara put a hand on Patsy's shoulder. "I have a pencil with me. Perhaps we should place this 'phone' of his on the rock and use that to press the button in case there's something spring-loaded inside."

Patsy ignored Clara's advice and pressed the button. "Arrh!!" Patsy and Clara screamed out in unison. Startled by the brightness of the screen lighting up after she'd pressed the button, Patsy threw the phone onto the sand.

Jai's face contorted as he cried out, "My phone!"

Colin raised the flintlock and pointed the sights toward the phone. "What kind of magic is in that box?"

With the rifle now pointed at something other than his face, Jai felt comfortable to lower his hands a little. "It's not magic, sir. It's technology, electronics, a type of science. Can I show you how it works?"

Patsy folded her arms and cocked her head to one side. "All magic is really just science. People only call it magic when they don't understand the science behind it."

Colin closed his eyes for a moment and grimaced. Why must she be so like her grandmother?

Patsy squatted down to pick up the phone, forcing her father to lower the rifle. "Patricia, what in God's name do you think you're doing?"

Patsy ignored him as she inspected the device. "Look, the glass is a bright blue, with little symbols inside coloured squares." She pointed it toward her father. "See?"

"Patricia, we can't know if it's safe. I want you to put it down now, or so help me there'll be hell to pay."

A voice called out from above them on the pathway. "Have you gone mad?"

Great, thought Colin, *just what we didn't need right now.* He turned around to face Patsy's grandmother, Neridah, as she came down the path wearing a green velvet dress with an elaborate white embroidered collar. Her mop of thick dark hair fell about her shoulders in a manner that suggested it had yet to be brushed since she'd woken. Colin set out to reply. "I—"

"Why are you waving that thing about in front of your daughter?"

Colin gestured toward Jai. "I was—"

Noticing the phone Patsy was holding and ignoring Colin, Neridah commented, "Oh, that looks interesting."

"It's his," said Patsy as she pointed at Jai.

Neridah looked at Jai and smiled. "Hello. My, what strange clothes you're wearing."

"He claims to be from the future," said Clara. She turned toward the pool. "He came out of there, and he's not even wet."

Neridah looked at Clara. "Well, if he says he's from the future, then I guess he probably is."

Clara held her hands against her cheeks as she shook her head. "No, he can't be. That's impossible."

"His coming from the future doesn't dictate that we should trust him," said Colin.

Clara stared at Colin. Her eyes suggested she was shocked that he could be entertaining the possibility that Jai had been telling the truth.

Neridah looked at Colin's flintlock, then to his face. "It doesn't mean you should be pointing that gun at him either, especially not when Patricia's already here." Clara's expression betrayed her continuing bewilderment at what she was hearing. "I mean really, Colin. Why even bother with your gun when it's so useless compared to what your daughter's capable of?"

"Do you really think it's wise to have this discussion in front of Miss Jenkins?" replied Colin.

Neridah shrugged her shoulders. "Um, begging your pardon, but didn't she just see someone come through the portal? Don't you think the cat's out of the bag now?"

"Could you please not talk about me as though I'm not here?" asked Clara.

Colin and Neridah both looked at Clara, then to each other, before realising that Patsy and Jai were standing together looking at his phone. Patsy looked up and said, "Jai just showed me how it works." She held up the phone so the screen was facing her father and grandmother. "Look, this is a photograph of his mother."

Neridah and Colin stepped closer to confirm what they were seeing. Colin turned to Neridah. "She looks just like you, only with red hair."

Neridah looked at Jai, then back to the photograph. She looked at Jai again. The colour drained out of her face as though she'd seen a ghost. "It can't be," she whispered. "You look just like—"

Clara said, "Could someone please have the courtesy to explain what's going on?"

Colin looked at Patsy. “Perhaps you should take Miss Jenkins up to have a chat to your mother, and then you can go and ask Darcy if we might be able to borrow some clothing from him so we can dress our new friend in a way that won’t disturb Cook and the other servants too much.” He turned to Jai. “And you, young man, might want to explain yourself in more detail while we wait for Patricia to return.”

CHAPTER 2

Jai stepped out of Darcy's bedroom and into the living area of the servants' quarters. With Darcy close behind, the boy paraded in front of Patsy and Neridah. He spread his arms out and asked, "Well, what do you reckon?" The trousers were baggy, but far too short for someone of Jai's height. Despite that, their looseness around his waist made it clear that, without the bulky suspenders, they'd soon be around his ankles. The shirt was much wider across the shoulders than Jai's frame, and even with the top button done up, it hung loose around his neck.

Patsy covered her mouth to hide a giggle, then Neridah raised her chin as she said, "You look far more presentable."

Darcy stepped forward and said, "Aye, but there's still one thing missing." He took off his flat cap and put it on Jai's head, pulling it down at the front as much as he could so Jai's eyes were hidden from view. He smirked as he turned to Patsy and Neridah. "We need to show mercy to the public at large and hide his face as best we can."

While everyone else in the room was laughing at his expense, Jai lifted the front of the cap, then turned to Darcy and asked, "What will you wear?"

"I've got another just like it… but I'd happily walk around with the sun in my eyes for a few days if that's the price of protecting the people from seeing too much of your face."

Jai smiled. "That's all well and good, but if you care that much, maybe you should stay indoors yourself."

Patsy said, "To be honest, your other clothes were a better fit, but at least you won't scare Cook now."

Darcy looked at her out of the corner of his eye. "Would you be sure of that? I've seen Cook jump at the sight of her own shadow."

"I've seen her jump at less than that!"

"Patricia!" Neridah glared at her granddaughter. "After everything that Cook has been through, don't you think she deserves more respect than that?"

Patsy cast her eyes down. "I'm sorry…" She glanced up at Darcy. He pulled a face and Patsy couldn't help but grin. She looked once more at Neridah's serious expression and burst out laughing. "I'm sorry, Nana-Neri, I just can't take you seriously when you're angry."

A subtle smile appeared on Neridah's face as she shook her head and stood up. "You most certainly are my granddaughter. I'd best go now and rescue your mother from Miss Jenkin's frantic questioning."

Patsy cast her eyes toward the ceiling and sighed. "I do hope she's alright. She was so distressed before."

Darcy said, "If you'd be asking me, I think it's about time she knew the truth about you lot."

Neridah glared at him then made her way to the front door, calling out as she went. "Well, Jai, all I can say is that I hope you've better manners than our friend Darcy."

Jai looked at Darcy. The Irish lad pulled a face as he shrugged his shoulders.

Patsy stood up and gestured to Jai. "Come on, I'll take you for a walk around the property."

•

Mrs Gladys Taylor stared at her new husband as their sulky approached the gate of Springwood Barracks. "Who'd have thought it, huh?" She turned her attention to her wedding band, twisting it as she spoke. "That you and I would end up hitched?"

Captain Taylor closed his eyes and grimaced. "I could really do without the reminder."

Gladys looked toward the barracks, then back to the Captain. "When we go in there, the men will expect us to behave like newlyweds."

The Captain stared straight ahead, refusing to answer.

"Don't worry yourself too much. I think I'll be more comfortable with the company of a bottle of rum than your good self anyway."

Captain Taylor turned to Gladys. "As much as it pains me to say it, that is completely unacceptable. I may be appalled by your presence, but the fact is, you are now my wife, and I will not tolerate any such behaviour, as I'm sure your host wouldn't either."

"Hah! What's she going to do about it? Be a nagging little voice in the back of my head? It only takes a few drinks to drown that out."

"Need I remind you that, as well as being my wife, you are the Governor's representative for education standards. How can you hope to muster the respect of the Blue Mountains community if you're falling around drunk in the mud? You need to tap into your host's experience if you want to pull this off."

A voice called out, "Congratulations, Captain." Captain Taylor and his bride turned to see where the voice had come from. A young lieutenant was running up to them. "Can I take your bags for you, sir?"

Captain Taylor brought the sulky to a halt. "Yes, of course."

The lieutenant looked at Gladys. "Welcome to Springwood Barracks, Mrs Taylor. We'll do our best to make you welcome."

Gladys cast a dismissive glance his way. "It's got to be better than the last time I was here."

"Excuse me, ma'am, when might that have been?"

Captain Taylor glared at his wife. "I think that she's referencing a visit to another barracks in Sydney. I don't believe she realises how different they can be."

An uncomfortable silence ensued as the three walked to the Captain's quarters. Once their bags were inside, the lieutenant said, "I'll be seeing you both in the mess hall for dinner then."

"Yes, quite." Captain Taylor closed the door as the lieutenant left the room. He turned and saw Gladys holding up an empty jar.

"We've got a problem."

"What do you mean, we've got a problem?"

"It's escaped."

Silence.

"The stringworm. It's managed to do a jump out of its jar."

"You must be joking."

"Trust me, I wouldn't joke about something like that."

"How? Isn't the lid still on?"

"You need more than a sealed jar to contain these things when they can smell something like that portal at the McIntyres'. That's the sort of place where they like to feed."

"But that's half a day's ride from here."

Gladys shook her head. "Well, it's gone, and that's the only thing that makes sense."

Captain Taylor stabbed a finger into his wife's chest. "Well, you, my dear, can be the one who tells Pritchard."

*

Patsy gestured toward the garden shed. "I've found all sorts of wonderful things in that shed, but Father gets quite cross if he knows I've been in there without his permission."

Jai glanced at the shed then turned to Patsy as they continued down the paddock. "I'm surprised I haven't met Reverend Casey yet."

Patsy laughed. "Why's that? It's not like he lives here."

"But I thought…" Jai let his words hang in mid-air.

Patsy stopped walking. "Oh, so is there something the boy from the future knows that I don't?" She spun around in a circle as though dancing. "Nana-Neri gets very angry with him sometimes." She paused and glanced up to the treetops. "Well, quite often really. She spends all week talking about how much she misses her Alfred"—she held her hands to her chest in a mocking fashion—"and how she's so looking forward to seeing him again." She spread her arms out. "Then, when he comes for dinner on the weekend, she almost always ends up arguing with him and storming off to her room in tears."

"Wow, I'm sorry to hear that. I just thought—"

Patsy cut him off and pointed to the bottom of the paddock. "Can you see that?"

"See what?"

"See how the trees look different there?"

"Oh yeah, and the light looks different too… more golden."

Patsy's face betrayed her excitement. "Krinkle-myst!"

Jai stared at her. "What do you mean?"

"Krinkle-myst, he's a wood-elf."

"My grandmother's told me stories about the legend of Krinkle-myst for as long as I can remember. But it's just stories."

Patsy gestured toward the shimmering portal leading to the forest that played host to Krinkle-myst's cabin. "That pathway, it only appears when he's here."

"Are you telling me he's real?"

Patsy picked up the hem of her dress and started running. "Of course he's real. Come on, he's probably here because of you."

Jai shook his head then started running after her. Once through the portal, he came to a standstill and turned around. "I can't see the house anymore."

Realising he wasn't following anymore, Patsy stopped as well. "Of course not, silly. We've passed through to another world."

"Oh yeah? And what world is this then?"

"Krinkle-myst says it's the world that no one's ever seen."

"Never heard of that one before. So, where is this Krinkle-myst?"

"He'll be in his cabin, working on one of his fairy tales."

"And how do we find his cabin?"

"By allowing ourselves to be there."

"By what?"

Patsy sighed. "For someone who's descended from a long line of witches, you don't seem to understand magic very well."

"You're still not making any sense."

Patsy looked up. "Or we could fly there."

"Fly?"

"You've never flown anywhere?"

"I've been on a plane and flown to Bali."

Patsy screwed up her face. "What's a plane?"

Jai smiled. "Planes are amazing. They're marvels of modern engineering."

Patsy stared at him.

"I guess that doesn't tell you much." He looked up for a moment and pondered how to explain a plane to someone who'd never even imagined such a thing before. "You know how a horse and carriage can carry people from one place to another?"

"Yes."

"Well, imagine a really big carriage, one that can carry hundreds of people and that flies through the air."

Patsy frowned at him.

"Seriously, I'm not making it up."

"How do they fly?"

"They have wings, like a bird, and really big engines."

"That sounds ridiculous."

"It's true."

"I'm going to get angry if you keep making fun of me."

"Seriously, I'm not lying."

"You wouldn't like it if I get angry."

"But I'm telling the truth." Jai could sense that she wasn't joking. He pulled his phone out of his pocket. "I think I might have a photo—"

A broad smile spread across Patsy's face as she looked past Jai's shoulder. "Pixie-dust!"

Jai turned around and saw the dancing ball of sparkles. "Oh, wow!"

"That's how we'll find Krinkle-myst's cabin. We'll follow the pixie-dust."

Jai tried to reach out and touch it, but it evaded his hand at every attempt, as though it were teasing him. Then it shot up high and started heading down the path.

"Come on, let's go." Patsy pushed herself up from the ground and was airborne in an instant. She moved about as though treading water in the air while waiting for Jai to do the same.

"What the… how'd you do that?"

"It's not so much that you do it, it's more that you let it happen." She reached down and took his hand. "Come on, just push off the ground."

Jai pulled his hand away. "No, I can't."

"If you want to be like that, then good luck keeping up." Patsy did a frog kick with her legs then started making sweeping actions with her arms to move through the air in the direction of the pixie-dust. Within seconds she had already travelled twenty paces.

Jai started running. "Wait! I can't keep up!"

Patsy was already out of sight up ahead. Her voice seemed distant. "Of course you can."

Jai kept putting one leg in front of the other, running faster than he ever had before. "I'll get lost out here."

Patsy's voice was barely audible. "Then you'd better keep up."

As he rounded a bend, Jai noticed a large tree trunk had fallen across the path. He was moving too fast to stop, so had little choice but to try and jump over it. He jumped high enough that his feet landed on the top of the log, then he pushed up and forward, determined to catch up to Patsy. He moved his arms as he'd seen Patsy move hers, hoping he might gain extra distance from his leap. The ground was moving rapidly beneath him, and yet he seemed to be maintaining his height.

Then he noticed the ground coming closer. He moved his arms again and imagined himself in the pool at his school's swimming carnival. He kicked with his feet and brought one arm at a time over his shoulder, as though swimming freestyle. Faster and faster, he stroked, not thinking of where he was, just the need to catch up to Patsy.

"Come on, the pixie-dust is way ahead of us now."

Jai could see Patsy up ahead now, and the treetops far below. "I can't believe it! I'm flying!"

"I don't really see it as flying. I think of it more as another kind of swimming."

"This is amazing!"

"Not as amazing as you expecting me to believe hundreds of people can fly in a box."

"But they do."

Patsy ignored him then pointed to a narrow stream of smoke up ahead. "That'll be from Krinkle-myst's chimney." She pushed against the air in front of her to slow herself down. Jai followed suit and started descending. "It's a lot quicker if you just allow yourself to follow the pixie-dust, but I could tell you weren't ready to try that yet."

Jai was looking below him at the approaching forest floor as he moved his legs as though pedalling a bicycle. "I can't believe how much this is like being in water."

"Air and water are very much the same as each other, you know. People just assume that because water is denser than air, that they can float in one but not the other. Anyone can swim through the air if they know how."

Once they landed, Jai's knees felt weak and he collapsed to the ground. "Whoa! I feel like I've run a marathon."

Patsy gave a reassuring smile as she offered a hand and helped him to his feet. "It's a bit like that the first time. It takes a bit more energy than swimming in water, but you move a lot faster."

Jai turned to face the little stone cabin. "There's no windows or doors, and it looks way too small for us to fit inside of it."

"It doesn't need doors or windows. Here, take my hand. Close your eyes and imagine you're inside. Allow yourself to be inside."

Jai did as she suggested, then heard the crackling of an open fire. He opened his eyes and looked at the room around them. There were two wooden chairs by the fire. A large cast iron pot was suspended from a tripod holding it over the flames. The steam rising from the pot carried aromas of cloves, mint and cinnamon. He turned to scan the rest of the room, finding it to be empty other than a small writing desk in the far corner. And sitting at that desk was a wood-elf, who wouldn't have been much taller than the height of Jai's knee.

Patsy ran toward the desk. "Krinkle-myst!"

Krinkle-myst turned and glanced over the top of his glasses. "Hello. You took your time getting here."

Patsy squatted low when she'd reached the desk, trying to bring her head down to Krinkle-myst's eye level. "I know. Jai's not used to allowing himself to move from one place to another."

Krinkle-myst glanced past Patsy to the nervous teenager standing near the fire. "Hmmph! Why does that not surprise me?" He pointed an accusing finger in Jai's direction. "There seems to be quite a few areas where you're lacking in wisdom, young man."

Jai opened his mouth to speak, but found himself lost for words when he noticed that he was now sitting in one of the chairs, with Patsy in the other. Krinkle-myst was standing by the fire, using a ladle to fill a metal cup with the sweet-smelling brew. He handed the cup to Jai. "Here, this will warm your soul and make you more comfortable."

As Jai wrapped a hand around the warm cup, he asked, "What is it?"

A smile filled the wood-elf's face as he looked up. "It's Mrs Krinkle-myst's special heart-warming recipe, perfected over thousands of millennia."

Jai took a sip. A warm glow embraced his taste buds, then spread through his mouth, oozing out to his cheeks before enveloping every part of his being with a sense of contentment. "Oh, wow. This is amazing." Krinkle-myst handed another cup of the elixir to Patsy. After she'd tried it, Jai could tell from her expression that it was having the same impact on her. He turned back to the wood-elf and whispered, "I feel so privileged."

"And so you should," Krinkle-myst snapped back at him.

Jai leaned back in his chair as Krinkle-myst stepped closer to him.

"Do you have any idea how much trouble you've caused me today?"

Jai held up his free hand in a look of surrender. He opened his mouth, but no words came out.

"As if one timeline isn't enough to look after! I was just about ready for Mrs Krinkle-myst and I to go on a holiday to one of the most beautiful places that no one's ever seen. Then along comes Jai, happily prancing his way through time and creating a whole new timeline for me to have to deal with."

"I, I didn't know."

"Then why'd you do it?"

"My little sister, and the Book of Wisdom. The Nasqa—"

"Yes, yes, I know all that already. I want to know what made you think that travelling through time might make things any better."

Jai looked across at Patsy. "All my life, my mother and grandmother have talked about the legendary Patsy McIntyre, and how no problem was ever too big to—"

Krinkle-myst reached across and covered Jai's mouth. "Now, just hold it right there. You don't want to make this worse by telling Patsy details about her future." He pulled his hand away and shook his head while holding a hand against his forehead. "Why? Why is it that nobody seems to understand time travel?"

Patsy said, "I remember when Kerridwen came, and the trouble that the time freezes—"

Krinkle-myst waved a hand at her dismissively. "Yes, yes, but that was just time freezes." He pointed at Jai. "This young man travelled over one hundred and fifty years through time."

Jai said, "But my grandmother had read about how to do that in the Book of Wisdom. Surely if it's in there, then there must be times when it's okay to do it."

"And you consider yourself a sound judge of when it's the right time to make such a choice?" asked Krinkle-myst.

"Look, I'm sorry. Okay?"

"No, it's not okay."

Patsy stood up and stamped a foot, causing a rumble to shake through the building. Jai and Krinkle-myst froze in response. Patsy took a step toward them. "We get it. Jai shouldn't have come here. But he's here. Is getting angry really going to help anything?"

Krinkle-myst sat in a small chair that had appeared behind him. "No, I guess not."

"I don't understand. You've always been so calm and measured in the past," Patsy said.

"I know. It's been a hard day." Krinkle-myst looked at Jai. "Have another sip on that elixir and I'll tell you a bit about time. You see, most people think of time from totally the wrong perspective. They see it in a linear fashion, believing the only thing that's real is the moment. That the past is fixed solid in history, and that the future is flexible." They had now transported to Krinkle-myst's writing desk, where he was drawing a line across a page. "They perceive time in a two-dimensional manner and as something that moves in one direction." When he'd finished drawing the line, they were back by the fire, with Krinkle-myst holding up the sheet of paper. He held it so the sheet faced Patsy and Jai. "This is how most people view time." He then turned the page, so they were looking down the length of the line. "But the correct way to view time is like this, with all points co-existing together. There is little relevance as to what is future or past unless you are sitting somewhere within that line. From outside the line, it's all one and the same moment."

Jai was focusing on the sheet Krinkle-myst was holding. "I'm really struggling to get my head around this."

"Of course you are. Anyone silly enough to use a portal to travel through time would struggle. Now, imagine that you are somewhere on this timeline, not knowing that everything that ever has happened, or ever will happen, is already defined. If you look back, what do you see?"

Jai looked at Patsy for reassurance before answering. She gave him a polite nod of encouragement. "Memories?"

Krinkle-myst smiled. "Exactly! But you can only see back so far. And the further back you look, the more those memories blur into those of parallel timelines, causing them to become distorted and inaccurate."

"So, if there's already multiple timelines, why should it be a problem if I've created another one?"

"Because you've created it using brute force rather than nature's way of just allowing them to unfurl, like a flower opening in spring. It's as though you've driven a bulldozer through a hundred and fifty years of past and future memories."

Patsy asked, "What do you mean by future memories?"

"I was wondering when someone would ask that one. The future is no different to the past, it's already happened. And the past is just as flexible as people perceive the future to be. Most people lack the comprehension, or even the ability, to see their future memories as clearly as they see their past. But there are some who do see them just as clearly."

"Clairvoyants?" asked Jai.

Krinkle-myst snapped a finger and pointed to Jai. "Now, I'm starting to think you might have promise. Yes! And there're others too." He looked toward Patsy. "The more powerful of the Crossworld Witches have always shown somewhat of a flair for seeing the future memories. But you have to be aware that, like with past memories, future memories are distorted by the parallel timelines."

Jai took another sip on his elixir, then asked, "These parallel timelines, are they related to the multiverse?"

Krinkle-myst smiled. "And…?"

"Well, they're all sort of connected, by strings of energy that pass through all of them… or something like that," said Jai.

"Yes, and that's important. Those strings create pathways through space, time, and different realities, different crossworlds. Most of the time, if someone uses a portal like the one on the McIntyre property, there is a magnetic repulsion that ensures one doesn't cross into a world that is close to the one you're already in. But there are other ways to pass through the Crossworlds that are more subtle. Sometimes, just being sad enough about an event in your past will actually shift you into a version of reality where whatever it was that happened was worse than it really was."

Patsy was getting more interested in the conversation now. "But if someone slips into another nearby crossworld like that, wouldn't they end up facing themselves?"

Krinkle-myst shook his head. "No, they effectively swap realities, so for the one in the world that is a sadder version of reality, they suddenly find things looking more positive. There's a blurring of realities for most people where they are able to drift from one reality to another. Sometimes it's driven by positive feelings, and sometimes by more negative ones." Krinkle-myst poured himself a cup of the elixir. "The problem we have now is that you, young man, have travelled into your past on the wrong timeline. Your reality is not the future of this Patricia McIntyre. You're interfering in the wrong timeline."

Jai and Patsy looked at each other, then Patsy turned to Krinkle-myst. "So, does that mean we're not related?"

Krinkle-myst looked upwards and shook his head before replying. "Of course you're still related. Relationships carry across timelines. If he were far enough removed that he were in a wholly different crossworld, then the connection becomes separate. But as it stands, he comes from what is a possible future for you, albeit an unlikely one." He turned to Jai. "And you've now effectively altered your past in a manner that's severed every timeline you've crossed and created whole new branches with unpredictable outcomes. Some of which will likely spread into this reality. These tears in the fabric of reality are hard to stop when they start to spread. They're like an infectious disease."

Lost for words, Jai buried his head in his hands.

Patsy looked at the wood-elf and said, "He was only trying to help his sister."

"The most calamitous events always start with the most noble of intentions."

"Is there anything we can do to fix it?"

"Not unless you're able to find your way to Jai's timeline and stop him from coming back."

Patsy stood up. "Come on Jai, let's go."

"Go where?" asked Jai.

Her eyes were narrow and focused as she glared at the wood-elf. "I'm going to consult the Book of Wisdom and find a way back to your timeline."

Krinkle-myst smiled and slapped his knee. "Now that's the Patsy McIntyre I'm used to."

In the next instant, Krinkle-myst had vanished.

•

Archbishop Darvos threw down his brandy then asked the Governor, "How'd you know the gravedigger would come to the cathedral? Hadn't you directed him to seek employment?"

Governor Pritchard smiled as he leaned back in his chair. "Come now, haven't you inhabited your host long enough to get a grip on how these creatures' minds work? This world has two types of hosts. There are those like Gladys, who long for the power we afford them, and the foolish ones who hanker for freedom, the ones who want to 'cleanse' themselves of us. As if the gravedigger was going to do as I'd asked after he'd been set free. Particularly when he'd just received more money than the poor wretch had ever seen in his miserable life."

"Well, I'm glad you warned me he was coming."

"So, you understand the problem now that he's confessed?"

"Oh, yes. This Reverend Casey, he needs to be dealt with sooner rather than later. I'll be heading straight to the railway station from here. We can't afford to have rogues like him out there when we've put so much effort into taking control of the churches in this country."

"I always knew you were the right choice to take over the bishop."

"Yes, but it's a shame about the arthritic knee in this body."

"Well, my friend, once you've dealt with our little problem, you can feel free to choose whatever host you please."

•

"Patricia!" Meredith was calling to her daughter as she walked down the paddock. She decided it would be prudent to check the garden shed before heading down the pathway to the pool in the creek. As she approached the wooden structure, she noticed the shimmer of golden light glowing at the edge of the bush, the portal to the forest that was home to Krinkle-myst's cabin.

Her pace slowed as she approached the portal, twisting her head as though it may help her see more of it. As it grew larger, she marvelled at how different the trees looked on the other side. Its shimmering light had her mesmerised. This was the first time she'd seen the path since her mother and Patsy had used it to hide from the soldiers a year ago. It was as though she could hear a song within the dancing sunbeams. The spell was broken when Patsy came racing through it, with Jai close behind. The boy tripped on the edge of the portal, bringing Patsy to the ground with him as he tumbled forward. The two of them looked at each other, then burst out laughing.

"Patricia!"

Patsy and Jai's laughter came to an abrupt halt when Patsy looked up and saw her mother's silhouette. It was clear from Meredith's stance that she was not impressed. Patsy looked back to Jai and couldn't help but let out a giggle.

"Patricia, this is no laughing matter."

"Sorry, Mother."

Meredith turned her attention to Jai. "And you must be the young man from the future that I've heard so much about this morning."

Jai got to his feet and offered Meredith his hand. "It's a pleasure to meet you, Mrs McIntyre."

Meredith glared at Jai's hand then looked back to Patsy. "You do recall, don't you, that the Education Department has sent a representative to Blackheath to check on how you are progressing under the tutelage of Miss Jenkins?"

Patsy rose to her feet, her eyes widening as she realised she'd forgotten all about the planned afternoon meeting. "I'm so sorry, Mother, I'd completely forgotten."

"Well, maybe you might be a little less forgetful if you actually considered asking my permission before leaping into other worlds."

Patsy sighed and lowered her head. "Sorry, Mother. It's just, I never know when the portal's going to appear. If I'd gone up to the house to let you know it was there, it may have been gone when I got back."

An uneasy silence followed. Meredith knew Patsy was right, but she certainly wasn't going to admit it. She chose to change the topic back to what was really bothering her. "The woman who's coming up from Sydney, we've been informed her name is Mrs Taylor."

Patsy replied, "Yes, I recall Miss Jenkins telling me that."

"Yes, well as it turns out, Mrs Taylor has only recently remarried. She was a widow. Her previous name was Mrs Bradshaw."

Patsy's jaw fell open.

"It gets even worse. She's now married to Captain Taylor, the man who tried to have your father hung last year. You need to lie low until she's gone, Patricia. I suggest you take Jai for a walk along the creek. She's not likely to want to look for you down there."

"But, what about Miss Jenkins, will she be alright? What if she loses her job because I'm not there?"

"She'll be fine, I'll see to that. You and Jai just need to get to the creek, and quickly. She'll be here soon, by my reckoning…"

•

Destellie rose from where she sat on the church steps, her eyes wide with excitement. She'd been there since just after sunrise when Felibrey had left. Inside the church, the Reverend Casey was up on a scaffold finishing the installation of a stained-glass window behind the altar. Destellie called out, "Reverend, he is almost here! And I could see that his cart is laid heavy with supplies. You were right."

The Reverend Alfred Casey kept his attention on the strip of window putty he was smoothing out. He checked the window was firmly in place before he turned to face Destellie. "I'm glad he's returned so soon. I felt certain he was ready for a trip into town. And far better that he does it on his own than appear too reliant on one such as myself." He climbed down the scaffold with the dexterity of a jungle primate. "Let's go out and give him the warm welcome he deserves."

Destellie ran to the door, pulling the hem of her long dress up so she could run faster. The Reverend smiled. Of all his disciples, it was Destellie who had most embraced the ways of this world. Felibrey arrived at the church entrance as she did. The Reverend's mind transported back to his teenage years as he watched them embrace, remembering the feeling of Neridah's warmth when they'd held each other close. The memory was just as fresh in his mind as it was the day it first happened. He closed his eyes and felt like he was falling as he remembered their lips coming together that day. The feelings that had overwhelmed him then had informed every decision he'd made since. He took a deep breath and whispered, "The sacrifices we make for love."

"How about you stop feeling sorry for yourself and do something about it?" The Reverend looked down at his shoulder to the pixie standing there with her arms folded.

Another voice caused him to turn the other way. "Come on, Talia, give the guy a break."

Talia pointed to Destellie and Felibrey as they remained oblivious to the rest of the world. "See that? That's what both Neridah and Alfred deserve. Forty years that poor woman spent wrapped in a cocoon in Sellemae's lair." She took to the air and hovered in front of the Reverend's nose, causing him to go cross-eyed. "What's the point in you spending all those years dedicated to rescuing her if now you deny her what these two lovebirds have?"

Bandah protested. "How many times do I have to tell you, he took a vow?"

Talia put her hands on her hips and glared at the Reverend. "Vows are made to be broken… as my husband of ten thousand years has been so deft at demonstrating."

Bandah looked away. "Not this again."

The Reverend took a step back, his brow transforming into a frown. He brushed Bandah off his shoulder, taking the pixie by surprise. "If you two don't mind, there is a happiness in this moment for two of my dear friends that I would like to share." He took a few long strides toward Felibrey and Destellie, then threw his arms around them both.

Talia stared at Bandah. "So much for that bond you were so proud of with your grundai."

Bandah shrugged his shoulders. "What can I say? That hasn't really been the same since he brought Neridah back."

"I don't understand these vows of his. Surely there's some way that he could nullify them or something."

"You'd think so, but that's not Alfred's way."

Talia shook her head. "I feel so sad for Neridah."

"I feel sad for both of them."

Talia nudged Bandah's shoulder. "Hey, do you feel like a bit of nectar? There're some really juicy flowers in a nearby crossworld. The place has a great vibe as well."

Bandah grinned. "Now you're talking my language."

They took each other's hands and vanished.

*

Patsy and Jai walked upstream. Jai kicked a stone as he said, "My mum's going to be so jealous when she finds out I met Krinkle-myst."

Patsy looked up at the boy who was staring into space. "You know what, Jai? As much as you only arrived this morning, I'm enjoying you being here. You make me happy."

Jai looked at her and let out a little laugh. "I guess that's to be expected. What, with us being related and all that. I never imagined it could be so cool to spend time with a great-great-ancestor."

"Oh, look!" Patsy pointed out a leech on a rock. Its head waved about as it tried to find the source of the blood it could smell. "We'll need to check our feet when we get back. I've often picked up a leech or two coming up to this part of the creek."

"Tell me about it. Trust me, it's just as bad in that regard a hundred and fifty years from now. Not that I've ever let a few leeches stop me." He looked around at the trees and took in a deep breath. "I've always loved it down here, and you'd be surprised how much the same it looks in the future as it does now." Jai pointed to what appeared to be another leech waving its head a metre or so ahead of them. "That's a big one."

Patsy let go of his hand and approached it. "I don't think it's a leech. It's looks somehow different."

Jai said, "It's like it's transparent."

Patsy picked up a stick and moved close to it. She crouched down and held the stick behind it. "Look, it's not really transparent, you can't see the stick behind it."

A few seconds later, the stick's image was where Patsy had expected it to be.

Jai's jaw dropped. "Time-displacement!"

Patsy turned to him and asked, "Could you please use words I understand?"

"Just watch, move the stick up again and it'll take a few seconds before its image disappears behind the leech."

Patsy moved the stick, but the image behind the transparent leech-like creature changed in ways they weren't expecting. Where they expected to see rock, they saw flower petals.

Jai put his hand on Patsy's shoulder. "This is getting freaky. And it's growing, really fast."

Before Patsy had a chance to respond, the stringworm lunged forward and expanded its sucker-like mouth to cover her left knee, the pressure of its mouth forcing the knee to bend.

"Argh!" She grabbed hold of Jai, eyes wide as she screamed, "Get it off me!"

Jai reached down and tried to grab the lips of its sucker-mouth, but his hand passed straight through it into a strange coldness. The sucker inched up Patsy's leg. She tried pushing against its mouth with her right foot, only to have the creature expand its mouth and start consuming the other leg.

Jai wrapped his arms around her shoulders. "Don't worry, I won't let you go."

Patsy's breaths were short and panicked as she reached her hand back and started drawing energy from across a myriad of crossworlds. The stringworm had consumed her legs almost to the waist by the time she flung her arm toward it, the ball of energy having no distance at all to travel before reaching its target.

There was a blinding flash on impact, then the stringworm doubled in size, its mouth now having reached her chest. The strength of the creature's movements were sucking Patsy deeper into its body, causing Jai's grip around her shoulders to slip. He watched on. In the space of a second, Patsy's head and shoulders disappeared, leaving just her right arm exposed. He grabbed hold of it in a two-handed monkey grip. He felt Patsy clasp her hand tight on his wrist, so much so that her fingernails bit into his flesh.

A moment later, his own arms had disappeared up to the shoulders. Although his arms felt cold, there was also a tingling sensation, almost what he would describe as an electric feeling. The next thing Jai knew, the stringworm had drawn in his whole body, with only his left foot remaining to be consumed. In desperation he'd managed to hook it around a tree. As the stringworm sucked harder, Jai felt his foot slip out of its shoe. Then came the sensation of falling.

Patsy and Jai maintained their grip on each other as they watched differing versions of the area around the creek flash before them. Although inside the stringworm's belly, they could see through it to the outside as they experienced a freefall through the Crossworlds and time.

In some worlds and times, the creek was much as Patsy knew it, in others it was dry, or part of a vast ocean, while in others it was filled with fantastical buildings and strange creatures.

The worlds and times flashed by at a rapidly accelerating pace as the stringworm digested its meal, feasting on the energy generated by their transitions through worlds. Once it had its fill, Patsy and Jai were ejected to a world in a time and place that neither recognised.

CHAPTER 3

Gladys Taylor settled into the seat of the sulky and took the reins. She looked down at her husband and smiled. "Are you sure you'd rather not be joining me?" she asked.

Captain Taylor closed his eyes and rubbed his brow. "It's humiliating enough having to call you my wife. I'll be damned if I'm going to let that pathetic scum who should have swung from the gallows bear witness to my torture."

Gladys leaned down and said, "Such a shame you see it that way. I'm learning to find the lighter side of our situation."

The captain looked up. "Well then, do us both a favour and get this over with. Find the worm and get rid of that wretched little witch so I can send you back to Sydney and we can be free of each other."

Gladys flicked the reins and the sulky began moving forward. She looked over her shoulder. A broad grin grew across her face. "Don't worry, I'll find the stringworm. It'll be close to the portal for sure. I don't know that I'll be in such a rush to be wanting to leave my husband's side, though. The soldiers all seem to think we make a grand looking couple." A haunting cackle filled the air as she rode off.

*

Jai ran his hand over the hard ground they had landed on. "It feels cold like cast iron." He looked across at Patsy. "I think it must be some kind of road."

She looked around and asked, "Where are the trees?"

Jai replied, "Forget about the trees, what was that? What just happened?"

"The only thing I know for sure is that we got dragged through too many crossworlds to count. But something else happened, too, something unfamiliar to me."

"What, like getting swallowed by some weird leech-like creature that displaces time?"

"That's it!" Patsy leaped to her feet. "Time! We've been dragged through time, as well."

"So, we've travelled across worlds, and through time, but we're effectively in the same place?" asked Jai.

"I think so."

"The portal, do you think there might be one here as well, in the same place?"

Patsy shrugged. "I don't know."

Jai smiled. "I've got an idea." He pulled his phone from the pocket of his borrowed trousers. “When I was close to the portal in our world and time, I could pick up a signal.”

“Pick up a signal? What’s that meant to mean? Could you please explain that in a way that makes sense?”

Jai ignored her as he unlocked his phone and stared at it as though willing it to find a signal. “It’s there, but it’s very weak.” He stood up and looked around. “The good news is, that means the portal is here. It must be.”

“I can’t see any sign of the creek anywhere.”

Jai pointed. “Look, over there.”

Patsy looked to where he was pointing. There was the rock, the one where Patsy had rescued a fairy two years earlier in her own world. It was surrounded by a mass of green slime. “It looks like there’s water in there.”

“Ewww!” said Jai. He pinched his nose to block out the smell as they approached the stagnant pool. He looked down at his phone again. “The signal’s definitely stronger as we get closer.” He tapped on the screen and said, “I’m turning on a tracking app.” Seeing the frown on Patsy’s face, it was clear to him that she’d need an explanation. “The tracking app will record how far we move and in what direction… without relying on satellites.” Patsy’s expression hadn’t changed. “Look, what matters is that it’ll help us get back here if we have to move away for some reason.” He slipped his phone back into his pocket and asked, “What was that thing anyway… you know, the thing that sucked us up and transported us here?”

Patsy shook her head. “I don’t know. I’ve never heard of anything like it.”

“Whatever it was, it’s not featured in any wildlife docos I’ve ever seen.”

His comment was met with another angry glare.

Jai opened his mouth, ready to provide an explanation, but then thought better of it.

An uncomfortable silence followed that felt like it lasted an eternity. Then, Patsy grabbed Jai's shoulder and pointed to a giant slug moving toward them through the thick green fog that obscured their surroundings. "What's that?"

Jai took a small step forward. "I don't know, but it looks a bit like it might have a human on its back." The slug was as big as a small house. It had reins, a bridle, and an elaborate saddle like you would expect of a horse in a parade for a monarch. A rider sat in the saddle wearing red military clothing similar to what the British soldiers wore in the American War of Independence. The face was hidden by a leather gas mask with large goggles.

The rider, holding what appeared to be a stockwhip, pointed at Patsy and Jai then yelled, "Bash wah!"

Jai looked at Patsy. "Any idea what he's saying?"

"She's telling us to stand up."

"She? How do you know?"

"I can sense it." Patsy tightened her grip on Jai's shoulder. "I suggest we do as she's asking."

"Do you recognise the language?"

"No, I just know how to listen. If you listen properly, every language makes sense, even animals."

"My grandmother says that, too. She reckons the birds in her garden always talk to her. Mum and I always thought she was just a bit on the crazy side."

"Vestey!"

Jai asked, "What was—"

The whip unfurled and a moment later was wrapped around Jai and Patsy. Patsy whispered, "She said 'silence.'"

The rider turned her stead and dragged the tightly bound Patsy and Jai into the fog.

*

Colin, Meredith, Neridah and Clara stood on the front veranda watching Gladys Taylor's sulky approach.

Meredith asked, "Why does it have to be her?"

Colin replied, "We both know why."

Clara looked from one to the other. "I'm still confused as to why you let Patricia go into hiding. What could she possibly have to fear when we're all present?"

Neridah continued watching the sulky as it came to a stop. Darcy made his way across from the stables to help Gladys Taylor down from the seat. Neridah glanced at Clara and replied, "I just hope you don't end up with a full answer to that. You've had enough surprises for one day."

As Clara watched the older woman in the heavy blue dress approach, she shielded her eyes, sure that the midday sun must have been playing tricks on her. There was something about the woman's shadow that disturbed her. She looked across at the other three who stood with her. "Do you see it?" she whispered to Colin, who was standing to her left.

"See what?"

"The shadow." As Clara turned back to face Gladys Taylor, the shadow's arms stretched out toward her in a way she knew was not possible when the sun was almost directly overhead. The jaws of the shadow's head opened wide, revealing a hideous array of sharp silhouetted teeth. She reached for her chest as her knees collapsed under her.

Colin managed to get an arm under Clara's shoulder before she blacked out completely.

Meredith raced into the house calling out, "Cook, we need cold water and wet towels. Miss Jenkins has passed out."

While Neridah and Colin lay Clara down on the veranda, Gladys came up the stairs and asked, "Would I be right in my assumption that this is the tutor?"

Neridah glared back at her. "A bit of concern would be welcome."

Gladys put her arms out as Darcy carried her bags up the stairs. "Welcome? Yes, a welcome would be nice. I accompanied my husband up from Sydney for the express purpose of seeing to it that a girl who appears absent is being properly tutored by a young woman who, it would seem, is incapable of dealing with the midday sun."

Colin looked at the bags. "I would hope you don't have any thoughts that you'll be staying here overnight. There's ample accommodation available in town."

Gladys walked straight past him and entered the house uninvited. "I'd appreciate a brandy while I wait for the girl to appear and for the tutor to recover."

Cook came out to the veranda with a jug of water and a wet towel. "Don't worry yourself, Mr McIntyre, sir. I'll look after her from here and see to her comfort when she comes to."

Colin looked at Neridah and whispered, "I should go inside and see to our guest's comfort. Can you make your way to the creek? Someone needs to check on Patricia and Jai. I've a bad feeling."

Neridah rose to her feet and made her way down the paddock toward the pathway leading to the pool and the creek that fed into it.

Gladys walked into the sitting room and looked toward the window. She smiled at the sight of Neridah walking through the paddock. If the young witch had chosen to hide near the portal and the stringworm had been attracted to it, then maybe things were destined to work out as planned after all.

*

"It smells like mint." Jai stared into the mist, sniffing as their captor hauled them along.

Patsy stumbled, pulling Jai to the ground with her. The slug continued its slow progress forward, dragging them along while they struggled to get back on their feet. "Can we focus on just trying to keep moving rather than what the fog smells or tastes like? It's not like I hadn't noticed." They were forced by the whip that bound them to walk sideways with their backs to each other. The leather of the whip was already making the flesh on Patsy's arm raw.

"Vestey!" The rider glared at them while holding up a blowpipe in a threatening manner.

Once the rider had turned forward again, Jai whispered, "Can't you use some magic or something?"

"Or something?" Patsy whispered back.

"You know, allow yourself to be somewhere or whatever."

"Whatever?" Patsy wanted Jai to see her face, so he could see just how ridiculous she thought his comment was. "You really think it's that simple?"

"I've read your books… you make it seem so simple in them."

"What do you mean, my books?"

"About your life, and how you learned about magic. You've written about a dozen from memory. I've read them all."

"Oh, really?"

"Yeah, the first one was called *Sellemae's Wrath*."

"Why would I want to write a book about that horrid creature?"

"I don't know, you tell me."

Patsy took a deep breath and spoke through clenched teeth. "You have no idea how annoying it is to have you tell me about something I haven't done yet and behave as though I should know all about it."

"Hey, what's your problem?"

"You're my problem!" Patsy's breaths were getting short and sharp.

"VESTEY!" The rider brought the blowpipe to her lips.

Oblivious to the rider and the blowpipe, Patsy stamped her foot. "I've had enough!" The ground shook, sending a shock wave up through the slug that threw the rider off balance as she blew into her pipe. A dart flew past Patsy's ear as she burst free of the stockwhip and pointed at Jai. "Krinkle-myst told you not to tell me about things I'm going to do in the future."

Jai turned to face her and put his hands in front of himself in a defensive gesture. "Hey, calm down will you."

"Calm down? You expect me to calm down?"

Jai pointed to the rider. "I can see you're upset, but can't we deal with this little problem first?"

Without looking, Patsy pushed a hand in the direction of the rider, sending a burst of energy forth that knocked her from her saddle.

"What captor?" Patsy's eyes bore into Jai so deep that he found himself backing away.

"Hey, my plan worked, okay?"

"What plan?" Her breathing was getting heavier. Energy was building around her hands that hung by her side.

"In the books, they said that when you get angry you sometimes release a burst of power."

Patsy responded with more heavy breaths delivered through clenched teeth. She was drawing back her right hand, her eyes still trained on Jai, when a giant hairy caterpillar landed behind him. It took them both by surprise.

Patsy yelled, "Duck!"

She lunged forward, hurling a ball of energy at the creature. No sooner had it been sent hurtling back than another had fallen and landed between them. It reared up, lifting its head high above Patsy, then opened its jaws. Jai had crash tackled it, bringing it to the ground. More caterpillars started falling, surrounding the two teenagers. One had reared up over Jai, but Patsy brought forth her left hand and sent it hurtling back. Again and again caterpillars reared up, only to have Patsy send them back. But Jai wasn't getting up. More caterpillars fell, some up them landing on the slug's back. The animal was screaming in pain as they crawled over its back.

"Flade." The rider was calling out to them and gesturing for them to follow her.

"Jai, we need to go."

He raised his head. "Urrgh…" He struggled to lift himself to an elbow.

"Are you okay?" Looking at his flesh told her he was anything but okay. Everywhere his skin had made contact with the caterpillar was now red and swollen with large lumps. Patsy grabbed hold of his arm, put it across the back of her neck, then grabbed him around the waist and tried to lift. Another caterpillar reared up, ready to lunge at them. A dart from the rider's blowpipe struck it in the eye, causing it to release a high-pitched scream. Jai was dead weight as Patsy started toward the rider. The adrenalin surging through her veins was all that allowed her to move forward. Passing the slug, she saw the caterpillars tearing away at its flesh. The life seemed to drain away from its cries. The rider came to her aide and took Jai's other arm over her shoulder.

The rider said, "Flade, lil sis bo carpee." *Hurry, or else he dies.* With the two of them supporting Jai, they managed to break into a laboured run from the scene. The caterpillars seemed more concerned by the feast they had captured than pursuing them.

•

The Reverend was tightening the strap on Elsa's saddle when a voice called from behind him. "I was hoping we could talk before you go to the McIntyres."

The Reverend turned. "Bordauex? I'll happily delay my departure, if only briefly, to share some words."

"I wish to follow in your path… to become a priest of this church."

The Reverend raised a heavy grey eyebrow in surprise. "So, you believe in what you have read of the Messiah?"

"I have read of many messiahs in many worlds. I believe in the shining light that they give to their followers. Whether the tales are factual or fabrications is not important to me. I care about the spreading of good messages in a way that people may respond to."

The Reverend nodded and looked to the ground for a moment as he collected his thoughts. He then looked Bordauex in the eye. "The thoughts you have expressed are not the thoughts that the Church wants to hear when someone expresses their wish to be ordained as a priest." He placed a hand on his disciple's shoulder. "But your heart is in very much the same place as my own. If being a priest is what you want, then I believe you'll make a fine one. I'll do all that I can to help you."

"Can you then train me?"

The Reverend put his left boot into the stirrup of Elsa's saddle, then mounted the horse. "No, that is something I cannot do. There is a seminary in Sydney where you can be trained. That is the only way. I'll make sure to contact the bishop and see what I can do to help you get a place there." Before Bordauex had a chance to respond, the Reverend had kicked his heels into Elsa's side and headed off toward the McIntyre property.

•

"What were those creatures?" asked Patsy in the rider's language.

"Oh, so you can speak the true words?"

"I need to only listen for a while before I can speak a language."

"There is only one language, everything else is akin to the noises animals make to each other."

Patsy opened her mouth to respond in a reflex reaction to the rider's closed-minded attitude. She managed to stop herself before the first words spilled out. *I need this woman's help if Jai's to have any chance of survival.* "Those creatures, what were they?"

The rider stopped and stared at Patsy through her grimy gasmask. Her voice muffled by its multi-layered filters that gave it an electronic sound. "How could the Enchantress not know of wrathapillars?"

"Enchantress?"

"Unlike most of our rebellious youth, I have bothered to study the prophecies of the ancients. 'She will be unknown until she breaks her bonds and strikes down her enemies with the power that comes from her hands.' Is that not what you have just done?"

"I very much doubt that my arrival here is what was foretold."

"We'll see what the Seer has to say when we reach the citadel."

Again, Patsy refrained from saying what first came to mind. She tried to bring the conversation back to the urgency of Jai's needs. "Is there a doctor at the citadel?"

"You use the words in a strange way. Your beast of burden needs a healer, not a doctor."

"He's no beast of burden. He's my friend."

The rider looked at Jai and sneered. "I've yet to meet a male who is not a burden."

"Well, then I'm sad for you. The reason he's hurt is because he put himself in harm's way to protect me. You were there. You saw him tackle the 'wrathapillar,' as you call it."

"And that is the only reason I'm prepared to risk my own status by taking him to the healer."

"We have just arrived here from far away. Where I come from, males and females are more equal."

The rider looked Patsy up and down. "You don't look like a coast dweller. But your clothes and use of words are strange. I know of no culture where a woman would call a male a friend." After a long pause she asked, "Where do you come from?"

"I come from this same place, but on a different plane and from a different time."

"I don't doubt that there is likely a truth in what you say, for you clearly are the Enchantress. But I won't pretend to understand. That is the job of the Seer, and hopefully she will help me to comprehend."

They walked on in silence, carrying the now unconscious Jai, whose feet dragged along the ground as they moved forward.

The green fog began to thin out, revealing a forest of what appeared to be gigantic mint plants. Up ahead, a massive wall loomed that appeared to be made of the same material as the ground they'd been walking on.

An ornate gate dominated the wall ahead of them. "Why the wall?" asked Patsy.

"I don't understand the question."

"The wall, why do you need it?"

"What meaning would life have without it?"

Patsy wished she hadn't asked.

"Halt, and state your business in the city."

"I am Keesnah, returning from patrol."

"Where be your stead?"

"Taken by wrathapillars."

"Who else accompanies you to the city gate?"

"I bring with me the Enchantress, whose coming was foretold. Her beast of burden is injured."

The gate opened a small amount and a round mechanical contraption approached the trio. It was covered in knobs and dials, with large keys for winding springs located in several spots around its spherical base. It moved as if on wheels, although Patsy couldn't locate where the wheels might be. A light rose out of the top and Patsy was blinded for a few seconds when it flashed. The contraption then retreated back through the gate which closed behind it.

"What now?" asked Patsy.

"We wait for approval. I have lost my steed. We will not be admitted into the city unless the Seer wishes to interview you."

*

Gladys downed her brandy in an unladylike fashion. She held the glass out toward Colin and asked, "Could I trouble you for another while we wait for the tutor and your daughter?"

Colin grimaced as he remembered the last time they had an unwelcomed guest who enjoyed downing his brandy in such a fashion. Regardless, he took the glass. "Yes, of course."

Gladys walked across to the window as Colin made his way to the small table where the brandy decanter sat. She smiled as she watched Neridah run up the paddock, waving her arms in a state of panic. Meredith met her halfway. Colin approached the window, handing Gladys her drink on the way. He glanced out at the scene unfolding in the paddock, then said, "Please excuse me, it seems there are things I must attend to."

Gladys threw down the second drink in the same way she had done with the first. "So it would seem. And that being the case, I think I shall leave and return another day when your tutor is better prepared."

"I'll only be a few minutes—"

"No, I'll be on my way." She strode past Colin and made her way out of the house, picking up her bags from where Darcy had left them just inside the front door. She ignored Cook and Clara as she carried her bags down the stairs, then tossed them onto the sulky in a haphazard fashion before climbing into the seat and driving off in a hurry.

*

The creaking of the gigantic gate startled Patsy. "What's happening?"

Keesnah turned to Patsy. "Enchantress?"

"Oh, sorry. I'd drifted off into a daydream. I wasn't quite sure where I was for a moment."

"It is written that the Enchantress inhabits many worlds. Perhaps your mind had drifted to another."

A dozen soldiers marched out, two carrying a canvas stretcher. They placed it on the ground next to Jai, then lifted him up and laid him on it. Another two clapped irons on Keesnah's ankles then placed a hessian sack over her head before marching her into the darkness within the gate. A woman who appeared to be a captain of some sort addressed Patsy. "The Seer will see you now."

Patsy looked at Jai. "And what about my friend?"

"The healer will see to his survival if the Seer is satisfied."

"Satisfied?"

"That you are indeed the Enchantress."

Patsy looked at Keesnah disappearing into the shadows with the soldiers. "And her?"

"Her fate will be decided by those who study the scriptures. That is to say, if the Seer deems you true."

"What if she doesn't?"

"Then she will be declared a burden."

Patsy needed to meet the Seer as soon as possible if there was to be any hope of Jai getting treatment. She looked down at her descendant. *I'm so sorry this has happened to you.*

The point of a spear against Patsy's back told her it was time to start walking. As she passed through the massive cast iron gates, her eyes adjusted to the dim light. There were hundreds of people gathered in silence to watch her entrance. Up ahead she saw what appeared to be a grand cathedral. Like the gate and the roads, it was made of cast iron.

"She has come to save us!" called a voice from the crowd. Everyone turned and pointed to the culprit. She cringed as the crowd parted to make way for an approaching soldier. "Please, I wish only to honour that which has been foretold."

"You blaspheme against your monarch." The soldier punched the woman in the stomach, causing her to double over in pain, then addressed the crowd. “See to it that she wears her shame till the moon has twice been full.”

The crowd continued pointing at her and began chanting, “Shame, shame, shame…”

“ENOUGH!” The crowd went silent and turned to face the cathedral. An old woman dressed in orange robes with gold embroidered trim was descending the stairs. She carried a large staff topped with an orange crystal. Despite her age, her voice boomed with authority. “Let no woman cast judgement on another this day until we know whether the Enchantress is truly among us.”

An instant later, Patsy and her escort had been transported to the steps of the cathedral, just below where the old Seer stood with her staff. “You know magic!” gasped Patsy.

The Seer smiled at Patsy. “You speak as one who understands such things. Come, allow yourself to join me inside, away from the brutality of these thugs.”

A moment later, Patsy and the Seer were seated in a gallery that overlooked the altar of the church. A ceremonial fire burned behind them in an ornate cast iron bowl that sat atop a pillar twice Patsy’s height. “My friend, can you save him?”

The Seer shook her head. “No, he is not of this world. The only one who can save him is you.”

“But I don’t know how.”

“Perhaps with some guidance you might. He can only be saved by one who knows him walking inside his mind and waking his soul.”

“Can you help me to do that?”

“I can help you and he prepare. But the real help you need comes from a book.” The Seer gestured to a golden shroud that covered a bookstand. “If the book accepts you, you will find the wisdom you need.”

Patsy rose to her feet then approached the bookstand. She took a deep breath before raising the shroud. "No! It can't be!" She dropped the shroud then turned back to the Seer. "It's the Book of Wisdom! How can it be here?"

The Seer laughed. "Didn't the wood-elf tell you the truth of the book? It exists in many worlds, and thus contains many points of view. How could it contain true wisdom if its words came just from one world's understanding?"

"So, this is the same as the one I'm familiar with?"

"Seeing I have read many of your passages, Patricia, or should I say, Patsy McIntyre, one would assume so."

"And, you know Krinkle-myst?"

"Is that what he calls himself?" Again, the Seer smiled. "All I know is, a wood-elf came to me in a dream and warned me of your coming."

"Warned you? That doesn't sound good."

"No, it doesn't, does it?"

*

Neridah arrived at the stables at the same time as the Reverend. "Patricia's gone!"

The Reverend could see the panic in Neridah's eyes as he dismounted Elsa. "What are you talking about? How is she gone?"

"Patricia and Jai. They went for a walk to hide from Mrs Taylor, who it turns out used to be Mrs Bradshaw, the tutor that Patricia couldn't get on with. Remember? She's the one who had been possessed by a mind thief. After Mrs Taylor left, we went looking for them. We can't find them anywhere, just some footprints down by the creek where they went to hide."

The Reverend nodded thoughtfully and leaned forward in the saddle. As he considered the news, he looked up and asked, "Have you made enquiries with the fairies?"

Neridah sneered and looked away. "That would mean talking to Mrs Smith. Can't Bandah and the pixies help instead?"

The Reverend handed Elsa's reins to Darcy who'd just emerged from the darkness of the stables. "It seems Bandah is somewhat distracted by other issues of late." He rubbed at his bearded chin. "With regards to Mrs Smith, is it not worthwhile dealing with the likes of her if it might help us find your granddaughter?"

"She's your gran—"

Neridah was interrupted by a voice with less volume, as though from someone much smaller. "You always talk about me as though I'm not here." The Reverend and Neridah looked down to see the old fairy that was Mrs Smith standing, hands on hips, just a few paces away from them.

Neridah glared at the fairy. Her fists clenched as all her muscles tightened. "Perhaps you would find that happened less often if you made your presence known before listening in to others' conversations."

"Hmmph!" Mrs Smith adopted a similar pose to the one Neridah had struck. "Perhaps I'd be more upfront about my presence if your words were generally kinder."

The Reverend closed his eyes and nodded in agreement. "Aye, I must admit, it would seem there is some truth in that."

Neridah's jaw dropped. "You must be joking!"

The only response she got was a raised and heavy grey eyebrow.

"I spent forty years bound up in a cocoon because of her. She kept us apart for four decades. I tried to help her, and she betrayed me. Haven't we both suffered enough as a result of her deceit?"

Mrs Smith shook her head. "I nearly died trying to help you deal with Kerridwen. Oh, and your pixie friend, Bandah? He would still be stuck in the void were it not for me."

Neridah rolled her eyes. "Oh, what a saint you are! I can't believe you would even consider comparing that to what Alfred and I went through thanks to your betrayal."

Mrs Smith said, "That's not what this is about. The girl's gone missing. I don't know where she is, but I want to help, and I think I might have a clue."

"I don't need to hear more of your lies." Neridah looked away.

The Reverend shook his head. "Can you not hear yourself, woman? I think you're being unnecessarily unkind."

"If that's how you feel, then I'm finished with this conversation." Neridah turned and stormed off toward the house.

The Reverend looked up to the sky as though it may deliver an answer to the question he didn't want to ask.

"So, do you want to know?" The fairy stood with her arms folded, her voice carrying the smug tone that suggested she knew she was now in control of the situation.

The Reverend turned his gaze toward Mrs Smith, then took a deep breath and closed his eyes. He reminded himself that anger would not help him convince the fairy to tell him what she knew. He opened his eyes and squatted to bring himself closer to her level. "Aye, I would very much like to know."

"I didn't see it myself, but I heard a rumour. My sisters were concerned. They see people coming from another time as a poor omen, so weren't prepared to keep a watch on the two of them themselves." She paused, as though wanting to wait for clarification that the Reverend understood.

"Go on, I'm listening."

"So, they asked a magpie to keep watch and report back to them." An uneasy pause followed before Mrs Smith took a deep breath and continued. "The magpie said it watched a worm, or a leech of some kind. It watched the creature devour them whole, but without increasing in size once they were consumed. It said that it was as though they were transported to another world."

The Reverend slowly rose to his feet. He'd never heard of such a thing before. "As hard as it is to believe what you're saying, I see no reason why you'd seek to deceive me right now."

"Thank you." Mrs Smith reached out and grabbed his trouser leg. "Despite everything from the past, I truly do wish to be of help."

The Reverend nodded in acknowledgement as he started to meander toward the house, pondering how to break the news to Patsy's family.

*

Silence hung over the crowd for several seconds after the Seer and Patsy disappeared. A lone voice then called out, "It's true, she really is the Enchantress that was foretold."

The crowd as one turned toward the woman who had spoken out. A pair of soldiers marched up to her and dragged her to the top of the stairs.

One of the soldiers addressed the crowd. "Do you before us declare that you have witnessed this one blaspheme?"

The crowd chanted, "Guilty as charged. Guilty as charged. Guilty..."

As the crowd continued their chant, a young woman, barely past the age of independent thought, strode through the middle of the crowd and up the stairs. She then turned to face them and called out, "All she is guilty of is speaking the truth." Shocked by the boldness of one so young, the crowd fell back to silence. "We have all seen for ourselves, the Enchantress is real. She disappeared and took the Seer with her." The crowd began murmuring among themselves. "The Seer has not dared to display her power in nearly fifty rotations around the sun. Surely this is a sign that we should stand up to those who have enslaved us for so—" She fell to the ground with a dart in the side of her neck.

A bugle sounded from the top of a building adjacent to the cathedral. It was less than half the church's height, but still imposing. A soldier wearing the trappings of high status within the military walked onto the building's upper balcony and held up a gigantic megaphone. A hollow electronic projection of her voice rang out over the square. "The population within this area is guilty of allowing one of its own to speak a heresy. Two score will now pay the price."

A battalion of soldiers rushed out of the building and collected forty women at random and dragged them into the shadows. The scene played out in eerie silence; no one wished to draw attention to themselves.

*

Gladys rode the sulky over the small bridge that crossed the creek a few minutes down the road from the McIntyre property. She led the horse and sulky down a side-track which travellers sometimes used to lead the horses to the creek for water. Once sure that the sulky was out of sight, she grabbed a glass jar from her bag and began making her way down the creek in search of the stringworm. She felt confident that if it had just enjoyed a meal, it would be more content to remain in the jar once captured.

It was slow going walking through the creek with the heavy dress weighing her down as it absorbed ever more water. She would have removed it were it not so difficult to do so. It was at times like this that the Nasqa holding her mind captive most missed its days as a gravedigger with all the simplicity that life had offered. She was halfway back to the McIntyre property when she heard voices approaching. *Damn that man's tenacity*, she thought. It sounded like Colin had enlisted the help of the stablehands in his bid to find his daughter. Gladys crouched low and pushed herself into the gap between the buttressed roots of a large tree. She closed her eyes and imagined the anger she'd have to face from her husband once she'd been caught and returned to him without the stringworm. A cold and empty feeling on the tip of her ring finger drew her attention.

No, it couldn't be!

The stringworm had already made her whole finger disappear as she struggled to get the lid off the jar. She hoped she might still be able to get it off her finger and capture it.

Then, the jar was gone, as was the hand holding it. Both arms were now consumed up to the elbows.

The voices were getting closer.

She had no choice. She'd have to either call out for help or accept being thrown into another time and plane with no hope of return. As she opened her mouth to call out, the world disappeared, and she found herself falling through an abyss. Countless worlds flashed by. It felt like an eternity had passed when she hit the ground with a thud. She coughed as she tried to breathe the methane-laden atmosphere. And the heat—it was sweltering, unbearably hot with clouds of fire filling the sky.

CHAPTER 4

Patsy closed her eyes and strained with the effort as she dragged the Book of Wisdom open to the page she had selected in her mind. She ran a finger over the soft vellum, feeling as though she could read the ink lettering with her fingertips. The young witch opened her eyes and scanned the page. "This can't be."

"Is it not as I told you it would be?" asked the Seer.

Patsy nodded. "It says that I have to allow myself to go inside his mind and become one with him." She turned and faced the Seer. "Are you sure this is the only way?"

The Seer took a deep breath and placed a withered hand on Patsy's shoulder. "He has reacted badly to the wrathapiller's poison. Far worse than any I have saved before. He is beyond the lotions I would normally apply being of any use."

"But you haven't even tried." The shakiness in Patsy's voice betrayed her desperation.

"Look at him, Patricia McIntyre, Crossworld Witch, Enchantress that the scriptures foretold, and then try to tell me that I lie."

Patsy wept as she looked at the unconscious boy who lay on a cot in the corner of the gallery. She walked the few paces it took to be by his side, then held his hand. It was cold, with little sign of life. She could see that the Seer was right. "What if I fail?"

"That's the wrong question."

Knowing the Seer was right, Patsy knelt down and closed her eyes and whispered, "You have to make it through this." Her words were for both Jai and herself. She took a breath, then allowed herself to be one with her descendent.

*

The Reverend and Neridah stood looking over Meredith's shoulder. She closed her eyes and ran her hand down the edge of the pages in the ornate and ancient Book of Wisdom, feeling for which one she should turn to. Using both hands, she opened the book to the page she'd sought in her mind.

At the top of the right-hand page was an illustration of a leech-like creature devouring a human forearm. The three of them gasped together as they stared at the illustration. They had to wait while they absorbed the page before them enough to read the language they'd never seen before. It was written in a script that had little in common with any they'd previously encountered in the book.

Neridah was the first to be able to translate the ancient script. "It's called a stringworm."

The three of them were all now able to read the text, digesting its words and trying to make sense of the strange syntax as they went.

Meredith held a hand against her heart as she said, "I feel more confident they're alive now."

The Reverend asked, "Aye, but where are they?"

Neridah replied, "According to this, they could be anywhere. It talks about not just different crossworlds, but different times and timelines."

The Reverend said, "It tells us nothing of how to find them."

Neridah said, "We need to search elsewhere in the book."

Meredith nodded in agreement, then closed her eyes as she again ran her fingers down the edge of the book while thinking about finding someone lost in place and time. She opened the book to another page, one that was dense with small text and the occasional equation that appeared similar to what one might find in a physics textbook.

"This will take time to make sense of," said the Reverend.

"We don't have time," replied Neridah.

Meredith turned to her mother. "We don't know that. We don't even know for sure that they were consumed by that thing."

Neridah's eyes narrowed as she prepared to counter her daughter. Then she felt the Reverend's firm hand on her shoulder. "Let's not bicker. To know one way or the other, we'll need to decipher this text."

Neridah bit her lower lip as she nodded in agreement.

Meredith said, "I'm going to grab a journal and take notes."

The Reverend agreed. "Aye, that's a good idea. I might do the same."

The three of them spent the next three hours reading, writing notes, and discussing points that made little sense on first reading. They were debating one particular point when there was a knock at the door. "I'll get it," said Meredith.

As Meredith made her way to the door, Neridah said to the Reverend,

"It's not worth the risk. We could end up lost in the void forever."

The Reverend replied, "I understand your reasons for feeling that way, and that's why I say we should take the book with us, just in case."

Meredith opened the door to see Colin's concerned face. "How's Clara?" asked Meredith.

"I think she's fine now. She said she saw Mrs Taylor's shadow move like it was the shadow of a monster. You know what that means," said Colin with a note of concern in his voice.

At the far end of the library, Neridah pointed to Meredith and lowered her voice to a whisper. "How can we be sure that you replacing Patricia in the Trilogy will even work?"

"It will work as long as she's replaced by someone of the same bloodline." The voice came from a small wood-elf who'd appeared at their feet. The Reverend and Neridah looked down at him, disbelief etched into their expressions. "I don't normally make house calls, but those two kids have created a hell of a mess. And I'd really like to see it cleaned up before it's too late to save this world and countless others."

Unaware of Krinkle-myst's appearance, Meredith slipped outside the library and pulled the door shut behind her. "Yes, and I must say, it comes as little surprise. It also confirms all our worst fears about the governor."

Colin asked her, "Have you had any luck?"

Back inside the room, debate was continuing. The Reverend looked at Krinkle-myst and said, "So, judging by what you say, it will indeed work if I take Patricia's place in the Trilogy."

The wood-elf shrugged his shoulders. "It's the only way you'll have a chance of tuning in to her among the vastness of all places and times."

"We've kept this truth secret for all these years." Neridah looked to the door, thinking of her daughter on the other side.

The Reverend replied, "She has to learn of the truth sometime."

"But does it have to be today? And what if we're wrong?"

Krinkle-myst reassured her. "I can tell you now, your granddaughter and Jai will sooner or later look to form a Trilogy themselves, wherever they are. While the time and world they've gone to can't be predicted, the geographic location can be. It will align to where we are now. And they more than likely will come across someone of the same bloodline and form their own Trilogy."

"How can you be sure of this?" asked the Reverend.

"Because it's already written as the most likely future history."

Neridah sighed then looked at the Reverend. "Well, it looks like it's time we have a little discussion with my daughter about the truth."

Outside, Meredith looked to the floor as she considered what to say. She then made direct eye contact as she told Colin what she knew of Patsy's fate in as few words as she could. "Patricia and Jai are lost in place and time. The only way we can find them is if Alfred, Mother and myself form our own Trilogy and surrender ourselves to the void. It's the only way that she'll ever be able to tune into the right time and place to return as we'd still be anchored to this one. We'd be like a beacon."

"Then why does it appear there's still debate going on?"

"If we're unsuccessful in finding her, there's a risk that we'll be unable to get back from the void. Being within the void requires someone outside of it to pull you out."

"I see." Colin nodded, then rubbed at his chin before asking, "What do you think?"

"I don't think there's any other choice."

"Then you have my support. Go, go and find our daughter."

*

"Jai?" Patsy looked around her and saw nothing but emptiness; her voice echoing through the void suggested that the empty space had boundaries. She took a few small and tentative steps forward. "Are you in here?"

A little girl's voice behind her said, "He's here. You just need to wake him." Patsy turned to see a girl with long dark hair wearing a white dress who wouldn't be older than four or five.

"Who are you?"

"I'm the Seer. I came to help you find him."

"But you're so young."

"My body can't survive if I leave it fully, so I could only send a small part of me."

"Well, thank you."

"There's another reason I came to join you."

"What's that?"

"We can talk in here without anyone hearing us."

"We were on our own in the cathedral's gallery too."

"No, we weren't," said the girl, "the soldiers have listening devices everywhere. They won't tolerate dissent."

"But aren't you revered by them?"

"They tolerate me, barely. They see my magic as a threat to their power, and accept my presence only if I toe the line and support their agenda."

"Can't you stop them?"

"I am old and on my own. I don't have enough strength. They killed my offspring when they were born because the scriptures foretold a Trilogy of Power that would oust them."

"Is that the same scripture that the rider I came across outside said foretold my coming?"

"Yes." She looked up at Patsy with sorrowful eyes. "Few understand its true meaning. They interpret the Trilogy as meaning I have offspring, but the truth is different. The Trilogy is formed after the arrival of the Enchantress. That's why it's so important that you save Jai."

"But a Trilogy requires three women of the same bloodline."

"The Book of Wisdom says it needs three generations of the same bloodline. It says nothing about gender."

"Even if that be the case, you and I are from different worlds."

"Different worlds perhaps, but I believe our bloodline is the same. I have traced back my family history and yours through the Book of Wisdom. It is identical until the time the gene cutters changed my world's history a century and a half ago."

"What's a gene cutter?"

"Do they not exist in your world?"

"Not that I know of."

"Do you know much about biology?"

"No, I've always found it quite boring."

"Hmph! Some help you'll be." The little girl who was the Seer grabbed Patsy's hand. "Come, we need to find Jai within this darkness before the soldiers realise what we're doing."

"With him not responding to my calls, I've no idea where to look. It's so dark in here."

"You need to find his energy veins."

"His what?"

"The focal points of his energy. Do you not know of them? Have your mother and grandmother taught you nothing?" The Seer reached out a finger and ran it along an imaginary line that ran from below Patsy's waist to above her head. As the girl's hand moved up, eight times Patsy felt a surge of energy between the girl's finger and a point within her that correlated with the path of the Seer's gesture. Each surge of energy felt unique and of varying strength, with the strongest surge coming from above her head. "It is through these energy veins that all living things draw the power that gives them life, and as the Enchantress, you can channel far more than others. Have you never wondered about how the energy you draw from the Crossworlds is channelled through your being? You must find these points within Jai and feed him from your own energy that he may again find his own."

"Why do I feel them now, when I'm already outside of my body?"

"The vision of yourself maintains a connection. Your body feels what your projection feels, and your projection feels what your body feels."

Patsy looked around her. "I guess that makes sense… in a strange kind of way. But how will I find them within Jai? Where do I look?"

"Don't look, feel. Feel each of your own energy veins and you will be drawn to his. That's if you allow it to be so."

Patsy nodded. "Okay, I'll give it a try." She closed her eyes and remembered where the first surge of energy had come from… near the base of her spine. She focused on the sensation and, despite the fact that her consciousness was already projected within Jai, she descended within herself on another layer. She focused on that one particular energy source and omitted all else from her mind. A moment later she became aware of the energy surrounding her, albeit very weak. She could sense the energy was in fact Jai's… that she had transported herself to his lowest energy vein. She opened her eyes and saw a disc of pulsing energy swirling around her. It reminded her of pictures in a book Miss Jenkins had shown her of the rings around Saturn. Only this ring was dim, as though ready to fade out altogether. Patsy focused again on her corresponding energy vein and then thought of her wish to share it with Jai. She could feel it emanating from the base of her spine and merging with Jai's, causing it to glow and spread.

"Good, you can move to the next one." The Seer's voice sounded distant, yet remained clear.

Without a word, Patsy focused on the next energy vein and repeated the procedure… again and again until she reached the vein behind the eyes.

"Be careful with this one, it will likely cause him to stir, and he may react with fear if he senses our presence."

"Then I'll reach out to him in an effort to soothe his fears." As Patsy repeated the procedure, she noticed something altogether different. A pulse of energy rose up through each of the energy veins, connecting them and flooding the darkness with colourful light in hues that defied description. Patsy couldn't help herself, she reached out with open palms, allowing the soothing energy to flow over them.

"Quickly! You must move to the last vein before the energy flow recedes like the tide."

The urgency in the Seer's voice jolted Patsy's mind back to her task. She focused on the crowning vein and found herself shooting upward as though being tossed up by a geyser of light and happiness.

She fell to the floor and realised her consciousness was back within her own body and that she'd been physically thrown back.

Jai was sitting bolt upright, his eyes wide open. "What was that?" he asked between frantic breaths.

The Seer, back within her decrepit frame, replied, "Your ancestor just rescued you from the jaws of certain death."

The main doors to the cathedral swung open with a bang. "Up there, in the gallery… seize them!" More doors were flung open and hundreds of boots thundered into the building. Several of the soldiers took out blowpipes and began firing darts up at the gallery, most of them falling short.

The Seer looked at Patsy and Jai. "We must now be the Trilogy. Both of you, take my hands and we will leave here."

Jai looked to Patsy and, when she nodded her approval, he stood up and took the Seer's hand.

•

"It would have been nice if you'd thought to tell me this sooner." Meredith's eyes were burning with rage.

Neridah reached out to put a hand on her shoulder, only to have it pushed away. "How could I tell you? I was taken away from you for forty years when you were just a baby."

"But you've been back for over two years now." She turned to the Reverend. "And as for you, you have no such excuse. All these years you've lived a lie as the rigid man of the cloth and family friend." She looked him up and down and sneered. "How can you live with yourself?"

The Reverend's voice was an uncharacteristic whisper. "Do you think it's been easy?"

"Try it from where I sit." She collapsed into a chair and burst into tears.

Neridah crouched down next to her daughter. "But we still have to find Patricia. And at least we now know that Alfred's bloodline matches hers."

"We? We now know? It seems to me I'm the only one that's been kept in the dark." She looked at the Reverend. "And don't you think that girl we're looking for deserves to know who you really are? The girl who used to fear you so much? How could you do it… those times you put the fear of God into her when she was younger."

The Reverend remained silent.

Meredith glared at him. "Is that really all you have to say?"

He glanced up. "I think it would be better for all concerned if she remains in the dark in this regard for the time being."

Meredith sneered as she replied, "Better for who?"

Again, the Reverend remained silent. Neridah took his hand in hers. He turned to her. When Neridah saw the forlorn look in his eyes, she leaned in to give him a hug of reassurance, retreating when she sensed his resistance.

Meredith watched on, struggling with how best to deal with this revelation of who her real father was.

This was too big to deal with now.

It would have to wait until she knew her daughter was safe.

She took a few deep breaths then stood up and said, "Okay, let's do this."

•

Destellie's hands lay on Felibrey's shoulders. "You've worked so hard today. It's little wonder you're tired."

Felibrey's yawn was involuntary and long. His eyelids almost obscured his pupils as he replied, "Yes, but it's worthwhile. I do so want to have the cottage finished before our wedding day."

The light of the full moon made the canvas of Felibrey's tent seem to glow behind Destellie's thick mop of dark curls. The lamplight highlighted the softness of her cheeks. "I do too, but are you sure you're not pushing yourself too hard?"

Felibrey put his hands on Destellie's hips and pulled her closer. He found the strength to lift his head and peer into Destellie's eyes, as though reaching in to touch her soul. The sound of frogs and flying foxes celebrating what was an unseasonably warm evening filled the silence while Felibrey searched for his words. "I have never before felt so motivated or driven. It gives me an energy I never knew I could possess."

"My beautiful Felibrey. How could any woman help but love you?" Her eyes closed as their lips came together. Her head swirled as she lost herself for a while in the pleasure of their kiss before her chin finally came to rest on Felibrey's shoulder. They enjoyed the stillness of the moment and the sounds of the night, their hearts beating in perfect rhythm. She gave him a gentle kiss on his neck, then said, "You need to sleep."

Felibrey nodded. "Yes, you're right." They loosened their embrace. "I'll walk you back to your tent."

Destellie took a step back and said, "No, really, I'm fine. You just get yourself to bed. It's only a short walk to my tent."

Again, Felibrey yawned. His eyes were almost shut when he said, "It's really no trouble."

Destellie took his hand and led him the one step it took to reach his cot then placed her hands on his shoulders, pushing him down till he was seated. He lifted his legs and stretched them out, pulling the blanket over himself. He lowered his head to the pillow and said, "As usual, you are right, my love."

Destellie kissed him on the forehead. "Sleep well, beautiful man."

Felibrey's eyes were already closed as he replied, "You too…" Within seconds, his breathing was replaced by a gentle snore.

Destellie waited a few minutes before leaving so as to make sure she didn't wake her fiancé. She emerged from the tent's entrance and looked toward the light at the Reverend's rebuilt house. The light in the windows and the distant sound of revelry told her the other disciples were still enjoying their evening meal and would be there for some time. The moon had only risen a short time ago, so it should be out just long enough for her to make her journey and get back with plenty of time to get an hour or so to sleep before the morning.

*

Instead of the usual instant transportation to where they were allowing themselves to be, the Trilogy of Patsy, Jai, and the Seer found itself caught up in the void between times and places. They were not alone. Jai was staring at the Reverend Alfred Casey, Patsy at her mother, and the Seer at Neridah.

The Reverend peered into Jai's face, studying as one would when seeing something unexpected in the mirror. He turned to Neridah. "You were right. To look at him is akin to looking at a younger version of myself."

Jai said, "I know the truth."

"And you'll not speak of it!" The Reverend's eyes burned with intensity to underscore the importance of his statement.

Patsy looked across and asked, "What truth?"

Meredith said, "The only truth that matters now is that we've found you."

"How?"

Neridah answered for her daughter. "It was Krinkle-myst. He told us that the bloodlines would match well enough for us to connect with you if your mother, Alfred, and I formed our own Trilogy and allowed ourselves to search for a matching one that contained you and Jai." Neridah glanced at the Seer. "You are obviously of our line in your world and time."

The Seer nodded. "The wood-elf gave me similar advice. He said that escape would only be possible if I formed a trilogy with the boy and the Enchantress, and that ours would be strengthened by yours. It made no sense to me at the time, as is always the way when wood-elves are involved."

Meredith said, "Patricia, you need to come home. Then we can send Jai back to his. Once he's gone, you'll need go to an earlier point in that timeline so you can stop him from coming in the first place and prevent the leakage from his reality into our own."

Jai replied. "But the Nasqa are close to taking total control in my world. They have to be stopped. If they unlock the full potential of the Book of Wisdom, they'll be able to follow my path into other timelines. They'll be stronger and harder to stop."

Neridah was firm in her response. "We can show you ways to fight the Nasqa." She turned her attention to Patsy. "We will act as a beacon for you to find your way home. When you're back, we'll need your help to pull us out from the void. Then you can each go where you need to in Jai's timeline and do what must be done."

Patsy asked, "What do you mean?"

Meredith's voice was starting to fade and Patsy struggled to hear what she was saying. "We have to go for now, or we won't be able to find our way back to be near the portal for you. Remember, you'll need Jai's metal box…" Meredith was starting to fade away. Patsy could still see her lips moving but could no longer hear her words.

As the Trilogy of Neridah, Meredith, and the Reverend dissolved into the distance, Jai thought he heard the Reverend's voice in his head. *Keep her safe.*

The darkness lifted, revealing that the Seer, Patsy, and Jai were in a humble wooden cabin with a small fire burning at one end of the room.

The furniture in the cabin was frugal and sparse. Patsy could smell spicy aromas coming from a large pot suspended over the fire on a tripod. Ignoring the hunger that gnawed at her belly, she turned to Jai. "Your phone… do you have it?"

Jai checked his pockets. "It's gone."

The Seer asked, "Are you looking for the magical metal box the boy had in his pocket?"

Patsy retorted, "It's not magic, it's science."

The Seer laughed. "As is all magic when fully understood." She looked toward Jai. "They will have taken your magical box to the Grand Field Commander of the military. She will have her best engineers try to unravel its mysteries as she watches over them." She scratched at her forehead then asked Patsy, "Why is this device so important?"

Jai answered on Patsy's behalf. "Because with it, we can locate the portal and tune it into my crossworld and time. It's the only way we can be sure of getting there."

Patsy tugged at the Seer's sleeve. "We need to go to this Commander and get Jai's phone. We need to do it now."

The Seer nodded her disapproval. "No, they'll be expecting us to try something direct like that. We need to create a distraction."

"Like what?"

The Seer looked up and smiled. "We need to set the beasts of burden free."

*

Twice Destellie had fallen into the creek, the second time grazing her elbow. She had to ensure she got back and took her washing to where the creek ran near the Reverend's property. That was the only way she'd be able to remove the muddy proof of her journey before Felibrey saw her. She'd explain away her injury by saying she'd lost her footing while carrying the basket of clothes. Although she would be tired herself after her long night, the herbs Destellie had slipped into Felibrey's dinner made her confident he would sleep late into the morning.

Now, after a walk of almost three hours, she had reached the pool at the bottom of the McIntyre property.

She sat on a rock to catch her breath and noticed that the frogs and flying foxes had fallen silent. It was only after having stopped that she became conscious of how cold her legs were with the wetness of her dress clinging to them. Her teeth chattered as she wrapped her arms around her shivering shoulders. Glancing up, she saw the moon had passed its zenith. She would have to act now. Destellie stood up and approached the pool's edge, reached down, and grabbed a pebble. Was she doing the right thing? She closed her eyes and thought of Felibrey and her deception. A tear ran down her cheek reminding her of how the emotions that had started as a rouse had now become quite real.

She loved him.

But there was no turning back.

Seeing the pitiful way that the other disciples had embraced this world and been enslaved by its customs filled her with disdain. Bordaeux even wanted to become a Christian priest!

She threw the pebble into the middle of the pool and watched its ripples spread out.

Instead of dissipating, the ripples grew in intensity. The still night became filled with a swirling gale, centred on the pool. Then a massive spray of water surged upward. The spiralling wind captured the water droplets and pushed them around until a shape emerged that hovered larger than life above Destellie. At first, it seemed nondescript. But as the howling wind grew stronger, the features became clear. A haggard vision of Kerridwen, with a garland of angry, snapping daisies, loomed tall. "You're late!"

Destellie went down on her knees and brought her hands together. "Oh, great Queen of the Crossworlds, I have done as you asked, but it took time to win Felibrey's heart, and he is the one who is closest to the priest."

One of the watery daisies in the apparition broke free and flew toward Destellie, turning to flame as it came near. Destellie was forced to push herself flat against the sandy bank at the pool's edge to avoid the flame. Kerridwen's voice carried her fury. "I don't want excuses, just facts. If you want to revel in the power of your own garland, you must do exactly as I say."

Tears were streaming down Destellie's cheeks. "I promise… whatever you wish." She looked up and tried to face the apparition, but the hateful rage that she saw within it compelled her to avert her eyes. Despite her words, she found herself wanting to ensure that, however this played out, she somehow protected Felibrey from the consequences.

"The fools think that the stable-boy, Darcy, is free of my command, but his will remains mine to control. You must use him to help you lure the witches to this spot when next the moon is full, that I may capture them in my garland and thus gain the strength needed to usurp my father." Kerridwen's tone softened. "Then, you will have your garland once more, and the eternal life that goes with it."

The wind died and the water dropped back to the pool. Destellie wept as the sounds of the night returned.

She'd made a big mistake.

She wasn't up to this. As much as she longed for the power of the garland, she now questioned the price.

A gentle hand touched her shoulder. She turned around and saw Darcy. His warm smile reassured her.

"It's okay. What she said is true. There is no resisting her power. Come on, I'll give you a ride back in a sulky so you can get a bit more sleep before the morning comes around. Don't worry about her anger and stuff. Kerridwen's pleased with what you've done so far. She told me herself."

•

Marji pushed the mush around his plate, eager to make sure there were no lip biters hidden in his meal. He was almost ready to decide it was safe when he noticed a telltale flash of reflection off a black nipper. He pushed his spoon down hard on it until he heard the popping sound that indicated he'd killed it. He scooped up the portion containing the dead parasite and flicked it out through the bars. "Nice try! You might want to use a smaller one next time." There was no reply. The guards must have retired early for the night, feeling confident there'd be no trouble now the men were all shackled and locked in their stalls. A scream rang out from one of the stalls to his right, telling Marji one of the men had found a lip cutter in his meal the hard way. It was a favourite sport among the guards, slipping the genetically engineered bugs into a man's dinner from time to time. They were like tiny crabs that, when placed in the mouth, would seek to escape by pinching down hard on the inside of the lip. The worst part of it wasn't so much the painful cut as the inevitable infection that would follow.

Marji scooped up a mouthful of the slop on his plate and slipped it into his mouth where he rolled it around for a while so saliva would mix with it, making it easier to digest. He peered out through the bars and wondered about the world outside, about whether the other lands were like this. He'd heard rumours about places where men and women were seen as equals, and where people moved about in mechanical carriages instead of riding on the back of slugs. A world where wrathapillars were small and almost harmless. *What's the point in dreams when reality is so harsh?* he thought to himself. Then they appeared, the Seer and two strangers wearing strange clothes, a boy and a girl, right here inside his stall. He sniffed his food, wondering if he may have been drugged with something that would have a telltale aroma.

The Seer looked at him and asked, "You, what's your name?"

Marji replied, "How did you get here?" He looked at Patsy and Jai. "And who are you two?"

"Hello, I'm Patsy, and this is a distant relative of mine." Jai waved as Patsy introduced him. "His name's Jai."

The Seer said, "It doesn't matter how we got here. What matters is that we need your help, and you need ours. Now, I asked you a question. I expect an answer."

Marji rubbed at the grey stubble on his chin. His grimy salt and pepper hair was tied back in a ponytail. "I'll answer your questions when you've answered mine."

The Seer took a deep breath and stared at the ground in an effort to contain her frustration.

Patsy stepped forward. "The Grand Field Commander has something that belongs to us, but we need to distract her if we're to get into her office and get it back. We figured the best way to do that would be if we helped all the males escape and stage a rebellion."

Marji laughed. "Such things take a great deal of time and planning. I still don't understand just how you've broken into my stall, and even if this is real. I'll need more proof if you're going to convince me to take you seriously.'

Without taking her eyes off Marji, Patsy lowered a hand and drew power from the Crossworlds. Marji felt compelled to hold his gaze on her as she furrowed her brow. Then she flung her arm back, sending the barred gate of the stall flying across the courtyard outside. She looked back through the opening it had created then flung her arms upward. A deafening roar of twisting metal followed as dozens of gates from other stalls were torn from their hinges and sent flying into the centre of the courtyard.

Marji's jaw dropped. "The Enchantress!" He stepped forward and went down on one knee, casting his eyes downward. "Forgive me, my name is Marji, Marji of the Seventy-Third Rank. I pledge my fealty."

Patsy put a hand on his shoulder and smiled. "I'm not the Enchantress, and I really don't want your fealty. My name is Patsy, and I come from another world and time. A world much like this in some ways, but very different in others. My mother and grandmother have sworn oaths to protect my world from evil. One day I'll take the same oath. But right now, I need to get back what the Commander has taken from us. And to do that, I really need you to draw the Commander's attention in a way that's good for you and the other men."

By now a hundred men had wandered out of their stalls in stunned silence. They gathered around Patsy and Marji.

Marji looked toward a cast iron barrier at the far end of the courtyard that would have been four times his height. "Beyond that gate are the slugs and catapults."

A guard had appeared on the top of the wall surrounding the courtyard. "They're escaping! To arms, my sisters!"

Patsy lunged in the direction of the gates with an arm extended. A ball of dancing energy flew toward the gates, pushing them into another crossworld.

Guards were rushing onto the wall. One of them stopped and called out, "The rider was right. The Enchantress is here! We must lay down our arms!"

The first guard retorted, "Your loyalty is with the realm, not some foolish, superstitious nonsense."

The second guard pointed to where slugs were now entering the courtyard. "Do you not trust your own eyes?"

The first guard took a blowpipe from her holster and sent a dart coated in wrathapillar poison into the second guard's neck. She collapsed to the ground dead. The first guard then raced to where a giant bell was suspended above the main gate to the courtyard. She leapt off the wall and grabbed the bell's chain, causing it to ring out through the city. She grimaced with pain at the deafening sound that reverberated through her head and body. Three times the metal ball on the chain struck home against the thick brass. On the third strike, it was too much for her. She released her grip then fell to the cast iron below.

Patsy lunged toward the main gate, tearing it from its hinges and sending it into a distant crossworld.

Marji and the hundred odd men looked at Patsy. Marji asked, "What now?"

Patsy said, "You lead them to freedom."

Marji looked around at the men. None of them had ever known what it meant to have hope, but he could sense something stirring in them now.

The Seer said, "You know the scriptures, do you not?"

Marji turned to her.

The Seer took a deep breath and closed her eyes as she focused on the words that she'd never thought would come to pass in her lifetime. "The Enchantress shall break the bonds of those who serve when she has become one of three. A humble beast of burden shall then rise forth and set men free that they may live as equals among the women." She walked up to him, her gaze piercing him with its intensity. "Step forth and meet your destiny, Marji of the Seventy-Fourth Rank."

He nodded, then took a step back and turned to address the others. "What say you? Do we rise?"

His question was met with a roaring approval.

He punched the air and roared as loud as he could. "Raid the armoury! Mount the slugs!"

No one noticed the Trilogy had disappeared.

*

The Grand Field Commander thundered with rage. "Let none of them escape. In the morning, I want to be there personally to see them fed to the wrathapillars."

"Of course, Commander, but what of the Seer and the Enchantress?"

"Enchantress? A girl performs a few parlour tricks, having obviously been trained by the Seer, and you fall for some superstitious claptrap?"

The sergeant at arms gestured toward Keesnah. The rider was tied by her limbs so she was spread-eagled between two columns. "And her?"

The Grand Field Commander sneered at the rider. "She won't be going anywhere. Come, we'll deal with the usurpers and then return to tease the truth out of her."

Keesnah struggled to watch the Grand Field Commander and her sergeant at arms leave through vision blurred by the bruising around her eyes. They were almost out of sight when she let out a gasp at the sight of Patsy, Jai, and the Seer appearing in the middle of the room. She prepared to call out, but the Seer held a finger to her lips then pointed at

Keesnah's mouth, compelling her to be quiet.

Patsy looked at the Seer and whispered, "That's something I haven't learned yet, how to make someone silent. I didn't even notice you draw power to do it."

The Seer replied, "That's because I didn't. I merely gave a look of authority, letting her know her interests would best be served by obeying the will of one whose power she fears."

In a hushed voice, Keesnah asked, "Why would you come to this room, like walking into the den of the hungry lion?"

"It is safe to enter the lion's den if you have first given it food to eat outside of its den, is it not?" The Seer walked over to Keesnah and began untying her bonds.

Keesnah's eyes betrayed her surprise. "You've come to set me free?"

"No, we've come for the beast of burden's metal box that is full of magical power. But I will not see someone suffer in bondage for no good reason. Did you see where the Commander left it?"

Jai scanned the room until his eyes fell upon the Grand Field Commander's desk. "No!" He raced across to inspect his phone. It had been taken from its case. The back had been removed in a clumsy manner, causing a few deep scratches. The battery had also been taken out along with the sim and memory cards. He picked up the sim and held it up. "I hope she hasn't managed to damage it."

Patsy walked across and asked, "Is that the source of its power?"

Jai pointed to the battery. "No, the power comes from the lithium battery." He then held the sim close to Patsy's face for emphasis. "This is the sim card. This is kind of what tells the phone which signal it should lock into. If this isn't working when we get to the portal, we'll never find my place and time."

Patsy stared at the bits of phone. "Can you put it back together?"

"Oh yeah." As he answered her, Jai was already halfway through reassembling the phone.

Keesnah asked, "When did you learn to speak in words rather than grunting as an animal?"

Jai stopped and turned around. "Why, I hadn't even noticed before. I can hear you as though you were speaking English."

The Seer said, "The Enchantress shared with you some of her power, that is how she saved you. It would seem some of her knowledge was shared as well." She paused before continuing. "Let's just hope you have also gained a part of her wisdom."

"How dare you!" The booming voice of the Grand Field Commander filled the room as she stood in the doorway. "Guards, seize them!"

Patsy looked at Jai, he'd just put the back on his phone. She then looked across at the Seer. "We need to go." As she spoke, a guard blew through her pipe, the dart aimed perfectly at Patsy's neck. It hit the wall as Patsy and the others disappeared.

•

Keesnah collapsed when they reappeared outside the walls. She sat up and hung her head between her bent knees as she struggled to recover from the torture she'd endured at the hands of the Commander.

Jai punched the air. "The sim's still working! Yes! We should be able to get a signal when we get back to the portal."

Keesnah looked up. "I don't understand. What sort of signal comes from a metal box that emits light? Is someone trying to contact you?"

Jai glanced across and smiled. "I can get signals and messages from people in lots of different ways. But the signal I'm talking about is like something that opens a door to them. And to get that signal, we just need to use the tracking app to find our way back to the portal."

"App? You can now speak in words rather than meaningless grunts, and yet still you use words that have no meaning."

Patsy smiled at Keesnah and offered her a hand getting to her feet. "Don't worry. I still find his metal box hard to comprehend as well." Patsy strained under the rider's weight, slipping the woman's arm over her shoulder once she was standing. She looked to the Seer then back to the rider. "You will come with us, won't you?"

Keesnah and the Seer looked at each other. The Seer nodded, then Keesnah turned to Patsy. "As the prophecies say, 'Two shall stand in defiance against the angry mob so as to facilitate the flight of the Enchantress that she may later return to set the world free.' We shall do what we can to make sure that you can go where you must. I believe in you. You truly are the one who was foretold."

"Oh, it's very sweet of you to have such faith in me. But really, I'm sure that the prophecies refer to someone else."

The Seer put an arm around Keesnah, allowing Patsy to release her hold. "It is also written of the Enchantress, 'She will be humble and deny the truth of her destiny until the day of her return.' You must go." A distant horn signalled that the city gates were opening. "The Commander's soldiers will be here soon, and they will not show you mercy."

"But won't that be the same for you?"

The Seer pushed her chest forward. "I am the Seer. The Commander may lack faith, but there are few among her armies that would dare to harm me."

Jai said, "Can't you and Keesnah just disappear if you're attacked?" He turned to Patsy. "Can't we all do that? There's no reason to leave them behind. They can come with us."

Patsy thought back to the admonishment they'd received from Krinkle-myst. "No, we can't."

"Why? Because some wood-elf got angry with you?" He gestured toward Keesnah and the Seer. "Their lives are at stake."

Patsy turned away to hide her tears. "I'm sorry…"

The Seer placed a hand on Jai's shoulder. "The Enchantress speaks the truth."

Jai pushed the hand away. "We can surely at least take them to the portal with us… do that thing of just letting ourselves be there."

The Seer shook her head. "I have no strength left to summon the power to do so. Such things take a great deal from one."

He turned to Patsy.

"I've drawn lots of power setting the men free. I want to save what strength I still have for if we need it."

"But you draw it from the Crossworlds."

"Do you think that's a trivial thing? I threw giant metal gates into other worlds with no knowledge of where they might fall. And every bit of power I draw comes from somewhere else. Do you know what the ramifications are for the worlds where it's come from? I don't. And if you think it's easy to draw that power, then think again. I'm tired. I don't know that I even have the strength to allow myself to be somewhere else right now."

Jai's jaw hung open. "I'm sorry. I just thought—"

"No, you didn't think, that's the problem." She was gulping for breath as tears streamed down her face. "All you seem to think about is what suits you. Do you have any idea what it's like to be me? What do you expect of me? You and everyone else, you all expect things of me. Do you think I asked for this? Do you think I actually wanted to be cast as someone who has to protect the world? And now, I'm apparently the

Enchantress!" She turned away from the now silent group. "I just want to go home and enjoy my studies with Miss Jenkins."

"There they are!" The call came from up above. A scout was mounted on a giant dragonfly swooping low so it was passing between the trees of mint. They could feel the wind of beating wings as it flew ahead of them. The dragonfly's pilot lifted a megaphone and looked over her shoulder, calling the advancing ground troops to action. "Fire at will!"

"Go now, run!" said the Seer.

"We can't leave you," said Jai.

Keesnah pleaded with him, "Just go, protect the Enchantress."

Patsy straightened up and grabbed Jai's arm. "They're right, we need to go." She looked at the rider. "I'll come back for you."

"I have no doubt that you will come back. It has been foretold. But now, Enchantress, you must go!"

Feeling uncomfortable with the burden of being labelled as the 'Enchantress,' Patsy asked, "Please, could you just call me Patsy?"

The air around them was filled by the whistling of flying darts. One dart found the Seer's sandal, missing her flesh by a finger width.

Jai looked up and pointed to the northeast. "The portal's that way. If we run, we can be there in a few minutes." He looked up. "The battery's getting low. If it runs out, we'll never find our way there."

The dragonfly was circling high above them. "Fire the catapults!"

Patsy grabbed Jai's arm, dragging him in the direction of the portal. "Come on then, let's go."

As they ran into the jungle of mint, Keesnah called out, "May speed be on your side, Enchantress… Patsy."

Wrathapillars fired from the catapults were landing all around Keesnah and the Seer. Seeing the Dragonfly change its course in an effort to follow Patsy and Jai, the Seer reached down and focused what strength she had left in drawing energy from the Crossworlds. The dragonfly was almost out of sight when she flung her arm skyward. The massive burst of energy she unleashed pushed the giant insect off its course and knocked the pilot off its back.

Keesnah and the Seer looked at each other as another rain of darts came down around them. Keesnah pulled one from her shoulder while the Seer had to pull one from her leg. The advancing soldiers emerged from the green fog with blowpipes ready for another attack. Keesnah and the Seer looked into each other's eyes and recited a line of the prophecy together. "And the two gave their lives that the Enchantress might survive and hence return in future times to free the people from tyranny."

*

Patsy and Jai could hear the fallen pilot calling out through her megaphone. "I will find you, Enchantress. You might as well accept your fate."

Jai looked in the direction of the sound. "What the—" He turned back to Patsy. "Didn't we see her fall from that thing she was riding?"

"I guess the mint must have broken her fall."

The megaphone echoed through the forest. "There is no escape. We know this forest better than you."

Jai said, "I think she's bluffing."

"How far away is the portal now?"

Jai looked at his phone. Colour drained from his features as the screen went blank. "The battery."

"The what?"

"The battery, it's dead. It's got no more power."

"Can you remember where it said the portal is?"

"Not well enough to be confident."

The hollow tone of the megaphone was getting closer. "I will find you."

Patsy reached out. "Give me the phone."

"Why?"

"Just give it to me." Patsy snatched the phone away from him then held it down low as she closed her eyes and concentrated until it was consumed in a glowing ball of energy. She relaxed and the glow subsided. She opened her eyes and handed the phone back to Jai. "Try it now."

"That's just great. It's probably fried now. We'll be stuck here."

"Just try it!"

The megaphone was getting louder. "I can hear you. Don't move. If you don't attempt another escape, your lives may be spared."

Feeling his heartbeat quicken, Jai had little choice but to trust that Patsy's attempt at charging the phone had worked. He pressed the power button. "I can't believe it. It's working!"

"Where's the map?"

"It's got to finish booting up first."

They started running in the direction they'd been heading before.

Still, the megaphone got closer. "They're escaping. Fire at them on sight."

A dart whistled past Patsy's ear. "How long does that take?"

"It's almost there." With his eyes fixed on the phone, Jai tripped on a fallen mint branch, sending the phone flying from his hands. It was just as well. A dart sped through the air where his neck would have otherwise been. The wind was knocked out of him as he hit the ground.

A robotic voice came from the device. "You are three minutes from your destination." Patsy went down on the ground to try and avoid what was now a shower of darts. She crawled through the slime and mud of the forest floor to grab the phone then scrambled back to Jai. The slime that now matted her hair and covered the front of her dress stank. She lay next to Jai and held the phone up to him. "Which way?" Still too winded to talk, he raised a finger and pointed.

"Gotcha!"

Patsy looked up and saw the pilot standing over them, bringing a blowpipe to her lips. Patsy wrapped an arm around Jai and allowed her mind to blend with his. He put up no resistance. She found the part of his mind that understood where the phone had told him the portal was located.

The pilot blew in her pipe. The dart embedded itself in the ground where Patsy and Jai had been.

*

Patsy was passed out when Jai came to, brought back to his senses by the now distant megaphone.

"I will find you. Your parlour tricks will not stop me."

He looked at the pool of thick green slime they'd been transported to. The large rock on the other side confirmed that Patsy had brought them to the right place.

He put a hand on her shoulder and gave it a little shake. There was no response. He bent down and checked she was still breathing. While there was still breath, it was shallow. He grabbed his phone and went through the contacts until he found his mother and called her. After three rings he heard a recorded message: "Hi, you've called Glenda. I'm either unavailable, or don't want to talk to you. Leave a message if you want, but I probably won't bother getting back to you." He shook his head. *Yep, that's Mum alright.*

The megaphone was getting closer again. "I know you're going to the slime pool. You can't fool me."

Jai tried calling his grandmother. Come on, pick up, Nan. It rang once… twice… three times.

The megaphone was getting closer. "I'm almost there. You might as well give up. We've got you surrounded now."

Come on Nan, Jai looked at Patsy. This is my fault. I never should have done this.

The ringing stopped. "Hello? Jai?"

"Nan! Thank God you answered. Are you at home?"

"Is that really you?" Her voice sounded more fragile than usual, huskier.

"Of course it's me. Just tell me, are you at home? I need you to open the portal."

"Where have you been?"

"I went to get help, remember?"

"But that was so long ago." Jai's Nan paused, then let out a little sob before continuing. "Your mother gave up on ever seeing you again."

"I've only been gone a few days."

"It's been almost fifteen years—"

"Nan, I need you to open the portal, now!"

"I never gave up—"

Jai looked up and saw two dragonflies circling overhead. "Nan, please! Where are you?"

"I'm sitting by the pool at the creek. I'm reading a wonderful book by—"

At least she was right there. There was still hope. "Nan, this is life or death, I need you to open the portal."

"Oh, well you should have said so earlier. Hold on a minute. I'll have it open for you in a jiffy."

"I've got no time to lose, Nan. I'm going to start moving into the water, and I'm going to trust that you can get it to open in time. I'm bringing Patricia McIntyre with me."

"That's nice, dear."

"I'm going to put you on speaker phone while I carry her into the portal."

"Oh, that's lovely that you don't want her feet to get wet."

Jai didn't bother replying. Nan had always been sharp and quick-witted in the past. It broke his heart to hear her sounding this way. He scooped up Patsy and placed the phone on her belly so he'd still be able to communicate with his Nan as he worked his way into the portal.

"This is your last chance to stop."

Jai looked over his shoulder and saw the pilot raising a blowpipe to her lips. He was knee-deep now in the pool, the stench of the slime assaulting his nostrils as he stirred it up. A dart whistled past his ear. "Come on, Nan. Please—"

"Just trying to remember the words, dear. It's been a long time, you know."

Another dart whistled past. The slime was starting to come to life, moving around him and becoming shallower in his immediate vicinity. *Thank you, Nan.*

More soldiers appeared on the bank with blowpipes. Then, Jai heard a thud. He looked over his shoulder and saw the pilot fall to the ground with a huge gash on his forehead where he'd been hit by a rock. There was a veritable sea of rocks flying out of the forest and taking down soldiers. Marji stepped forward and called out, "Go! Get the Enchantress to safety."

CHAPTER 5

The slimy water swirled around Jai as he carried the unconscious Patsy into the portal. In amongst the thundering sounds of the vortex he heard a woman gasp. Looking over his shoulder he saw the shimmering ghost-like images of Neridah, Meredith, and the Reverend. Meredith had her hands against her cheeks and was struggling to breathe on seeing her daughter look so lifeless.

"This way, laddie," said the Reverend. "Time to bring her home. Then we can send you back to your time and nurse her back to health to do what must be done."

Jai looked at Patsy's face, then looked in the direction he'd been heading. The water was becoming clearer, and he could see his Nan waiting for him on the bank of the pool. He turned back to the Trinity. "No, she needs to help me find my sister and get the Book of Wisdom back first."

Neridah's phantom image stamped its foot. "Jai! That's wrong and it's selfish! She needs help, help that you won't be able to give her. Bring her back, now!"

Meredith was crying. She reached out. "Please, Jai, please bring my baby back to me."

The Reverend stabbed a finger in Jai's direction. "We put ourselves into the void to help you. We did that to provide you with a beacon to find your way back to the right place and time. We trusted that you would come back and then pull us free of the void. What you're proposing is a betrayal of that trust."

Jai said, "I'm sorry. This is what I have to do." He turned his back on the Trinity and made his way toward his Nan.

*

"Well, that didn't go well." Neridah avoided eye contact with the other two.

Meredith replied, "I'm not surprised. A little disappointed, but not surprised."

"I expected better of the boy," said the Reverend, his eyes cast low.

Neridah glared at him. "Oh? What, because he looks like you? Do you expect him to do what you believe he should do just to please you? Would you have behaved any differently at that age? How's it feel to see yourself in the mirror? Are you comfortable with what you see?"

"Mother, that's enough. We're stuck in this void until Patricia can pull us out. Jai's made his decision, and we have no choice but to live with it. Even if that means we're stuck in this situation for weeks on end." An uncomfortable silence ensued as the reality of Meredith's statement sank in.

*

Gladys doubled over as she coughed, gagging as she took in another deep breath of the putrid smoke-filled air. It reeked of sulphur and bile. She was drenched in sweat and wondered how long her decrepit body would cope. Most other Nasqa would have departed the body by now, seeking an escape to a different crossworld. But not this one. This one had learned to enjoy the pain and suffering of the host's body. Let her feel it, while I revel in her agony. And besides, this was a different timeline. The Nasqa had no familiarity with what worlds lay nearby so likely wouldn't be able to access other crossworlds without some sort of assistance.

A gust of wind drew her attention. She turned and saw a shaft of light with swirling flames around it. The portal—that's where the portal must be. It's opened!

She ran toward it, not caring as her dress caught fire. There's a pathway out of this inferno. As she neared the swirling tornado of fire, she could sense it was retracting, as though getting ready to close. She threw herself forward, diving in as it snapped shut. Gladys Taylor disappeared with it.

*

Destellie sang as she washed her clothes in the creek. It was a chore she loathed, but she found singing made it more bearable.

Felibrey's voice from behind caused her to jump. "Your singing is so sweet it puts the birds to shame."

She turned and forced a smile. "It's only so sweet because it's a song I learned from them. The magpies are quite generous in sharing their knowledge of songs and melodies." She put her washing aside and turned to face where he sat on a rock next to her. They shared a morning kiss and embraced, moving their chins to rest on each other's shoulders. "You slept late."

"Yes, but I feel much better for it." They relaxed their embrace before Felibrey asked, "Have you seen the Reverend this morning? He was supposed to show me how to fix the roof shingles in place. But he never returned from the McIntyre's last night."

"I wouldn't worry. It's not unusual for him to stay the night there."

"Yes, but when he does, he normally returns early."

Destellie looked up and listened to a magpie warbling in a tree. It sang a song about the freshness of worms collected after rain. She wondered as she listened whether any of the local wildlife would betray her deception. "Felibrey, have you ever thought that maybe we'd be better moving to Sydney, or another place? Maybe even the goldfields?"

"But that would be breaking the promise we made to the Reverend."

"Did we? Did we ever really make a promise to him? Maybe we should think about the promise we're preparing to make to each other. Maybe we should start a new life, away from where anyone we know might find us."

*

Nan stared at Jai. "How is it that you haven't aged?"

"I told you on the phone. To me, I've only been gone a few days."

Nan looked at Patsy's limp form as Jai lowered her to the sandy part of the bank. "Oh my. This doesn't look good."

Jai's voice was soft. "Her breathing is shallow."

Nan closed her eyes as she passed a hand over Patsy. "She's exhausted herself. She needs sleep more than anything else, and a good bath. She'll likely catch a cold if she stays in those putrid wet rags much longer. We can't risk that with the weak state she's in." She looked up at Jai. "So, this really is Patricia McIntyre?"

Jai ignored the question. He was more interested in how the woman he'd last seen a few days ago had aged so much. "How long did you say I've been gone?"

Nan sighed. "Almost fifteen years."

He could see all those years and more etched into Nan's face as he explored the deep lines that told a tale of sadness and loss. So different from the face he was familiar with that had lit up the world of his youth with happiness and joy. "I'm so sorry, Nan." He went to give her a hug only to be pushed away.

Nan pulled her head as far from him as she could, pinching her nose at the same time. "We need to get you and this young lady up to the house and get you both cleaned up. We can hug and chat all you want later." She picked up her book and started up the steps. Jai marvelled at how, apart from a good deal of wear, the pathway hadn't changed since Patsy's grandfather had first cut the stairway out of the sandstone. Nan turned and glared back at him. "Come on then." She looked him up and down. "That shower isn't going to come to you."

Jai put his phone in his pocket and squatted down in readiness to pick up Patsy again. He was just starting to slip his arms under her when a pair of pixies appeared. They fluttered above Patsy, inspecting her. Having not encountered them before, Jai leaned back to try to create a safe distance between them. "What the—"

Bandah looked up and said, "What the what? What's your name kid, and what are you doing bringing Patsy into this timeline?"

"I..." Jai couldn't get the words out.

On hearing the pixie's voice, Nan stopped and turned around. "Bandah?"

Talia landed on Patsy's cheek and lifted an eyelid. "She'll be okay. Just needs a little laughter to bring her smile back."

Bandah turned away from Jai and asked Talia, "A bit of tickle therapy perhaps?"

Talia nodded. "Yep, unless you can think of another way to make someone laugh in their sleep."

Bandah positioned himself just under Patsy's chin then started beating his wings against her neck. A few seconds later, a giggle escaped her lips. Talia joined Bandah in the exercise, causing Patsy's eyes to open wide as she burst into a fit of laughter. "Oh, I'm laughing too much. I can't breathe. Stop it." She started to swat at her neck with her hands. "Please, stop it!"

Satisfied their job was done, Bandah and Talia drew their wings back in while Patsy took in a few deep breaths. She looked at the pixies and asked, "What was that for? What are you even doing here?"

Bandah replied, "You're asking us what we're doing here? Are you even aware of where you are?"

Patsy looked around. "I'm home." She looked up at Jai and smiled. "We made it." She looked across at Nan and asked, "Who are you? Where's Mother and Nana-Neri?"

Jai gestured towards Nan. "Patsy, meet Nan. Nan, meet Patsy."

Bandah said, "You still haven't told us who you are, kid."

Nan said, "Well, Bandah, if you and Talia had bothered to check in on me anytime in the past thirty-five years, you'd know that this is my grandson, Jai."

Talia asked Nan, "So, where's Glenda?" She cast a quick glance at Bandah. "She always was a little cutie."

The lines in Nan's face seemed to deepen as she responded. "We don't talk anymore."

"What do you mean?" asked Jai. "Where is Mum? I tried to call her when we first reached the portal, but she wouldn't answer."

"She didn't take it well when you didn't come back. With the Nasqa having taken Melanie, and you seemingly lost forever after entering the portal, she decided to devote herself to trying to find your sister. She reformed her band and uses touring as a means of trying to locate her… and to finance the search."

"The Crimson Dockers are back together?"

Nan nodded. "It's the worst thing she could have done. I never did approve of how she used her magic to make that band stand out. And as for the other band members…"

"Has she had any luck finding Mel?"

"Yes, just recently. She's being held by the Nasqa somewhere in Sydney, so your mother's based herself there now so she can pinpoint exactly where." Nan looked at Patsy. She was shivering and her teeth were chattering. "Come on, let's get you up to the house for a shower. I'll see if I can find something you can wear while we wash your dress." She turned to the pixies. "Are you two going to join us?"

"Absolutely," replied Bandah. He landed on Jai's shoulder. "And you, young man, are going to answer my questions as we head up there."

"We can't leave the portal yet," said Patsy. "My family, they're trapped in the void. Mother, Nana-Neri, and the Reverend, they formed a Trilogy and entered the void to help Jai and I find our way back to my timeline. They can't get out of there without my help, and I can only do that from there. They're stuck until I get back."

Bandah and Talia looked at each other. "That's not good," said Bandah.

Talia replied, "I'll go and let them know what's happening. With a bit of luck, Mrs Smith and I might be able to team up to peel back the veil to the void enough to pull them out."

"You can't, though, it's a different timeline. We don't belong there, just like Patsy doesn't belong here in this one."

"Have you got a better idea?"

Bandah thought about it. His answer was soft, almost inaudible. "No. Just be careful not to connect with yourself while you're there."

Patsy asked, "I don't understand, how will you find the right timeline… there's so many?"

"The void intersects them all. That's why it's so dangerous to be trapped in there." Talia turned to Bandah. "I know it's a long shot, but I've got to give it a try."

•

Colin grabbed his flintlock and walked out to the veranda when he heard the sound of the approaching horses. His heart sank at the sight of Captain Taylor and six other soldiers, no doubt all controlled by Nasqa. "Captain Taylor, I can't say that it's a pleasure to see you."

"Nor I, you murdering bastard."

"I beg your pardon."

Captain Taylor glanced across at the rider next to him. "Arrest this man and clap him in irons." He turned back to Colin. "This time I promise, you will hang."

Clara Jenkins and Cook raced onto the veranda as one soldier took Colin's flintlock and the other attached irons to his wrists and ankles. Clara looked at Colin and asked, "What's happening?"

Colin was silent.

She turned to Captain Taylor. "What's the meaning of this?" As she watched the Captain and his men, she noticed their shadows followed different movements and represented creatures just as ghastly as those in Gladys Taylor's shadow. She turned her attention to the captain. "What is he accused of?"

"He is guilty of the murder of my wife. Her sulky was found abandoned down the road, and her footprints led to this property."

Cook tried to reach out to Colin but was pushed back by one of the soldiers. "Don't you worry, Mr McIntyre, sir. I'll go and talk to Vincent, he'll know what to do."

Captain Taylor laughed. "Mr Donaldson won't be much help to you." As he spoke, another soldier rode into the property, leading Gladys Taylor's sulky. Vincent Donaldson was in the seat, weighed down by the chains on his wrists and ankles. There was a large gash over his closed and blackened right eye. "My poor wife's sulky and horse were found on Mr Donaldson's property. He is clearly an accessory to the fact. I intend to see the two of them hang side by side."

Cook burst into tears. "Please, God, please, please tell me this isn't happening." Cook started to sway, and then her knees gave way. Clara caught her before she collapsed, struggling to hold the woman's weight.

"We'll go down to Sydney. We'll take this to the governor if we have to."

Captain Taylor's laughter grew louder. "Oh, please do."

Jimmy and Darcy O'Sullivan ran across from the stables. Jimmy called out, "Oi! What in the name of God is goin' on here?"

Captain Taylor turned to one of his soldiers and said, "If that man utters another word, I want you to shoot him." The soldier smiled as he lifted a pistol and pointed it in Jimmy's direction. Jimmy stopped running, his mouth hanging open. Darcy continued up to the veranda to help Clara support Cook.

*

Gladys emerged from the stinking pool of swirling slime. The soggy remains of her dress and petticoat were blackened and hung from her wiry frame like lichen. Darts covered in wrathapillar poison whistled through the air around her, some striking her, some striking the myriad other creatures that had taken advantage of the portal opening in countless worlds scattered across different timelines. There were giant rodents, griffins, fairies, and other creatures Gladys couldn't recognise. Someone had been careless when they'd opened this portal, allowing a chaos of creatures who had no place in this crossworld or timeline to come flooding in. Gladys smiled. She liked chaos.

Feeling her leg muscles weakening from the impact of the poison darts, the Nasqa within Gladys let go. The life drained from her as she fell to the ground. The hint of a smile on her face suggested there was somehow a final moment of peace, an uncomfortable end to a life spent seeking empowerment through being controlled by another. The Nasqa swept through the air and through the minds of the soldiers on the bank as it sought a new host, searching for a mind that displayed weak character. Then it found a mind that had all the traits it was looking for. Disregard for what mattered and a willingness to change one's values to suit the occasion.

The Nasqa that had once inhabited Sean O'Malley, then Gladys Taylor, now took control of the Grand Field Commander.

*

Patsy was stunned by how the library was the same now as it had been a hundred and fifty years ago. The only noticeable difference? The Book of Wisdom was nowhere to be seen. She stood at its empty stand.

"Please, do sit down," said Nan.

Patsy looked around and saw that Nan had taken a seat at the main desk where her father normally sat and was gesturing for Jai and herself to take seats across from her. She hesitated before taking tentative steps toward the desk.

Jai had already taken a seat. "What's wrong?" he asked.

Patsy seemed oblivious to his presence. "It feels so weird. I'm being treated as a guest in my own home." It didn't help that she was wearing clothes unlike any she'd worn before. And that shower… the hot beads of water raining down on her, cleaning away the grime of another world. That, in itself, was as strange and frightening as anything she'd experienced during this new adventure.

"Of course it does," said Nan. "This must be very difficult for you."

Patsy nodded in response, then glanced at Jai. "I'm sorry, I didn't realise. It must have been like this for you, too, when you arrived."

"Not really," said Jai. "Mum used to drag me and Mel around on tour all the time. I've spent most of my life living out of a suitcase. I'd been around the world twice by the time I was ten. It was only when Mel got taken that she stopped touring and broke up the band."

"What's this 'band' that you keep talking about?"

"The Crimson Dockers? Punk and grunge rediscovered with a touch of alternative folk for good measure. Mum wrote every lyric and note of every song."

"That's not helping me."

"Perhaps this will help." Nan powered up her tablet then opened a page promoting the Crimson Dockers' next gig. "The Crimson Dockers are playing at the Sydney Opera House tomorrow night." She looked at Jai. "Your mother always sends me two tickets and backstage passes. I've never used them, but I think you two need to go down there for this one."

Jai asked, "Will you come with us?"

Nan sighed. "No. There's only two tickets." A tear started to well up in the corner of her eye and her voice became shaky. "But even if there were three, I really don't think I could—"

Seeing her distress, Jai raced around the desk and threw his arms around Nan. She buried her head in his shoulder and sobbed.

*

As the sulky entered Springwood Barracks, Colin noticed something very different from the last time he'd entered the compound a year earlier. This time, every face looked toward him with contempt. This time, every soldier was clearly Nasqa.

He looked at the gallows that were under construction. It occurred to him that this time would be different. This time there wasn't even going to be a trial. He looked across at Vincent and found himself lost for words. Meredith, Neridah, and the Reverend were trapped in limbo in an effort to bring back his lost daughter. For the first time in his life, Colin McIntyre could see no hope of salvation.

CHAPTER 6

Patsy had always wanted to ride on a train. She'd never dreamed that the first time she did so it would be powered by electricity rather than steam. The bra that Nan had insisted she had to wear felt uncomfortable, but she liked the t-shirt with its image of a sultry looking Stevie Nicks, the word 'Witch' scrawled across the top in red. Nan had bought her the shirt during their morning shopping escapade. She was still trying to get used to the feel of the jeans and struggled to understand how something with several tears in it could be sold as 'new.'

"Just wait until you see the Opera House. That will seriously blow your mind," said Jai.

Why is he taking so much joy in this? Patsy really didn't like the side of Jai she was seeing now. Almost every minute since she'd arrived in this time had been an overload of new concepts and ideas to absorb, and

Jai seemed to take pleasure in watching her struggle to take it all in.

"There it is." Jai was pointing out the window to the most unusual building Patsy had ever seen. But what amazed her more was the bridge they were crossing and the size of the buildings behind the Opera House. She wondered what could possibly be contained within those structures. What purpose did they serve? She opened her mouth to ask, but then decided it might just lead to even greater confusion.

•

The crisp winter morning was filled with a symphony of bird songs. A few soldiers were up and about to watch Colin and Vincent being marched to the gallows.

No words were spoken as the nooses were secured around their necks.

Colin looked across at Vincent with his swollen and blackened eye. He felt gratitude for everything Vincent had done to support him and his family. He also felt an overwhelming sense of guilt. Vincent had never even met Gladys. He had no real connection to the issues that caused Captain Taylor to be so full of hate. He opened his mouth to say something, to express his sorrow. To confess his culpability for what was about to befall them. His jaw hung limp; He could find no words.

A lever was pulled.

Captain Taylor smiled then walked away as Colin McIntyre and Vincent Donaldson's lives came to an end.

•

Patsy scanned the orchestra members then turned to Jai and whispered, "Which one is her?"

Jai laughed. “This is just the orchestra, the backup musicians. Mum will be out soon enough. And trust me, you’ll know it’s her when she appears. She looks a lot like your grandmother.”

The melody the orchestra was playing started to change, becoming a repetitious string of a few bars.

The audience saw it as a sign that the band was preparing to start and, at the end of each repetition, they chanted, “Crimson!”

“What are they saying?” asked Patsy. “Is it meant to be some sort of incantation?”

“Not really, they’re calling for the band to come out and start playing.”

“But the orchestra is already playing.”

The crowd began stomping their feet with each repetition of the chant.

Jai laughed, “You ain’t seen nothing yet, Pats.”

Patsy looked away and crossed her arms, disappointed by the lack of substance in Jai’s answer. The chant of the crowd was getting so loud that it started to hurt her ears. Then the room went dark and the loudest sound Patsy had ever heard filled the auditorium as a spot of light focused on the woman strutting onto the stage holding a guitar.

The crowd erupted and got to their feet.

Patsy stared at the close-up images on large screens behind the stage. She placed a hand on Jai’s shoulder and yelled in his ear, “She looks like Nana-Neri!”

Jai smiled.

Glenda Williams strummed the guitar again then threw her arm out at the audience as she yelled out, “Hey there, Sydney. Are you ready to rock?”

The crowd roared, “YES!”

“I didn’t hear you. ARE YOU READY TO ROCK?”

"YES!"

Patsy watched in stunned awe as Glenda dropped her right hand, strumming the guitar before reaching into the Crossworlds to draw power. A dancing ball of energy built up around her hand. Patsy turned to Jai. "What's she doing?"

Jai shrugged his shoulders. "She's building the suspense."

Glenda yelled to the audience. "We are the Crimson Dockers and we are here to rock your world!" She threw her arm forward and released the ball of energy. It exploded above the crowd. The stage lit up and the band swung into the first number, "Refrained Power."

Patsy asked Jai, "Why would she use her power that way?"

"That's part of what draws people to the shows."

"But where's the danger?"

"What are you talking about? There's no danger. It's just entertainment."

"But the consequences… that power comes from elsewhere. You know that!"

Patsy chose not to say anything more and tried to make out what Glenda was singing.

If you knew what I can do
You'd think it can't be true
I hold back
You don't know
Hidden power
Desperate needs
If you knew you'd get on your knees
Don't you know how it's been for me?
Refrained Power!

She held the microphone out to the audience. The crowd sang out in unison, "Refrained Power!" Patsy was shocked when she realised she'd been swept up in the chorus and was singing along herself.

Glenda took a step back as the lead guitarist ran toward the front of the stage then went down on his knees, momentum carrying him forward as his fingertips danced along the fret board. As Patsy tried to follow the movement of his hands, she noticed something disturbing… the shadows. She looked around the stage to the other band members. How could Glenda spend so much time with these people and not know? Patsy nudged Jai with her elbow. He ignored her, continuing to shake his head wildly in time with the music. She grabbed hold of him with both hands and shook him until he stopped. She yelled into his ear, struggling to be heard over the amplified music and the roar of the crowd: "Look at them!"

"Who?"

Patsy pointed to the band members. "Don't you see it?"

"What?"

"Their shadows. They're moving differently."

"That's the light show."

"What?"

"Look, there's lights flashing on and off and swinging around everywhere."

"The shadows, they're moving."

Jai pointed to the lighting grid. "The lights are moving."

"It's not just the lights."

Jai shook his head. "It's just a light show."

"They're Nasqa."

"It's a light show." Patsy's glare told him she wasn't convinced. "My mum's a witch." Patsy's expression didn't change. "Wouldn't she know if they're Nasqa?"

Patsy crossed her arms and sat down. They had seats at the front of a side box near the stage. As she watched Glenda's performance, Patsy pondered how she felt about meeting this woman whose use of magic was so careless. How would Krinkle-myst feel about this woman? It made her appreciate how much she'd learned about the importance of thinking before using magic herself.

•

Jai pulled out his phone and showed the security guard his backstage pass. The guard laughed when he looked at the fifteen-year-old device. "Hey kid, it's a wonder that antique even works. Very retro, dude." He looked across at Patsy. "Where's yours?"

Jai answered for her. "She doesn't have one."

"Is that so?"

"A phone… she doesn't have one. I've got both our tickets on mine." He swiped to reveal the second pass. "See?"

"Yeah, well, you know what, this party's no place for kids anyway—"

"Don't you realise who I am?" Jai shoved his phone in the guard's face. "See who issued the ticket? I'm her son."

"Sorry kid, even if you are, the rules are the rules. No under eighteens allowed."

Patsy asked Jai, "Where do we need to go?"

Jai pointed past the guard to a room down the corridor filled with music and laughter. "The backstage party's in there."

Patsy grabbed Jai's arm. "Okay, well let's go."

The security guard staggered back a few steps and clutched his chest hoping it might slow the sudden increase in his heart rate. He'd been talking to a couple of young teenagers, he was sure of it. But now, there was no one there. He grabbed his walkie talkie, wondering if he should call the guard inside the party to see if anyone matching their description was inside, then thought better of it. He needed this job, and he was already on his last warning after having been caught drinking on the job in the past. The last thing he wanted now was to give his superiors reason to question his sobriety.

*

"Jai?" Glenda took a step closer and reached out to touch her son's face. She didn't dare blink in case it might cause him to vanish. "Oh my God, it really is you." She burst into tears as she threw her arms around him. "I thought I'd lost you."

Jai cried, too, as he responded in kind to his mother's embrace. "I promised you I'd come back."

Glenda struggled to get the words out through her tears. "Yes, you did. My beautiful boy. But that was so long ago. I'm so sorry Jai… I'd given up hope." Glenda relaxed her grip then noticed his companion. She studied Patsy's face, moving her head around as she scanned every detail. "You're her, aren't you?" Before Patsy had a chance to respond, Glenda turned back to her son. "I can't believe it, you succeeded! You brought back Patricia McIntyre." Again, she threw her arms around her son and cried into his shoulder. "How could I have been so foolish as to give up on you?"

"It's okay, Mum, it's been quite a journey."

"I've felt so guilty all these years. I'm so sorry."

"No, I'm the one who should be sorry."

"You've been gone fifteen years, but haven't aged a bit."

Jai thought to himself, *You look like crap, Mum, what have you been doing to yourself?* He took a step back and said, "You look great yourself, Mum."

Seeing through his deception, she bit her lower lip and nodded. She pulled her son toward her then gave him another hug. "I should never have risked losing you. It was the most stupid thing I've ever done." She released her hold on him and offered her hand to Patsy. "I am so pleased to meet you, Patricia. I've read so much about you."

Patsy looked at Glenda's outstretched hand and wasn't sure how to respond. She raised her own but didn't make contact with Glenda's. Seeing Patsy's discomfort with the procedure, Glenda instead threw her arms around her. "Stuff the handshakes, you're family." Patsy couldn't help but smile at the genuine warmth she felt in Glenda's embrace. There was more she had in common with Neridah than just her appearance. Glenda took a step back and looked over her shoulder to the rest of the people enjoying the feast and drinks at the backstage party. "We really should join them for a while. Some of them paid a lot of money to attend this party, and I really need to meet and greet as many as I can before we go."

Jai asked, "Do you mind if Patsy and I just sit back here and wait for you to be finished?"

"No way! Come and join the party. You and Patricia need to meet the band."

Jai glanced across at Patsy, his expression betraying his disappointment.

Patsy thought about the disturbing shadows she'd seen cast by the band members. She forced a smile and said, "I'd really like to meet them. Thank you."

Having absorbed so many new things throughout the day, Patsy felt like she was walking through a dream as they navigated their way through the party. She'd never seen so much food laid out on tables before, even when her parents had entertained for dozens of guests on special occasions. Then, she saw the guitarist, and watched his shadow harass the young woman he was talking to. Patsy grabbed Glenda's arm. "He's Nasqa!"

"Well, duh…" Glenda rolled her eyes and sighed, waving her hand in a manner that suggested she found it tedious to have to explain what was so obvious to her. Seeing the look of confusion in Patsy's expression, Glenda softened her tone and whispered into Patsy's ear. "Keep your friends close, and your enemies closer."

Patsy stepped back and shook her head. "This is wrong."

"Is it?" Glenda put her hands on Patsy's shoulders and looked into her eyes. She spoke slowly, as though she were speaking to someone with a poor understanding of English. "I'm trying to find my daughter."

Feeling patronised, Patsy took another step back to take her shoulders beyond Glenda's reach. "What you do on stage, that's wrong, too."

"Excuse me?" Glenda paused before asking, "Are you casting judgement on me?"

Patsy shot back, "I don't need to. You know it's wrong."

"Huh?" Glenda turned to Jai. "Do you understand any of this?"

Jai took a deep breath before responding. "Umm… after what I've seen in the past few days, I think it might be worthwhile listening to her."

Unimpressed by her son's response, Glenda turned back to Patsy. "Now, you listen to me. I've spent fifteen years putting this plan into place—"

A tall man with an effeminate voice came up behind Glenda and put his arms around her. "When are you going to join the party? Your fans await. They've paid top dollar for a piece of you—" He froze mid-sentence, as did the rest of the room.

Patsy's breathing was short and her arms were outstretched. Glenda glared at her. "A time freeze? You've done a time freeze?"

"On everyone in the room but us."

Glenda's words were barely audible. "And you did it without even reciting a spell?"

"I don't need words when I'm angry."

Glenda held up her arms in an effort to somehow shield the room from Patsy. "Whatever you're thinking of doing, please don't. I've spent too much time setting this up."

"You've spent fifteen years drawing energy from other worlds for no reason. You've been pandering to the Nasqa." Patsy stepped around Glenda and approached the lead guitarist. "I'll show you how to deal with a mind thief."

The guitarist's eyes widened. The Nasqa possessing him struggled to break free of the time freeze. "Please, not the void, anything but that!"

"Oh, so you know who I am?"

"Every Nasqa knows about your sadistic madness, how could we not?"

Patsy reached into the musician's chest and ripped out the Nasqa, then held it up high. "Tell me where she is, or so help me, you'll be spread across a hundred unattached realms in the void."

Detached from the musician's body, the Nasqa had to communicate using its thoughts. *I can't…*

Patsy reached down with her free hand and opened a connection to the void. "Are you sure about that?"

Please… I can't… the consequences…

Patsy pushed part of the Nasqa into the void then slammed the opening shut, leaving part of the Nasqa lost for eternity. "Are the consequences as bad as what you're facing now?" Patsy opened another connection to the void. "Last chance." She started moving the Nasqa toward the void.

No… I'll tell you. Just please, promise me you'll help me get to somewhere I can be safe.

The Nasqa controlling the drummer broke free of the time freeze, just enough to call out, "Don't do it. Don't be a fool." His face screwed up in a sneer. "You know what happens to traitors."

Patsy turned to Glenda and extended the hand that held the shadowy apparition of the Nasqa. "Here, hold this."

"What?" Glenda took a step back.

"Just grab hold of it, with your mind as well as your hand."

"Eww!" Glenda looked at Patsy and asked, "Are you for real?"

Jai stepped forward. "I'll hold it for you."

"You're not strong enough. She needs to."

Glenda protested, "This is madness."

"Just take it."

Glenda took a tentative step forward and reached out, wrapping her right hand around the Nasqa. As soon as Patsy released her hold on the shadowy form it started thrashing about like an eel on the end of a fishing line. "Whoah!" Glenda brought up her other hand and tightened her grip.

Patsy walked over to the drummer and ripped the Nasqa from his chest. "So, you think you're stronger than him?"

That one's always been weak.

"You don't fear the void?"

I don't fear anything.

Patsy tore the Nasqa in two, throwing one half into the void.

You'll never find the girl, nor your precious little book. It's ours now.

She threw the other half into the void as well, not caring whether or not it would be able to reconnect with the other part of itself.

Glenda was still struggling to hold the Nasqa. When Patsy approached, it broke free and was gone. Patsy looked around and saw the bass player. His long hair was halfway down his back and looked like it hadn't been washed in a long time. His beard was just as long and dirty. His eyes darted back and forth as he tried to break out of the time freeze.

"The time freeze won't last much longer, but however long it does, it'll be longer than the time it takes for my patience to run out."

"You… you're insane."

"No, I'm just angry." Patsy was raising her arm, ready to reach into his chest.

The words spilled out of the bass player's mouth in rapid succession. "She's at the Art Gallery. The director… she had a secret apartment created for her. She has the book on display in her office." An uneasy pause followed, filled only by the terrified man hyperventilating. "Can I go now?"

"If I ever feel your presence in this world again, so help me…"

"I get the picture."

A ghostly shadow came out of the bass player and disappeared, leaving the freed bass player locked in the time freeze. Glenda stood behind Jai and grabbed his shoulders as she addressed Patsy. "I don't want you going anywhere near my son ever again."

Jai looked over his shoulder. "Huh?"

Patsy's jaw dropped. "What?"

"You heard me. I want you to stay away from my son."

"But… I just got rid of three mind thieves and found out where your daughter is—"

"You were cruel."

"But they were Nasqa."

"Cruelty is still cruelty, no matter who it's perpetrated against."

Her jaw hanging open, Patsy glanced at Jai. He shrugged his shoulders and said, "I kinda agree with Mum on the cruelty bit."

"But… they're Nasqa… mind thieves. They are the great nuisance of the Crossworlds."

Glenda replied, "Does that justify tearing them into pieces like that? Do you take joy in telling them they face an eternity of pain and suffering?"

Feeling weakness in her knees, Patsy stumbled to a nearby chair and sat down. "But your daughter—"

"But this, but that—for someone with such a big reputation, you're pretty damn good at making excuses. Of course I want my daughter back, but not at any cost. You can measure a person's worth by how they treat their foes."

Patsy leaned forward, her head almost dangling between her knees. Her voice was barely audible. "You shouldn't use magic the way you do."

Glenda's fingernails dug into Jai's shoulder as her muscles tightened. Her breaths were coming in short gasps and her teeth were clenched. "Excuse me?"

Patsy raised her head a little, just enough to make eye contact. "The magic you use on stage, it has consequences—"

"Don't give me that mumbo-jumbo. You're as bad as my mother." She released her grip on Jai's shoulder and grabbed her bag from a nearby table. "Come on, Jai, we're leaving. I've had enough of this."

Jai took a step back from her. "No!"

"What do you mean, no?" She glared at Patsy. "What have you done to my son?"

Jai stood with his arms straight by his side and his fists clenched. "I mean no."

"Well, that's just great, isn't it? I thought you were with me on this. For fifteen years I thought I'd lost you. Just when I thought I'd got you back, it turns out that I've lost you anyway."

"It's not like that. I'm sorry it's taken so long. It must have hurt real bad. But I'm not going to walk out that door with you now."

Glenda stood with her mouth open and a hand against her chest. "My poor baby! What has she done to you?"

"You can drop the act, Mum. I agree with you about what she did to the Nasqa, but we've still got to try and get Mel back."

Glenda slipped the bag off her shoulder and slammed it down on the table. "Ugh! You saw what the little monster just did here. Can you imagine what else she's capable of?"

Glenda spun around at the sound of Patsy's voice. "Not as much as what we're capable of if we work together."

"Come again?"

Patsy stood up. "We can form a Trinity that the Nasqa will fear so much they'll likely flee this world without us having to even threaten them."

"Oh really, just like that? And how do you propose we form this Trinity? We're kind of short one generation of witches."

Jai said, "I've been in a Trinity of Power with her before. And she's right. The Nasqa will fear us if we work together."

"You've done what?" she looked at Patsy. "Is there no end to your madness?"

"She saved my life, Mum. We wouldn't be here talking now if not for her courage and determination."

"You did see what I saw?"

"Yes, but trust me, she really is our best hope."

"They're going to be waiting for you." The three of them turned around to see the drummer addressing them. The time freeze had lifted.

The bass player was struggling to get to his feet. "Oh man, these clothes stink." He looked at Patsy and said, "I'd love to stick around and thank you, but I've got to get home and have a shower… and a change of clothes."

Glenda asked, "You are aware of what she did to that thing?"

"Oh yeah. And I'll be forever in her debt."

"What she did was cruel."

"Oh yeah? Let me tell you, Glenda, you don't know what cruelty is until you have one of those things controlling you."

The lead guitarist strode across and pushed against the drummer's shoulder. "Is that so? Maybe you shouldn't have resisted, you little wuss."

The bass player turned back from making his way to the door and wedged himself between them, pushing against the guitarist. "Hey, go easy. What's your beef?"

"The Crimson Dockers never would've been a hit without our little friends driving us. Do you really think any of us can play like that without them?" He turned and pointed an accusing finger at Patsy. "And it's all your fault."

Patsy's voice was deadpan. "Of course you can. You just have to believe in yourself. It was your hands doing the playing."

The band manager, an old hippie with long grey hair tied back in a ponytail, came across. "Hey, is there a problem here?" He looked over his shoulder to the crowd of party guests staring at the band members. "There's a whole lot of people hanging out to meet you guys."

The guitarist replied, "I was just in the process of telling Glenda and the boys that I quit."

"What are you talking about?"

The guitarist looked across at Jai and Glenda, then turned his attention to Patsy as he sneered, "Let's just put it down to family issues." He turned and took long strides as he departed, turning to flick the room the bird as he walked out the door.

The manager stood staring at the now empty doorway as if he might somehow be able to will the musician back.

"It's okay, Rick, let him go." Glenda put her bag back over her shoulder. "I've got a few family issues of my own that I need to deal with." She glared at Patsy. "Are you coming or what?" As the three of them left the party Glenda muttered under her breath, "This really goes against my better judgement, but it seems I don't have much choice."

*

Kellie Mercier, director of the Art Gallery of New South Wales, strolled through the door leading to the secret apartment. Her simple alpaca wool dress clung to her slender figure. "Hello, my dear."

Mel was slumped in a luxurious leather couch. She looked up from her book and replied, "Hello, Mother."

Kellie ran a hand through her silver, shoulder-length hair. "I've just learned we're likely to have some visitors shortly."

A smile erupted across Mel's face. "Really? It's been so long since we've had visitors! Is it Uncle Ben and Aunty Jan?" She put her book aside. "Uncle Ben always brings me new books to read. And I do so enjoy Aunty Jan's stories about going to the moon when she was in Buzz Aldrin's body."

Kellie smiled as she watched Mel's enthusiasm.

Mel noticed a tear running down Kellie's cheek. "What's wrong, Mother?"

Kellie sighed. "I so wish I could say it was our kin who are coming."

"Who is it then?"

"It's your birth mother. She's with her son."

Mel's eyes lit up. "I get to see my brother?"

"Darling, this is serious. They want to take you away from me."

"But why would they want to do that?"

"They're being influenced by someone else. A ghost from the past. Someone so evil the very thought of her sends a shiver up my spine. She's caused more harm to the Nasqa than anyone else in history. She's obsessed with keeping us from helping humanity reach its fullest potential."

Mel's expression conveyed her lack of understanding. "Who is this ghost? Why would anyone want to interfere with the Nasqa's benevolence?"

Kellie took a seat next to her on the couch. "Well, 'ghost' probably isn't the best term. One of your ancestors has travelled through time, with the sole aim of trying to take you away from me."

"Why would anyone want to do that? I'm happy here with you."

"I know you are." She placed a hand on Mel's knee. "But there are those who are motivated by greed and a lust for power. That's why I've had to be so careful about protecting you from the rest of the world."

"Protecting me? Sometimes I wonder why that's even necessary."

"Have I not given you everything you've ever wanted? Would I do for a prisoner the things I do for you? Yes, I'm protecting you, from monsters like the one who's on her way here now."

Mel cast her eyes downward. "Mother, I do love being here with you. But I wonder sometimes, when will I be able to leave the gallery building? I want to walk through the city with everyone else."

"Melanie." Kellie's voice took on a more serious tone. "We've been through this a thousand times. Do we really have to go over it again? You know I don't like having to repeat myself."

Mel shook her head then started to cry.

Kellie stood up and threw her arms into the air. "For fifteen years I've been trying to tell you. Read the book with me and I'll be able to fully protect you. Then, and only then, will it be safe for you to go out into the city."

"But you know what happens when I try to read it. It's like it gets angry with me and pushes me away."

"Melanie! You're twenty-three years old. You're not a little girl anymore. How on Earth do you expect the Nasqa to help humanity find a better future if you're not prepared to conquer your fears?"

"Why don't you just read it yourself then?"

"You know that's not possible."

"Why?"

"I'm trying to protect you."

"That's not an answer."

"Don't you want to protect me too?"

"How am I meant to do that?"

"If we go into my office now and we read the book together, we can stop your birth mother from taking you away." There was a long pause. "Do you remember the last time we read it together… when you were fourteen?"

Mel nodded.

"Do you remember what we did afterwards?"

"We went for a walk in the Botanic Gardens."

"And wasn't that a lovely day?"

Mel looked up at Kellie. “But the dreams I had after that… the ones with the wood-elf. He told me that I shouldn’t read it with you.”

Kellie sat next to her again and put an arm around her shoulders. “Oh, my poor baby. They were just dreams. And you do remember what I’ve told you about wood-elves, I hope?”

Mel nodded. “They can’t be trusted.”

“That’s right.” Kellie gave Mel a big hug. “As long as you trust in me, I promise I’ll keep you safe. But for me to be able to fulfill that promise, we need to read the book together. And we need to read it now.” Kellie relaxed her hold on Mel then looked into her eyes and smiled. “You know what? If we can use the book to get rid of your birth mother, and make sure that she never comes back, I think it might just be safe enough for you to go out into the city.”

Mel’s eyes widened. “Really?”

Kellie’s grin grew as she nodded. “Yes! You’d be able to go wherever you want.”

Mel threw her arms around Kellie. “Oh, thank you, Mother.” After a long hug she stood up and declared, “Okay, I’ll do it. Let’s go to your office and do some reading.”

•

“I’m sorry about your band.” Patsy was right behind Glenda and Jai.

“Oh yeah? You could’ve fooled me.” Glenda refused to look over her shoulder as she addressed Patsy while they walked down the corridor toward her dressing room.

“Don’t worry, she’ll get over it.” Jai’s voice was almost a whisper.

“Are you sure about that?” replied Patsy.

Glenda came to a dead stop just outside the dressing room door and spun around. "What did I tell you about staying away from my son? Just because I'm willing to give this Trinity thing of yours a shot, doesn't mean I'm happy for you to talk to him."

Jai asked, "Don't you think that's being a little unrealistic?"

Glenda's sharp glare switched its hold from Patsy to her son. "I think everything about this girl is unrealistic, especially her reputation for performing good deeds."

"Whatever you may think of me, Jai's still right." Patsy took a deep breath. *Stay calm. Getting angry isn't going to help.* "If we want the Trinity to work, we need to be thinking in harmony with each other."

"Well, that's just great, isn't it? How's this going to work anyway? I thought it was supposed to be three consecutive generations of women to make a Trinity work."

"That's ideal, but not necessary. As long as we're all the same bloodline, we can make it work."

"I think you're just making this up."

Patsy closed her eyes. *This is her problem, don't let it be yours.*

"Mum, haven't you listened to anything either of us has said? I told you, I've already been in a Trinity with her. That's how we escaped."

"How do you know it was a real Trinity and not just her telling you that's what it was? You never used to talk to me like that. What's she done to you?"

"I'm not a little kid anymore, Mum!"

"Oh, really? All of fifteen years old and all grown up, huh? You have no idea what I've been through for you."

"How about what I've been through for you?"

"Excuse me! Ever tried giving birth? Have you been through that for me?"

"How appropriate. You decide to talk about giving birth while you're treating me like a baby."

"You are a baby. You're my baby."

"I wish I'd stayed in Patsy's time. Her family were—"

"Stop it!" Patsy clenched her fists and stamped a foot for emphasis. The resulting shockwave shook the building and sent Glenda and Jai to the floor. Glenda's head hit hard against the door frame of her dressing room.

Seeing his mother slumped in the doorway, Jai lurched across and cupped his hand under the back of her head. "Are you alright, Mum?" Glenda's hair felt warm, wet, and sticky. There was blood, and lots of it. A small puddle was forming on the floor.

Glenda groaned, "Yes, I'll be okay."

"Is anyone hurt?" The three of them turned around to see a security guard at the end of the corridor. He started running toward them when he noticed the dark red pool of blood in the doorway.

Glenda looked at Patsy and said, "Okay, you made your point. If we're going to do this, we'll need to go now, otherwise we'll just end up spending the night waiting for stitches at the hospital."

Patsy pushed a hand toward the guard causing him to appear as though running in extreme slow motion.

Glenda's jaw dropped. "How did you do that?"

"The three of us being together makes all our powers stronger."

"All of us?" Glenda looked at Jai then back to Patsy. "Last I knew, Jai didn't have any powers."

"When Patsy saved my life, she had to share some of her powers with me."

Glenda shook her head. "I'm scared of what the devil in the detail is to this story." She glanced at the guard still inching toward them. "Let's just get this over with."

Patsy wrapped her arms around them, closed her eyes, and said, "Imagine we're at the Art Gallery."

The guard came to a stop at the empty door, puzzled by how the trio had disappeared. This was the second time tonight he'd imagined seeing people who turned out to not be there. But the pool of blood was real. He looked inside the empty dressing room then squatted to inspect the scarlet evidence of Glenda's injury.

•

"I don't understand." Patsy was looking at the contemporary works filling the walls around them. "Weren't we supposed to be going to an art gallery?"

Glenda stood up and approached a large canvas with a heavily textured splash of black paint going from one corner to another. "Invigorating, isn't it?"

"Shh!" said Jai. "There's bound to be security guards."

Glenda shook her head, "No, it's all electronic these days, all driven by AI." She pointed to the myriad of small, dark domes attached to the ceiling. "See all those cameras? They'll have detected us and notified the police by now. So, I guess we'd better be quick."

"We can put the building in a time freeze if we need to," said Patsy.

"We? Don't you mean you?" replied Glenda.

Patsy looked around at the size of the building with its cavernous halls disappearing in every direction and metal staircases leading to levels above and below where they stood. "It's too big for me to do on my own straight after allowing us to be here. We'd need to do it together."

Glenda's expression made her cynicism obvious. "Maybe we should just forget that for now and focus on things we're all a bit more familiar with."

Patsy's bewildered expression made it clear these surroundings were anything but familiar to her.

Jai headed toward the static escalators. "Shouldn't we be heading down to the basement if time's an issue?"

"Yes," replied Glenda. She looked at Patsy. "Come on, we can't waste time spacing out on the art."

"But they're not in the basement. I can tell. They're with the Book of Wisdom."

"And you know this because?"

"I've written in the Book of Wisdom, I'm attached to it." Patsy continued staring into space. "And I've written so much more in it now than I had in my time… I feel like I'm part of it, like I can see everything around it."

Glenda's expression changed. She could tell that Patsy was telling the truth.

"There's two women. They've opened the book. One is older with straight silver hair that's down to her shoulders. The other one is younger. She has long, wavy, red hair and freckles."

Glenda gasped. "Melanie!"

"The older woman can't make out the words in the book, but the younger one can. She's reading it out to her… she's reading the Book of Wisdom to a Nasqa!" Patsy looked around at Glenda and Jai. "We have to stop her."

"Well, that is kinda why we're here," replied Glenda.

"Do you know where they are?" asked Jai.

"I don't need to. Take my hands. I can take us to where the book is."

*

Melanie gasped and stepped back, her hand grabbing at her chest when the Book of Wisdom slammed shut.

"What was that?" asked Kellie.

She turned when a voice from behind her spoke out. "It was me."

Kellie and Mel glared at Patsy. She looked somehow more powerful as she stood in her torn jeans and t-shirt than Kellie had expected. Her steely gaze spoke of a confidence beyond her years. Hands on hips, she was flanked by Glenda and Jai. Kellie took a step toward the trio, ensuring that she placed herself between them and Mel. "Well, well, well. I'd been told you three might by dropping by." She tapped a finger against her chin while she looked Patsy up and down. "I'm not sure if I prefer your quaint nineteenth-century attire or your new look. They're both rather dull, I must say."

"What are you talking about?" Patsy's expression betrayed a hairline crack in her confidence. She tried to cover for it by sneering as she followed up. "I don't know you."

"Ah, yes, but I know you." Kellie was grinning as she waved a finger in the air for emphasis. "You were always quite a thorn in my side. Back in the day, when I inhabited Governor Pritchard's body, you caused all manner of problems for me and my men as we tried to maintain order. Every time I hatched a plan to get my hands on the book, there was Patricia McIntyre, always getting in the way."

"And now I'm here to get it back."

Kellie put her hands up in mock fear. "Oh no, the cranky little witch has come to take her book away."

"You can keep the damn book." Glenda stepped forward and continued. "I'm just here to take my daughter back."

"No!" Patsy snapped.

"My, we are a united team, aren't we? The aging, wounded hippie who relies on misusing magic to make a living, her hapless adolescent son, and a cranky little girl who's nowhere near the height of her powers." She turned back to Glenda. "Oh, and please, do try not to bleed too much on the carpet. It's awfully difficult to get out, you know."

Mel looked at Glenda. "Why are you doing this? Why would I want to go with you?"

"I'm your mother."

"Then why didn't you act like one? This is where I belong"—she stepped up to Kellie and took her hand—"with my real mother."

A tear rolled down Glenda's cheek. "But I..." Her jaw hung open, but she couldn't find any words.

Kellie grinned. "See? You really are wasting your time." She put an arm around Mel. "How about you three toddle off now and stop upsetting my daughter?" She blew Glenda a kiss. "Nice of you to drop by."

Glenda's expression went blank as she lowered her hand and started drawing energy from the Crossworlds. She whispered, "I'm not leaving without my daughter." Her breaths were growing short and sharp.

Kellie snickered then turned her attention to Jai as he stepped forward to address his sister. "Mel, do you remember me?"

Mel choked back a tear as she looked at him. "Yes, of course I do." She pulled away from Kellie and took a step toward him. A nervous giggle escaped as she said, "It's funny, you seemed so much bigger in my memories."

"Well, hey, you were only eight, so that's to be expected." He took a step closer. "I've risked my life travelling through time trying to find you, and well, I'm kinda sorry that it's taken me fifteen years to get here." He reached out to her. "Please, Mel, let's go home and make up for those years we lost." He glared at Kellie. "Years we lost because of what she's done to you."

"What's she's done to me?"

"Can't you see? She's turned you against us."

"How can you say that?" Mel turned to Kellie for reassurance then looked back to Jai. "She's been kinder than your mother ever was. I feel loved. I never knew how that felt before Mother rescued me."

"Then do it for us, for you and me."

"I can't, and I don't want to. Can't you see? I could never do that to her, not after what she's done for me."

"She's Nasqa, a mind thief. She takes over people's lives, and when one life wears out, she takes another."

"No, you're wrong to judge her like that. The Nasqa are doing everything they can to make the world a place that's safe for humanity. The human race is forever staging wars, trying to tear one another down. That doesn't help us, and it doesn't help the Nasqa. They benefit from humanity being stable and happy as much as we do."

Patsy sneered. "The Nasqa just want to enslave people, nothing more, nothing less."

Mel shook her head. "No, they're not like that." She looked at Kellie. "Mother is the kindest person I know."

That was enough for Glenda. "In that case, I need to get you out to meet a few more people." She lurched forward and hurled a ball of energy at Kellie, only to find herself flying backwards.

Kellie laughed. "You really should be more careful, what with that nasty wound and all."

Patsy also threw her hand forward, only to find that she too was flung backwards as the energy rebounded off Kellie and went straight back to her.

Kellie walked up to Patsy and stood over her stunned face. "Melanie and I found a wonderful little spell to protect us from magic that comes from anyone in her own bloodline. Let's see now…" She smiled before continuing. "That would equal all of you." She leaned over so her face was near Patsy's. "Oh, and that little trick you learned from your friend Kerridwen… the one about reaching in to grab me out of this body? You'll be in a whole world of pain if you try that one."

The sound of approaching sirens caused Kellie to look over her shoulder to the window. "That'll be the police on their way to lock you up for breaking into the gallery." She turned to Mel. "Your brother's still standing there like a stunned mullet. Perhaps you should do something about that, before he gets any heroic ideas?"

Mel shook her head. "But… I can't, Mother. He's my brother."

"Melanie, you know I wouldn't ask you to do this if it wasn't absolutely necessary. You need to show him your power, or he's liable to do something stupid."

"What, like this?" Jai charged at Kellie and lunged. Seeing Kellie threatened forced Mel to act. She extended her hand toward Jai. He became airborne, hitting his head hard as he landed. The impact left him unconscious.

Mel ran up and crouched next to his slumped form. "Oh, why did you have to go and threaten Mother like that?"

Kellie looked at Patsy and Glenda. "Either of you two want to have another try?" She approached Patsy, who was still winded from the impact of her attempt at bringing down her tormentor. "What's the matter, Witch? Cat got your tongue?"

Patsy wasn't paying attention. She was focused on Mel. With Jai unconscious, the Trinity was broken. But a new one existed. With three generations of women from the same bloodline present, the Trinity was like a magnetic force drawing the three together. Patsy opened her mind to Mel's, revealing all she knew about the Nasqa. *Reach out to your mother, learn the truth.* Mel turned to Glenda.

Kellie gave Patsy a short kick in the stomach. “Hey, I’m talking to you.”

Patsy spluttered up some blood, then smiled. “You’re making a big mistake.”

Two police officers accompanied by the representative of the gallery’s security firm entered the director’s office. “What seems to be the problem here?”

Patsy gestured toward the three of them and locked them in a time freeze.

“Really?” Kellie looked at the frozen officers then turned her attention back to Patsy, bringing her foot back in preparation for another kick. “You are just so annoying.”

“I wouldn’t do that if I were you.” Glenda had got to her feet and was reaching into the Crossworlds to draw power for another strike at Kellie.

“You don’t learn, do you?” Kellie looked at Mel. “Could you please do something about that birth mother of yours?” Mel drew her arm back to draw power herself. Glenda swung her arm, this time letting a cord of energy come forth from her hand, almost like she was swinging a rope. It pulled a nearby marble bust from its plinth, sending it hurtling toward Kellie, not caring that Patsy was also in its path. Mel threw her arm forward in response. The bust shattered, its pieces flying back toward Glenda. A large piece struck her on the head, causing her to fall to the ground, blood gushing from a fresh wound above her right eye.

Kellie turned her attention back to Patsy. “Try holding a time freeze after this.” She put as much energy as she could into swinging her foot.

“No, Mother, wait!”

Kellie’s foot stopped just short of making contact with Patsy again. She turned to Mel.

"We should let the police deal with them."

"Why?"

"Because we're better than them. You're better than them."

"If we want the police to help, we need to knock her out of action to break the time freeze."

Mel thought of all the images Patsy and Glenda had filled her head with. Nasqa being ripped from bodies by pixies, by Kerridwen, and by Patsy. Nasqa torn apart and hurled into the void. Nasqa treated like vermin. She joined her mother standing over her. "Please Mother, let me look after this." She drew her arm up then slammed a ball of energy into Patsy's head.

*

Patsy's head hurt. She had no idea where she was. To make it worse, the constant, high-pitched 'bing' that she heard every few seconds was annoying beyond belief. She tried opening her eyes, but the bright light made the pain in her head worse. When she closed her eyes again, it felt like the room was spinning, making her want to vomit.

Bing!... Bing!... Bing!

Then she felt the thing in her arm. She grabbed hold of it, then a hand grabbed hold of hers. "Whoa, whoa, whoa. Slow down, Pats."

She forced herself to open her eyes at the sound of Jai's voice. "Where am I?"

"Royal Prince Alfred Hospital. You've been out for most of the day."

"What's this thing in my arm?"

"It's called an IV drip." Jai pointed to the plastic bag hovering above Patsy's head. "It's like a kind of food that gets fed straight into your blood."

"Then, why am I so hungry?"

Jai laughed. "Don't worry, now that you're awake, you'll be able to eat something soon." He looked over his shoulder to the door. "Right after the police have finished questioning you."

"Urgh! Let's just get out of here. We've still got to get your sister back."

Jai went silent.

Bing!... Bing!... Bing!

"What is that noise?"

"It's monitoring your pulse."

"Why?"

"Patsy, you almost died. My sister, she hit you hard. The doctors say you've got a really bad concussion."

The memory of the look in Mel's eyes as she threw her arm toward Patsy swamped through her head, causing it to spin once more. Seeing Patsy's eyes roll up into her head, Jai grabbed hold of her, wrapping his arms around her shoulders. "Hey, it's going to be okay." Again, he looked over his shoulder, then back to Patsy. "You've got no choice. When the police come in, you'll have to answer their questions. Mum's told them you're my cousin, Jess. That your Mum's name is Paula, and you came down with me to watch Mum's band."

Before Patsy had a chance to reply, the door opened and two police officers walked through, a man who was taller than anyone Patsy had ever met and a woman whose face lit up as she approached the bed. "Hey you, welcome back to the land of the living."

The tall officer looked at Jai "Shouldn't you be checking on your Mum?"

Jai nodded and started towards the door. "I'll see you soon, Jess."

•

"So, what else did they ask you?" Glenda cast a glance at Patsy via the rearview mirror as they sped along the freeway on their way back to the Blue Mountains.

"I don't remember."

"What do you mean, 'you don't remember'?"

"Go easy on her Mum, she's got a concussion."

Glenda looked across at her son in the passenger seat. "Yeah, and I've got a dozen stitches in my head. Despite everything, I still stuck my neck out for her and lied to the cops on her behalf, so I figure the least she could do is give a few honest answers."

"Really, I can't remember," Patsy protested.

"Yeah, you said that before. Perhaps you can try harder."

"They kept asking me questions that I didn't know how to answer."

Glenda looked at the road ahead and nodded before responding. "Well, there you go. The girl who had all the answers when she arrived, declaring she was going to save us all, is suddenly lost for words."

Silence.

"Did you tell them about how you broke up my band?"

More silence.

"Or, how you destroyed any chance of me getting my daughter back?"

"Mum, don't you think you've made your point already?"

"No, I don't. How do you sum up fifteen years of planning to get your baby back being flushed down the toilet by a teenager's arrogance in twenty questions? Do you have an answer for that? I've got no choice but to ferry her back to my home just to be rid of her. So, please excuse me for wanting to get a few answers on the way."

Patsy whispered, "I'm sorry."

Silence.

*

Patsy and Jai walked down the steps toward the pool. "I'll come back soon and we'll try again."

"No, Patsy, it's not worth it. Mum's never going to trust you, ever."

"I know that. But you still trust me, don't you? And Nan, she still talks to me."

Jai let out a sigh. "You saved my life and risked your own doing it. I'll always be grateful for that. But that was in a different world, one where we were both out of place. This is my world, and somehow, your moral judgements don't work as well here as they did when we were facing blow darts and wrathapillars."

"I'm sorry."

"Yeah, so am I."

Patsy felt a hammer banging in her head that reminded her of the noise from the machine in the hospital.

As she approached the water's edge, she found herself focusing on the need to get back home so she could release the people she loved most in the world from the void. She longed for her family, for Cook's food, and Clara's conversation. She longed for the reassurance of her father's moral authority and strength.

She wanted to go home and lick her wounds.

Jai grabbed her shoulder. "Hey, snap out of it, Pats. You can't wander into the pool without saying goodbye. This is the last time we'll ever see each other."

"It doesn't have to be."

"Umm, you might want to talk to my mum about that. Actually, on second thoughts, that's probably not a good idea."

The water in the pool was stirring, beckoning Patsy to return to where she belonged.

She started walking into the water. What would her family make of her new clothing? How would she face telling them about her failure? Most important of all, would Glenda and Jai be able to strike up a new plan to get Mel back?

"It's not your fault." It was as though Jai was reading her mind. "You risked your life to try. And hey, that Nasqa had done a real job on Mel. I don't know that any plan would've worked."

A hint of a smile appeared on Patsy's otherwise dour expression.

"Hey!" Jai followed her into the water. He handed Patsy his phone. "Take this, that way I can message you and let you know when we succeed in getting Mel back. As long as the phone is near the portal, it should work."

"But don't you need it?"

"I need a new one anyway… Take this one, and we can keep in touch."

"Won't that upset your mother?"

"She doesn't have to know."

"Goodbye and thank you… thank you for everything." Patsy turned away and walked into the vortex.

"See you, Pats. Take care of yourself."

•

"It's about time." Neridah's frustration was obvious as she berated her granddaughter.

"Aye, it feels as though we've been trapped in here for an eternity." The Reverend's gaze carried an unspoken accusation.

Meredith's tone was softer. "I'm just glad you made it back safely."

The water swirled around Patsy as she approached the shore,

clutching Jai's phone to her chest. "I'm sorry, I didn't feel like I had a choice." She looked up, preparing to continue, but the three images grew more distant and were breaking apart. Patsy's heart raced as she reached out to try and grab hold of them. "I'm going to get you out of there… I promise!" *Surely they'll be okay. It's only because I'm coming out of the portal that they've disappeared… surely.*

The wind was howling as she emerged from the pool. The trees had all been stripped of their leaves and a gritty dust made it difficult to see far ahead. She reached the shore, then turned around and saw the wind had swept all the water from the pool outside of the vortex itself. Trees had fallen across the sandstone steps that led up to the paddock. She held one arm up to shield her eyes from the dust as she fought against the wind and struggled to get up the stairs. Her mother, Nana-Neri, and the Reverend would just have to wait a bit longer. To try and rescue them in this storm would be unthinkable.

As she worked her way through the paddock toward the house, the dust-filled wind tore at Patsy's flesh and clothing. She put the phone in her back pocket and tucked her t-shirt into her jeans to try and keep it from blowing up like a loose-fitting dress on a windy day.

On nearing the house, she saw that nothing remained of the stables other than their framework. The front door and most of the window shutters had been stripped from the house. She watched in horror as parts of the veranda were torn away, disintegrating into dust as they hurtled through the air.

Falling in through the front door brought some respite from the gale. She yelled as loud as she could to try to be heard above the wind's deafening howl. "Father!" There was no answer. "Cook! Father! Is there anyone here?" She thought for a moment that she could hear someone crying in one of the rooms. She made her way along the corridor, then opened the imposing door to the library. Inside, she found Clara Jenkins huddled in the corner holding Ferdinand.

She ran across to her tutor. "Miss Jenkins, what's going on? Where's Father?"

Clara struggled to get the words out through her tears. "Your father… I'm so sorry… he's… he was taken away by Captain Taylor. He… he's dead."

The words didn't register, didn't seem real. "What about Cook, where's Cook?"

Clara sat shaking her head. She looked down at the cat she was rocking back and forth.

"Where's Cook?"

"I watched it happen."

"Watched what happen?"

"The storm. It took Cook. It took everyone."

"Miss Jenkins, you're not making sense."

"I saw it with my own eyes."

"What did you see?"

"The dust… this storm… it's not of this world."

Clara released the cat, then threw her arms around Patsy, crying into her shoulder. Patsy returned the hug and watched as Ferdinand ran out the door, disintegrating into dust and drifting away on the wind as he went. Patsy struggled to comprehend what she'd just seen. "Did Cook do that? Turn into dust… then blow away in the wind?"

There was no answer. Patsy hugged her tutor tighter, feeling a desperate need for her familiar warmth and reassurance. Instead, Clara disintegrated in Patsy's arms. Clothing, flesh, hair, all turned to dust and blew away.

Patsy looked around at what was left in the room. The Book of

Wisdom was on its stand. Her only hope would lie within its pages, of that, she was sure. But she'd have to take it somewhere safe. She tried a time-freeze, but it was ineffective.

Krinkle-myst's cabin! Being outside the known universe, that was bound to be safe. She grabbed the book and allowed herself to be at the bottom of the paddock near the portal that led to the land that no one's ever seen.

CHAPTER 7

Patsy plummeted then slammed into the ground near the bottom of the paddock. She found herself a few paces away from the wood-elf. Krinkle-myst watched Patsy struggle to lift herself from the ground. It appeared the wind had little effect on him.

The Book of Wisdom landed with a thud between them. Patsy called out to the wood-elf, but her words disappeared into the wind.

She rose to her knees, then looked into the wood-elf's eyes, his stature being such that, even on her knees, she was still almost twice his height. "I need to get them back."

The wood-elf gestured toward the book. "You won't find the answer in there."

"That can't be. It must be in there somewhere. I need to take the book to your cabin so I can find the answer."

"The land that no one's ever seen won't let you in, not until you repair the damage you and your friend have done to the fabric holding the timelines together."

"But how can I do that without the book to guide me? I can't even form a Trinity of Power. Everyone's gone."

"And there won't ever be another Trinity unless you can repair the damage. Thanks to your reckless actions, history is now being wiped away from countless millions of timelines. If you don't act soon, all timelines within this range of crossworlds will be gone, and all that will be left of it is you. You and an empty universe."

Dust combined with Patsy's tears to create brown streaks on her cheeks. "I can't do anything right."

"Feeling sorry for yourself won't help anyone."

"I just make everything worse."

"Well, it's about time you look at turning that trend around."

"I don't know how."

"You'd better come up with something... and sooner rather than later."

She looked around. There was no sign of the house now at the top of the hill, and all the trees were gone. She had no way of knowing where she was. "How can I undo any of this? I don't even know where to start."

"You can start by going back to Jai's timeline, to the moment before the foolish boy decided to play the hero, and you can stop him."

"That's easy for you to say. I don't even know how to find my way to the right timeline."

"Do I really have to spell everything out for you?"

Patsy started sobbing. "I'll just make things worse if I try to fix it."

Krinkle-myst looked around, then turned back to Patsy. "I have to say, making things worse than they already are would be quite a feat."

Patsy nodded, wiping her eyes dry. "Okay, I'll try. But please, you must have some idea of how I can get there."

"You've carved out a deep trail. It's like when you walk through long grass. The more you walk a certain path, the more pronounced it becomes." He pointed to her back pocket. "And his phone will help guide you. It feels compelled to return to its own time. You can force it with your will to guide you so that you arrive a few minutes earlier than when he left to come here."

"Then what?"

"Stop him."

"How?"

"You'll work it out."

"And after that?"

"Then, the timelines will be restored to what they were, and no one but you will remember what happened."

"What about you?"

"I think I'd rather forget. But my burden is that I always end up remembering these things." Krinkle-myst removed his glasses and rubbed at his right eye. "Now, I'm going back to the land that no one's ever seen so Mrs Krinkle-myst can help me get a speck of dust out of my eye."

"Wait! Before you go… how am I going to find the portal when everything's already turned to dust?"

"You're really not very good at listening, are you?"

"But—" Patsy found herself talking to the wind. The wood-elf was gone.

Now, with the timelines progressively turning to dust, she felt more alone than ever before.

You're really not good at listening…

Listening to what?

Patsy tried to shut out the sound of the wind and reflected on what Krinkle-myst might have been talking about. What had he discussed with her recently? What was new to her in what he'd been saying? She thought back to when she and Jai had been to see him and he'd tried to explain about the timelines, about future and past memories. What she needed was somewhere in what he'd had to say about the timelines.

Sometimes, just being sad enough about an event in your past will actually shift you into a version of reality where whatever it was that happened was worse than it really was.

The parallel timelines. The way he'd spoken about them suggested they were almost countless in number. And, if it was possible to slip between them, maybe Patsy could communicate with versions of herself in different timelines. Maybe she could find one where the portal hadn't yet turned to dust. Maybe that other version of herself could guide her to the portal… despite everything of substance in this one having turned to dust. She thought of what she'd learned from the Seer when going inside Jai, how she'd gone deep within herself to help him. She'd felt the connection then, the connection to versions of herself in other timelines.

The tears stopped and Patsy's sadness was flushed away by grim determination.

She could do this.

She had to.

•

Patsy closed her eyes and allowed herself to accept the sound of the wind for what it was.

She allowed herself to accept the pain of her loss.

She allowed herself to accept the guilt.

Most of all, she allowed herself to be at peace with herself as she sought guidance to the portal. Millions of Patsy McIntyres were experiencing the destruction of their universe, but only one had any understanding as to why it was happening. And those Patsy McIntyres who were lost in confusion about what was happening were drawn to this one who knew. They were drawn to her pleading for guidance. Most important of all, there were those who lived in worlds where the portal hadn't yet been wiped away, not many, but enough.

With her eyes closed, she started walking. She could feel a picture around her coming into focus of how the property was before the dust, how it still existed in some worlds.

She walked further, becoming more confident with each step.

Then, as she neared the pathway leading down to the pool that housed the portal, the image started to fade. The pathway leading to the pool was vanishing from the parallel universes at an increasing pace. But she was getting close now, close enough that she could feel the power of the portal. She held Jai's phone and felt it pulling her toward the portal.

She had to be careful with the placement of her feet. There were no carved steps anymore, just a steep slope of dust.

The vision that had guided her was completely gone by the time the sloping dust had levelled out, indicating to her she had reached the location of the portal. She kept her eyes closed as she walked into the centre of where the pool would have been and became conscious of a shift in how the dust was moving. It was swirling around her.

She knew she was successful when she opened her eyes and saw water instead of dust. She'd arrived in Jai's timeline.

*

Glenda embraced her son. “Don’t forget to call me when you get there. As long as you’re near the portal, the phone should work.”

“Don’t worry, Mum.” Jai pulled away from her and walked toward the pool.

“And remember, you’ll need to call me when you’re ready to come back so I can open the portal.”

“Yeah, I got that the first ten thousand times you told me.” He looked back over his shoulder. “Are you going to open it up or what?”

Glenda’s expression went blank. She stared past her son toward the pool. “It looks like I don’t need to.”

Jai turned back toward the pool to see the water in the middle was swirling. The centre shallowed to reveal an adolescent girl in torn jeans and a tattered Stevie Nicks t-shirt. Her long hair was matted and she was covered in dirt and scratches. Her face reminded him of photos he’d seen of his grandmother as a young girl. Could it be?

Glenda and Jai approached the edge of the pool as Patsy made her way toward the shore. Glenda’s voice trembled as she asked, “Who are you, and what do you want?”

A tear welled up in Patsy’s eye as she looked at Glenda and saw Nana-Neri in every feature… Nana-Neri who’d turned to dust while trapped in the void. Could she stop that happening?

“Hello, I’m waiting. Who are you and what do you want?”

She even sounds like Nana-Neri. Patsy looked at Jai and thought of how much younger he looked now than the boy she’d shared so much with as they’d laid the groundwork for the destruction of everything. *All that we went through… and for what?* She took a deep breath to compose herself. “I’m Patricia, Patricia McIntyre. I’ve come to stop you from making a big mistake, the biggest mistake anyone could ever make.”

"I didn't know they wore jeans and t-shirts in the nineteenth century."

Patsy looked at Glenda. "Your mother bought me these fifteen years from now."

"I don't believe you." Glenda positioned herself to be standing between Patsy and her son. "Your timing seems like a coincidence too extreme to be possible. Tell me the truth. Who are you, and how could you know what we have planned?"

As Patsy continued moving toward them, Glenda and Jai were stepping back. Glenda was lowering her hand to draw power from the Crossworlds. Patsy pleaded with her. "What you're about to do, it's a terrible mistake."

"Stop right there."

"The consequences…" Patsy looked to the ground, choking back tears. "Everything will be lost."

"It can't be as bad as the consequences of not going," said Jai. "I need to find my sister."

Glenda turned to her son. "What did I tell you about not telling anyone about this?"

"I swear, Mum, I never breathed a word to anyone before now." Jai gestured toward Patsy. "What if she really is who she says she is?"

"More likely the Nasqa have found out what we're doing." She addressed Patsy. "You might as well leave her body now. We're not fooled." She turned back to Jai. "I'm going to open the portal, are you ready?"

"You can't! You can't do it! I can't let you!" Patsy collapsed on the shore as the water settled behind her. She was still clutching the phone. She buried her face in the sand for a while, sobbing, before lifting her head and looking at Jai through the haze of her tears. "If you go, then everyone dies."

Glenda glared at Jai then turned back to Patsy and said, "You don't look capable of stopping anything to me. And you still haven't answered my question. Who are you really?"

Jai ignored his mother and asked, "How do you know what I'm planning to do?"

"Because we already did it. You came back to my time." Patsy reflected on all that had happened, sifting through the events, searching for the right ones to mention, the ones most likely to be believed. "We found your sister, and the Book of Wisdom. The Nasqa were keeping her hidden at the Art Gallery, fifteen years from now. We went in there to try and get her back."

"And?" asked Glenda.

"The consequences…"

"Urgh… you'll have to do better than that."

"I can prove it." Patsy held up the phone.

Glenda held her hand up behind her shoulder, ready to strike. "I'm running out of patience."

Patsy struggled to her feet, holding the phone as high as she could. "When Jai came through the portal, he used this as proof of who he was." She extended her arm toward Glenda, offering her the phone.

"Drop it now, or so help me… I'll blast you right back into that pool you came out of."

"Give it a rest, Mum." Jai stepped forward and reached out to take the phone.

"You gave it to me just before I left, so we could stay in touch."

Jai took the phone and unlocked it. He looked at the log of call records. Then he checked the photos. "I think you'd better look at this, Mum."

CHAPTER 8

Patsy blinked and found herself at the top of the stairs leading down to the pool. She heard a little giggle followed by Clara's voice. "It wouldn't be a surprise if I tell you."

Patsy looked over her shoulder to see Clara carrying a picnic basket. "Is it a book? A book about biology?"

Clara stopped in her tracks. "I must say, you never cease to amaze me." She pulled the book out from the basket and handed it to Patsy. "It's by a scientist called Charles Darwin. It's called *On the Origin of Species.*"

Patsy smiled as she took the book.

She was back.

By preventing Jai from making his journey, she'd been snapped back to the moment before he arrived. She was in a dress, and she felt clean. Yet the memories of what had happened raced around her head.

"Are you okay?" asked Clara.

"Yes, I'm fine, thank you. I'm just so overwhelmed that somehow you must have guessed I've been secretly longing to learn more about biology."

Clara smiled. "I can't begin to tell you what a relief it is to hear you say that. I know how much you love physics, but I really wanted to help you expand your horizons."

Patsy threw her arms around Clara. "Thank you. You're the best tutor a girl could ever hope for."

*

Patsy watched from behind a bush at the bottom of the paddock as Gladys Taylor's sulky arrived. Her father, mother, and tutor waited on the front veranda steps to greet her.

There was something that wasn't right. She shouldn't have accepted her parents' suggestion that she make herself scarce during the woman's visit. She had to go back up there, in case something went wrong. She liked Miss Jenkins too much to see her forced to endure an inquisition from that crabby old monster without Patsy's support. She stood up to make her way up to the house. She was about to take her first step when she heard a voice from behind her. "We need to talk."

She turned and responded to the wood-elf. "Okay, but first, I need to make sure nothing goes wrong for my family."

"They'll be fine. We need to talk, now!" In that instant, they were both transported to Krinkle-myst's cabin

"I did what you asked. I went back and stopped Jai."

"Yes, you did. And, I must say, you did it well. You demonstrated that you do actually listen, after all." He took a seat by the fire and gestured for Patsy to do the same.

"So, why is it so urgent that we talk now?"

"A change you triggered in another timeline will now have to be followed through. You've repaired the damage done before, to this world, and countless others. But that repair is fragile, to say the least."

"But why is it so urgent to tell me this now?"

"Because the events playing out now at your home must take place. In order for this timeline to line up with another. Otherwise, the fabric of reality will start to unravel again, but starting from a different time and place where it would be impossible to repair the damage." He took a sip from a goblet of warm mead that appeared in his hand while he talked. "You need to understand that reality, all of it, is an illusion. That's why it's so fragile, and why it's so malleable to those who understand the science behind it."

"Why are you telling me this now?"

"Because the prophecies of another world have said that the Enchantress shall return. The history of that future is already in place. If it is not fulfilled, reality, as you understand it, will cease to exist. And there are dark forces that work tirelessly to make that come to pass. The Enchantress must return."

Patsy's shoulders slumped. The burden of being a Crossworld Witch weighed heavily on her. *I haven't even taken the same oath as Mother or Nana-Neri. It's not fair.*

"Of course it's fair!"

"Don't you think it's rude to read people's minds?"

"Not when they scream their thoughts out so loud."

"All I want right now is to spend time with Miss Jenkins and my family. I want to be like a normal girl for a while."

"A normal girl, huh? A totally normal girl with an insatiable appetite for knowledge about physics and biology rather than needlework and flower arranging?"

"I've seen the future. It will be normal, and only having an interest in needlework would be awful. I can't imagine what could be worse."

Krinkle-myst nodded and smiled. He liked the young woman Patsy was growing into. "Don't worry, you'll have plenty of time to spend with your family and tutor before the Enchantress must return. In the meantime, the best way to prepare yourself will be to enjoy life."

"So, when the time comes, how will I find my way back there?"

"The way back will find you."

Patsy looked around. The cabin and the wood-elf were gone. She was back at the bottom of the paddock. She looked up to the house just in time to see Gladys Taylor's sulky disappearing from view.

•

Colin grabbed his flintlock and walked out to the veranda when he heard the sound of the approaching horses. His heart sank at the sight of Captain Taylor and six other soldiers, no doubt all controlled by Nasqa. "Captain Taylor, I can't say that it's a pleasure to see you."

"Nor I, you murdering bastard."

"I beg your pardon."

Captain Taylor glanced across at the rider next to him. "Arrest this man and clap him in irons." He turned back to Colin. "This time I promise, you will hang."

Neridah and Meredith raced onto the veranda as one soldier took Colin's flintlock and the other attached irons to his wrists and ankles. Meredith glared at Captain Taylor. "What's happening?"

Captain Taylor ordered his soldiers, "You can arrest these two as well, as accessories."

Patsy appeared at the door, accompanied by Clara. "Let them go!"

"Corporal, if that girl so much as raises a finger, I want you to shoot her father." The corporal raised a pistol, held it up next to Colin's temple, and pulled back the safety.

Patsy glared at the Captain, watching his shadow as it seemingly mocked her. She cast her gaze across all the gathered soldiers. "Nasqa, all of you."

Meredith looked at Clara's puzzled expression, then turned to Patsy. "Patricia! Discretion, remember?"

Clara looked between the two, unable to comprehend what Meredith was talking about.

Neridah whispered to Meredith, "I think the time for secrets has passed. It's time to act."

Meredith nodded and reached out to take hold of Colin's hand. "We'll ride to Sydney and appeal to the Governor."

Captain Taylor laughed. "Please, by all means. I'm sure that would make the Governor's day." He turned to his troops, encouraging them to join him in laughing off the suggestion. The corporal joined in the laughter, lowering his pistol for a moment.

They had to take advantage of this opportunity, or they may not get another. Neridah reached back to take Patsy's hand and gave her a knowing nod while reaching out to take Meredith's at the same time. Patsy raised her free hand and took hold of Clara's.

One of the soldiers asked, "What are they doing?"

Captain Taylor's eyes filled with rage when he realised what was happening.

"Now!" said Neridah.

The corporal raised his pistol's muzzle back to Colin's head and pulled the trigger.

The bullet ricocheted off the hardwood post of the veranda. Colin, the witches, and Clara had vanished.

*

Clara collapsed into a high back leather chair in the library. "What just happened?"

Neridah replied, "We'll explain later." She turned to Patsy. "Drawing the Nasqa out of them, how do you do it?"

Patsy shrugged her shoulders. "It's like allowing yourself to be somewhere, you just let it happen. It's only hard if you try. It's throwing them into the void that's harder."

"We won't have time for that part. We'll need to hope the soldiers are strong enough to block them getting back in." Neridah looked at Meredith. "It's our only chance. We need to split up and keep moving so they're confused. We can pick them off, one by one."

They could hear boots on the floorboards just inside the front door. A soldier's voice called out. "Show yourselves, I know you're in here somewhere."

Colin grabbed a pistol from the drawer of his desk. He looked at his wife and daughter. Sending them into harm's way went against every ideal he held dear, but he knew there was no other choice. "Go, I'll see to it that Miss Jenkins is kept safe."

Clara gasped and held a hand to her breast when the witches vanished. "Surely, this is some mad dream."

Colin stood in front of her, his arm raised, pointing the pistol at the closed library door. "I wish, for all our sakes, that could be the case."

*

The Nasqa inhabiting Captain Taylor could sense Patsy's jump as she moved from the library to be standing in the front doorway. He pulled out his pistol as he turned to face her, but she was already gone. Her presence was close, he could feel it. Then came the tap at his shoulder. As he turned to face her, Patsy reached into his chest and pulled out the Nasqa. Holding the shadowy phantom aloft, she said, "I could so easily open the void and send you there, but I'll show you mercy if you promise to leave this world and never return."

You speak of mercy? Patricia McIntyre dares to speak of mercy? You don't know the meaning of the word.

Resisting the temptation to open the void, Patsy flung the Nasqa aside. "I don't have time for this." She looked down at the Captain, who'd collapsed to the floor "Don't let it back in. It can't take you over again if you actively refuse. I need you to stand guard at the door and make sure none of the others enter the house. Do you understand?"

Captain Taylor was still looking to the floor as he nodded in agreement. By the time he looked up, Patsy was gone.

*

The Nasqa slipped through the door to the library as it sought a new host. There was no point trying Colin, as delicious as that irony would be. His steadfast determination in this moment made his mind an impenetrable fortress. But the young woman? She was anxious and filled with uncertainty and fear. Her mind was like an open door.

Clara was mopping tears from her eyes with an embroidered handkerchief as she struggled to take in breaths between her sobs. *How can this be happening? What the hell is going on? How can any of this be real?*

A voice in the back of her mind reached out with soothing words. *Relax a little, and all will be clear.* From Clara's perspective, it was a welcome suggestion.

•

Jimmy and Darcy O'Sullivan were tending the horses in the stables when the thundering of hoofs heralded the arrival of Captain Taylor and his troops. Jimmy put a hand to his chest, feeling the scar he still bore from the last time Captain Taylor's troops had visited the McIntyre property. They walked out into the paddock and watched as the discussion between Colin and the Captain unfolded with the witches and Clara in the background. Darcy asked, "Should we go up there and see if they need a hand?"

Before Jimmy had a chance to answer, the McIntyre ensemble had vanished. The Captain raced inside while the other soldiers scattered. "By all the saints in heaven, what just happened?"

"They ran inside. Didn't you see?"

Jimmy shook his head. "No one moves that fast." He started walking toward the house but was distracted by the sound of a sulky entering the property. A soldier was driving it and Vincent Donaldson was onboard, battered and in chains. Jimmy turned to Darcy. Father and son exchanged a knowing look then started running to Vincent's aid. The soldier turned the sulky and charged at Jimmy while reaching back to grab a rifle. Darcy, adrenalin pumping, moved quickly. He grabbed the soldier around the shoulders and dragged him from the driver's seat, taking his rifle as the soldier fell to the ground. Jimmy managed to clamber on board and brought the sulky to a stop, then looked up to see an approaching soldier raise his rifle.

"Put your hands up behind your head and dismount, now."

Neridah appeared behind the soldier and tapped him on the shoulder. He turned. Horror filled his eyes as Neridah reached into his chest and pulled out the shadowy Nasqa. It thrashed about in her hands, desperate to break free. Four of the remaining soldiers were running toward the sulky. The fifth had collapsed after Meredith had torn out his tormentor.

Neridah lifted the soldier's chin. "Be strong, don't give it a chance to find its way back in."

Jimmy watched on as Patsy appeared in front of the charging soldiers, causing them to hesitate. She reached into one soldier's chest with her left hand and into another's with her right. At the same time, the other two found themselves face to face with Neridah and Meredith.

A woman's voice called out from the top of the hill. "Stop!" The three witches looked up and saw Clara and Colin standing on the veranda. Clara holding Colin's revolver to his head. "If any one of you so much as moves, or vanishes, so help me, I will shoot."

Patsy stared at Clara, fully aware it was the Nasqa she'd just before shown mercy to who was talking through her tutor. She looked at the revolver and focused, visualising it in the emptiness of the void. She closed her eyes. The image was clear. She reopened them and smiled. Clara was shocked when the weight of the weapon was gone from her hand. Colin turned to her and said, "I suggest you leave Miss Jenkins in peace." He looked at his daughter, who was walking up to the house wearing a heavy frown, then turned back to Clara. "I really don't think you want to be facing my daughter again."

Clara said, "This isn't over, I will be back." With that, the Nasqa drifted from Clara's body and disappeared into a neighbouring crossworld.

Clara fainted and fell, Colin catching her before she hit the deck of the veranda.

Jimmy watched in horror as it all unfolded, triggering memories of what had occurred the year before. Memories that he'd so far managed to suppress. He resolved in that moment that it was time for he and Darcy to look for work in Sydney.

CHAPTER 9

Destellie knocked at the door of the McIntyre homestead. She was looking out at the rising full moon when Meredith answered the door. "Hello, Destellie. Are you nervous about tomorrow?"

Destellie looked coy as she gave a little giggle. "I guess so. I can't quite believe that this time tomorrow I'll be a married woman."

Meredith took Destellie's hands in hers. "We're all so happy for you."

"Thank you. And thank you for agreeing to join me tonight. I can't imagine a better way to enjoy my final night as a single woman than dancing around a fire with my wonderful bridesmaids."

Patsy came running down the stairs calling out, "Come on, Nana-Neri. Desttie's already here." Patsy ran out the front door and threw her arms around Destellie. The bride-to-be swept her up and swung her around.

"How blessed am I to have such a wondrous greeting?"

Colin and the Reverend came out of the library as Neridah descended the stairs, pulling on her gloves. The Reverend looked at Neridah in her emerald-green velvet dress with black lace trim. "That's a good deal of trouble you've gone to for a dance by the fire."

Neridah grinned as she flicked a glove his way. "Oh, do be quiet. A dance by the fire's as good a reason as any to dress up."

As the three of them reached the door, Colin said, "Jimmy tells me that Darcy will be playing his harmonica for you."

Meredith said, "It's so sad that they'll be leaving after the wedding."

Colin nodded. "Yes, but can you blame him? He's doing what he believes is best for Darcy. That's what's guided his decisions for as long as I've known the man."

Cook's voice called from the end of the corridor. "Thank goodness I caught you before you'd left." She hurried along the corridor carrying a wicker basket with a tea towel draped over the top. "When I learned of your plans, I took it upon myself to prepare a pot of soup for you." She handed the basket to Destellie. "There's also bread and cheese in there." She looked Destellie up and down. "Can I get you a blanket? You'll likely catch a chill wearing that skimpy dress and shawl."

Destellie took the basket and gave Cook a warm smile. "Thank you so much, Cook. I'll be fine. Darcy told me he'd be spending the day collecting wood for the fire and I rarely feel the cold, but I do appreciate your concern." She turned to Patsy, Meredith and Neridah. "Shall we go?"

Meredith turned to Colin. "Can I trust you and Alfred to be sensible while we're gone?"

"We'll be fine, we have much to discuss."

The Reverend slapped a hand on Colin's shoulder. "Aye, like whether it's brandy or rum that better warms the soul while playing a meaningful game of checkers."

Patsy turned and looked toward the entrance to the property when she heard the sound of a horse pulling a sulky. "It's Mr Donaldson."

Meredith glanced at Cook. "I think it's time you take that apron off and enjoy your night off."

Cook blushed as she hurriedly removed the apron. "Is there anything else you'll be needing before I go?"

Colin reached across and grabbed the apron out of her hands. "Cook, you need to go now, and make sure you have a good time. I'll be most disappointed if we see you back here before Monday morning."

"Thank you, Mr McIntyre, sir. I'll do my best to enjoy myself, sir."

As Cook made her way down to meet Vincent, Neridah lit a hurricane lamp that sat on a small table by the front door. She held it up and asked, "Shall we make our way down, ladies?"

The moon had risen above the treeline as the witches and Destellie made their way down the paddock. The Reverend's eyes followed with Neridah as she held up the lamp to light the way. Colin said, "It's not too late, you know. No one will hold it against you if you recant your vows."

The Reverend's eyes remained locked on the only woman he'd ever loved. "It wouldn't be fair to her. Physically, I'm forty years her senior."

"Maybe you should let her be the judge of how fair it would be." Colin turned and made his way back into the house, unaware the man he'd just spoken to was in fact his father-in-law. The Reverend stared into the darkness, wondering about what might have been if events had played out differently in his youth.

•

Felibrey was glad for the full moon. It would be enough light for him to nail the last of the roof shingles in place so the cottage would be weatherproof in time for the first night he and Destellie would spend together as husband and wife. It took him by surprise when he climbed the ladder and found Mrs Smith waiting for him on the roof. "You don't deserve this."

Felibrey blushed. "I know, she's so amazing. I still struggle to believe that such a woman would want to commit to a life shared with one such as myself."

The old fairy smacked a hand against her forehead. "Urgh! That's not what I meant. You deserve better." She leaned forward to make a point of staring into his eyes. "You poor, lovesick fool. You've been around for how many thousands of years, and you still don't see what's going on?"

"I don't understand."

"You've been played for a fool. The frogs and crickets have been gossiping about it for weeks."

"What do mean?"

"I mean, your fiancé has been meeting with Kerridwen in secret. This marriage is just a ruse… a means of luring the witches into a trap, which is playing out right now."

"That can't be, the hunter is long gone."

"Oh no. I can assure you, she is fighting to find a way back. She promised Destellie a garland of power in exchange for leading the witches to her… tonight, while the moon is full."

Felibrey opened his mouth to respond, but no words came. He clung tight to the ladder as his world crumbled to dust around him.

•

Darcy sat on a rock by the fire playing an Irish ballad on his harmonica while watching Destellie and the witches descend the stairs. The flames danced as though in time to his music, a plethora of frogs providing a steady rhythm.

Destellie opened her arms and spun around on reaching the bottom of the stairs. “What a beautiful night to dance in the moonlight.”

Meredith pulled her shawl tight around her and approached the fire. “It’s a bit chilly for me to dance. I think I’ll settle for warming myself by the fire.”

Patsy skipped across the sand. “I’ll dance with you, Desttie. I so love to dance. Come on, Nana-Neri.”

Neridah slipped her shoes off at the bottom of the stairs. “I must admit the feeling of the sand underfoot is quite nice.”

Destellie danced in a sweeping arc, then reached out and took Neridah’s hand. “Yes, it’s so soothing.” She pulled Neridah along as Darcy stepped up the tempo. “It’s wonderful to feel so alive.”

Patsy looked across the fire at her grandmother and giggled, then did a pirouette as she passed Meredith. “Come on, Mother, dance with us.”

Darcy rose up to his feet and beckoned Meredith to join them as he took his place in the procession dancing around the flames. Their pace quickened, and Meredith began to feel intoxicated as they all twirled around her again and again. She wasn’t aware of when she’d thrown her shawl aside, but she was now dancing with them.

None of them had noticed the vortex beginning to form in the centre of the pool.

*

Felibrey ran to the stables, straight to the stall of a black stallion that had only recently been broken in. He grabbed the lead rope as he entered the stall, then jumped on the horse’s back, threaded the rope through the halter, and kicked his heels into the massive stallion's side, driving it into the night.

He leaned forward as the horse thundered down the road away from the small village that had grown around the church as the Reverend's disciples had built their homes. "We must fly like the wind, my dear friend."

After what felt like little more than a minute to Felibrey, they reached the bridge that crossed the creek upstream from the McIntyre property. Felibrey pulled hard on the left of the reins. The stallion responded by leaping off the bridge, hooves causing wild splashes as it began navigating its way down the creek.

Water and mud flew up into Felibrey's face and he had to duck so his head was against the horse's neck on many occasions to avoid low lying branches. In the thousands of years he'd been alive, he'd never before been consumed by such a sense of urgency. It didn't matter that Destellie had betrayed him. She was in danger. He had to reach her before she was lost to him forever.

*

Jimmy O'Sullivan walked across to the stables. He was anxious to ensure he had everything packed and ready so he and Darcy could make their way to Sydney after the celebrations had finished. He smiled at the distant sound of laughter from the pool at the bottom of the paddock. It was good that Darcy was enjoying himself on what would be their last night at the property. Then something struck him. The tunes Darcy were playing bore no resemblance to anything Jimmy had heard him play before.

Curious, he made his way down the paddock to take a closer look. On reaching the bottom he peered through the trees, trying to make out what was happening. He felt a tightness in his chest, reminding him of the gunshot wound he'd received a year earlier when Kerridwen had tried to take his son away from him. Blood pulsed in his temples. He raced down the pathway as quick as his legs would carry him.

*

Patsy had never enjoyed dancing so much. They were all holding hands now. She looked at Darcy and marvelled at how he could play the harmonica so well with no hands holding the instrument. How was that even possible? The chorus of the frogs, the screeching of the flying foxes, and the crackling of the fire filled the background as well as any orchestra could. The tempo built and they all threw themselves further into the dance. Meredith was laughing with delight. Neridah's eyes were closed as she lost herself in the celebration. The flames rose higher and spiralled their way into the night sky. The vortex in the pool threw up a waterspout that wound its way into the centre of the dancers, weaving between the flames in a perfect harmony of fire and water. The very air itself joined the circling dancers, creating a wind that moved with them, lifting them off the ground. Each of them rose up and down in a random pattern that mimicked the flickering of the flames. Their laughter grew louder as the pace increased.

The water and flames crept together, weaving through each other to form a shape… the shape of a woman… the shape of Kerridwen, the hunter.

The image of the hunter laughed.

A sound like thunder in the distance merged with the music of the night like a drum roll anticipating a musical crescendo. Kerridwen's sculptured image of pulsating fire and water called to the dancers,

"Come to me now. Come to me and become one with my garland of power."

The dancers picked up speed, moving so fast they became a blur as they drifted in toward the centre. The hunter's image laughed louder as she spread her arms, ready to embrace the dancers and pull them into her garland.

The thundering drum roll grew louder. Then it became clear. Kerridwen realised too late. The drum roll wasn't thunder but the sound of an approaching stallion. She turned to face it as Felibrey compelled the majestic horse to leap into the midst of the spiralling flames and water. The collision triggered a flash of lightning and a deafening crack of genuine thunder. The image of Kerridwen was split down the middle, as is a tree when struck by lightning. Felibrey leapt from his mount and grabbed hold of Destellie, pulling her to ground. The image of Kerridwen pulled itself back together, rage writ large upon her face.

Darcy and the witches continued their dance. But their momentum had slowed so they appeared more to be spinning about in a dazed frenzy.

Jimmy O'Sullivan burst onto the beach, reached up and grabbed hold of his son's leg and pulled him down to the ground. With the circle broken, the witches fell, only to be swept up again as the flames and water reshaped themselves. The ground shook. The flames flickered in and out of the semblance of Kerridwen with the witches spinning around like leaves caught in the wind. The stallion reared up, fearful of what was taking place. Felibrey leapt up and grabbed hold of the reins then managed to clamber onto the great beast's back. "Come, my friend. One more time and we'll be rid of her." He willed the horse to leap into the flames once more.

Kerridwen screamed, "Damn you all!"

An explosion erupted as she blew apart, sending all of them flying back. Jimmy was flung hard against a nearby tree. The water receded, flickering ashes rose up, drifting in and out of a vague semblance of the hunter. Kerridwen's voice was unmistakable in the crackling remnants of the fire. "I will see to it that you suffer as you serve me, you pathetic little witches."

Neridah rose to her feet and reached back to draw energy from the Crossworlds. Patsy grabbed her hand and said, "No, that's what she wants. It's like last time. She's weak. She's trying to goad us into using our powers against her so she can absorb them." Patsy approached the remains of the fire.

Kerridwen laughed, "You think you can be rid of me that easily, witch? Or should I say, Enchantress?" Patsy kicked sand into the flames. Kerridwen laughed again. "You'll serve me yet, little Patsy." The laughter continued, becoming less and less until its last vestiges were extinguished along with the last of the embers.

Colin's voice boomed from the top of the path. "What's happened here?" Patsy looked up to see her father and the Reverend coming down the steps holding a lantern. Neridah ran up to the Reverend, who took her in his arms and held her tight. Colin saw his wife sitting by Darcy while Jimmy lay unmoving on the ground. He raced to be by her side. Darcy was wailing, tears streaming down his cheeks.

"I'm sorry, Dad. I'm so sorry..."

Meredith held Jimmy's wrist. She looked at Darcy and realised there were no words she could offer that would provide any comfort.

Colin asked, "Is there anything you can do for him?"

Meredith shook her head. She grabbed Colin's arm. "There's no pulse, and he's stopped breathing." She buried her face in Colin's shoulder and wept.

Destellie's cry echoed through the night. "Help me, please, somebody!"

They all turned and saw that she was trying to pull Felibrey's limp body from underneath that of the stallion in the shallows of the pool. The Reverend and Colin went to her aid and worked together in silence to pull his lifeless body free.

Destellie was inconsolable. "I'm so sorry. This is all my fault. My beautiful Felibrey… what have I… how did this…"

The Reverend put a hand on her shoulder. "Blaming yourself won't bring him back, and it won't do anything to help you. There were many forces at play here." He looked across at Darcy, whose eyes betrayed his sense of guilt. He turned back to Felibrey's fiancé. "You and the boy were merely pawns. No one here will hold either of you responsible, that is a promise."

*

Patsy ran up the stairs, Meredith calling after her, "Patricia, where do you think you're going?"

She stopped and yelled at her mother, "He should have warned me!"

"Who?"

Tears ran down Patsy's face as she cried out, "You wouldn't understand." She turned from her mother and continued up the stairs.

"Patricia, come back!" Meredith started walking toward the stairs but then felt Colin's firm grip on her shoulder.

"Let her go." Colin whispered in his wife's ear. "She's been through so much. She needs to let it out. Don't worry, she'll be back."

Meredith took Colin's hand and held it against her cheek as she nodded in agreement.

*

Patsy raced along the bottom of the paddock. "Krinkle-myst! Let me in! Let me in! I need to talk to you!"

She reached the spot where the portal would normally appear, only to find there was the same darkness there as the surrounding bush. "Krinkle-myst!" Patsy looked up at the night sky and screamed at the moon and stars, "Where are you!" She fell to her knees. "Why didn't you warn me?" Her vision was blurred by the flood of tears, her voice choking on her sobs. "I could have saved them." She buried her face in her hands and kept repeating, "I could have saved them..."

"You don't know that."

Patsy looked up. She was in Krinkle-myst's cabin, next to his fireplace. The wood-elf was sitting at his writing desk with his back to her. "Why?" she asked.

"Why what?" The movement of his quill suggested he was more concerned about his writing than about Patsy's questions.

"Why didn't you warn me? I could have saved them. They didn't need to die."

"You don't know that."

"You could have warned me. Now Felibrey and Jimmy are dead... why?"

Krinkle-myst's quill stopped moving. "What was it you said to your mother just a moment ago? Oh, that's right... you wouldn't understand." The quill started its movement across the page again.

Patsy blinked and found she was back in the paddock with nothing but the sound of crickets around her. She got to her feet, her mind feeling empty as she traipsed back to the pathway. It was as though there was no room left for any kind of thoughts or feelings in her head. She'd never felt quite so numb.

The young witch worked her way down the stairs, wanting to wake up from this nightmare. She looked down at Destellie wailing over Felibrey's body and Darcy clinging to his dead father. A grim realisation flooded through her. She finally understood why her mother had hidden the truth from her about their family when she was younger. She understood why she'd wanted to protect her from the burden they carried, and why she'd hoped Patsy would never need to learn of it.

Meredith met her daughter at the bottom of the stairs. Patsy buried herself in the warmth of her mother's embrace.

EPILOGUE

Patsy turned to Clara as they walked down the path to the pool, the tutor carrying a picnic hamper. "I got a letter from Darcy yesterday."

"Oh, how is he?" asked Clara.

"He started a new job last week. He's learning to be a carpenter."

"That's nice. Do you think he's happy?"

"I hope so. Mother and Nana-Neri said he can never be happy here after what happened last year."

Clara paused and took a deep breath. She tried to avoid thinking about those events—events that had challenged everything she'd ever understood about the world. She gave a gentle nod and said, "I think they're quite right in that regard."

"Oh, and he said he ran into Bordauex. Apparently, the archbishop has taken a great interest in the Reverend Casey's work and wants to travel up here soon to meet with him."

"Oh? Well that should be interesting."

Ferdinand came running down the steps, catching up to them as they reached the bottom of the pathway. Patsy picked him up then asked, "Miss Jenkins, would it be okay if I call you Clara? I feel like you're more of a friend than a tutor now."

Clara smiled and said, "I'd like that very much, but not in front of your parents."

They made their way to the rock where they always sat for their picnics. Patsy noticed the corner of a dark, rectangular metal object sticking out of the sand near the edge of the pool. She raced down and picked it up, brushing the sand off it. Jai's phone!

"What is it?" asked Clara.

"Oh, just something I thought I'd lost."

"Show me."

Patsy looked over her shoulder. She blushed as she kept the phone hidden from view. "I'd rather not, if that's okay. To be honest, it's a little embarrassing."

"Ah!" Clara gave a knowing smile. "I kept diaries like that when I was your age. Don't worry, I won't pry."

Shielding the phone from Clara's view, Patsy turned it on, remembering all the step-by-step instructions Jai had given her like it was yesterday. Her intuition told her to tap the text message icon.

There was a photo of Jai with his mother and little sister standing next to the Book of Wisdom, on its stand in the library where it belonged.

Patsy smiled at the image then scrolled down to read Jai's message.

Hi Patricia,

I just wanted to thank you. Mum and I followed up on your tip about the gallery, and you were right. It took a year of planning, but we got Mel back last week, and the Book of Wisdom. Ever since you talked me out of our original plan, I've been having the craziest dream about what would have happened if you hadn't stopped me. The bit that always stands out the most is where we end up meeting the legendary Krinkle-myst and he lectures us about future history. I'd love to know if maybe you've had the same dream.

Patsy closed her eyes and bit down on her lower lip while holding the phone to her chest. When she opened her eyes, she smiled and hurled the phone into the middle of the pool.

Clara called out, "Bravo! Sometimes that's the best way to treat past embarrassments."

Patsy let out a little giggle as she walked back up the beach and sat next to Clara on the rock. "Actually, it's not so much that it's embarrassing, just something I need to put behind me. It's not really something I want to talk about though, if that's okay."

"Of course it is. But as you said, we're friends. So please, if there's ever anything you ever need to talk about, you can trust that it will never go past the two of us."

Patsy threw her arms around Clara. "Thank you."

As Clara started unpacking the picnic basket, she noticed a bit of movement near Patsy's foot. "Is that a leech?"

Patsy looked down and saw how the light refracted as it passed through the waving, over-sized head of the leech-like worm.

The stringworm latched onto Patsy's foot before she had a chance to pull it away.

THE END

www.ingramcontent.com/pod-product-compliance
Lightning Source LLC
Chambersburg PA
CBHW020718310726
48979CB00004B/975

* 9 7 8 0 6 4 5 6 5 8 1 8 7 *